THE

BAD SEED

BATTLE FOR THE HEAVENS

To Karen, Welcome to my world

MICHAEL LACKEY

Original theme composed by Michael Christopher

An Apollo Publication
www.apollopublications.com

THE BAD SEED

Text Copyright © 2015, 2017 by Michael Lackey

Apollo Publications Inc. www.apollopublications.com

Printed in the United States of America

First Hardcover Edition, January 2017
 ISBN: 978-1-64084-177-2 PDF
 ISBN: 978-1-64084-178-9 EPub
 ISBN: 978-1-64084-179-6 MOBI
 ISBN: 978-1-64084-180-2 Paperback
 ISBN: 978-1-64084-181-9 Hardback
 ISBN: 978-1-64084-182-6 Delux Edition
SAN: 990-4514

This book is dedicated to my wife, April, and daughter, Christian. Without your support, love and understanding, I could not have done this. You have always been and always will be my reason.

Also, to my dog, Maddie. She always helps me write by laying behind my chair and snoring. Good dog, Maddie. Good girl!

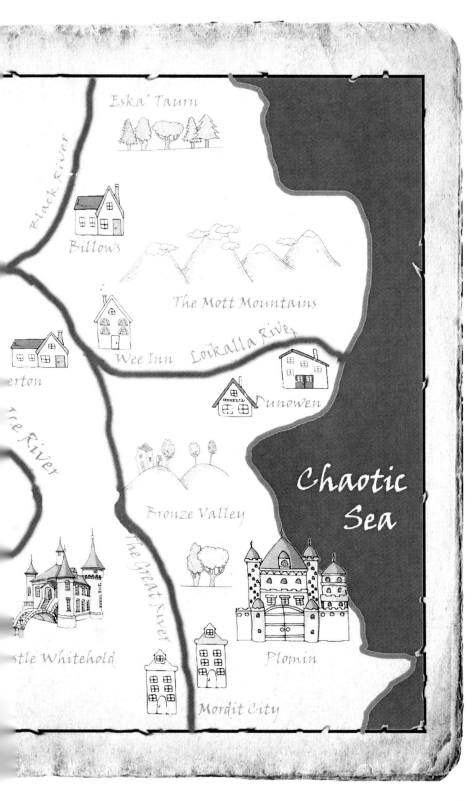

1
Seed Planted

Whitehold was the center of the commonwealth in Cyreus, a realm ruled by King Gabriel, filled with lush farm lands surrounding a large castle that housed a city within itself. As the morning dew burned off the leaves and birds sang the arrival of a new day, we find a house in the corner of a little farm, just outside the city of Whitehold. A quiet homestead brimming with crops and livestock to be delivered to the people. This particular farm is home to the Morelys.

As the warm sun peeked over the treetops, the Morely family started their morning routine.

"Zachery, will you please gather me some of the herbs from the garden?" Elizabeth asked. "Your father is bringing me the eggs."

Zachery, the eldest child to George and Elizabeth Morely, walked from the house, bag in hand, to do as his mother asked. He was a young man on the brink of adulthood with broad shoulders carrying a head full of dark hair that shimmered in the morning light. His eyes full of wonder and expectation of a life he longed to live. After celebrating his fifteenth season day, he stood nearly as tall as his father. As he made his way to the garden, he grabbed his wooden sword and wrapped his dirt stained cloak his mother had made him around his neck.

"I understand, sire. A mission to the garden sounds like you need a King's Guard!" He then pretended he was a member of the King's Guard, protecting the King and going on adventures. Zachery could always be found carrying that wooden sword, and his makeshift cloak with the King's colors on it. Zachery always knew he was not destined to be a poor farmer. He longed for the time he could leave his humdrum days behind.

This was no usual day for him as it turned out. As he rounded the hedges to the open garden plot, there in the back he caught the sight of a dark figure. Zachery ducked behind the hedges, hoping not to be seen. He watched the gloomy silhouette fade in and out of the shadows.

"Was father expecting someone? That doesn't look like anyone I know," Zachery whispered to himself.

He held his breath, listening to the pounding beat of his heart as it tried to escape his chest. With every second, it grew louder until Zachery thought for sure the dark one would hear him. The skies dimmed, the wind picked up and started to swirl around the shadowy individual.

"I see you, boy," the stranger spoke. "No one can hide from my sight."

Startled, Zachery asked, "Who are you? Wha. . .what do you want?"

An echoing, unnatural voice, that resonated through Zachery's very bones answered, "Today, the seed is planted. All shall kneel before him. He is the bringer of death. Spread his warning, and prepare for doom. Your people will suffer in his wake. The light will shine no more. Our time has come. Darkness will grow. Night has fallen." Then in a puff of black and purple smoke, the dark figure vanished into thin air.

Horrified, Zachery ran back to retrieve his father, skidding to a sudden stop. George was busy with the chickens in the coop when Zachery came rushing in nearly out of breath.

"F-Father! Come quickly! A demon is in the garden!" he yelled pointing out. "His voice sounded as if it would force itself into my mind. It was as if he was standing right next to me, but I could see him in the shadows of the garden. You will not believe what he told me. He said a seed was planted, and we were all going to suffer. He called this seed the bringer of death that we should prepare for doom! Do you think we are in danger?"

George's eyes grew wide. For a moment, Zachery thought his father was as terrified as he was. Then, George burst out laughing, brushing tears from his eyes with the back of his hands. "A fine prank, my boy! A demon? Here? What does he want? Some milk and herbs for his travels?"

Zachery's eyes showed the fear he felt inside. "It is not a joke! Please, we need to do something. Come, I'll show you where he was."

He could tell his son was truly terrified of something. "All right, we will go see this demon." Playing along, he called for their dog. "Duke! Let's go see a demon, boy!"

If only he knew that at that moment forward, his world would change forever. As he followed Zachery and Duke out of the coop, his eyes fell onto the spot where Zachery said the stranger stood. It was now a ring of smoldering ash, and in the center of the ring grew a small, single sapling.

George approached the circle, confused; he tried to figure out what it was. "Well, would you look at that! This was not here yesterday. How did you do this?" he asked turning to his son.

Zachery gave his father a wide-eyed look. "See, I told you. Someone or something was here. He stood right here."

Duke, the family dog, went to investigate for himself. Sniffing as if he knew this was an unmarked tree, he crossed the circle of ash. Breaking the circle triggered the evil inside. Consumed by the tree, Duke's face slowly disappeared into the sapling as the trunk acted as if it was feeding on him. The animal howled in pain and struggled to break free. Although, the more he fought, the tighter it held on to its' prey. As Duke sank into the tree's trunk, the bark seemed to contour and shift into the shape of the poor dog as the sapling swallowed him before their eyes. After the tree consumed the poor animal, they could see it grow in size.

"Father, did you see that?" Zachery shouted.

George grabbed his son in one hand and ran home frantically shouting, "We have to tell King Gabriel! He has to know!"

My morning started off very dark that day. I had no idea how dark my world would get. I'm Zachery Morely, and the tale you are about to read changed our worlds forever. You will hear of heroes and kingdoms uniting to be stronger. I'll be here to give you insight.

Once they returned home, George tried to explain to Elizabeth what they had seen. "I know what I saw. That tree is not normal. It ate Duke! I don't know what it's able to do. I have to tell Gabriel."

Despite believing her husband's story, Elizabeth shook her head. She was too worried that people would blame them for the sapling and not believe they were trying to help. "George Morely, if you go around telling folks that story, they will surely lock you in the lowest part of the dungeons!"

"Elizabeth, listen to me," George pleaded. "We have to think of the others and protect them. I saw it, Elizabeth, I saw it. I know Gabriel will believe me and send help. I have to get the news to the King."

***

As they prepared the horses for the trip, George told Elizabeth to keep their other child safe and inside the house.

"No matter what, you and Launa must stay away from the garden. Do not let anyone near the spot where the tree is. I feel in my soul that it is shrouded in darkness, and is not of this world," he confessed.

She kissed her husband softly on the lips. "I promise. And please, be safe. Take care of Zachery. You know he loves Gabriel and the castle. Do not allow him to wander and get lost. I need you both to come back to me. I mean it, George."

She then hugged her men and sent them on their way. The journey to the castle was a day's ride. They could make it by nightfall. If they knew what was coming, they would have made it faster.

What trouble could a tree cause? A paltry tree? I wish that's all we had to deal with from that garden.

As the men rode to the castle, Elizabeth kept her daughter inside and warned her neighbors the best she could. Launa grumbled and complained, but did as she was told. What they didn't realize was while they were holed up inside, animals were making their way to the circle, drawn by a strange curiosity to the sapling. As the animals crept closer to the circle, like the Morely's dog, they too were consumed. Every time one was taken, the sapling grew bigger. This was no ordinary tree sapling. Who was that vile man who left it here?

I always enjoyed going to Castle Whitehold, seeing the knights in their shiny armor, Zachery thought. *All the Lords and Ladies dressed in the finest clothes of the land. I was lucky to have what clothes I had on, and I did not understand why? As farmers, we did not have the finer things. Mother usually made our clothes and toys, but we knew the king! Father was his best childhood friend! That had to count for something.*

2
The Old Man

That evening, as George and Zachery made their way to the castle, they stopped to let the horses rest and to grab some supper at a local pub outside of Castle Whitehold. Being close to the castle, this was no filthy tavern run by scoundrels. It was well-respected by the people. They entered the large, blue doorway to see all the patrons turn their heads toward them.

"Why are they looking at us that way, Father?" Zachery asked.

George knew why. "We are not the type of people who frequent this tavern, Son. We are simple farmers, not wealthy Lords."

"That old man isn't either." Zachery pointed to a strange old man walking from table to table.

"End of days!" the old man cried. "Everyone will die! We need to protect the champion of light!"

Most of the patrons ignored him and went about their meals and ale. After what Zachery had seen, he found this ragtag gentleman amusing, and decided to listen to him banter with himself closely.

As George and Zachery sat at a nearby table, the old man stopped in his tracks as if something grabbed his attention. He turned toward the boy and said, "The champion is not yet born to this world. He must be protected at all cost, until his eighteenth season. Till then, we are all at *his* mercy!"

Stunned by the old man's words, Zachery glanced at his father for answers. George was busy trying to get the barmaid's attention, acting as if he didn't know the old man was even there.

"If this so-called Champion is not born yet, then how will we know who he is?" Zachery asked. "And who will he protect us from?"

In a blink of an eye, the old man stood inches away from him. Face-to-face, close enough for Zachery to see that under his nasty brown hood, his eyes were white as milk and he carried the stench of burning flesh that emanated from his skin, filling the air around them. His robes looked to be unwashed for weeks. Zachery couldn't tell if it was green or brown, or even dark gray.

"The new mother that carries the child has hair of flames as the dragon's breath. Her skin is as the moon that hangs high at night, and is protected by a fierce dire wolf that would lay down its own life for hers. Tread softly, for she does not know the gift she carries. This child is our only hope to stop the three. Save him, or we all lose. Seek the answers of the wise."

As the old man spoke these final words, his eyes rolled back into his head and he slumped over the table. Instantly, the old man burst into flames sending the patrons into a frenzy. Ale was spilled, food dropped. Some of the women ran for the doorway as others fainted to the floor. A short fellow, that had a little too much ale, pulled his sword and swung wildly. George grabbed his son away from their table as the barmaids splashed buckets of water on the corpse.

"What kind of establishment is this? The king will hear of this!" one of the older patrons shouted.

Zachery watched as they dragged the poor decrepit man's body outside, trying to let what he had just heard and seen sink in.

He told his father what the old man had said before he burst into flames. Knowing his son to be truthful, especially after doubting him at the garden, he took his words as sincere, but feared King Gabriel's men would lock him up for witchcraft if spoken outside the two of them.

"I know I doubted you at the garden, son, and I do believe you. Let's just keep quiet about it for now. We do not want a bunch of scared mothers trying to hide their babies now do we?"

***

As they started for the castle again, Zachery turned to his father. "Are you scared of what we have seen? Are we in danger?"

George thought for a minute, and then replied, "Fear is normal for every man. If he tells you he is unafraid, then he is a fool. Courage does not quench fear—it is the strength to overcome it. So yes, I am afraid, but I have faith in our King, he will have answers. All will be well." George gave his son a smile and disheveled his hair, just as he did when Zachery was a small child and the two made their way to Castle Whitehold, and King Gabriel himself.

I hated when he would mess my hair. I was fifteen, not five! My father knew I was practically a man now. We would get ready soon for my sixteenth season day. I would be taking more responsibilities around the farm. I guess, since I was the first born, it may have been more difficult to let go of the notion I'm was longer a child.

Soon they would find themselves in council with the king, not many people could command such a private meeting, but Gabriel felt a bond with George.

The two had known each other since childhood, before Gabriel was king. At one point, close as brothers. Zachery had heard the story a thousand times, he could nearly tell it word for word just as his father did.

**

As a child, Gabriel was quite an adventurer, always running away from his royal nannies in search of danger. One morning, George and his father, Doron, were in the woods hunting.

"An honest man will provide for his family with what the Gods provide for them, son." Doron would always tell him.

Gabriel had escaped his nanny's clutches, again, and ran through the same patch of forest. The feeling of freedom was what Gabriel craved. He ran simply so he could feel the wind brush his face. He made the mistake of enjoying it too much. He closed his eyes and suddenly, a root caught his foot sending him flying over a small cliff, down into a ravine.

Coming to an abrupt stop, the young prince found himself stuck to the ground. "EWW! What is this mess? I. . . I cannot move!"

He had rolled into the web of a Highland ground spider, extremely sticky, and if you're alone, deadly.

"Help! Someone, please help! Is anyone there?" Gabriel began to squirm to try to free himself and yell for help. The more he moved, the more tangled he became.

George was close by and heard the screams.

"Someone is in trouble," he said to himself.

He followed the noise and with wide eyes, found the spider inching closer to its meal. He drew his bow and began to stream a volley of arrows into the creature. With each arrow, George took a step closer to Gabriel, making sure to keep his footing and not suffer the same fate. Reeling in pain, the spider made a quick jump in the boy's direction, but George was ready.

"We will not be a meal today!" He pulled a dagger from his boot, stabbing it deep into the eye of the spider. Slime and blood spewed everywhere. These woods were George's home and he knew the creatures who crept here. He had knowledge that the spider's brain was directly behind the eyes. He retracted the dagger and cut Gabriel free from the web. The spider lay slumped in a heap at their feet.

Shocked from what he had seen right at his own eyes, Gabriel was in awe of George's bravery. "Thank you so much! Name your price, and it shall be yours! Thank you!"

Before George could open his mouth to speak, Doron appeared on the scene and seeing the bloody spider, pulled his son towards him and held him tight.

"How did you do that? How did you defeat the spider alone?" Doron asked.

George gave a wink. "I remembered what you said about their tiny brains. I heard someone needed help, and I could not be afraid."

Doron and George then glanced at the young lad George had saved. He then stood, brushed off his elegant clothes and introduced himself. "I am Prince Gabriel of Whitehold, and I am forever in your debt."

"Well, my young prince," Doron began, "we need to help you find your way home."

From that day forward, the Morely family held a special place with the King's family, even a place at court when he was older, if he ever wanted it. However, George always declined. "Our place is the farm."

The boys kept in touch through their growing years, but with Gabriel becoming king, sooner than expected with the sudden passing of his father, and George's father wishing to stay a simple farmer, it was hard on the boys. Occasionally, Gabriel would long for his freedom. Freedom from the day-to-day duties of being king. He would slip to the stables and find a horse. He always found himself at the Morely's home. Always by George's side.

"One day, George, you and I will have a marvelous adventure," Gabriel always told him.

"We had our adventures already, my Lord, or have you forgotten the spider? That was plenty!" George would always laugh and say. "You just concentrate on ruling the realm, and I'll make sure the farm is here any time you want to visit."

Gabriel knew that George would always be there for him, even if it were to hide him away from the day-to-day royal affairs.

My dad was always brave. Even as a child, he was a hero. I hoped when I needed to be brave, I could be half the man he was. Gabriel became the youngest king ever to rule over Castle Whitehold at the age of his fifteenth season. This makes me stop and think, he became the leader of all these people at the same age I was when this started. Could I handle that much responsibility if it were handed to me? I always dreamed of adventure, like King Gabriel did, but I knew my adventure was to stay at the farm. I would love to have stayed at that farm.

3
The King's New Bride

The two soon arrived at castle Whitehold. The glorious structure stood taller than any in the realm. Even with the sun low behind the hills, the majestic structure still shone bright. White block with bold, black metal fixtures around the massive gates sparkled at night. The King's colors flew atop the towers, glorious blues and golds, welcoming all who came.

George was known at the castle. The guards offered no resistance when he asked for council with King Gabriel. They ushered him and Zachery inside the private section.

"We need to see King Gabriel, it's urgent," George told the guard.

The King's top adviser, Xavier, overheard the request. "I will handle master Morely from here. You are excused."

The guard gave a slight nod of the head and went back to his patrol.

In the castle, George and Zachery waited in the war room. "I will alert the King to your arrival, good sir," Xavier said.

George smiled. "Thank you, Xavier. You are a great man."

After a bit of a wait, the door opened and in walked the King.

He was a tall, strong man with hair that resembled the sea, tossed, dark, and just a touch of mystery. His stern gaze faded into a smile as he saw his close friends. George stood and embraced Gabriel. "We need to talk, old friend." He began telling Gabriel of the strange visitor and in his wake the corrupt sapling he left behind. "Gabriel, we have known each other for a long time. You must believe me when I say the kingdom is in trouble. This...this demonic sapling has the power to kill."

The King was concerned by this. He paced the floor stroking his stubbly beard, deep in thought, dropping himself into a large chair at the head of the table. He was discussing a strategy with George when a knock came at the door. "Enter," replied Gabriel.

Zachery was admiring the many banners hanging on the wall when a very beautiful woman came in. Her eyes held a gentle calmness. She had an awkward shyness about her as if she did not belong. From her royal looking headdress to her flowing gown, she was dressed similar to a...queen? George looked to Gabriel, waiting for some explanation.

Gabriel rose from his chair, walked to the woman and helped her to a seat. He kissed her on the cheek and turned to George. "I know this will come as a surprise, my old friend, but I have married. This is my wife, Queen Natallia."

We didn't know this woman. Father was in shock. How could he marry without him there? He couldn't have, could he? Many questions arose about her, but we had to trust in the king.

Natallia smiled. "So this is the famous George I have heard so much about."

George could see why Gabriel would fall for such a beautiful woman, no question there. The questions George had were "when" and "where". "How did this come about? Why have *I* not heard of this?"

Gabriel replied, "My King's Guards and I were on a diplomatic mission trip to Tralla, in the Northern Realms. She and her brother were in the streets looking for work and shelter. There was something about her that drew my attention. Their entire village had been raided by orcs. Everyone was slain. They only survived because of her brother, Antoine's, bravery and great cunning. He is her protector. I'll let him finish the story. He is never too far from her side." He raised his hand and motioned to the King's Guard to let him in.

Antoine walked into the room. A tall, massive, beast of a man carrying a sword the size of a child.

The king asked him to share the story of their village to the visitors.

Nodding his head, Antoine began to share his story. "Our village was no stranger to the orcs's terror, but this was no ordinary food raid. We were thrown out of our window by our father who told us to run. Our father was a master with blades, he taught me how to handle a sword from the time I could walk, but even he wasn't enough to fend off the attack. He sacrificed himself to save us. We could hear the massacre behind us. As we broke through the tree line, we were surrounded by another troop of deadly orcs. We hid at the butcher's shop under a pile of animal carcasses. They had a fresh kill of wolves from the day before. The stench of the flesh masked our scent. Luckily, they were quick and did not stay in our village very long. Like I said, we were used to the orcs raiding the village, but they never were this brutal before. The bloodshed and carnage was awful. It was as if they were mad with rage. After a day, we left searching for food and shelter."

"That's where Gabriel found us," Natallia suddenly added. "He could have just tossed some coins our way or passed by without even a glance. Our eyes locked together, and it was the fates telling us we were each other's destiny. I pray and thank the Gods, old and new, every day he was sent our way, for without him I do not know what we would have done. Where we would have ended up."

George looked confused and amazed as Antoine and Natallia told their story.

"Dear George, I have heard more about you than anything or anyone else in this kingdom. It is truly a pleasure to finally meet you," Queen Natallia said softly.

"All your questions will be answered later, I promise you.," King Gabriel assured. We haven't even made a true royal announcement. The people need a royal wedding, but we could not wait. We were married in secret before we left Tralla. The people know of their queen, words spread fast from the castle walls. All of them are just waiting for the festivities, but we have more pressing matters to attend to. Please tell me more of this stranger that came to your garden."

George told the group all about the happenings at his farm, then Zachery stood and told them of the old man and his prophecy at the pub, how he swore they had to find the champion and protect him.

"This strange old man seemed to know something. Why would he be trying to get people to listen, and what killed him?" asked Zachery.

George covered his eyes and lowered his head hearing Zachery speak up.

Antoine laughed and asked, "Dear boy, do you believe we are to wait on this unknown champion 'til his eighteenth day of season and do nothing?"

"No," answered King Gabriel. "We will send Rodderick and some of the War Council to investigate this sapling and find this stranger. They will pluck this threat or return with a way to destroy it."

Natallia rose. "Excuse me, dear husband. I must attend to the kitchen and make plans for the banquet." She smiled at George and Zachery. "It was truly an honor to meet you both." Then the queen departed and left them to their business.

"I know you have questions, dear friend," Gabriel assured George, "and I will gladly answer them at another time. Now, we will assemble the War Council with Rodderick. Tell him all you know of this stranger and the sapling. When this is over, we will share an ale and you can tell everyone the story of how I am the reason you met Elizabeth." With a laugh and a wink, Gabriel rose and embraced George. Zachery knew his father and the king were like brothers, and if anyone could do anything with the stranger, surely Gabriel could. Gabriel loved the Morely's and their quiet little farm; if anyone or anything were threatening their well-being, he would put an end to it as soon as possible.

King Gabriel was like an uncle to me. His shiny armor and stern face was a comfort to me, even as it struck fear in the ones who opposed him. We were going home, and I got to ride with the knights of Castle Whitehold! This had turned out to be a fantastic journey! I often dreamed of adventures with the King's Guard! Father always said he thought Gabriel was a bad influence on me, and then he laughed and would punch Gabriel in the arm.

4

Sapling No More

The members of the War Council led by Sir Rodderick were a small but lethal bunch, trained to be the best fighters in not only Whitehold, but the surrounding realms as well. A total of ten men, including Sir Rodderick, traveled back to the Morely farm. What a grand site they were. All the War Council rode white steeds and bore the glorious blue colors of King Gabriel, trimmed with gold on their breastplates. Zachery rode up front looking like he belonged to the group.

"You know, I will be a member of the War Council someday. I might even become a King's Guard!" Zachery told Sir Rodderick.

The noble Sir Rodderick didn't make a sound, but Zachery could see the hint of a smile forming on his lips.

Rodderick was a mountain of a man, a head higher than an average man. Many of the men whispered myths about him. The good knight looked to be a God in the flesh. With his bald head and soot black beard, he was a sight to behold. Most men had to look up to see his eyes, and when they saw them, they always felt uneasy about it. Sir Rodderick was never defeated in battle, but gave all glory to his king in victory. If you were a friend, Rodderick was as gentle as a lamb. If you found yourself as an enemy, he was as ferocious as a lion. No other knight could compare to his loyalty.

George just laughed at the sight and wondered to himself, was he seeing a glimpse of his son's future. He had always fancied the armor and style of the War Council and King's Guard. George shook off the thought, because when they arrived home something was wrong.

It had been a total of five days since George and Zachery left and the sapling had consumed their dog. Elizabeth ran out to meet them, clearly disturbed. "The tree! Stay away from it! The tree! It will consume everything! We are all in danger!"

George grabbed the distraught woman and held her tight in his arms to try and calm her. "Elizabeth! Calm yourself, slow down and tell me what has happened. Is Launa all right?"

All the poor woman could do was nod her head and point in the direction of the garden.

Rodderick told his men to be on the ready and the group made way to see for themselves. "War Council! To arms! Spread out, let's find this tree," commanded Sir Rodderick.

When they approached the garden, George gasped. "Oh my Gods, what has happened?!"

Elizabeth still had a hold of her husband's hand and replied, "It was horrible. We could hear it all. Animals were being drawn out of the forest into the circle. I stood at a distance, just to watch. It was horrible, George. One by one, each consumed and with each the tree grew bigger and bigger. One night, we heard this commotion from the woods like an animal that was hurt. It was a wild dog trying to fight the urge to go near the tree. It seemed as if the more it resisted, the more pain it was in. I couldn't bear to hear the poor animal's screams of pain. I took the bow from the house and killed it myself. I wanted to put it out of its misery."

In the five days they were gone of what had been just a small sapling had now grown to a tall tree whose trunk was almost as big as the smoldering circle around it. They all wondered what kind of sorcery could have brought this upon them? As they stood astounded, one of the War Council stepped closer to the tree.

"Sir Rodderick! Look at the trunk. I can see the faces! There's a deer with antlers!"

I could clearly see the face of the deer in the tree's trunk. It had the look of terror. I wondered to myself, how many poor animals had it taken to get the once small sapling to its enormous size? We were only gone for five days. What would have happened if we were gone longer?

One of the Council members drew his sharp blade.

"Do not get close, Jonas!" Sir Rodderick shouted. "We don't know how it will react to humans." Jonas was careful about not crossing the circle and sliced at a branch cutting the end cleanly off.

At the branch's severed end, it was not sap, but blood.

In the distance, they heard sounds of dark laughter, coming closer to them, surrounding them. Zachery turned a sickly, pale color.

"My Gods, it is the same man as before," he whispered to his father.

The sound mocked them, taunting them as if the dark figure was standing beside them.

Rodderick looked to George. "If the thing can bleed, it can die! Get us all the oil you have. Let's see how it likes being firewood."

George and the others went to fetch the oil. "It is not much, but it is all we have," George told him. When they had it all in the garden, the War Council doused the tree from afar and threw a lit torch. The tree blazed up, the heat pushed all back from where they were standing. Hisses and moaning but worst of all, laughter could be heard coming directly from the tree. Now the men were frightened.

The sound of the laughter was the same voice I heard when the stranger was here. What was this thing? I prayed to the Gods this was the answer to this problem.

After the fire died down, the tree still stood. One by one, the leaves grew back. The laughing continued. All could hear it, as if someone or something right beside them, but no one was around.

Lucas, the second in command behind Rodderick, was a very

aggressive soldier. He told them, "I want to see more blood!" He took a spear hurled it through the air and found his mark, the center of the trunk. A piercing shriek was heard from the tree as blood spilled from the spear tip. The shriek echoed throughout the valley, scattering animals everywhere. Birds darkened the skies fleeing from the site. The hold on all the animals had been broken for the moment.

"Well done, Lucas!" one of the men shouted.

Suddenly, the tree moved. Branches, used like arms, removed the spear and tossed it straight back at Lucas. He barely shifted out of the way as the spear zipped passed him, stopping as it shattered against a large stone.

The War Council had seen enough to take back to King Gabriel. They knew this would be declared a state of royal emergency. A scowl appeared over Rodderick's face as he assigned some of the group to stay.

"Lucas, take four of the men and form a perimeter around this garden. Kill any animal that tries to enter, and turn away any villagers. Nothing comes close to that tree. Nothing. We can't have it feeding and getting larger."

They had to come up with a plan. As long as the tree stood, everyone was in danger. They had to deal with this soon or there would not be any animals left in the valley. Rodderick told the Morelys his idea.

"The men will stay and keep an eye on the garden, you can sleep easy tonight, and these are my best men." He watched with concern as Lucas and the men set up their camp around the tree. "May the Gods be with them." They would make sure it did not feed until Rodderick could return.

As big as the tree had grown, I didn't think there were any animals left in the whole forest! I slept better that night knowing some of the War Council stayed behind. What would King Gabriel do now? How could we destroy this demon of a tree? Where did the stranger go, and who was he? Too many questions without answers, for me.

5

Evil Has a Name

Upon his return to the castle, Rodderick told the remaining King's Guard, War Council, and King Gabriel what he had witnessed.

"This tree, sire, is not from this world. It beckons the animals from the forest to feed. We have to destroy it as soon as possible," Rodderick said.

Gabriel's brow furrowed. "Feed? This tree feeds on living things?"

"Yes, sire. I saw it with my own eyes. These animals are in pain from some unseen source, forcing them to the Morely garden."

Eyes wide open now, Gabriel asked, "A tree that can consume living creatures? This worries me, Rodderick. Is there anything that we can do?"

The group conceived a plan of attack to destroy this demon monstrosity. Gabriel told them, "I will equip my guards with elven steel swords, they are some of the hardest and sharpest blades ever known. The front line will have poisoned-tipped arrows, I'm hoping that if the steel does not kill it, the poison would." The king looked to Rodderick, "Assemble our best men."

Gabriel went to address his men, "If this thing bleeds, let's see how much blood is in it! We cannot allow this atrocity into our land and let it continue to feed on the creatures that live here. What if it can devour a man? We will not let that happen!"

With a cheer and salute to their king, the men set out for the farm without delay.

***

I was relieved to see the War Council still at their post. Their presence gave us peace, knowing they were willing to stand up for the people. For all our safety, I wanted to have my garden back and let the men go home.

Upon reaching the farm, Rodderick found the men he had left and listened to their report.

"The animals, sir, have gone insane. We killed dozens, all trying to make their way to the tree. We burned the carcasses because we were not sure if they were tainted," Lucas said, while pointing to a smoldering pile of ashes.

"Good work, men!" Rodderick began to set orders. "Lucas, you and the men from the original group, stand down. Take your rest. This time, that damned tree is coming down."

As Lucas and the others took their leave, Rodderick wasted no time.

"Front line at the ready! Aim true and make it count!" Rodderick said.

When the new guards saw the tree, some prayed to their gods, a few cried, and others vomited at the sight of something they couldn't understand. This could be the end of their world as they know it. All the men were willing to lay their lives down for their king and the people of their realm.

The front-line archers set up with the swordsmen behind them at the ready. They dipped their arrowheads into poison at their feet, and with the order, they fired. All arrows found their mark in the trunk with dozens of thuds as the tips buried into the bark. Blood spewed from the wounds, coating the ground and shrieks of pain rang out as the tree began to move again.

"Help us, Gods of old. We need you now," one of the swordsmen prayed softly.

The sounds shifted from pain, to laughter, to a piercing howl. The dreadful plant stopped its movement. The same voice as before surrounded them all; unnatural, booming in their ears the men turned to find the source.

"Try as you may, he shall rule this day. The light will go dim, all shall kneel before him!"

"That voice, where is it coming from?" one of the men shouted. Seeing this, Lucas and the others, although tired, came to aid their commander.

The tree started to move again. The limbs now grabbed the arrows and pulled them from its trunk as if it had hands. Once all were out, the limbs began to hurl them back at the knights.

"SHIELDS!" Rodderick commanded. The swordsmen moved in front of the archers. It was too late for two of the men. The arrows found their mark deep within their chests. "Hold your line! Back battalion! Post your arms and get ready!"

As the tree threw the last arrow, Rodderick shouted, "BATTALIONS MOVE IN! DO NOT cross that line! Let's see how it handles itself without its branches!"

The swords battalion moved in. The sharp elven blades severed the smaller limbs with little effort. Suddenly, it was as if the demon could learn from their movements. The next soldier moved in and slashed. Then a larger limb swooped down, acting as a shield on a gladiator's arm. It blocked the sword as a smaller limb thrusted up and pierced his armor, tearing him asunder. The tree acted as a seasoned fighter. One by one, it bested them, throwing their lifeless bodies to the ground haphazardly.

Seeing his men being laid to waste, Rodderick felt the blood boil inside him, sending him into a rage. The knight took up his great axe and charged the demon.

This is what the tree wanted. It threw all the other warriors aside. Their battered bodies scattered about and the limbs opened up in invitation. With a resounding battle cry, Rodderick swung his axe, making sure he was clear of the circle. Roots sprung from the ground, grabbing at his ankles, sending him to the ground with a thump. The roots began to tear his armored war boots away, rendering him helpless, and began to pull him closer. All the limbs wrapped around him, dragging him into the trunk, while tearing at his body. The poor knight screamed in pain as the tree controlled him like a puppet master with his marionette.

Zachery watched in horror. With a violent tug, the limbs pulled him into the trunk. Like the deer, they could see Sir Rodderick's face from inside the trunk. In a flash, he was gone. Everyone could still hear him screaming in pain. Black smoke filled the air around them. The ground began to rumble and quake, with the consumption of Rodderick, the tree expanded to fill the circle of ash. A loud boom shook the entire farm.

Suddenly, the tree appeared to stop and wilt before their very eyes. At that moment, Rodderick's mortally wounded body slammed onto the ground spewed out and rejected. The tree shook, limbs fell off, and the bark slowly turned black.

As they watched with wondering eyes, the tree burst into flames. Within moments, the tree was gone, but the circle remained. Rodderick's naked body lay motionless inside the circle. Blood trickled from the wounds, staining the grass a crimson red. The few remaining knights and people around began to shout:

"RODDERICK! RODDERICK! RODDERICK!"

Sir Rodderick had given his life in sacrifice to save them all, a true champion of the realm. Songs would be written in his honor. Men would name sons after him. Oh, the feast they would have for him tonight in the great hall.

Sir Lucas sent the men in to collect the body of their fallen champion, but as they drew closer, Rodderick, moved.

He stood with his bare back to the people. Slowly standing fully upright, he began to twitch. His skin started to darken the color of soot, turning to bark. You could hear his bones breaking inside his body, molding and conforming to a form that was not his. He turned to the guards, and they watched him fully transform. The bark hardened as armor; no longer the king's shining Champion, but a dark and sinister being. His eyes seem to have burned from their sockets and now replaced by red, glowing coals. A fiery cloak appeared on his back with the symbol of a dark tree upon it.

He reached down, grasped Rodderick's mighty war axe and proclaimed: "I am Dori'naur, the first. We will deliver this world unto our own. You will serve us or suffer."

Hearing this, the remaining knights took up arms.

"Suffer it is, then. So be it!" Dori'naur stretched out his left arm and a mighty shield appeared to grow from his forearm. The same dark tree of his cloak graced the front of the bulwark. Knights rushed in, and the demon slew them like insects drawn into a flame. Such power had never been seen before. Dark magic of this kind was thought to be long gone since the War of the Gods. These were King's Guards and War Council members, swatted away like children. The massacre was gruesome. The men lay dead around the demon like the proud first kills of a hunt.

Then Dori'naur turned to the Morelys and rest of the farm folk. "Serve us or suffer. We will bring pain to all that defy us. Kneel, or be struck down."

As the people began to fall to their knees, George grabbed Zachery and told him, "Run, get the horse and warn Gabriel. Tell him I will take care of everyone here as best as I can. GO!"

Zachery bolted for the barn, George stood between his son and the demon, ready to defend him. Zachery grabbed a horse and started for the castle, thinking he would be stopped, but Dori'naur released him.

The dark demon sneered. "Good, run boy! Tell your people we are here! Tell your king I am the new ruler, and I will be taking my castle soon. Now, we find the vessel and destroy the Champion of Light."

I didn't want to leave my family, but someone had to warn the king. The way that Rodderick's body had been disfigured and maimed turned my stomach. I was on my way to Castle Whitehold, possibly for the last time. I had always craved adventure as a King's Guard. It seemed adventure found me. My horse's every stride was a prayer sent to protect my family. I look back now and wonder what would have happened if I had stayed.

6

Mother of the Champion

Zachery rode that poor horse harder than it has been worked in its life. He knew he had to make it to Castle Whitehold and warn King Gabriel. He made the day and a half ride in record time.

He reached the castle gates, and his poor horse collapsed under him. The animal had served his purpose for the greater good.

"Quickly! I must see the king!" Zachery shouted.

The guards escorted Zachery straight to King Gabriel's war room. Once all were present, Zachery told his news of the tree's growth, the animals drawn into it, and of Rodderick's bravery only to fall to the demon now known as Dori'naur the First.

"The first of what?" asked Antoine.

"He didn't say. Just that we would be delivered to their world. All would serve or suffer. He saw me leave and told me to say that he was coming to claim *his* castle," Zachery finished.

Gabriel slowly stroked his unshaven beard, thinking aloud. "How could one creature defeat almost a whole squad of King's Guard? And Rodderick? You say this demon is using his body now?"

Zachery nodded. "It is as if he is no longer Rodderick. He acted like the demon has taken his mind, body, and soul. Please, you have to remember that."

Antoine added, "Something has to be done about this Dori'naur. Or not only will this realm and kingdom fall, but all of Amundiss will be at his mercy."

Gabriel looked to Antoine, "Gather what men we have left and wait for me. We will make plans to travel to the Morely farm and I will see to this Dori'naur. First, I have to take care of Zachery."

***

The king took Zachery to his private dining room and called for some food and drink. When Queen Natallia came in to check on him, Zachery noticed something. He leaped to his feet and exclaimed, "She has red hair!"

Natallia turned sharply, startled by his outburst. Long, bright, red hair flowed down her back. Gems and ribbons were braided into the plait. Zachery's head spun. He could now clearly hear what the old man had told him over and over.

"Do you remember the prophecy from the old man? He said the Champion was not born yet. That he would be delivered from a mother with hair of flames, skin of the pale moon high in the sky. My lady, your hair is the brightest red I have ever seen, and you have skin of porcelain! Clearly beautiful." Zachery ventured a guess, "Any chance, my Queen, would you be with child?"

Natallia was startled and began to blush while resting a hand on her stomach.

Gabriel stood. "Natallia, my love, is it true? Are you with child?"

Natallia sat down, looking at Zachery."How do you know? I have told no one, not even Antoine. My handmaidens and I just recently left the physician. Our child cannot be this champion, for that would mean this demon would be hunting for us and stop at nothing to strike me down!"

Gabriel stopped and asked Zachery, "Wait, was there not a third detail as to the identity of the mother?"

Zachery hung his head, starting to doubt himself. "Yes, that she would be protected by a dire wolf that would lay down its life to protect her."

Gabriel started to sigh in relief. Zachery insisted, "She has to be the one, my Lord. Why else would the fates lead her to you, and you to us at this moment?"

Gabriel looked at Zachery. "Dire wolves are long gone from this land, my boy. All were killed or driven out."

Natallia agreed. "Yes, the men of our village back home would set out in hunting parties to rid them. The wolves would terrorize the village; some took children from their homes. Our father always warned us to stay clear of these beasts if we ever heard their howls," she added.

"Why would the orcs and dire wolves attack your village so often?" Zachery asked, but was interrupted.

Just then, the door opened. "Apologies, my king. I heard a commotion." It was Antoine, looking after his sister.

"Sir Antoine, clearly we are quite well. Feel free to see for yourself." Gabriel scolded.

"Wait!" shouted Zachery. "Your cloak? What is that fur? I have never seen it in these lands."

Antoine stroked the fur, "My boy, this is the pelt of a dire wolf. These skins saved our lives during the orc attack. That is why I wear it as a symbol that I will protect my family at all cost."

I knew it! I knew she was the one! Antoine was the dire wolf! Clearly, he would lay down his life for the queen, just like the prophecy said.

Zachery leaned back into his seat and smiled. "Do you not see? It is the last detail. She is protected by a dire wolf! She carries the hope of us all, and must be protected."

Antoine looked very confused. "She carries our hope? This is not possible. Natallia, are you with child? Why have you not told me?"

They did not want to believe; they did not want the safety of all Amundiss to fall to them. With it said aloud, they could feel the truth surrounding them, comforting them, as well as scaring them.

Antoine, seated now, had both hands rubbing his temples. "How will we protect the Queen and her unborn child? If Dori'naur gets word of this news he will stop at nothing to kill her, even if she is not the true mother, he would kill her just to cross her off as a possibility."

Zachery suggested, "We need to find a safe place. Surely there is someone who could help us. Do we know of anyone that could have knowledge of this Dori'naur?"

"I may know of one who could help us," Gabriel said. "If he will help us. We have to go in secret and hope to the Gods we can travel unnoticed."

Zachery looked to his king. "Where is this place?"

Gabriel responded, "We travel to the country of Kelendar, to a city called, Weelinn. Last I heard, he still lived there. I hope he is still there."

"Who is this man? And can he be trusted?" asked Antoine.

Gabriel replied, "His name is Benzoete. Possibly the last High Elf wizard in Amundiss. He may be our only chance." The king summoned his most trusted adviser, Xavier.

Once inside the war room, Gabriel explained. "We must leave, Xavier, the kingdom is in danger."

Xavier was a wise old man. He had learned, over the decades of serving the kings of Whitehold, his place was to advise, not to meddle. "What can you tell me of these plans, sire? Your people will need to know of these dangers."

They explained to Xavier of their need to travel in secret, and of Dori'naur's presence. "Please, make sure the people of the realms know of this danger so they can try and prepare. The people of Whitehold will face these dangers first. They will rise up in my name, but we cannot have that. I feel if they think I have fled, they will not resist."

"Some will still stand for your honor, my Lord…others will fear they have no choice. I will do as you ask, sire." Xavier bowed to his king.

Gabriel motioned for him to rise. With a warm embrace, Gabriel whispered in his ear, "You have served me and my family well. I love you like family, dear friend."

Xavier exited, and they set out on their way.

A real elven wizard? I had never seen an elf, let alone a wizard. If this Benzoete could help us, we needed to find him fast. My family, and my world were in danger. I had to try to save them. This adventure started with a battle of King's Guards, and now I traveled to meet a High Elf wizard. My life would never be the same from that day on.

MICHAEL LACKEY

7

Wizard of Weelinn

The king laid a book on the table that held accounts of all major events, places, and people of Amundiss dating back centuries. He opened the book and read:

"Once, the High Elf wizards were a large and powerful group. They were handpicked by the Gods to serve the Light. Centuries past, the group was nearly destroyed in battle against the fallen God, Craotonus. Craotonus fought for supreme rule of Amundiss, and only by the wizard's sacrifice was he conquered, and sealed inside a tomb deep in the center of the world. The battle nearly wiped out the order of high wizards. Only three remained, and none were ever named to take the other's places."

"My father wrote that passage. He spoke of meeting an elven wizard. Benzoete was one of these. His knowledge spans the thousands of years he walked this life, fighting evil and caring for others. If anyone can help us, it must be him," Gabriel told them.

They set out on their journey to Weelinn with handful of what was left of the King's Guard. They traveled in small groups, apart from each other as to not draw attention.

Xavier sent out royal messengers, carrying the message: "Danger is at our door. Prepare your home for the worst, but do not resist. King Gabriel of Whitehold has fled and will return when possible. Your king asks this of you: May the Gods be with the king!" The people in Whitehold respected their king and would be crushed to hear that he fled, but still will have faith in their ruler.

King Gabriel hoped this was the best way to help his people and keep them alive. He thought with him gone it would be easier for them to serve Dori'naur and not rise up in his honor against the monster. There would be less bloodshed if they were to do as Dori'naur commanded. If he only knew what the demon was capable of.

Along the way, Zachery overhead the quiet moment between Natallia and Gabriel. Natallia asked Gabriel, "How are we going to help our child? How can we protect a baby when we cannot protect ourselves or our kingdom? Can this wizard ensure us safety?"

Gabriel took her hand in his. "I promise you, we will do all that is possible to keep our child safe. I will shake the heavens to grab the God's attention if I have to."

I wanted the God's attention already. I needed to protect my family, but did not know how to do it. We were a ragtag bunch of heroes following a notion to a wizard that may or may not even still be there. If he was there, I hoped we could convince him to help us.

***

Along the way, they detoured and stopped in a small dwarven village called Bronze Valley, where the noble Black Clan Dwarves mined for precious gems and hidden treasures. There was a dwarf here that Gabriel wanted to visit, a blacksmith by the name of Bainebeard. They got a room for the night at the local inn under false names. As the Knights tended to the horses and wagons,

Gabriel, Natallia, Antoine, and Zachery went to the tavern for food and ale.

The dwarves had a taste for ale. The pub was filled with dirty miners sharing stories of treasure they had found. Zachery looked around the room, noticing that was taller than most of the patrons having never seen a Dwarf before he found this humorous. Suddenly, something caught Zachery's eye, or someone rather. It was the crazy old man from the pub in Whitehold that told him of the prophecy of the Champion.

"YOU!" shouted Zachery. "I saw you die! I saw you burst into flames and dragged out of the pub!"

The old man turned to face Zachery, the same milk-white eyes, and the burning stench even worse now. "The child will be known. He will be coming. Protect the champion at all cost, or all lives will be lost."

Zachery had a puzzled look on his face. "Why are you speaking this way? Tell us what you know. How do we protect the child?" Zachery expected King Gabriel to confront the old man when he noticed the king wasn't moving. No one moved. No sounds, not even the insects on the floor moved.

All were frozen in place. One of the pub servers was in mid fall, mugs of ale suspended in air.

Zachery turned back to the old man again, who was inches away from his face. "You hold the key, you will soon see. The champion will grow, but no one here will know."

The boy stumbled backward over his stool. "I hold the key? How. . . How am I important? I'm just a farm boy!"

"Everyone is more than they are. A farm boy can soar to the stars."

In an instant, the old man once again was gone in a burst of flames. This time he didn't leave his body, just a smoke ring that floated aimlessly out the window.

The tavern sounds came back and all was normal. The poor pub server hit the floor with a thud as ale splashed around her. The dwarves loved it. A burst of laughter arose.

"Did you see him?" Zachery asked. "He was just here!"

King Gabriel grabbed Zachery, and sat him down, "Quiet, boy! Do not draw attention to us. We do not need eyes upon us at this time."

Zachery pleaded with Gabriel, quietly this time. "The old man was here. He spoke more of the prophecy."

Gabriel moved his hand downward, indicating, not now. "We will speak of this later."

Once they gave the food to the others and returned to their room, Zachery told them what the old man had said this time.

"You hold the key to what?" asked Antoine.

Zachery shrugged his shoulders with no words for him.

Natallia asked, "The main question is how my child will grow with no one here knowing? No one? Does this mean us also?"

Again, Zachey was at a loss for words.

Plenty of questions arose from the old man's last visit. Everyone hoped Benzoete had the answers.

It made me uneasy that I seemed to be the only one getting these visits from the old man. I thought I was going insane. I did not understand what importance my role was going to be to this group. I now held the key to success? I needed answers, fast.

***

Before they left Bronze Valley, King Gabriel purchased a sword that none had believed existed. It was rumored that Bainebeard, the blacksmith, had a blade crafted by one of the original kings. This sword was forged by an ancient dwarf named Ferralloy. He called it, "Fuascailte," which translated into Redemption. The sword was said to be forged from scales of a dragon—the most feared, most devastating, fierce dragons of ancient times. The scales came from Fraener, a dragon that was once a Dwarf-king, leader of the Iron Army. Fraener was transformed by greed and terrorized the people. They would forfeit all their treasure and wealth, or lose their lives.

Ferralloy defeated the dragon, and as it lay at the steps of doom, Fraener once more was a dwarf. Fraener asked Ferralloy to help him receive salvation for his sins against this world. Ferralloy found four scales of the former dragon lying under the fallen dwarf leader. They were as hard and sharp as the beast's own teeth. Ferralloy forged the sword from the scales using a method said to be used by the Gods. He then had it blessed by a holy high priestess, enchanting it with holy powers. Ferralloy used the blade to destroy mountain crags. A vile, disgusting, and evil assemblage of creatures, born from the belly of darkness. An experiment gone wrong by dwarven chemists seeking a way to mine treasure faster.

Ferralloy was chosen to be the dwarven king after defeating Fraener and his bravery against the mountain crags. He forged the Iron Army into a fierce war machine. Legend states if the blade is used against evil, it would never break or dull, thus giving Fraener his redemption and a chance to meet his Gods in the afterlife.

After all the things that have been witnessed lately, Zachery thought that sounded reasonable. King Gabriel said he thought a blade like this would come in handy against a demon, and for the price he paid for it, it better.

"What happened to all the other dwarves?" Zachery asked. "Why are there so few here in the valley?"

Gabriel looked into the distance. "They, like the elves, lost faith in humanity and set themselves apart from the rest of the world. They keep to the mountains and do not let any outsiders within their iron-walled cities."

Zachery just shook his head, "Sad to think they live their lives secluded and alone."

Now, we were talking about dragons? How could this be? This was turning into a trip full of nightmares. I wondered what would it take for the dwarves to be involved with Amundiss again? Would they ever want to?

8

Friends in Need

The next morning, Zachery woke to the sounds of talking. Or rather bickering. One of the King's Guards, who had been on watch during the night, told of a stranger that came into town. He was horribly scarred and clearly afraid. He claimed to be from Whitehold, sent to deliver a message from "The true king and ruler, Dori'naur's people."

"Tell me, son, what did this man say?" asked Gabriel.

The young guard struggled to speak. "Your majesty, he was not of his right mind. The man had been forced to deliver this message by torture."

Gabriel looked him in the eyes. "I am aware of this. Now tell me the message, please."

He straightened his back, swallowed his fear and spoke. "A price has been put upon the heads of the false king and queen, Gabriel and Natallia. Rewards to the one that brings them to Dori'naur's castle dead or alive."

"Some of the Queen's handmaidens must have overheard the

physician tell Natallia she was with child, and broke under the torture from Dori'naur. The knight said the traveler looked to be starved and beaten," Antoine said, sadly.

Before the guard went to rejoin the others, he mentioned one last thing. "The strange markings on his body were made to resemble tree bark. This demon is making the people in his likeness."

The people were being tortured until they broke to Dori'naur's will, or killed and tossed to the side. King Gabriel was furious at the news. "We leave now! We have to make it to Weelinn as soon as we can. This Benzoete has to help us in some way."

I desperately wanted to find out about my parents, but I knew we could not disclose our location. I would have to wait and pray to the Gods they were safe.

***

George kept a watch on the demon's actions, trying to stay out of sight. Dori'naur had started his reign of terror, with the people of Whitehold. Just as he had promised in the garden, all would either serve or suffer. The ones that would not break found a blade across their necks. George and Elizabeth were no fools. They knew what it would take to keep their family safe, so they played their part as servant to the demon.

"Please, George, we must do as he says," pleaded Elizabeth. George cupped his hands around her face, her big brown eyes filling with tears. "I have spoken to Xavier, the king's advisor. He tells me that Gabriel has taken the queen and Zachery to Weelinn. We need to find others willing to fight and wait for our chance to escape. I know Gabriel, and he will not just flee. We need to help as many people as we can."

Dori'naur's first task was to make the people look the part of his subjects by scarring their bodies to resemble his own tree-like form. The evil new King of Whitehold started assembling an army, knowing that, with numbers, it would be easier to overthrow all the surrounding realms.

Standing atop of a statue of Gabriel's father, King Owin, in the courtyard, he called. "Good people of Whitehold, hear your new ruler. I require an army. Any volunteers that heed my call will be rewarded for their loyalty." Some of the men wishing to protect their families stepped forward reluctantly. As the men lined up before their new ruler, Dori'naur pointed to the women watching from the side. "I have a task for your males. I hope, for your sakes, they can carry it out. We will crush this former king and the Vessel of Light!"

Dori'naur knew he was on the right trail sending the bounties for Gabriel and Natallia. He planned on ending this threat before it had a chance to even begin. The people of Whitehold did not want to carry out the demon's wishes, but found they had little choice. Against George's advice, a militia had formed one night to try to destroy the demon at the castle.

***

"Please, I am begging you to wait. Give us a little time to plan our escape," George pleaded with the men.

Twenty men decided to try and defeat the demon.

One of the men told him, "We understand if you are afraid, George. Stay back and protect Elizabeth and Launa."

Jacorry, one of the willing fighters added, "If we fail, please help our families to safety."

George nodded his head solemnly and gathered the families outside leading them to a hidden shack which had been overlooked by the demon's gaze.

The small army fighting against Dori'naur found that killing a demon was not an easy task. They attacked while they thought the demon rested. Their rotting corpses now hang naked at the gates as a reminder to all of the promises he made. Each body had a message carved in it, for all to see: "Serve or Suffer."

Dori'naur now knew that Natallia was with child and on the run. We

just hoped we could out run the news of the demon's bounties.
***

With the news from the stranger, King Gabriel was even more on edge now that Dori'naur knew Natallia was with child. They rode for Weelinn as hard and fast as their horses could carry them. When they arrived at the city's gates, they found a party of hooded men waiting for them. The King's Guard drew their swords and prepared to defend their king.

Gabriel held his right hand up. "Easy, men. From whom do we have the pleasure of welcome my, good man?"

The tall man in the front stepped forward and removed his hood.

Zachery gasped. "You're an elf!" He had never seen an elf before.

He had hair as black as night, pulled to one side in a tight braid. His skin was a pale color that seemed to shimmer in the light highlighting the scar that ran from the left eye to his right cheek. A snarl came across his face. "My name is Elos. I most certainly am not a man. My master, Benzoete, is expecting you."

Gabriel climbed down from the wagon. "How is Benzoete expecting us? How did he know we were coming?"

Elos made a pathetic attempt at a grin. "Master Benzoete knows more than your pitiful life span will allow to be told. Follow us, and you will be taken care of."

The small band of elves took the group into the city. Weelinn was the central hub of merchants, the center of all trade. Buildings with people selling anything imaginable lined the city streets, fish merchants, fur traders, an odd man with a monkey telling fortunes. Weelinn had whatever goods you needed, and a nightlife that no one could resist. Another common seller was the flesh peddlers who drew patrons from all the realms.

The group followed a winding road leading to a tall building in the center of the city. Round and made of a light-colored brick, it looked as if it could touch the clouds. It was surrounded by several smaller buildings connected as one, and he structure resembled a cogwheel that had fallen out of a large machine. They approached a large blue door with strange brass hardware that looked like small hands holding the door in place. Elos turned to the group again. "My master only requires the four to come," he said, pointing to Gabriel, Natallia, Antoine, and Zachery.

"Make a perimeter around the building. No one is to disturb us. If we need you, we will call for you." Gabriel told the guards. The men saluted their king, and then followed his orders.

Elves! I could not believe we had actually found them. I hoped this Benzoete is nicer than the group he had sent to welcome us. The Gods were on our side that day.

They followed Elos up a winding staircase that led to a very large and cluttered library. The room looked as if it were larger than what the outside portrayed. Windows lined the walls, allowing a wave of sunlight to burst in. Dust fluttered in the air flying off shelves that haven't been cleaned in years. Books were as far as the eye could see on bookshelves made to look like a maze throughout the room. Standing behind a desk, mumbling to himself, was an old elf with long white hair pulled back in a braid. He wore red and gold robes that had several burn marks on it.

The elderly elf looked up. "Welcome, friends. Are you well? How was your trip?"

Zachery's jaw dropped and then exclaimed, "YOU! You are the man from the pub that told me of the prophecy! I saw you die! Twice!"

Benzoete let out a hearty laugh. "My boy, you saw only what I wanted you to see. I had to convince you of the story, so you would believe. I had to act in secret so the prying eyes and ears around you would not be alarmed. I knew when you told dear Gabriel, he would think of me and want answers. His father, Owin, spoke of me highly, did he not?"

"Yes, my father told stories of the great wizard Benzoete, with his endless knowledge and answers. How do you know of Dori'naur and that our child is the Champion?" Gabriel asked, looking very confused.

Benzoete walked over to a large basin filled with water surrounded by blood red candles. "When you are connected to the Water of Life, nothing escapes your gaze. I have seen these demons and I have seen your child. All of these acts can be altered, so we have to protect this child, for he holds our future. But only, if allowed to mature and harness his power."

Natallia rested a hand on her stomach. "What power will he be born with?"

"In due time, my Lady. We must concentrate on your and the child's protection," Benzoete said.

Antoine listened closely. "But how do we protect my sister and her child?"

Before the wizard could explain, Zachery stood and spoke. "In Bronze Valley you told me that the child would grow but no one here would know. Also, that I was the key. Please, tell me what needs to be done."

Benzoete walked over to a shelf and started fumbling through his books on his desk.

"Ah, here it is. The Book of the Ancients." The old wizard passed page after page until he reached a passage and read aloud. "*Tel yeste' en' nelde will come e'a. Atara whos findl s en' flames, helma en' I moon, ar' proto ed I' Dire Draug, Sha deli var.*"

Elos smiled, but the rest of the group remained confused. Benzoete rolled his eyes and translated, forgive me. "The first of three will come as the tree. A champion of light will come into sight. The mother whose hair is of the flames, skin of the pale moon, and protected by the Dire Wolf, she shall deliver."

Natallia looked faint, grasping Gabriel's arm. "How does this book know of me and our child?"

Benzoete walked over and placed a hand on her shoulder. "My dear, we are all connected in this life force. What shall come has already happened and what has happened shall come again.

Everything revolves in life's circle, if it is not broken. The future is set, unless we change it. I have fought these demons before, we need your child to be the turning factor."

Gabriel looked hard at the old elf. "All right, then what do these Life Waters say we need to do? We have a world to save. We will not allow this demon to have his way with our people."

Benzoete clasped his hands together and said, "Talking to you is as if I'm speaking with King Owin again. I knew the Waters had chosen correctly."

King Gabriel spoke, and it stirred the inner fire in all of us. I wanted to serve him and fight 'til life's last breath. I just hoped we could save our world before our last breath occurred.

9

New Family Found

Benzoete turned to Zachery. "You hold the key. Do you think it was chance that your father found the soon-to-be king in the forest that day?"

Gabriel looked to him with utter confusion, the feeling shared among them all. Benzoete asked the boy. "What do you know of your grandmother child? Your father's mother."

"She died of the fever when my father was very young. He was too young even to remember her," Zachery said.

George rarely spoke of her, at least to Zachery.

"Yes, George told me the same when we were growing up. What does his mother have to do with this?" asked Gabriel.

With a gentle smile and warm eyes, Benzoete looked to Gabriel. "Your meeting in the forest was more than happenstance. It was the fates moving the pawns of life in the direction they needed to be moved." The wizard looked to Zachery and asked. "Do you have the dagger that your father used that day to slay the spider?"

He reached for his boot. "I am growing tired of wanting to ask how you know these things!" As Zachery pulled the dagger from his boot, Benzoete stretched forth his hand, waiting for it. The wizard's next statement changed Zachery, forever.

As Benzoete gazed in remembrance at the blade, his fingers fumbled over the shiny gold gems stones encased in a brass handle. "I asked about your grandmother because she was special to me. Well, she is special to me. You see, I can assure you she did not die of fever. She did not die at all. She is my daughter," he said.

The room suddenly fell silent.

Zachery's words seemed to not want to be spoken. "How. . . How could this be? How could my grandmother be an elf? How could. . . Why did. . . How could my father lie to me and keep this secret from everyone?" Zachery said, as his mind flooded with questions.

"They had to keep it a secret, because for an elf and a human to become involved, laws of life had to be broken. When they learned that a child had been conceived, she had a choice. Valindra could renounce her elven heritage, her immortality, everything that made her elvish," Benzoete explained. "Or renounce her husband and child."

Zachery, who was usually reserved, could not hold it in. "And she did not? What kind of mother does not do everything in her power to be with her child?"

Benzoete gently sat him back down. "The kind of elvish mother who has a child with one of the noblest humans I have ever known. Doron, your grandfather, did not allow Valindra to give up her gifts. He told her that after he was gone, George would need someone looking after him, even if it was from afar. They made the choice to sacrifice their love for their child."

"If she had made the choice to renounce her gifts, they could have lived as a family. Is that not better for all of them?" asked Gabriel.

Elos, who had been standing quietly by, stepped forward. "Elves are known for their gifts. Master Benzoete, is one of three Grand High Wizards left in all of Amundiss. I am but his apprentice in the Light. If the magic possessed in their bloodline passed to their half-blood child, he would have been taken from them to train. The Elven Order of Magic would have not given them a choice. George would have been taken to Eska'Taurn. With the choice your grandmother made, he was guaranteed to know at least one parent, instead of risking him being taken from both. Very few of our race still possess the power of the magics."

"George was watched very carefully, but he never showed signs of his elvish side being present," Benzoete explained. "The elven order of magics made sure he was human dominant." He twirled the dagger in his hand. "This dagger was a gift from the old gods to my father's father; it was forged in the flames of the high elves by the Gods, given as a token of their love. It has been passed down to each generation and used in the great War of the Gods that sent Craotonus into exile. It has seen many years in the hands of high elves, and now it is proudly in your possession, my child."

Benzoete waved his hand and made a bookshelf slide to one side. As the shelf shifted, books fell to the floor, forcing a cloud of dust up. Zachery's eyes widened for hidden behind the shelf was a hollowed out portion of the wall. Inside the hole in the wall was something very unusual. Zachery's first thought was a giant lizard, bigger than he had ever seen running around the farmhouse. As he stepped closer, he could see rows of sharp teeth leading up to the hollow eye sockets of a once majestic beast: a real dragon skull.

"Dragons hold a special magic within them, even after death. They are fierce fighting creatures that cannot easily be tamed," Benzoete told them.

Antoine laughed, "You speak of them as if they still exist. We all know the fables. The last ones were killed over three-thousand years ago!"

Benzoete stared coldly at Antoine. "Yes, where do you think *this* skull came from? Your people, *Humans*, destroy all things they do not understand. Dragons need leaders, a rider to control them."

Antoine slapped his knee. "Dragon Riders were a myth mothers told their children to calm them before bed. Magical protectors of the realm! No man has ever had the power to control a dragon!"

Elos stepped toward Antoine, clenching his fists to hold back his anger. "You are correct, no mere human could ever harness the power of a Dragon Rider; the High Elves were the original riders. Elves and dragons shared a connection, and if the elf had the rider's bloodline, they were as one. These magical creatures were beautiful to behold and deadly to oppose."

Zachery shouted to get the adults attention. "What does this have to do with me? I am not special. I know both my parents and they are just simple farmers."

The room fell silent. They knew they did not need to fight amongst themselves.

Benzoete came to him, leaned down and looked him in the eyes. "Dear boy, everyone is special. That is the one thing humans seem to forget. Alas, in your situation, I believe you are more than you think. We believe the magic skipped your father and lies dormant inside of you.

"That is what drew Dori'naur to your garden. He believed it was the champion's home. Come, take the dagger. Insert it into skull of the dragon. Find the slot in the top, just behind where the eyes once were. Close your eyes and concentrate on what brings you happiness. Let the Light wash over you and feel what the beast is telling you."

Zachery stepped up to the skull. He found the opening and traced it with his finger. As he brought the blade closer, the eyes started glowing. He shoved the blade in up to the hilt. Grasping the handle with both hands, he closed his eyes and thought of home. His father, mother, even his sister, that is where he wanted to be most of all.

"Home. I just want to go home. To sleep in my own bed and smell my mother's cooking in the morning." Those were the people Zachery wanted to protect most.

Benzoete stood behind him, chanting in an elvish tongue. The eyes of the skull glowed brighter red; a light aura shone around the room giving the dust the appearance of flames. Suddenly, a vision of the Morely farm appeared in Zachery's head and he smiled. Zachery released the handle and stepped back. Home. Home with his family is what made him happy. All the years of yearning for adventure, and home was what simply excited him now. The group stood as one, in awe of what they had just seen, no doubt wondering the same thing: did this mean Zachery was to be a wizard?

"Very good, Zachery. Now, I am certain you are the one." Benzoete took the dagger from the skull and presented it back to him.

"I am the one, for what? What does all this mean?" he asked.

Benzoete flashed a warm smile at him. "You carry the blood of the Rider. You will protect the Champion of Light until your power, and his, is at full strength. Your powers combined will defeat the demons and save our world from extinction. The blood of the heavens will free us from this terror. As for the rest of us, we will endure many hardships as the journey will be long. Our mission is clear, survival. Your mission, my young Morely, is to protect and hide."

The old wizard turned Zachery to face the others in the room. "Behold! The line is intact once more. I give you, the *Dragon Rider!*"

Me, a Dragon Rider? My head spun out of control when I heard this. The only good thing inside my thoughts that day was seeing Morely Farm again, even if it was in a vision. All this was hard to comprehend, especially that my grandfather was a High Elf wizard!

10
Dori'naur Keeps His Word

At castle Whitehold, Dori'naur spread fear among the people. Anyone who spoke against him as the new king and ruler found themselves with cold steel against their necks. The men were put into his army and sent to other realms; if they opposed they were beaten until submission or death; either served Dori'naur's liking, while the women and children were used as servants or spies. Any others were used for sport and his amusement. When the demon grew bored, he would have the good people of Whitehold fight each other to the death as he watched.

"You puny sacks of bone are worthless. One slice, and you bleed everywhere. I need entertainment! Find me someone who can fight!" Dori'naur bellowed out to his servants.

If the people would not fight, he would have them slowly tortured and killed as everyone was forced to watch. Somehow, George and Elizabeth managed to stay away from the demon during all of his misdeeds. Keeping to the back towers and remote storage shacks behind the castle, they kept a small group of refugees on the move, trying to stay ahead of Dori'naur's sight. George felt he had a responsibility to keep as many people safe as possible, which meant keeping them from the demon's army and out of the clutches of the ones who followed him out of fear.

From behind a pillar leading to the kitchen, George whispered to Elizabeth, "How many more came in today?"

"I counted twenty. Mostly scared women and children," she answered.

George shook his head in disbelief. "Try to talk to them. We have to get as many away from here as soon as we can. I fear if we stay much longer, we may fall to the demon, or worse, Launa could."

The Morelys hid as many people as they could, but it seemed more and more came from other towns and realms daily. Dori'naur's army ransacked small villages and brought the survivors to fill ranks wherever needed. Any women found to be with child was brought directly to him. The things done to these women were horrible.

"I see you are with child. Who were your parents?" Dori'naur asked.

"Just simple folk, your Grace. I beg you, don't hurt my baby!" The woman said, clearly distraught.

Dori'naur ran a cold, crusted finger along her belly, studying her child from the outside in. The woman trembled with fear.

"Is it you Champion?" Dori'naur asked as his finger pierced her stomach. The woman screamed in pain and fright. Blood flowed down his hand and puddled on the floor. "Bah! You are not the vessel!" He sent the woman flying with a smash from the back of his hand.

George and his refugees knew they had a long journey ahead of them while the champion grew in strength, but they had faith. Faith that their world would be saved and the demon would be sent back to the hell from where he came. Faith was a big word for George and Elizabeth because they had to keep their trust in Gabriel to keep Zachery safe. Little did they know it would be their son doing the saving.

My father may not have had the magical powers of the High Elves, but he did possess some rare and unique traits: bravery, compassion, and love for his fellow man.

***

Dori'naur stood before his army and gave the command. "Bring me the head of this Queen and rewards will be yours! Fail me and you will feel my thorns from the inside out!"

Dori'naur was a force never dealt with before, not at least in this century. The people could hardly withstand this much punishment. Everything was coming together just as the demon had planned. "Soon, I will sacrifice the vessel of the Champion of Light, open the pathway for my brother, and bring this world to its knees." He said as he sat on the king's throne.

Dori'naur hefted the skull of one of the villagers in his hand, looked straight into its eye sockets. "I told them this world would be ours for the taking," he cackled. "They could not destroy us the first time, and now the High Elves are scattered. I will find the vessel and end her life. Without the Champion, the Heavens will fall to our master."

Dori'naur brought pain and destruction to every realm, with little effort. Faith, hope, and the willingness to survive was all the people had. They had to persevere. George kept the illusion of loyalty to Dori'naur to avoid his family's heads on spikes. Why was the demon so obsessed with death?

These were good people. We were determined to stop this suffering. We needed the Light to shine again over every being of this world.

Dori'naur had decided his castle needed a few upgrades. The once very proud and noble throne of King Gabriel was now adorned with the skulls of his people. Hundreds of skulls lined the structure spilling out across the floor like a carpet. The walls were now coated red with the blood of Whitehold's citizens. He covered the king's family crest with the skull and crossbones of Xavier, the king's adviser. As a lesson to the others in loyalty, he left poor Xavier's face intact, showing the fear the old man had at the time of his demise.

"This! This is a throne room fit for a ruler! This is the throne of a true king and champion!" Dori'naur boasted.

The new army of the demon flooded the realms, and brought back stories of fear. The news of Dori'naur swept over the lands like wildfire. The people were afraid and his fear is what seemed to fuel him in his ways of evil. There was a method to his madness; he was preparing the world for something even greater than himself. A force thought to be gone long ago. "Soon, revenge will fall on those who wronged us. The Heavens will shake at our feet." Dori'naur said as he smashed the skull against the wall.

The lives of so many had already been lost. Amundiss had been cast into a dark and dangerous time. The Light was needed more than ever.

11

A Visit from Beyond

The Book of the Ancients was a worn, cracked, dusty old book, not beautiful by any means. It had been passed down through the centuries by the elven wizards. Written by the hands of the Gods themselves, it has proven to be a worthy guide for the High Elves.

Benzoete ran his crooked fingers along the leather cover and a smile emerged on his face with the memory of his mother reading to him from these very pages rushing through his mind. He opened it up to a section of pages and enumerated his plan.

"Zachery and the queen are not safe here, nor in any region or realm we might choose to go to in this world. I have used the Book of the Ancients and Waters of Life to search for a place that will serve as a safe haven."

Antoine asked, "You say they are not safe in this world. What does that mean?"

"I have used the Book of the Ancients to search the Waters of Life, and found a new world that will nurture them both while they harness their powers," Benzoete explained. "It will provide protection from Dori'naur and his forces. I trust the people in this room. No one else can know of this plan. I will use the book as a map, then open a portal to the new world."

"How will we fit in this new world? Will we be in danger from the people there?" Zachery asked.

"Yes, should one of us go with them to help protect them there?" asked Gabriel.

Benzoete shook his head. "No, we need everyone else here. This world is much like our own, except they have yet to harness magic. That is a good thing. Without magic, it will be very difficult for Dori'naur to locate them. They will blend in nicely and not cause alarm, as long as they keep out of sight when communicating back here and during the boy's training. I fear if we do not succeed in killing the demon brethren, they will target this world next. The brethren fought during the War of the Gods. They are ruthless and unmerciful. Our wizards could barely hold them back then. With our ranks almost extinct we need the Champion of Light. We will need his power to defeat them."

Not only was our world at stake, but the fate of these good people hung in the balance of our success. The weight of responsibility that hung on me then, and my then fifteen seasons old shoulders was heavy. I could feel the fear and doubt swell inside me waiting to burst.

Gabriel had a concerned look on his face. "How will we explain the Queen's whereabouts when the demon's forces come for her?" he asked. "We have to make them believe she is still here. Keep them from finding their true location."

Elos looked to his master, and then back to the king, "We have that under control, for now. You will have to trust us."

Antoine didn't like the sound of that. "Right now, we have no choice. You are our only line of hope against this monster. We will do as you say. We are in your hands."

Benzoete clapped his hands together and smiled. "Wonderful! We will get started tomorrow." He wrapped his staff on the door loudly and called for a chambermaid. In walked a thin elvish girl dressed in white linens. "This is El'nora. She will attend to your every need. Your men downstairs are being fed and will have a warm place to rest for tonight. They must not know of this, no one can. El'nora will show you to your chambers now. If you need anything, please let her know. Try to get a peaceful night's rest, you will need it."

Antoine leaned close to Gabriel's ear, "Was she standing guard at the door, or trying to listen?"

"She did enter rather quickly. She is Elven, surely she is loyal to Benzoete." Gabriel said.

With that, Benzoete and Elos exited and El'nora showed them to their rooms. She led them down a long hallway, with many doors that followed a circular pattern. One by one she opened the door, checked the bed linens, and slowly bowed her head to each all while never speaking a word, or making eye contact, acting nervous for some reason. The next morning the group would embark on a journey that no one ever thought possible.

My room was huge, nearly the size of our barn back home. Smelled a lot better, too. The walls were lined with portraits of elven leaders and bookcases filled with books I could not read. I was not used to the royal like conditions by any means, and the added pressure of what would come the next morning had me terrified. I didn't think I would be able to sleep a wink, and with what happened next, I really thought I had gone insane.

***

That night, Zachery lay awake wondering whether he would ever see his family again. "I pray to the old Gods and new. I pray to the fates and creators. Please keep my family safe, see them through this."

He knew the dangers that lay before him if they stayed and the dangers of an unknown new world they would have to face. Thinking of the danger all these people would face with Dori'naur and his army was unbearable. His mind began to wander and to doubt.

"How could a farm boy and an unborn child be the hope of a whole world? Or two worlds now, for that matter? I am not a warrior, or savior. I cannot defeat this demon," Zachery wondered aloud.

Not only defeating Dori'naur, but as well as these Brethren the demon provided the way for.

"Benzoete seemed to have confidence in me, but why? Because my grandmother was an elf? I am not trained in combat, and I doubt my skills in milking cows and feeding chickens will defeat demons." Zachery covered his face with his hands and just lay there quietly.

He was finally able to fall asleep though in a state of slumber, his mind still churned with questions. Visions of his home burned to the ground while a mad demon stood laughing at him, gave his body no rest. He tossed and turned, sweat rolling from his brow. Suddenly, from beyond his dream world, he heard a voice softly call to him.

"Zachery, wake my child." It belonged to the voice of a woman, but from where?

He rose from his bed, and wiped the sleep from his eyes, to see who had come. "Natallia, is that you?"

At the foot of his bed stood a beautiful woman with long black hair. Her skin shone like a bright, glowing light. Her voice, like that of angels, calmed his spirit and made him feel safe. She wore a white robe trimmed in gold, with a symbol of a black dragon down the sleeve. Sparkles of light twinkled around her as if she was a goddess.

"Hello, young one. My name is Valindra, I am your grandmother. I can only stay a moment before my window closes, but I need you to know your power is within you. Search diligently for it. You remind me so much of your father when he was your age."

Zachery leaned forward in his bed to get closer. He should have been frightened, but the curiosity and awe of the moment proved more powerful. Her voice soothed him, as if he already knew who she was. "How are you here?" he asked.

"I am not. It is a window of illusion. I am in the elven homeland of Eska'Taurn," Valindra explained.

"What power do I have? I'm just a child," Zachery pleaded.

Valindra winked at him. "You have the blood of the Dragon Rider. Our people were tamers of these magnificent beasts for centuries. I came to reassure you that you are the one and that all the riders doubted themselves. This is a great honor and responsibility, young one. You have a destiny, grab hold of it. My father, your great-grandfather allowed me to come to you. I do not know when or if I can again. Please tell my son, your father, that I love him from the moon and back, and he was never away from my sight. As you always will be, my child. May the Goddess watch over you."

A shower of twinkling light drifted down from above her. Resembling embers dancing above a fire, they fell over her and with that, she was gone, fading away from sight.

It was hard to explain, but her words did bring him serenity. He had never known his grandmother, and now he knew she would be with him every step. Even just as an inner thought, it was still a comfort to have her. Zachery drifted off to sleep much easier this time. His head filled with thoughts of dragons and what it would be like to have one with him along the way.

Meeting my grandmother that night was just what I needed to get me through. My head overflowed with questions, thoughts, and fears but she helped me see that I was not alone and never would be. I could not wait to see my father and tell him of this!

-

12

Next Stop: A New World

The next morning, Zachery woke to the smell of fresh bread, bacon, and eggs straight from the kiln. He almost forgot where he was.

"Something smells good. Mother has the stove hot this morning." Zachery thought while rubbing his eyes.

Gabriel knocked on his door and stepped inside. "Benzoete's plan is to perform the ritual after breakfast, to not alarm anyone that you and Natallia have gone."

Gabriel followed Zachery down the hall to the winding staircase that would take them to the main floor. As they walked to the formal dining room, those in attendance not already seated to eat, bowed to their king. The two entered the dining room from the main entrance that resembled the front gate of a castle. A hush came across the crowd as a voice announced, "His highness. King Gabriel of Whitehold and master Morely." Everyone stood and bowed to their king, then returned to their meal. They arrived at a table set for the royal breakfast at Castle Whitehold. Fitting, since the king himself, had a seat at the head of the massive table. Maidens walked from person to person, filling glasses and piling plates high with food.

Zachery looked around the room in awe. "I have never seen so much food at one setting. This is amazing."

As everyone enjoyed their meal Benzoete stood. "Greetings to all our new friends. It is an honor to dine with his grace, King Gabriel and the beautiful Queen Natallia of Castle Whitehold. Today marks a historic day for all; we, the elves of Eska'Taurn who have made our way here in Weelinn, join forces with the army of Whitehold to find a way to crush this threat that has been lain at our door. Like the original elders of ancient times, we will prevail. I and my advisers will work diligently with the king and his men to defeat Dori'naur before he can cause more havoc and horror on all the good people of Amundiss."

The cheers from the dining area were deafening; the High Elf wizard spoke with such encouragement. Adrenaline was raging as it stirred everyone to do their part in this war. Zachery was ready. He understood he had to sacrifice to gain.

Benzoete was a natural speaker. He sparked a fire in everyone. I believed we could have ended Dori'naur right then! His wisdom and passion were plain to see, and it was reassuring, knowing the journey we were about to embark on.

Zachery knew they had to fight to be able to win, and win they would. He would be ready when asked to do his part, whatever tasks lay before him.

After the meal, Benzoete made a fictitious announcement. "I hope the food was as good as the company to all. Please, eat your fill and feel free to take as much as you would like back to your homes. I have instructed the good maidens to see that each and every one of you has food for your bellies. Elos and I will be joining the royal party in my library to help with a plan."

They were instead going to a secret temple located inside the structure only the High Elf wizard and his apprentice knew about. Benzoete placed an arm around Zachery's shoulders and leaned close to his ear. "Do not be afraid once we are back in my library. There is an elven temple hidden inside, we will be safe. Nod if you understand." Zachery took a deep breath, and nodded his head once. After they excused themselves, Benzoete led the party through a large door that opened to a staircase lined with brass rails. As they entered the library, guards were placed at the entrance of the library door with strict orders not to let anyone inside, anyone at all.

Once everyone was in place and accounted for, Benzoete waved his hand and spoke. "*Kella tora, strall en' tel i.*"

Books began to fly from a set of bookshelves directly in the back portion of the room. The books hovered in a small circle at the top of the room while candles shook and flew out of their holders. The two bookcases slide across the walls, revealing an open, dark doorway with strange writing starting at the floor of the left side, winding all the way around the circular top, to the floor on the right. The smell that escaped from the pitch black void was damp and musky.

"Once we descend into the stairwell, I will close the entrance. Only I can reopen it. No one will come looking here for you, for only Elos and I know of this place. If this fails, and something happens to me, you all will perish inside the temple." Benzoete searched their faces and saw they were ready and understood the consequences.

Elos was the first to enter the stairwell. As he walked, the torches on either side of the walls lit one by one. After the last one entered, Benzoete spoke again. "*Amalla en' tora shall en' tora Dien.*"

The doorway closed and they could hear the room return to the way it was when they entered. When the sound of books returned to their resting places upon the shelves and the thud of the bookcases sliding back against the wall was heard, they knew there was no turning back.

Gabriel patted Zachery on the back. "I have faith in you."

Five little words that seemed to wash the fear and doubt from his mind. They had a duty to all the people to give them a chance to live. They continued down the stairwell until it opened to a massive temple floor. The walls were decorated with artifacts from Eska'Taurn. In the center of the round room stood an altar of pure white marble surrounded by seven blood red candles.

Benzoete laid a hand on young Zachery's shoulder. "It's time. We must stay strong and say our farewells."

Elos stood beside the altar, lighting the candles with a long, skinny, golden torch. He had changed into a white robe trimmed in gold crested with a dragon on the front, much like the one Valindra wore when she visited Zachery. Benzoete walked to a shelf and retrieved a book that looked like the Book of the Ancients, but this version seemed alive. Bones protected the cover and when in the wizard's hands it seemed to move out of the way for him to open it. He placed it on a stand beside the altar. Elos handed Benzoete a robe that was like his own. Benzoete tied the gold frayed cord around his waist as he motioned with his hands, "Please, Queen Natallia, you and young Morely join me at the altar. The rest of you, stand to the outer edges and do not speak during the ritual."

Natallia leaned toward Gabriel. "I love you, my dear husband. You have brought me more happiness than I could have ever deserved." She leaned forward for a kiss.

"This is not a farewell kiss, my love." Gabriel put a hand on her stomach. "We shall be together again, as a family. I trust in Benzoete. We will win this war against the demons. Then we will sit at Castle Whitehold with our son at our side."

Natallia wanted to believe that very badly. She longed for this to be over and to have her life back to normal. She hugged her brother Antoine, and said her goodbyes.

"I need to go with you. To protect you. I need you to be safe," Antoine told her.

Natallia kissed his cheek and wiped the single tear off his face. "You have protected me my whole life. Now I need you to protect Gabriel. I want him in one piece when I return."

She walked over to stand beside Benzoete at the altar.

Gabriel stopped Zachery. "I have known your father nearly my entire life, we are as brothers. I know he would be proud of the man that he has raised, and I promise you, he will know of your bravery and courage."

As the king extended his hand, Zachery realized he was a man now. Childhood was left behind that door in the old wizard's library. He stepped up and listened as Benzoete shared what little advice he had of the new world to help them on this new journey.

"First thing, you are no longer Queen of Whitehold or anything for that matter. You have to tell anyone that asks you hail from a place called England. Do not tell anyone where you are really from. You will have to fit in and make your way among these people, find work, find a home," he told them.

I knew this was my destiny. I would train to be a Dragon Rider. A chuckle escaped from inside me. A Dragon Rider in a land without dragons, magic, or my family. This was going to be hard, but it had to work. I would make this work somehow.

Benzoete handed Natallia an emerald stone attached to a necklace. "I will be able to communicate with you from time to time, but only for brief moments. Wear this. It will let you know when we can talk. Keep it hidden under your garments so as not to attract thieves.

At the time it alerts you, you must find a mirror in your home and wait to see me." He searched their faces to see if they understood. With that, he gave a nod to Elos.

A chant started from the apprentice, and Benzoete extended a hand to help Natallia onto the altar. Next, Zachery. The kind old wizard smiled. "Close your eyes and concentrate. May the Gods be with you, and soon we will be back together, stronger than ever."

He joined Elos in chanting the ritual. The air started to swirl. All the candles around the altar flared up, and strange symbols flew around them, as if they were ricocheting off the walls. A giant, swirling portal opened above the altar. Benzoete and Elos backed away from them, hands stretched toward the portal, the two elves were chanting together as one. Louder and louder. "*Kella tor' en Kello dah tri oss!*"

The portal fell upon the altar. Light shone so bright the ones standing around the altar had to shield their eyes.

"I love you, my darling!" Gabriel shouted to Natallia. "Be strong and know I am with you!"

The air became normal again as the candles flickered. Natallia and Zachery were gone. Gabriel rushed to Benzoete. "Did it work? Are they alright?"

Benzoete walked over to a mirror, waved his hand, and the mirror rippled like water. He gazed into it. "Yes, I can see them. They are on a hill overlooking a small town with strange buildings. It is in their hands now. They have to establish themselves as a part of that world. Once they do that, we will be able to communicate briefly with them."

13

The Queen Has Fallen

At Castle Whitehold, Dori'naur was busy adding fresh skulls to adorn his throne when a captain of the Dark Guard escorted a servant from Weelinn into the throne room.

"What do you want, maggot? I have pressing matters to attend. This had better be useful or you will become a wall fixture!" Dori'naur sneered.

It was El'nora, the chambermaid from Benzoete's tower. She fell before him landing on her face. "I have come looking for safety for me and my family in return for the information you seek," said the woman.

Dori'naur was intrigued. "The value of this information will determine the value of your safety. Speak."

El'nora knelt before him weeping. "My Lord, the king and queen are in Weelinn seeking help from my master, Benzoete."

"Former king!" Dori'naur shouted. "I am the ruler of this land until my master takes his rightful place."

"My apologies, my Lord. I do not wish to offend. The former

ruler and his party are in Weelinn. I stood outside the door trying to listen to their plan. Alas, the doors are thick in the tower, I could only hear pieces. Master Benzoete has a plan that will protect the former queen and her child. Whatever the plan is, I know it is soon. You will have to act fast." El'nora stood waiting for Dori'naur to react.

The demon cackled. "So, they think they can hide from us? We shall rain death upon them and deliver the vessel of light back to ash!" Dori'naur beamed with delight. "Captain, take the woman to the gates." He threw a handful of gold at the servant for her information. "Run. The next time we meet, I will not be so gracious."

Dori'naur decided his new army would march into Weelinn and destroy them. He stepped through the doorway leading out to a balcony, overlooking the courtyard where his army trained. "Attention my army! The enemy has been discovered. Your services are required to assist your masters. If you fail terrible, excruciating pain can be expected, but riches will befall the one that brings us the head of the false queen! Take this city of Weelinn and shake it from its foundation!"

The army of the dark one stirred. Avoiding harm to these people was unavoidable, they had to do his bidding. Steeling themselves, they marched for Weelinn.

***

Dori'naur was not the only one with spies in the realm. Benzoete's great power allowed him to hear the news the wind brought of the army headed their way. He and Elos went to the Waters of Life to see the events unfolding.

"We have to act quickly, my master. We do not have much time to prepare," Elos said to Benzoete.

They rushed to Gabriel and Benzoete explained what they had seen. "We need to bring haste to our plan, Dori'naur marches on the city. He must have had a spy amongst my ranks."

"Natallia is safe, far away from here. Let them come!" Antoine growled with hate.

Gabriel looked to the wizard. "What will happen when they march on the city and find she is not here?"

Elos shifted his eyes to Benzoete and back to Gabriel. "We have a plan of sorts, to buy us some time. It is not a very moral plan, but it may be our best chance."

At this time, any plan will be a good plan. They did not know exactly how many of the demon's army would descend on the city, but knew they would not stop until they had delivered the queen back to the demon.

"We have the corpse of a woman in the same age range as the queen. She was with child at the time of her demise. She was ill and came here looking for help. Her ailment had progressed and even my magic could not help her; fever ran through her body, killing her and the child. She had no family that she spoke of. We were preparing her for burial when you arrived. I can use a spell of illusion to transform her into Natallia. It should buy us the time we need to get to a safer place and plan our next move." Benzoete explained.

As the sun slowly sank down behind the hills, an alarm sounded. The army had arrived. The elven guards, the city defense, and the king's guard were ready.

The army broke through the main gates and poured into the city. The sound of steel rang through the streets and alleyways. Death, destruction, and bloodshed was everywhere. Antoine and Gabriel ran into the fray, swords blazing in the haze of the setting sun, trying to help the men.

"We have to delay them. Benzoete needs more time!" Antoine shouted as he sliced through one of the former citizens of Whitehold.

Gabriel retorted. "How many must we kill? These are good people who are simply scared."

As the army pushed through the city, the High Elf wizard said an enchantment over the body of the dead woman and she transformed into an exact replica of the beautiful Queen Natallia. He and Elos took the body to the ground floor, set her hands with rope and, with her body between them, carried her out to the streets. Benzoete placed his hand on the back of the corpse, directly behind her heart and whispered, *"Hillin ter fret, Tella' no ray."* The woman's body began to twitch.

"We have what you want!" shouted Elos. "Take her and leave; we want no more bloodshed!"

They shoved the twitching body into the alley. The dark army rushed to the queen, trying to be the first to take her head and claim their prize. The illusion worked to perfection. Dori'naur's people greedily fought against each other in hope of receiving the rewards. With all the confusion, this gave the defenders a chance to swoop in and attack the distracted army. The more they killed today, the less they had to worry about later.

The guards who rushed to defend their queen were fooled by the illusion.

"Save the queen! They have abandoned her!" One of the King's Guards shouted.

The King's Guard fought fearlessly, trying to save a woman who was not their queen and already dead. The men fought fearlessly. They started to devour the attacking army, swords found their marks and laid waste to those carrying out the evil demon's commands. Pushed back by the horde of attackers, the army was finally able to get to the woman.

One of the dark one's soldiers had sliced her head clean off her at the shoulders. Excited, he hoisted his prize and ran for the gates. Another of the army tripped him and delivered a sword through the back. The new victor snatched up the head and jumped on a horse as a horn sounded and the army retreated.

Antoine and Gabriel had to play their parts as well to avoid suspicion. They rushed to the fallen woman, swords at the ready.

"Run to your master! Tell him to be ready, for I will have vengeance! The light shall burn him and we will send him straight back to hell!" shouted Antoine.

Gabriel held the woman's body, weeping uncontrollably. It was not hard to let his emotions flow. He had just sent his true love and unborn child to a world they did not know.

"No, Natallia! No! This is not the way it is supposed to be!" sobbed the king.

He was unsure of their safety and wondered if he would ever see them again. They had to move fast and determine their next step in the plan. The illusion would not fool Dori'naur for very long and when he found out he was tricked, nothing would contain the rampage and violence that he would unleash. They had to brace for the worse and hope for the best. They sent prayers to the Gods that Natallia and Zachery were safe.

MICHAEL LACKEY

14
Celebration at
Castle Whitehold

As the demon's army returned from Weelinn, all seemed to be lost. Dori'naur was pleased with his subjects when the head of the queen was presented to him.

"We will have nothing to stop us. No one to stand in our way. Hear me my master, your day of reckoning will come." Dori'naur growled while holding the linen bag containing the woman's head.

That night, Dori'naur had planned a grand feast as a reward for their achievement. He gathered the people into the courtyard for all to witness his triumphant victory. The servants prepared tables full of food and wine. As the sun began to set, the celebration was set to begin.

Dori'naur held the bag high above his head. "Behold! The vessel of Light is within our grasp. We have toiled countless centuries on these worthless pieces of rocks you call home. Staying hidden in the shadows until we could gather strength. Waiting for the day the vessel would appear to us again. It slipped our grasps before, but now it is OURS! The other Gods will tremble at your presence!

Today, we take what is rightfully ours. . . EVERYTHING!"

Dori'naur continued his speech, the people cheering for him out of fear, knowing all was lost now. Fear overcame them, the point was clear, they had to serve or die. Some of the people, who could not bear this, had taken their own lives to avoid bearing witness to a world under Dori'naur and his brethrens' control.

The demon summoned a fireball from above with demonic language. "*Chuny mar della Qur!*"

The people cowered down in fear, as it crashed into a giant cauldron lighting a demonic fire glowing bright red and blue. He had the person who retrieved the prize stand alongside him on stage. As promised, he would bestow great riches and honor unto him.

"I, Dori'naur the First, loyal subject of the Remissum, offers this sacrifice. Our time is now. Our time is forever. Our time is always. I give back to the ashes, this vessel. Grant me the sight and wisdom to ready this world for your coming."

With that, Dori'naur tossed the head into the fire. Again, the remaining people cheered for their new ruler. As the sacrifice burned and disappeared into ash, Dori'naur noticed there was no change. This was the wrong person. They had failed him.

Clearly distraught, the demon began to shout. "You have failed me! Useless bags of flesh!" Dori'naur's eyes began to glow brighter and flames could be seen swirling around him. "This is not the vessel of Light! It is an illusion to trick us! Those damned elves!"

The people stopped their cheering and cowered in fear again. Some, ran for their lives. The one who presented the head to Dori'naur was still on stage, watching his hope fade to terror, and was the first unfortunate subject. Dori'naur grabbed him by the throat and lifted him off the ground.

"You will not fail me again, you will not fail anyone again. You wanted the reward? I wanted success!"

Saying that, he flicked his wrist and the man's neck snapped, almost separating his head from the body. The demon tossed the lifeless man into the cauldron.

"None of you shall fail us again!" Dori'naur stretched forth his hands. A ring of fire appeared around all who remained in the courtyard. Roots sprang up from the ground, wrapping around the people's ankles. "I warned you not to fail us. I told you of the pain you would suffer if you did. Humans are useless, unreliable, and weak. Always have been and always will be, but we know how to remedy this problem."

With a booming voice he spoke in the demonic tongue once more. "*Kur dey jus! Gree hu nuu!*"

The roots pierced the skin of the people; they all cried out in pain. Sounds of torture and demonic laughter echoed off the walls of the courtyard. The roots entered their veins, traveling through their bodies until it reached their hearts. Their bodies flailed on the ground as the roots ripped the skin from their flesh, replacing it with bark-like armor to resemble their master. The poisonous venom of the thorns turned the people's love for one another into pure hatred. Their spirits broken, hearts crushed, and replaced with a black seed of evil, shattering their free will. Bones snapped inside the bodies, conforming to a new likeness. Their very souls turned black as the moonless night. They now knew only how to serve Dori'naur. They became the essence of Dori'naur himself. As it ended, they all stood as one, at attention before their master.

"Yes, very good indeed! We should have started this way." The demon let out an ear-piercing roar. "The vessel will be ours. The Remissum will rule all. We will deliver all worlds unto him."

Who was The Remissum? Was he the dark figure I saw in the garden that started all this? When the people who managed to flee told Gabriel of these things, it was clear that Amundiss was in grave danger. Things did not look good at this point. The bright spot was that Queen Natallia and I were safe in this new world away from the demon and his new army, for now.

During the start of the celebration, George and Elizabeth were able to use all the festivities as a distraction.

"Our time is now, are the people ready?" George asked her.

Elizabeth had tears in her eyes, "Yes. Do you think this is best? Can we survive?"

"We will surely die inside the castle. We will search for Gabriel, he should have a plan," George said.

They took Launa and whoever was willing to try, and exited the castle in search of a safer location. This was a good decision otherwise they would suffer the demon's wrath along with the others.

"Quickly, we have horses and a few buggies waiting outside the south wall. Take only what you need." George told the people.

George knew if he was going to protect his family he could not do it within the walls of Castle Whitehold. This new ragtag bunch of refugees had to stay on the run and try to find Gabriel and Natallia. George knew of a quiet place his father took him as a boy. The town of Casterton was a small town with few people, mostly farmers that stayed to themselves unless they needed to trade some of their wares for materials they needed. Something about this quiet town always made George feel good, like a home away from home. He felt a connection to this place and never knew why. Maybe it was out of the way enough to buy them time to regroup and find the others.

George knew that Gabriel would not stand idly by and let the demons take over his world: he needed an army of his own. George and Elizabeth were busy trying to give him that army. George knew this fight was his.

15

Benzoete Helped to Rewrite the Ancients

Inside Benzoete's library, Gabriel and Antoine sat and waited patiently in some chairs that smelled of smoke and water.

"It worries me that everything this wizard has smells of smoke," Antoine said.

Gabriel covered his nose and tried to mask the smell.

Elos walked in. "The illusion has worked for now. It will buy us precious time, but he will discover that he was tricked and Natallia is still alive."

Benzoete entered the room with a rather confused look upon his face. Elos looked to him and asked, "Master, have you fallen ill."

"No, good Elos, I am well. It's this." Benzoete held out one of the Books of the Ancients. "I have studied the Books of the Ancients many, many times in my centuries. Yet I have never come across this chapter. I retrieved the book to come and speak with you, dropped it, and when it opened, it opened to this part."

Elos went to his master to see for himself. "How can this be? This portion was not there earlier, I am sure of it. It spoke of the Champion being aided by the new Dragon Rider in a new world."

Gabriel looked shocked. "What else does this new chapter say? Does it reveal how Natallia and our child will fare in this new world?"

A puzzled Benzoete read the new passage again. "It speaks of dangers, turmoil, and death. That we are not safe here, we need to go to a new place, a safer place, as the vessel has done."

Antoine asked, "Where can we go that is safer? Can we too, go to the new world now?"

"I will not abandon the people of this world. They will need someone to look to until the Champion and the others return." Gabriel said pounding his fist into his hand.

The old wizard walked over to his desk, pulled up a chair, and pushed other books to the floor in a cloud of dust. He placed the open book on top of the now cleared desk and began to read. "We need to head north. We will be going to a place not many have come back from. We need to go to the Valley of Ice Shadows in the outer realm of Ndoren'Ba. There we will find the Tomb of the First Elders."

Gabriel stood, threw on a cloak, and grabbed his sword, Fuascailte and said, "Then north it is. I will get Lucas to ready the men."

"My king there is more you need to know." Benzoete stopped him. "We will need to find George Morely. He will be the key to helping me in opening the door to the tomb. It speaks of heavy blood magic sealing the doorway. If anyone tried to open it besides two male descendants of an Elder, grave dangers will be unleashed around the tomb with death in its wake. My mother was Aliz'Ra, the second seat of the elders." Benzoete explained.

Antoine said, "So that makes Morely a descendant of hers as well."

"Where is Aliz'Ra now? Can she be of any help to us?" Gabriel asked.

"Sadly, she perished in the original War of the Gods. Craotonus and his minions were too much for us. She gave her life for me and a few other high elves to get away. Her last words to me were, 'Carry the fight for the Light close to heart, for it would come again.' She smiled and ran into the minion army taking many down with her which gave us the distraction we needed to flee." Benzoete lowered his head to wipe the tears from his face.

At that moment, all seemed to know how they all were connected in this, even Elos, the stoic, stone-faced elf. As a child, he watched as his father was torn to shreds by the minions during this war. They all had sacrifice. They all had loved ones lost to a cause that was not their doing. For some, this was not the first war. For others, the feelings were fresh and felt like scars of the heart.

Gabriel asked them, "You said there was a minion army? Can we expect that as well?"

Benzoete raised his head, "I would say most definitely. We must prepare for everything we know and some of what we do not."

"After we find the Morelys, and make it through this Valley of Ice Shadows to the tomb, what then?" Antoine asked Benzoete "How do we know what we find inside will help us defeat this demon Dori'naur?"

Elos approached the warrior. He pointed in the direction of Benzoete and said, "Faith my new friend. Our ancestors gave their lives to defeat these minions centuries ago. I have faith they will show us how to do it again."

Gabriel walked over to an open window. "Where are you, George? I need you once more old friend."

***

Gabriel sent Lucas to ready the men as Antoine assisted the elven wizards gather supplies for a trip to find Benzoete's half-elf grandson, George Morely.

"This is going to be a long and weary journey. I will not lie to you, good men," Gabriel had said as the men got ready. "I will also understand and relinquish you of your vows if you wish to stay behind. Most of us will not make it. Those of us that do survive will be helping to ensure our future generations can live in peace without the fear of Dori'naur or his people."

Gabriel finished his orders and none of the men chose to stay. "We do not need vows or titles to know what is right, my king. We will follow you. We will fight with you. And if our name is called to go to the afterlife, we will die for you." Lucas said as he pounded his chest in salute. In unison, the entire group pounded their armor. This group was loyal to the end.

Gabriel knelt before his people, "Then my vow to you, is that I will give every ounce of my soul to free this world." He stood and saluted the men with a pound of his chest.

***

"How far is this Valley of Ice Shadows? I have never heard of this place," Antoine asked.

Benzoete replied, "No one knows for sure. The ones who have gone looking for this place either perished along the way or came back insane, mad out of their mind. With a hell-bent demon hunting us and unable to locate the whereabouts of my grandson, it will definitely take longer than we can afford."

Elos shook his head and looked to his master then walked over to the cauldron with the Waters of Life. Concentrating on George and Elizabeth Morely, the waters began to bubble and churn and Elos could see them. "They have hidden themselves with a group of refugees inside a temple in Casterton."

Benzoete beamed with delight. "Well done, Elos! I see the student is ready to be a teacher. Casterton is only a two-day ride from here. We will have a head start since the demon does not know this yet. We go there first, then on to the Valley of Ice Shadows."

Little did the group of heroes know, standing under that window had been a scared and frail woman who desperately wanted to gain favor with the demon. She now had a bargaining chip of information to go to Castle Whitehold with.

Seemed my father's elven heritage was coming into play after all. I just hoped he handled the news of his mother well, we did not need him to have a mental breakdown on everyone now. Not being this close to an answer.

***

Dori'naur now knew that Natallia and her unborn child still lived. He had mutated the good people of Whitehold into a new army he could control. Spies in every direction kept their eyes open for news of the queen's location wanting to gain favor with the demon.

"We have to find this champion. My brother and I have battled the light before and it burned beyond belief. I must prepare this world before your arrival and dispose of this threat. If I can ready this world and have my brother join me, the brethren can devour everything and prepare for your coming, helping you to gather your strength so even the Champion of Light cannot mettle." Dori'naur spoke to the shadowy figure in the corner of his chambers.

Just then a servant burst in the room and the figure hissed and disappeared in a cloud of black and purple smoke. "My Lord, we have news!"

Dori'naur spun around and pinned the servant to the wall with thorns. "Do not disturb me without notice!"

The servant gasped for air. "But…but my Lord, we know where Benzoete and Gabriel are going. They go to find George Morely in a place called Casterton. He holds some key to unlocking the secrets from the first War of the Gods." As the air returned to the servant, and he peeled himself off the wall, he ran for the door.

Dori'naur sneered a hateful smile. "They think they can find a way to defeat us? So did their first elders! My master will gain his strength and nothing will stand in our way. I will eliminate this vessel in your name."

The people were a good, loyal group, but even this proved too much for some. In a way, if you did not have faith in your king, all looked lost. Trust in the Light. All shadows will disappear soon enough.

16

A Strange Yet Familiar New World

In the new world, Natallia and Zachery woke up to find themselves outside a busy little town. Strange looking people walked up and down crude, makeshift roads. All the buildings were made of what looked to be wood. None big enough to be a castle.

"Now remember Zachery, you are my son. We are here looking for work and shelter because my husband died shortly after we arrived here from. . . oh. . . from. . ." Natallia was at a loss.

"England, my lady," Zachery answered with a smile.

"You have to call me mother from now on. Royal titles are gone." Natallia reminded him.

They brushed themselves off and headed for the town. "Shall we go and meet our new neighbors?" Natallia asked.

Zachery took a deep breath. "Yes, Mother, I am ready."

They hoped the people were friendly because they desperately needed to blend in. So they went in cautiously, taking everything they saw in. The people dressed oddly but rode in carriages and on horseback that was at least like home. The two entered a building and found it was a pub of some kind.

"The last time I entered a strange pub, Benzoete burst into flames in front of me," Zachery told her.

Natallia saw a man sitting at a table wearing a black hat with holes in it along with dusty old smelly clothes, and a leather belt with a metal object in it. Too short to be a dagger. His attire was not any kind of armor that they had seen before. How could this protect him in battle?

She walked up to him and asked, "Excuse me, kind sir. My son and I are in need of work and a place to rest. Can you help us?"

The stranger looked them both up and down, then rubbed the stubble on his chin. "You two ain't from around here, are ya? Where are ya from? Why you come to these parts?"

Their first test. "We are from England. We came here with my husband hoping to start a new life, but he sadly died from fever shortly after we arrived. He left us with nothing and nowhere to go. Me with child and one to raise. Please, can you help us?" Natallia told that story like it was the truth, almost having herself believing it.

An older woman, wearing an apron over an old dress with flowers on it walked up and slapped the strange man in the back of the head. "Now Jeb, this is no way to be treating visitors!"

She wiped her hands down the front of her apron and stretched it out for a handshake. "My name is Miss Lizzy. I own this here pub and be needin' some help around here. It's just me and my granddaughter, Cassy. If you're interested, I will pay you an honest wage, let you and yer boy stay in the back, ifen you ain't afraid of working."

Miss Lizzy was a bold woman. Her hair was white as snow and her face looked as if it had seen a thousand winters.

Zachery was just baffled by her language. He could barely understand what she was saying. "Yes! Yes, thank you, Miss Lizzy! We are honored by your kindness," shouted Natallia, as she grasped the older woman's hand.

Zachery could not take it any longer he had to find out where Benzoete had sent them.

"Miss Lizzy, is it? By chance is that short for Elizabeth?" Zachery hoped for some little sentiment from home.

"No, child, my given name is Eliza. Folks just starting calling me Miss Lizzy, hee hee," she said as she slapped her knee.

Zachery smiled and said, "If I may ask, where exactly are we?"

Miss Lizzy let out a huge laugh for such a tiny old woman. "Now hunny, you are smack dab in the middle of Southland, Georgia. Just outside of Savannah."

Well, they did not know what a Savannah or a Georgia was, but it reminded Zachery of his father and that was comfort enough. It was not home, but it would make do.

I was worried at this point and confused for the most part. I could not help to think, oh Benzoete, where had you sent us?

Miss Lizzy took them to their room and helped get them settled in. She was a kind and helpful woman. Just being around her made them feel like they found a good place.

It would some take time to get use to this new place, but knowing they were safe from Dori'naur made them feel a little more at ease.

The next morning, Natallia and Zachery went down to start their new jobs helping Miss Lizzy.

"Well, good morning my new sunshines!" chimed Miss Lizzy. "Today, we start your training as my saloon help. Natallia, I'm gonn' have you cleaning tables and gettin' folks seated. If they are needin' a drank, you can fetch that from the bar. Be nice to the men folk and sometimes they will throw a little extra coin your way."

Natallia had no idea what she was talking about, but she watched close as Miss Lizzy went through the motions and she was sure she would get the hang of it.

"Next my good boy, you will be responsible for fixin' things around here and for my farm. Doin' a lot of cleanin' and stayin' out of the way at night in the saloon. How are you at gatherin' eggs and milkin' cows?" She asked him.

Zachery was excited, it sounded like life back on his family's farm. "I am an expert at those things Miss Lizzy!" said Zachery.

Over the next few months, they seemed to find their way just fine. Making new friends, and learning their way around this new land. Natallia's stomach grew, and people wanted to rub it for some strange reason, but it made them smile. Zachery seemed to find a very special friend. He was very smitten with Miss Lizzy's granddaughter, Cassy. The two were inseparable, since they were so close in age. Cassy was a fiery little blonde girl with a spunky attitude that taught Zachery the ways of life in "The South," as she called it.

"First thing you need to learn is how to skip a rock," Cassy said while holding a smooth stone in her hand. "Hold it like this in your fingers, pointing with the first one." Cassy threw the rock across the lake and watched it skip along four or five times.

"Wow! Let me try it." Zachery picked a stone and threw as hard as he could. Only to hear a loud plop and watched it sink.

Cassy could not help herself and was unable to hide her big smile; she started to giggle as he just watched it disappear.

She helped him with history lessons as well. He blamed his lack of knowledge on his being from another country. He would take his information and pass it on to Natallia at night. Cassy told him about how Georgia was busy trying to rebuild.

It appeared this land has just ended a war, a Civil War is the term they used. The people of the "northern states " were at odds with the people here in the south. She told him about this powerful man named Sherman that marched an army through here, leaving a path of destruction sixty miles wide and three-hundred miles long, burning everything in his wake. Hearing this made Zachery wonder if they left the shadows of one demon just to be caught in another? Cassy told him not to worry that all that ended a little over fifteen years ago. They were at peace and simply wanted to rebuild their lands.

When needed, the green stone that Benzoete gave Natallia worked, but very briefly. It would start to vibrate, ever so slightly.

"Zachery, I think it's Benzoete and he needs to speak to us. Please go bar the door," Natallia said.

The pendant she wore seemed to glow as she approached a mirror. After Zachery was sure the door was closed tight, Natallia went to the mirror and held the stone in her hand. The mirror started to ripple like a lake after a pebble has been tossed in.

"Natallia? Are you there, my queen?" asked Benzoete.

"Yes, we are here. How are Gabriel and my brother?" responded Natallia.

Gabriel stepped into view. "We are well my darling. We have located George and Elizabeth and we are going to meet them. Please tell Zachery for me. Once we find them we will try to talk again. Until then we will be traveling a lot. I love you, my queen, please keep you and our son safe. I will count the moments until I have you both safe, here with me."

Natallia began to cry and placed her hand on the mirror. "I love you as well, my darling. Please stay safe."

With that, the mirror went back to normal and all she could see was herself. The Queen sat on the bed with her face in her hands weeping. Zachery tried to comfort her, but inside he struggled with his own need for that comfort.

I thought I was handling this new adventure well enough, until I heard Gabriel talk of my family and how I could possibly talk with them soon. Soon would not have come fast enough.

17
Reunion of
Brothers

Gabriel and his band of heroes traveled to Casterton, a small
town at the foot of the mountains that was used for passing traders
to barter their wares. They continued searching for George and
Elizabeth Morely, though Elos had seen that they were using a
temple as their hideout while George recruited new members for a
refugee army.

The trip was not long from Weelinn. They had stayed to the
shadows and did not follow the main roads to avoid drawing
attention to themselves. Once they had arrived in Casterton,
Gabriel looked to Elos. "I have visited here with my father when I
was a boy. There is only one temple that I know of here. It stands
tall with many windows stained beautiful colors like the rainbow. It
has a cellar door on the back. If I know George, that is where they
are."

"I saw the multi-colored windows in the vision, it must be the
same temple. We need to approach them with caution, we do not

know what they have seen the demon do," explained Elos.

Gabriel led them through the quiet town. The people were scattered and hiding for news of the demon and his army was spreading. "Here is the old schoolhouse my father would bring toys and clothing to. The people of Casterton had very little, he wanted to help any way he could. The temple was just behind here."

Within moments, they slowly entered the cellar.

"Someone is coming! Everyone hide until I give the signal," ordered George.

Footsteps could be heard coming down the stairwell. George drew his sword and hid behind some boxes stacked to the side of the wall.

"George Morely! Do not make me come all the way in there to get you!" laughed Gabriel.

George slowly stepped from his hiding place. "Gabriel? Is that really you? By the Gods, how did you find us?" George lowered his sword.

George and Gabriel embraced each other in a tight bear hug, and thanked the Gods each one was safe. George let out a loud whistle, and then shouted to his wife. "Elizabeth! It's Gabriel!"

Behind Gabriel, the others came into view. "This is Benzoete, the High Elf wizard from Weelinn, and his apprentice, Elos. They found you," Gabriel explained.

The others began filtering into sight. "Gabriel, where is Zachery? Does he still live?" Elizabeth asked with a worried look on her face. She held Launa tightly in her arms.

Benzoete clasped his hands together, smiled and said, "Your boy is safe, my lady. He is protecting the queen. We must get to a safer place than this so we can talk further. I will try to explain all you need to know. I know of a place not far from here."

The town of Casterton was known for its quiet people and its glorious mountains surrounding the town. The newly formed refugee army was small, but loyal. They loaded up their supplies and followed Benzoete to the outskirts of town.

"You have been busy my friend. How did you convince these

people to come with you?" Gabriel asked.

"You would not believe the carnage back at Castle Whitehold. People are being forced to do the demon's bidding. So, the choice was simple, try to escape, or die at our own hands," George explained.

Gabriel's eyes stung from the tears of anger rolling down his cheeks.

"How many have perished? How many are still suffering because of this monster?" Gabriel asked.

George lowered his head, "More than we can count. We escaped during the queen's celebration of death. When he found out the people had failed him, the sounds of chaos echoed off the walls. I did not see what Dori'naur did to them, but I feel it was worse than death."

Along the way, they found others that were willing to fight for their home and families. An army was forming.

Benzoete led them to a remote mountain baseline filled with trees. With a wave of the wizard's hand, the brush and heavy weeds parted revealing a doorway lined with strange markings and glowing runes.

"I have lived here my whole life, been all over these mountains. How have I never seen this?" asked Liam, a new recruit from Casterton.

"Simple my good man. This is an elven sanctuary, hidden to all human eyes. Only seen when the elven wizard that hid it, chooses to reveal it," Benzoete answered with a twinkle in his eyes, "in this case, that wizard is me."

The High Elf went to the door, placed his hands on two runes in the center and with a low whisper the door opened. As they stepped inside, torches lit themselves. Once all were inside, the door closed behind them and Benzoete waved his hand once more.

"We will be safe for now. The door is sealed and hidden," he said.

Looking around, the room was very deceiving. It was much larger than expected and lined with bookshelves and a large, square table in the center, piled with books. Armor of all different sizes stood at attention along the far wall. The ceiling was alive with sparkling dots mirroring stars in the sky.

"What is this place?" asked George.

"It is a safe haven for our kind. It has been used to harbor master Benzoete and others during times of distress and danger. A place they could come and study the elements while they were devising a plan of action for the situation," Elos stated.

"Or if I just wanted to be alone with my books." Benzoete winked.

"We have to tell you, George, Zachery is safe. He and Natallia were sent to a new world to hide them from Dori'naur. He is a very brave young man. I promised him I would make sure you knew that." Gabriel told George and Elizabeth.

They explained how Benzoete summoned the portal and can communicate with them briefly when needed. Then Benzoete looked to George. "There is one more matter I need to tell you about. You are going to want to sit down for this, and keep an open mind."

I desperately wanted to hear from my family. I waited for the call. It pained my heart to be away from them while the queen and I were away.

Benzoete started to explain all they knew to George. "First of all, I used the Book of the Ancients to foretell the madness that came into our world. It spoke of how during the War of the Gods, the original three elders fought alongside the Gods and tried to defeat Craotonus and his minions."

"I was a part of that war, even though I was young and new to the High Elf wizard order," Benzoete continued.

"I felt I needed to stand by my mother's side, as she was the second seat of the original elders. Her name was Aliz'Ra, and she was the bravest person I have known. After we sent Natallia and Zachery to the new world, it changed things. It rewrote some of the pages in the Book of Ancients. As if, by us sending them to safety, a key appeared that unlocked more information for us. The new pages speak of a place we need to locate. A dangerous place. It is called the Tomb of the Elders, located inside the Valley of Ice Shadows."

George looked confused. "I thought this Valley of Ice Shadows was only a myth. A place made up, stories told to children that misbehaved. My father told of this place, but he never spoke of this Tomb of the Elders. Some of the older people I spoke with around the realm told stories of the chaos and death inside the Valley of Ice Shadows. I took them for insane."

Elos walked over to George. "It was a myth, our people thought. This is considered holy ground, the remains of the beginning of our race. No one has ever found the tomb because no one ever knew where to look. Most of the people who went out looking for it never came back. The ones that did simply gave up looking."

"Very well, so now we know this place exists and where to look for it. What does this have to do with me and why do we need to go there?" George asked.

Benzoete shifted uncomfortably in his chair, searching for a way to begin, "The Book states that to open the tomb it takes two males from the bloodline of an original elder." He looked up and Gabriel gave him a reassuring nod. "If anyone tried to open the door without this key element, death was certain for all around the tomb."

"Again, what does this have to do with a farmer from Whitehold?" George asked, impatient.

Antoine laughed, "You sound just like your son, thinking you are less than important."

"That is what I am trying to explain. I will ask you the same question I asked your young Morely. What do you remember of your mother, George?" Benzoete asked.

With that question, George was uneasy now. "I remember nothing of her.

She died of the fever right after I was born. I was raised by my father. He told me stories of her, about her beauty, her wisdom, and her laugh. Oh, how he loved her laugh."

George smiled as the memories of his father flooded his mind. Benzoete laid his hand on George's knee. "He was the most noble human I have ever had the honor of knowing."

George stood up, knocking his chair over. "Wait, you knew my father? How?"

At that moment, twinkling gold lights fell beside Benzoete. A beautiful elven woman now stood at his side. "Hello, George, my name is Valindra. I am your mother."

Gabriel was at George's side now. "My friend, I know this is a lot to bear at one time, but what they are telling you is the truth. Your bloodline is part of the elven original elders. Zachery is the next Dragon Rider. His power has laid dormant all these years."

George was shocked, just shaking his head, clasping his hands behind his head. His mouth moved, but no words came out.

Elizabeth sat quietly during all the conversation but she just had to know. "If you are George's mother, why have you not visited him before now? How could you let him believe you to be dead? As a mother, I could not bear to not have my children in my life."

Valindra lowered her head. "Not a day passes that I do not look in on my son and his family and wish I could be a part of his life. I am so very proud of the man he has become. I see Doron in him so much. We had fallen in love by accident; humans and elves together was against the laws of nature. I was at the River Quoye admiring how beautiful it was. Doron came up on horseback, he was going fishing. He thought he was alone and I startled him, causing him to fall from his horse. That is how he got the scar on his right cheek, just below the eye. I could not help but laugh at him."

George smiled. "I remember that scar. He told me it was a constant reminder of you. Of course, he did not say he was frightened and fell from a horse, but he would say that is the day when his heart went to the woman he loved and if it took almost losing an eye, he would gladly give it."

Valindra ran a finger over a ring on her left hand, "We had to make a choice, George. The laws of nature state if a child was conceived from elf and man and showed magical gifts, the child would be taken to Eska'Taurn for training. Any elf that so wished could enter our homeland at this time, but once inside, you were bound to the city behind the locked barrier. We made the choice for me to go back to the home of the elves, because if you showed signs of magic you would be brought here and I would raise you. If the magic skipped you, you would remain with him. We felt we had to sacrifice our life together to guarantee your life with at least one loving parent."

With that, George started to cry. "I have missed so much, a whole other part of my life. My father made sure I knew of love and family. He would tell me stories of how my mother was the brightest part of his life before I came along."

His father was all he had ever known, and now he realized just how much Doron and Valindra had sacrificed for him, mainly their love for one another. "After father passed on to the afterlife, I felt alone. That is, prior to meeting Elizabeth. Now, I know I was never alone. I do not know how much you saw of our life, but he loved you until his last breath."

Valindra smiled as she wiped tears from her face. "I was there, watching as you cared for him. I desperately wanted to help you, to hold you, to let you know everything. I went to him one last time. Father permitted me to visit, as I am now with you. I saw the man I love and told him I loved him, one last time. I am proud to be your mother, George. I thank the Gods for the man who is my son."

"What do I need to do? I have to make things right to get my son back home," said George.

"We make our way to the Valley of Ice Shadows," Benzoete replied. "We find my mother's tomb, and we learn how to send these demons back to the depths of hell where they belong. Demons are not truly killed by mortal hands. We need a way to destroy them, and keep them from being summoned ever again."

The vision of Valindra stayed a bit longer before it dwindled away. George knew he had to be brave for not only Zachery, but he had to protect Elizabeth and Launa as well. Whatever he had to do, whatever he had to become, be it elf or man, he would. The group got a good night's rest knowing they were safe inside the mountain. What they did not know was that Dori'naur had become impatient and with the news from the Weelinn spy El'nora, he made plans for reinforcements and was on the way there.

18

Two Are Worse Than One

Dori'naur had spies in every corner of the realms. The people saw what happened to the army for failing him. Their minds wiped clean, their hearts turned black as night, and their bodies disfigured and tormented. They were afraid of death, or far worse. Dori'naur needed to ensure the death of the Vessel of Light, if it was not Queen Natallia, he would clear any and all obstacles toward his objective. The barkers, as they were called, roamed the lands looking for any woman with child with strict orders to kill them and bring their heads to their master. They left a trail of terror from one realm to the next. Dori'naur did not know that Natallia was long gone, safe in a new world beyond his clutches.

Feeling sure that his new army would carry out this plan flawlessly, he made preparations to summon his brother. Together they would prepare this world to be devoured by The Remissum. They would help him regain full strength to rule over the worlds as it should have been. With his army of barkers terrorizing the realms and preparing to go to Casterton to find the group of refugees,

Dori'naur made his way back to the Morely farm, to that spot in the garden where he first entered this world was. The ash circle still imprinted on the ground where the mighty tree had once stood.

"Your time is now my brother. Heed my call and join me," Dori'naur said in a low voice.

Once he was in the garden, he took a staff with strange markings on it and traced a large triangle around the outside of the ash circle. Dori'naur stood at the northern tip of the triangle, stamped the staff into the ground, igniting the markings into flames. He closed his eyes, stretched forth his hands and started a demonic chant, *"Trask nar, del'nor. Trask nor, Vari'te no."*

The flames of the triangle turned a sickening shade of green. Lightning crashed through the skies, thunder rolling in the distance. Dori'naur's eyes were ablaze with green fire now. With a booming shout, *"TELLO DRI'NOR RAUKO'!"* A blinding light flooded the garden.

A rather large, hulking figure stood in the center of the triangle. He was in front of Dori'naur with a hood draped over his face, heavy leather armor adorned with deadly spikes upon his shoulders and legs. A mighty war bow was strapped to his back and razor sharp fist blades on each hand. This new fearsome figure raised his head, pulled back his hood to reveal a skinless face, of only bone and chain. Inside the eye sockets glowed the same fiery embers that glowed inside of Dori'naur's eyes.

"Welcome, Brother. We have work to do," Dorin'naur told him.

A sneer came across the second demon's face. Hard to tell without skin, but his fangs gave the appearance of smiling. He lifted his arms and turned his hands down toward the ground. "Join me, my children. I am in need of your services once more." The other tips of the triangle began to glow and an eerie green smoke rose around. Standing inside the smoke were two monstrous hellhounds. "I have awakened!" The hounds moved to either side of their master. "I am Rauko' the Hunter! Disciple of The Remissum!"

Dori'naur smiled and said, "Let it begin."

The demon brothers returned to Castle Whitehold. Dori'naur told Rauko' of the information concerning King Gabriel and the refugee army forming in Casterton. "This information can prove vital. The humans want to hide from us, they plan to defeat us," Dori'naur told him. "They planned for this before, Brother. The elves are scattered, what is left of them. They will not be a threat," he assured.

Rauko' was not convinced that this was all they needed to know. "I will take a group of your minions back to this place called Weelinn. I will leave no stone untouched and will drain all information from the puny humans." Dori'naur knew his brother would complete this task with ease, "Yes, this is the will of The Remissum. As you do this, I will send the rest to Casterton to start the demise of the former King of Whitehold!"

Now with the Brethren on Amundiss, their work to break this world would truly begin. They were the servants to The Remissum, a cruel and nefarious being hell-bent on revenge. He was Craotonus, the God cast out from the heavens because of his greed and attempts of malice on the other Gods.

He christened himself with the name The Remissum or "the unforgiven" meaning he shall never enter the heavens as a God again. He is destined to live out eternity as a demon.

After the War of the Gods, The Remissum was weakened very badly. He and his minions of evil lay dormant for centuries waiting for him to regain enough strength to wage war upon the Gods once more. He was to consume the innocence of the worlds that the Gods created to regain full power.

The Brethren prepared the worlds by totally decimating—to the point of surrender by the people. As The Remissum consumed the poor souls of the worlds they conquered, he became more powerful. His mission was that if he could not enter the heavens as a God, he would enter it as a conqueror. They needed to find the vessel and destroy the Champion of Light, or risk the champion reaching full power and sending The Remissum back to hell where he would be forced to over again, or worse, face eternal death. It has taken three thousand years to reach this point, and failure was not an option.

Rauko' took an army of the barkers Dori'naur had created into Weelinn. He and his hellhounds were powerful and no match for the remaining people inside the city. Rauko' sent the barkers in groups; one group was to round up all the females appearing to be with child. A second group stormed Benzoete's tower, capturing the elves inside. Some elves escaped to the lower chambers to try and hide from the chaos, yet Rauko' still sent his hellhounds in to grab themselves a little snack.

The beasts were enormous. The first was a red male with a bad drooling problem. Rauko' called him, Varg; and a female that was nearly as large, with fur a lovely shade of green and smelled of rotting meat left in the sun for days; her name was Shaaux.

The hounds tore into the city, pouncing on the unsuspecting citizens, tearing them to shreds. A city watchman came to help, and successfully he buried his spear into the hind leg of Varg. Shaaux turned on the man locking her powerful jaws upon his upper torso while Varg took hold of his lower half. A human tug of war ensued until Shaaux bit down and severed the man in half. The beasts continued to wreak havoc until called back by their master.

The barkers finally had corralled all the women and all the elves that were a part of Benzoete's house and Rauko' assembled them before him in the great square of the city. He stepped forward and announced, "My name is Rauko', the Hunter. I will ask one question and one question only to each of you. Give me what I want, and no one suffers. Refuse my request, and you become my pets next meal."

The first of the citizens was shoved before the demon. "Where is the Vessel of Light?" he asked.

Trembling the man responded, "I do not know, my lord! I am but a simple merchant. Have mercy upon us!"

With a lightning quick thrust, Rauko' pierced the man through the chest with his fist blades, picking him off the ground and tossed him to the hellhounds. "Next one!" he shouted. One by one they are asked the same question and if they responded with the wrong answer, or they refused to respond at all, they shared the same fate.

That is until they came to Maddisin, a young elven woman who worked for the high wizard order. She fell to her knees before Rauko', "My Lord, I know where they need to be. Please spare us and the information is yours."

Rauko' stepped forward, helped her to her feet, then ran a finger down her cheek and asked his question.

"They search for a place of myth called, the Valley of Ice Shadows," Maddisin continued. "It holds a tomb of the first elders. Inside the tomb is the key to defeating you. They are on their way to the city of Casteron now. I do not know why and that is the truth, I swear it by the Goddess."

Rauko' looked to the people and said, "Now was that hard? All you had to do is cooperate. I told you if you answer my question correctly, you would not suffer."

Maddisin let out a sigh of relief and turned with a smile to her family. As the demon turned to walk away he looked to his army, "Kill them all, leave no one alive, but kill them quickly, as to not suffer. When you are finished, place the bodies at the front gates as a reminder to always do as you are told." With that, he laughed and walk away.

"You said if we tell you what we know, we would not die!" Maddisin yelled to the dark one.

Rauko' stopped and said over his shoulder, "No, my dear. I said no one would suffer. I will allow you to die swiftly." He raised his hand and snapped his fingers. The Hounds and all barkers rushed in, one could hear the carnage of the good people of Weelinn being destroyed for miles away. The Brethren already knew of the refugee army needing to find George Morely and King Gabriel in Casterton, and now they know why.

Rauko' was even deadlier than Dori'naur, if that is possible. I hoped my father and King Gabriel could find this Valley and learn how to destroy these demons fast. If these two are just the servants, I could not imagine their master. The world would surely turn dark for eternity.

19

Clash at Casterton

With the information gained from Weelinn and their spies, the demon brothers gave orders to their army to kill all the refugees hiding at Casterton, gather any information they could on the vessel of light, and return when victorious. Dori'naur and Rauko' had wreaked havoc across the realms. The search for Natallia was riddled with bloodshed and bodies from one city to the next, as The Remissum fed on the souls of the innocents. Chaos and carnage abounded to flush out the Champion of Light. How much more could this world take? How could these people stand to wait until the Champion is into his eighteenth season?

Gabriel, George, and Antoine trained any that wanted to fight for the Light. A word was sent from the scouts who had seen that the army of barkers was headed to Casterton.

Gabriel prepared the refugee army for battle, "We will fight until life's breath has left us! We will fight until the Gods call us to the afterlife! We will fight until this evil is gone from our world and all is returned to proper place! These men were once our friends, our neighbors, and our family, yet you cannot think of them that way any longer. They will not know you. All they know is death, destruction, and chaos! Do not waiver from this or you will not survive!"

Elizabeth and the other women took the children and supplies and left for their next destination to wait for the survivors of this battle. Elizabeth, in her own right, had turned into a very honorable leader, taking charge of the remaining women and children, helping to keep them safe and on the move when needed. Every child she helped along the way, she saw Zachery's face, and wished he was with her. A mother's love is a bond not easily broken. She channeled that spirit into helping the others.

A horn sounded from the front lines signaling that the barkers were here. Antoine took his band of ragtag refugees to flank the right side while George lead his team through the left side along the tree line. Gabriel stood like a statue on the front, hand at the ready on the hilt of his sword Fuascailte.

When the barkers came close he gave the order, "Fire!" Elos and Benzoete were positioned at either side of the main gates, arms stretched forth, magically calling down fire from the heavens. As the rain of fire slowed the evil army, Antoine and George moved their units in while Gabriel drew his blessed sword and gave the order to move in and help the others.

The demonic army had no remorse for themselves or the men they were sent to fight. All they knew was bloodshed. Mindless killers. On their hands, claws had formed, the tree bark that now covered their bodies, acting as living armor. As the blades found their mark and sliced the barkers, they would heal as fast as the cut formed. The easiest way to defeat them was from behind and hope to land the blade just right across the neck to sever the head from the body because when the head is removed from the body it is turned into ash. However, this was no easy task. Usually, it took one man to last long enough in combat to allow another to land the killing blow.

The sounds of metal clashing rang throughout the hills of

Casterton. The smell of burning flesh from the wizard fire was unbearable, choking their men. The refugee army was being pushed back.

Antoine urged Gabriel to pull back. "You have to run! You must make it back! We will hold them off, giving you time to escape and find the others."

For Gabriel, time slowed down to a stop. He looked over his shoulder and saw his men valiantly fighting. Fighting and dying. These men were willing to lay down their lives for the good of others, for the belief in their king.

"NO! I will not leave my people to die as I run! We will fight as one and die as one!" Gabriel shouted as he ran headlong into the army, slashing with all his might causing Fuascailte to start to glow. His first swing connected and split one of the barkers completely in half.

Seeing this brought memories back for Benzoete of his mother's unselfish sacrifice to save him and the other elves in the first War of the Gods. Benzoete motioned to Elos, "Concentrate fire around the king, push back as many as we can!"

The men saw their king rush in, fearlessly fighting for them and heard his mighty battle cry. Seeing this caused a rush of second wind filled their souls with a fever of honor; their blood boiled. As the refugees pushed back the demon army a figure appeared at the edge of the trees. A hooded man with a bow who then proved his accuracy was amazing. His arrows hit each and every one of their marks, piercing the skulls of the barkers, stopping them in their tracks. The refugees were winning! The demons were now on the defensive. One by one their bodies were turned to ash.

A roar of cheers arose from the refugee army. "The barkers are running!" one shouted.

"All hail King Gabriel!" another yelled out.

As the last of the barkers retreated to Castle Whitehold, back to their masters, the stranger came up to the group. "Thank the Gods, I thought I would never find you," he said as he removed his hood.

Antoine stepped between the stranger and Gabriel, "And you

are?"

The stranger smiled and said, "My name is Saduj Proditor. I am from the southern realm of Black Falls Mountain, just outside of Mordit City. I came to aid in the fight, for my people found a way to stop the minions."

As they settled down to care for the wounded and prepare to meet Elizabeth the next morning, the stranger told them of the method used to make the special arrows he used to kill the barkers with one shot.

"My people are Gods fearing people, so when the demon's minions came into Mordit City looking for the Vessel of Light we knew that something had to be done. Our priests prayed and were shown a special metal that is blessed by the Old Gods themselves. We harvested all we could find and made weapons. My aim is the best in all the realms, so I made my arrows, others made swords, and others daggers to protect their families. I came looking for you hoping to end this once and for all."

Gabriel took one of the arrows to examine the tip. "What makes this steel so special?" he asked.

Saduj then replied, "The rock where we gathered the steel from is the site where one of the Old Gods stood and chose the original elders of the new home, Eska'Taurn. Three new elders were appointed and asked to set out for a new way. Those who did not wish to leave journeyed to Eska'Taurn, where they would live out their days. At least that is what we are to believe, for elves were here centuries before man."

Benzoete leaned forward in his chair, rubbing the sides of his head with the first two fingers of his hands, "I do recall my mother speaking of a place in the southern realms where this call was made. Alas, I do not remember her saying it was a place called Mordit City."

"Maybe you remember the elven name of Terra'Fayoak," Saduj laughed. "When man moved in after the elves abandoned it the name was changed."

Benzoete sat straight up. "Yes, yes, that was the name. I was testing your authenticity. Well done my boy! We have to be careful letting people we know nothing about into our inner circle."

Gabriel stood and stretched forth a hand to Saduj. "Welcome, we need all the trained men we can find, and with this new steel on your arrows, we hold an advantage."

Antoine still seemed skeptical, "I'll have the men gather the arrows before we leave tomorrow; we will need as many as we can locate."

The next morning the refugees packed up and headed north the meet with Elizabeth and the others. They would try to find the Tomb of the Elders, but no one could foresee how long that will take or what perils lay ahead of them along the way. Their journey would take them far into the northern realms, places no man has seen in centuries.

The path was laid out for Benzoete in the Book of the Ancients and he hoped to gather more information as they went along. No one has ever made it back from a journey to the Tombs the same way they left. That is, if they came back at all. What secrets are hidden within, once the tombs were found?

20

Antoine Seeks
Answers

The next stop was a small town by the name of Billows. When the battle at Casterton started, Elizabeth and the other women headed north ahead of the men. They stopped at Billows to set up camp and ready themselves to care for the wounded that made it through the fight alive.

"We have to be ready for anything, ready to help where we're needed," Elizabeth told the others.

As the wounded warriors made their way to their new base camp, Antoine rode up beside Benzoete. "I have a question that has consumed me ever since this started. If you can kindly answer it for me."

Benzoete turned to him and gave a nod. "If I can answer, I will gladly shed light upon the subject."

Antoine stopped his horse, and looked to the wizard with tears in his eyes. "Why is my family cursed with this? Why has my sister been given the burden of carrying the Champion? What have we done to deserve this horror?"

The good elf placed a hand on Antoine's shoulder. "My boy this is not a curse. I will give you full details of what I know after we settle in at Billows. Know this, you and your sister have been destined for this since birth and the reason your parents fought so hard to save you from the orc attack. Now, come let us find the others. I can see the entrance to Billows just ahead." The two rode on as the others were filing into the town.

Elizabeth ran out to meet George with Launa tagging along behind her. "Every time we are separated, I had always wondered if this is the last time I will see your face. I do not know how much more of this I can take."

George took her into his arms. "Even if we are apart, know this. I will always be with you. I gave you my heart many years ago because I knew you would take care of it. Now, with this threat upon us, I would not have it any other way. I fight to ensure the safety of you and Launa. When we are reunited with Zachery, we will fight as a family for it is the right thing to do. We must keep the Light shining throughout Amundiss." The two shared a kiss when George felt a tug at his armor.

"There is my princess!" He tossed her into the air. "You're getting to be a big girl! You will be grown before I know it." George longed for the day he and his family could settle back into their small farmhouse and for everything be normal. Time will only tell.

After everyone had a chance to eat and have their wounds cared for, Benzoete motioned for Antoine to follow him. He led him to a small room in the back of the stables where a barrel had been placed with candles lit around it. On a table beside the barrel was the Book of Ancients, opened to a page near the front.

"You asked me why your family was cursed with the burden of the Champion of Light. This was no curse it was a choice. A choice made many centuries ago by your ancestors. Do you know why the orcs were attacking your village that day?" asked Benzoete.

Antoine looked confused but answered, "Because they were looking for food and resources to carry back to their village. It happened more than once, it was not a rare occurrence."

"Yes, it was not rare for your village. The orcs did not raid any other village, at least, not to the extent of the carnage they laid on yours. What made yours so special? Why on this day did they bring so much death and destruction?" Antoine did not know how to answer this. "I will show you why." Benzoete pointed to the Book and read:

"The days of the great war were hard to bear. The Gods knew they needed to create a vessel to nurture a Champion of their Light. This Champion would harness the power of the Light and be able to use this power to banish demons into the pits of Hell. They asked their most trusted angels to stay on earth and continue the line of Light. The angels had the choice to stay and fight for the Gods, or return to the heavens. The Champion can only be born to a mature female descendant while the males will possess powers of war. These males will use their power to protect and honor the Light in all forms, any deviation from this will draw them to evil and be damned."

Benzoete looked to Antoine. "You see, my child, you and Natallia are descendants of that first line of angels left here to protect this world and deliver a Champion of Light. Natallia is the first female of your line in centuries to live to a mature age. The orcs were acting on their instincts of darkness, trying to kill her before she reached adulthood. The orc race is a brutal race indeed, but flat out massacre is not in their nature. They were guided by darkness, looking to dim the Light one more time."

Antoine searched his memories, trying to find the truth in this. He recalled his father telling him he was to protect his sister from all dangers, no matter the cost. "My father taught me the way of the sword, told me to use this talent for the Light, to protect my sister and all innocents. Our parents were always protective of us. I thought it was normal. I see now, it goes beyond parental love. Does this mean we are angels?" asked Antoine.

"Your bloodline is from the ancient angels that came to this world. You and your sister and all before you were half angel and half human. The females in the bloodline were the only ones who could produce a champion. The males in the bloodline were unrivaled in fighting and celebrated battle leaders, sworn to protect. If the Champion of Light can rid this world of the demons, he will fulfill the destiny of your people. He then can take a wife and live a somewhat normal life. You also can marry and have children. Just know, as long as there is darkness, your children will be hunted, especially the females. Darkness is never truly gone. As long as there is light, there will be shadows."

Angels. They were direct descendants of angels. This simplified why their father fought so valiantly to defend his children, not only for the love he possessed for them but also for the love he had for the innocent lives still on this world. Antoine knew he had to protect Natallia. She held the hope for all mankind.

"Thank you for sharing this with me. It has provided a clear picture for me. I have one last question. You read that if there is any deviation from this, if one of our blood turned from the Light, they will be damned. In what way?" Antoine asked.

Benzoete's face became stern and still, "Dori'naur and his brother both were once angels that turned from the Light. An angel not in the Light is damned to be a demon."

This answer shook Antoine to his core. Dori'naur and Rauko' were angels at one point. He and Natallia were in direct relation to the demons.

They rejoined the others at the fire to share stories and ale. Gabriel and George were telling stories from their childhood and the children were having play sword fights with sticks. These brave people were the last hope to save their world, and they were bound and determined to do it. They were going to find the Tomb of the Elders, and they would bring back the Champion of Light and a new Dragon Rider to put an end to these demons for all eternity.

The group laughed, drank and shared stories of battle and loves lost. Saduj, the newest member of the refugee army was eager to get to know his new companions, "Good people! Let us celebrate today's victory in the name of our king, all hail King Gabriel!"

A deafening cheer arose from the patrons of the pub. "GAB-RI-EL! GAB-RI-EL! GAB-RI-EL!" they all shouted.

Saduj lifted his mug to Gabriel. "Raise your mugs and honor yourselves for a well won victory!"

The group gave themselves a toast and a pat on the back. George and Elizabeth took their leave to tend to Launa. Gabriel and Antoine were making sure the men stayed within their limits for they were leaving at first light toward what they hoped was the Valley of Ice Shadows.

Benzoete and Elos talked of old tales with Saduj of Mordit City, back before man took it over when it was still called, Terra'Fayoak. Suddenly, Lucas, the first of the King's Guard, fell to his knees knocking plates and mugs to the floor. Grasping at his throat for air. Benzoete rushed over and tried to help but it was too late; he was gone.

"This was poison!" declared Benzoete. "I have seen this before. The red marks along his throat are signs of Crimsunrain, a deadly plant that constricts its victim's airway until they suffocate. This plant was thought to be extinguished over two centuries ago."

"Then where would it have come from? Who could have access to a plant that has not grown for over two thousand years?" asked Elos.

Gabriel instructed the men to take Lucas out and ready him for a hero's burial. "Well, we don't know that is what happened here. We cannot be afraid of our own shadows for the real shadows await us, and we need to have a clear mind to overcome them."

As the people retired to their sleeping quarters with heavy hearts, Benzoete stopped Gabriel. "My king, I know that is Crimsunrain, my people used it against our adversaries until we felt it was too dangerous to be left growing wild. We gave the orders to destroy all the plants and seeds to keep it from dangerous hands."

Gabriel leaned in close in case anyone was near. "I know you speak the truth, but without proof we cannot let the men think we have more dangers to consider than we already do. We will find the ones responsible and deal with them quietly."

With the death of Lucas, the group traveled solemnly for days to come. He was a trusted and proven warrior. He would be missed. Antoine had the feeling something was wrong, that something was out of place. He kept it to himself and rode silently, until he could find proof, as well as pondering this new family information he had received.

21

Brothers Grim

"What do we hope to find within the Elders tomb?" asked Antoine.

"During the great War of the Gods, the first elders were hand chosen by the old Gods to carry out works for the Light. Given as a gift, the first elders possessed a great weapon to battle the evil minions of Craotonus. This gift was forged in the heavens by the Gods themselves a blade made from their immortal and holy blood. This blade was a deep crimson color with its hilt formed from the purest gold mined from the mountains of Terra'Fayoak. They called it the Bloodblade. When used in battle against the minions, it would destroy the very essence inside them, returning them to the ashes of creation." Elos explained.

"The Bloodblade served a great use for the elders, it won many a battle where the outcome should have gone the other way. The second seat of the first elders was held by a High Elf mage named Aliz'Ra, my mother. She wielded the Bloodblade with deadly precision," Benzoete said.

"During one of the biggest battles of the war, this was the turning tide that sent the minions of hell back to where they belong. Aliz'Ra and a troop of her wizards were pushing back a large group of minions when the ground started to quake and the air seemed to get thin and dark. Inside a black and purple swirl of mist, Craotonus himself appeared and led the fight. In the troop of elven wizards was a very young elf new to the order. That elf was me.

"Aliz'Ra knew she had to protect the others and help get them to safety. She gave me the order to retreat and help the other soldiers while she served as a distraction. I thought she was to protect us from the rear and be right behind us, alas I was wrong. Her plan was not to be a distraction, but to also confront the evil God and end the war right there. She waited to see her followers get to a safe distance before charging in.

"Craotonus reared back and let out a bloodcurdling roar sending the minions into a frenzy. They were no match for Aliz'Ra and the Bloodblade. She cut them to pieces and made her advance toward the demon himself. Craotonus then summoned a portal to flee and fight another day after seeing the determination in her eyes and the blade of the Gods in her hand.

'Stand and fight me coward!' she shouted.

"Craotonus laughed. 'We will meet again, dear wizard. Next time you will not fare so well!'

"As the portal opened and the demon jumped through, so did my mother. She knew wherever they went she had to end this. The remaining wizards and I saw her rush in and when the portal closed, the last minions were defeated." Benzoete choked as the words came out, trying to hide his emotion. "But she did not return and I feared the worst"

"'We need to find her, she will need our help against the demon!' I shouted. 'I saw Malotorin, the first seat of the elders standing before us, badly wounded.'

"'She will give all to defeat this threat, as we all have. The Light will guide her and help her. I just hope it is enough, for I fear we cannot endure much more,' he told me.

"I did not want to accept that there was nothing more to do for my mother. I wanted to continue the fight as long as I had breath in me. To this day, I keep up my search for her, for I know this was not the end of her, I feel it."

Benzoete composed himself and continued the story. "It was not long after the battle Malotorin succumbed to his wounds and passed to the afterlife. Craotonus and his followers were not seen since the battle that took him and Aliz'Ra from us. Everyone believed the war to be over and peace would follow. Chrin'lolas, an elderly elf, held the last seat of the first elders, and decided it was time to leave Terra'Fayoak to search out new lands for the elves. This marked the dawning of a new time, a new way, and a new life.

"As Chrin'lolas struggled to lead the elven people alone, he was visited by one of the old Gods, Hagorith, in person, atop the mountains of Terra'Fayoak.

"'You have served us well Chrin'lolas, you are deserving of rest. Search out a place to lay the body of your fallen elder, and prepare it as your own. We will watch over you, but your days are short. The minions of evil still lurk, as from the Light there will always be shadows cast. We fear the blade of our blood is lost to you, take this.

"'When we saw our brother, Craotonus, had turned to evil and darkness we wept for him. Our tears collected as one at our feet. It formed a powerful gem that when forged into a blessed blade will become a powerful weapon. It holds the power to banish evil and shed Light upon the world. Craotonus is a celestial being and the only way to truly destroy him is with the power of another celestial being. This gem holds our essence, keep it safe. We fear it will be needed.' Hagorith told him."

"So Hagorith told him to prepare his own grave?" asked Antoine.

Elos replied, "Yes, we believe the Gods delivered Aliz'Ra's body to him after the tomb was prepared."

Benzoete seemed to lose himself in the story. "Chrin'lolas took the gem and spoke the name, 'Heaven's Tear'. The gem shined bright in his hands and felt warm to the touch. Chrin'lolas took a group of our most trained high elf wizards and set out for the final resting place of the first elders. Before he left, he appointed me a true high wizard and placed me in a position to lead. Along with myself, keeping with tradition, Chrin'lolas appointed two others. I still remember his speech to the people."

Benzoete straightened his robe, and reenacted as if he was the former leader.

"'Today marks a day true to elven history.' he said to his people, 'We must make our way to the other realms and start anew. I give you Calaerphen, he will lead whoever will follow him to the realms of the sea. Gailben, she will lead those of you who wish to live out your time in the peace of the mountains, stretching forth to the heavens. Lastly, we have Benzoete, son of our own Aliz'Ra. He has been tasked to lead you to the cities, markets, and trade ways. We need to branch out, to spread our race. We need to help those who need us. Foremost, we will help our own kind whenever the need is present.

"'Families, you must choose your leader and follow them. If you do not choose, and wish to make the journey, Eska'Taurn will be opened and waiting for all who wish to settle there. Once the families enter Eska'Taurn, the doors will be sealed to guarantee our races survival, all who wish to return can enter, but no one shall leave.

"'Choose well and live in peace. I am taking the remains of our dear elders to our final resting place deep within the catacombs of the ice. Go forth and make our race proud of the sacrifices we have been able to endure. My last request of you is this, honor me as your Elder. Go in peace, and go find happiness.'

"Hearing the last speech of Elder Chrin'lolas, I made a vow before the Gods, 'I will strive to honor my mother, and the elders in their name. I will choose the Light over the darkness and fight for those who the Light shines upon,' he said.

"In the speech Chrin'lolas said he took the remains to their final resting place, I assumed they had found my mother, or her remains delivered, and felt overwhelmed by sadness. She had given her life for her people." Benzoete began to cry remembering.

Benzoete would spend centuries fighting the darkness and helping all that needed him as he settled into the commerce city of Weelinn. While researching in his library he discovered the Book of the Ancients. With that discovery, all of history would be mapped out and Benzoete did not like the outcome he saw. So now the refugee army searched for the Tomb of the First Elders and so does the Demon Brethren. If they can find it, can the demons open it? If Benzoete and George get there first and are able to open it, can they bear what lies inside of it? What memories will flood Benzoete with the opening of his mother's tomb?

22

Zachery Feels A Jolt

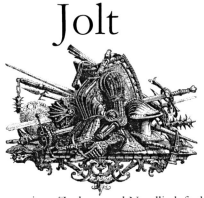

It has been ten years since Zachery and Natallia left their home of Amundiss. The two are still trying to blend in. They live in Southland, Georgia and have learned their new home is on a place called Earth. A fair and simple world; filled with new adventures and things to learn. They have met some truly nice people willing to help them and go out of their way to help them fit in. The most important ones so far have been an old woman named Miss Lizzy and her granddaughter, Cassy. Now, Miss Lizzy is a wrinkly, loud, and a genuinely outspoken old woman, but she does not hesitate to help someone in need. She and Cassy have provided a lot of information about Earth, and in particular, Georgia.

"Zachery, for you to be an adult, you don't know much," Cassy told him.

"Have you ever been to England? Things are much different there than here. I bet you would feel lost also," said Zachery.

The biggest news on Earth the last ten years, well as far as they were concerned, was Natallia giving birth to a healthy baby boy.

Yes, the Champion of Light was born. A strong baby boy born without tears. He came into this world that is not his, only to leave it to save another. Gabriel had been able to see his son on occasion through the mirror, needing to be wary as not to scare the lad. With magic being their only form of communication to their home world, they had to be careful. A few years ago, Miss Lizzy heard Natallia speaking with Benzoete her from the hall. She had to explain cautiously.

"Natty, you aight in there? I hear voices," Missy Lizzy called through the door.

Natallia swung the door open, "Oh, that! I pretend sometimes to talk to my husband, and that day he asked what our plans should be for Billy. It kind of helps me cope and stay sane." She said in a panic.

Miss Lizzy rubbed her stubbly chin. "I can see that. Motherhood can be a rough one when going at it alone."

Natallia named the prince Tradan, after her father, but around others here they just called him Billy. "Prince Tradan of Whitehold. That is a fine, upstanding name fit for royalty," Gabriel said as he gazed upon his son the first time. He wept at the first glance of his son. He knew now they had to keep fighting the demons. They had to try and save as many people as possible, for one day his son would take the throne and he needed a kingdom to come back to.

***

The last ten years for the refugees had not been a pleasant journey and rough many times over, but after the prince was born, they knew the final years were upon them. Tradan will soon celebrate his tenth season or as they are called on Earth, his birthday.

"His tenth season is upon us, he needs to start training, my lady. Elos and I have searched the pages of the Book as best we can. Do not try to force it on the child. He is born of an Angelic race, if he is ready, he will take to it grandly," Benzoete told her through the mirror one day. He had given them pointers on how to ease Tradan into his training to have his power develop.

As for Zachery, his training as the next Dragon Rider was an intense but slow process. He has taken the teachings from Benzoete and Elos and tried to apply them, some went well, some not so much. One night he almost burned down Miss Lizzy's barn while trying to channel the inner fire of the Rider. He told Benzoete what happened and it seemed to puzzle the old wizard. "You say you were trying to channel the power of inner fire and you started a blaze around you?" he asked Zachery.

"Yes, at least, I think I started it. I was concentrating like you said, searching my inner thoughts, seeing the fire and trying to control it within my mind. As I chanted the words I felt a warm glow about me. It frightened the horses. They scared me and my thoughts went to protection. I opened my eyes to see flames emitting from my hands catching the hay on fire," replied Zachery.

"That power is difficult for someone just learning their magic," Benzoete said. "I know you have been training hard for these past ten years, but that is still advanced. It requires a stable source of inner power, or someone else to act as a generator to help boost the power."

Zachery laughed. "You know magic is not on this world yet. I was just lucky Miss Lizzy came as quick as she did to help me put the flames out."

Benzoete stroked his long white beard, furrowing his wrinkly brow. "Be careful, young one. If this Miss Lizzy had seen you channeling the magic, I can only assume panic and chaos would fall upon that world."

I was not sure what I felt during that training session. I know it felt as if my entire body was tingling and ready to burst into flames along with that barn.

Zachery was able to speak to his parents from time to time,

which helped him tremendously. He had grown fond of Cassy and wished he could tell her about his life and introduce her to his parents, maybe someday. "You should see her! My heart felt as if it would leap from my chest the first time I laid my eyes on her. Even as children, I knew she was the one for me like mother is for you. I'm overwhelmed with emotion when we are near. I know she thinks me a fool. But enough about me, how is Launa fairing without me? She miss me yet?" he asked with a smile.

"We are keeping a watchful eye on your little sister. Well, she is not that little anymore. She will be in her sixteenth season soon," Elizabeth said.

A hard lump formed in Zachery's throat. "Sixteenth? She is the age now that I was when this began. I can't believe she is growing up without me." He couldn't believe he was gone this long.

"Do not worry. She knows how important her big brother is and what work you are doing there. We are very proud of you, Son."

***

Whenever Zachery felt down and needed to talk, he found comfort in talking to Miss Lizzy. He just couldn't say everything. They would do their chores together and talk for hours. She would tell him of her life. "You know, boy, you remind me of my son, Benji. He was a feisty young man, just like you. I lost him way too early."

"I am so sorry, Miss Lizzy. What happened to him?" Zachery asked.

Miss Lizzy had no problems speaking her mind, but when it came to her son the words still stung to speak. "We had three strangers come through the town we were livin'. Now these fellers were bad. They were tryin' to take over everything in the town, but my Benji and some others stood up to them. It wasn't pretty, but fighting never is. He was lost to me during that fight. I miss him something awful. He was my only child, just tryin' to save the people he loved."

Zachery loved hearing stories of Miss Lizzy's past, especially when she talked of Benji. "What happened to the three bad men, Miss Lizzy? How were they defeated?" asked Zachery.

Miss Lizzy sat down on a barrel with a plop. "Well, when tha other people saw that some was standing up to them, more joined in. We had to have tha others help to do any good, these were very powerful men. More powerful than I had ever seen. They brought in weapons we wern't use to. It took all the town folk standing together along with the local sheriff to send them where they belong. We lost a lot of good people during that time, besides my Benji. Sometimes, the right thing to do ain't easy, but it still gotta be done. We knew they were not gone for good, but we sent 'em high tailin it out of our town."

Zachery took inspiration from these stories. He knew that Dori'naur had summoned his brother Rauko' and they had all of Whitehold, and the surrounding realms, under their control. Zachery knew that for his world to survive they had to band together, like the people from the town Miss Lizzy lived, and stand up to the brethren and their master. He had to become the Dragon Rider. Tradan had to harness the power of the Light and together burn away the evil corrupting Amundiss. He had begun to worry this Tomb of the Elders they had told him about was just a myth. Ten years and the group did not even know if they were close.

***

With Tradan's tenth season upon them, they knew they had to start telling him of his heritage, and his responsibility of being the Champion of Light. Natallia hoped this would not be too much for the young prince to handle. Once he knew where he was from, she would then tell him he was also part angel. She knew how difficult that news was for her to understand when Antoine and Benzoete had told her.

They took him to Natallia's room to wait for the sign from

Benzoete.

"We need to tell you something. You realize we are not from here, don't you?" Natallia asked Tradan.

The boy nodded. "Yes ma'am, you and Daddy came from England."

"Well, that is not the truth. We feel it's time you knew your birthright and destiny. We have to prepare you for something bigger than anything you could imagine. I know that you are still very young, but you have shown maturity beyond your ten years. I know you can handle this and just know we are here to help you," Natallia elaborated. "I know we said your father died from the fever before you were born, again that is not true." She looked to Zachery, who gave her a reassuring nod. "We come from a wonderful place called Amundiss, your father is King Gabriel of Whitehold, and you are the prince. We were sent here by a powerful wizard, named Benzoete for our protection. You have to keep this our secret and not tell anyone. Anyone at all. Especially Miss Lizzy, I don't think her old heart could take the truth."

Tradan sat on the edge of the bed with a confused and puzzled look on his face. "I'm not sure what part of the world this Amundiss is at. Have we studied it in school? Wait, is this some kind of joke? There is no such thing as wizards!"

"It is not a part of this world, Prince Tradan, and not a joke. Amundiss is another world, much like this one, only we have magic and knights," Zachery said.

"Are you ready for the biggest part?" asked Natallia.

Tradan looked scared and a little upset. "So, all this time our whole life has been a lie? I knew you two were keeping something from me, but I didn't know it was this big. How can I have proof this is true?"

Natallia laid her hand on his shoulder. "That is the big part I spoke about. Tradan, would you like to meet your father?"

"He's here? How? Where?" Tradan exclaimed, searching the room.

Natallia touched the green amulet hanging around her neck and the mirror began to ripple. Tradan's eyes were as big as plates, peering into the big floor mirror when the image of a man, standing in armor appeared.

"Hello, my son. I have waited a long, long time to talk to you. Anything you need to ask, we will be glad to answer you." Gabriel was more nervous now than in any battle he had faced in his life. His heart was pounding, his palms sweating, and his voice even cracked as he spoke.

"We?" gasped Tradan as he stumbled backward, falling to the floor.

Another image appeared beside Gabriel. "Well, hello, there my good Prince! I am Benzoete, High Elven Wizard of Eska'Taurn, at your service!"

Tradan let out a shout at the site of the old wizard. Natallia bent down to Tradan, and helped him to his feet. "We are all here for you. You are very important to the survival of our world and possibly this one as well."

Suddenly, Zachery stumbled backward, knocking pictures to the floor. "My eyes! Burning again! I...I see someone. Something! NO, get out of my head!"

Benzoete called out for Zachery. "Zachery! What is it? What do you see?"

Zachery slowly stood, his eyes glowing like hot coals. His hands stretched out in front of him smoking as if they could erupt at any moment. "Zachery, calm your mind. Take control of your inner dragon." Benzoete said, trying to calm him down.

"I saw Amundiss burning. I saw Dori'naur and Rauko' staring back at me. They could see me! I don't think they know where we are, but they now know we are no longer on Amundiss! They stood side by side with a third figure behind them, standing on the king's throne as it burned."

Benzoete started pacing the floor. They could see him walk in and out of sight in the mirror. He wondered which form of magic they were using to find them. Then it hit him. "Craotonus!" he said aloud. "The Remissum is almost to full power. He was the third figure, I'm sure of it. We need to act fast. We need to hit them and possibly try to buy more time for Tradan and Zachery."

Gabriel looked on in bewilderment. "I love you, my dear ones. We will speak again, soon"

Zachery's powers are almost to full capacity. Soon he will be ready to herald the call. Can the refugee army and their king stall the demons for eight more years?

I felt the power of evil course through me, burning from the inside out. I was sure they knew where we were, and I hoped my power would be enough for now if somehow they came here. Doubts plagued my thoughts and fear swelled inside me, but I knew protecting the Champion is all that mattered. He was our only hope. I feared even more for the safety of our families back on Amundiss. May the Gods be with us all.

23
The Journey To Doochary

During those ten years, the refugee army has looked for the Valley of Ice Shadows with little success. Occasionally, they had to defend themselves from an army of barkers, or a group of bounty hunting scoundrels, and nature herself. Along the way, they lost many good people, though they also gained some new people willing to help defend their king and fight for the Light.

"We need to pay close attention to everyone coming and going. Something is not right in our group, hasn't been for a while now," Benzoete quietly told Gabriel.

Gabriel nodded his head in agreement. "I already have Antoine checking all the new recruits. If they are hiding something, I hope he will find it."

Benzoete feared someone had sabotaged some of their plans and possibly even murdered someone. With the price that the demons had placed on all their heads, they had to be very careful. A new recruit had caught Antoine's eye, but not as a threat. This recruit was Andrea Aravena from Dunowen, a small town they traveled through searching for clues and the direction for the Tomb.

"You there, what is your name girl?" Antoine asked as he grabbed the shoulder of a new recruit.

She turned quickly, and Antoine found a short blade placed right against his manhood. "First off, as you can see, I am no girl," she corrected. Antoine gasped, knowing she had caught him off guard. "The name is Andrea. Andrea Aravena." She placed the dagger back in its sheath. Antoine gathered himself.

"A pleasure, my lady. Please, if you need anything, do not hesitate to ask for me. . . ask it of me." He turned a pale shade of red and turned to walk away.

Andrea was the daughter of a blacksmith. He taught her how to use a sword better than most of the knights in the King's Guard. She could handle herself in a fight and was very beautiful with eyes that shimmered like a dark pool of midnight. When she removed her helmet, short braids of raven hair fell around her alluring ebony face. She was Antoine's kind of woman.

Over the next few weeks, she and Antoine had been the bane of many barkers. Together they made quite the team. One evening, Gabriel walked up to Antoine, outside the main tent. "This is the first time, I believe, I have seen you smile! Could the mighty Antoine finally have met his match in love and war?" he said with a chuckle. Antoine gave him a playful punch but did not deny the claim.

As the group camped outside El'Arsha, several of the men fell ill and were in need of medicine. Benzoete took Gabriel off to the side to talk in private. "My king, I fear we have not found our traitor. These men show signs of poison, not a powerful poison, but poison regardless. They will need special herbs to counter the effects."

Gabriel paced back and forth, slowly stroking his now graying beard. "We can't just accuse anyone without proof. We have to have hope Antoine can find something or someone that doesn't belong. Take Elos and some of the others to find your herbs, we will camp here until the men are well."

Gabriel desperately wanted to talk to Natallia and Tradan. Although an army of people surrounded him, he felt so very lonely.

"My dearest Natallia, if only you could hear me. I look to the heavens wishing I could hold you again, wanting to embrace my son and look upon him with my own eyes without magic. I fear we have traveled in circles, looking at all the wrong places. It has been ten long years of fighting and running and I feel we are no closer to the Tomb than we were when we started. I am not a young man anymore. I pray to the Gods that they give us a sign as to where to go as well as to watch over you in this new land." When he turned back towards the camp, his sword knocked the Book of the Ancients off the table Benzoete was using. The pages fell open and a beam of moonlight highlighted a section of the page:

"The meek search for what is not found. The brave search for what is needed. The cretin does not search for anything. All that is needed shall come to pass through Doochary. All that is useless shall fall to the wayside. Search your heart and let the light show you the way. Be at the ready, for treachery abounds and fulfillment is near. Follow the path of one thousand eyes and all shall see. Lose oneself in the path and forever be lost."

Gabriel's prayer had been answered! He called for Antoine, "How far are we from Doochary?"

"Only a day's ride my Lord. What reason do we have in Doochary? It is mainly trappers and hunters," he asked.

He lifted the book and showed him the passage. "The Gods are ready to end this; we must ready ourselves." Antoine eagerly stated.

"Be ready, when the wizards return and the men are well, we will be on the move," the king said, excitedly shaking Antoine by the shoulders.

***

The next day, Benzoete and Elos entered their tent to brew the herbs into medicines, finding their king sitting there patiently.

"We have our way," Gabriel began.

A confused Benzoete looked at his king holding the Book of Ancients, and saw him smile bigger than he has in a long while. "Catching up on some reading my Lord?"

"You can say that. I have been shown the way to the tombs," he replied as he stood.

"Not possible, that is an ancient book of elven descent," Elos retorted spitefully. Hearing his words, he bowed his head. "No disrespect, my Lord, but not to a human."

"Well, the Gods must be human and want a human to know the way," laughed Gabriel.

He pushed the book forward on the table and pointed to the passage. "Have you heard of this Path of a Thousand Eyes? Also, how far past Doochary is it?"

Benzoete sat at the table, and looked over the passage several times. "The path has always been a myth to my people. It is said to be very dangerous. Can it be, this is the pathway that leads to the Valley of Ice Shadows? This could be the reason no one has ever found the Tombs. The path makes you face your inner self, makes you search your soul. The ones that enter and do not survive, their eyes become part of the path as your body withers away."

"You make it sound like a lovely place," said Antoine, emerging at the tent's entrance. "When do we leave?"

Gabriel looked to Benzoete. "Once we enter Doochary, how do we know where this path is?"

Benzoete sat up abruptly. "It's been right there all this time. How have we been so blind? The path to my mother's tomb was this close and we did not know?"

Gabriel grabbed the old wizard. "Benzoete! How do we find the path?"

He shook his head, trying to think clearly. "I'm so sorry. I do not know what came over me. The path is said to be guarded by an ancient warrior. His eyes were removed and in their place are two seeing stones, his damnation for being disloyal to the Gods. He is able to sense all movement but unable to behold beauty, for his loyalty was broken for a beautiful woman who deceived him. Only one can face him per day and if he is defeated, he allows your party to pass."

"And if this warrior defeats his opponent?" Antoine questioned.

"Death. He will fight to kill whoever faces him," Elos stated.

Gabriel glanced back to the book. "Any answers in there as to where to look for this path?"

Elos laughed, rubbing his fingers on each side of his head, at the temples. "If the legend is correct, once you stop searching for it, you will find it. It's said that the city to which it hides is the hardest part. Once we reach Doochary, I feel we will not have trouble finding what we need."

"Are the men going to be able to travel come morning?" asked the king.

Benzoete nodded to Gabriel. "My herbs will work their magic overnight, all should be well come the morrow. Know this, my king, the warrior is not the hardest part of the path, even knowing if you lose to him, you lose your life. The path is spawned from ancient magic, I fear for those who enter."

Gabriel turned to Antoine, pondering these warnings. "I will give the men the choice. They have all served me and the Light well. I cannot force them into a war that we know nothing of. If they choose to not face the Path of a Thousand Eyes, their service will no longer be binding and they will be free to stay here or travel home. We will address the men after sunrise."

***

That night, Gabriel stood alone outside his tent, watching the stars, contemplating the events that stood before him the coming day. He heard a noise behind him drawing his mighty sword, Fuascailte. "This might be a bad idea for you, friend," Gabriel said. He suspected the traitor.

Gabriel turned and standing before him was a dwarf. He wore all gold armor, shining brightly in the moonlight. He held a large helmet, shaped like the head of a dragon, under his arm. He flashed a smile to Gabriel. "HA! Everything I ever did was a bad idea lad. This is one of my better ones!"

"Who are you, and where did you come from?" demanded Gabriel.

"Well, laddie, the most important question is where I be going? The name is Freaner, and to finally rest in the afterlife with me forefathers is the answer, thanks be to you," Freaner told him.

The king looked stunned. He lowered his sword, now knowing it would not do any good against him. "How are you here? You're dead," Gabriel asked.

Fraener just grinned a wide grin. "Yes, I am. Been gone a long time now. This is me last wish. I came to you to offer a gift, a gift for helping me reach my Redemption. You are a very noble human, King Gabriel, and your quest against evil has set me free." The dwarf reached out his hand. "I have been watching you and your group, and you impress me. There is more to you than ya know. You remind me of me self, back in the Iron Army days. You'll be needin' this tho. I fear there is much evil in your path." In his hand, he held a shiny, solid gold talisman attached to a golden chain. "Wear this laddie, it will help ya on yer travels and fight against the shadows."

Gabriel took the talisman and ran his fingers along the edges, noticing the symbol of an eagle in flight embedded on it. Then a bright light shone from Fraener. Moonlight danced all over the reborn dwarven king. His golden armor replaced with the robes of the ancient dwarf king. He had been redeemed and now will find a much-needed rest.

"How will this help me?" asked Gabriel.

With a wink Fraener said. "When things look darkest, and you think all is lost. Hold fast to it. Think about why yer doin' this. Who you be doin' this fer. The eagle has the best eyes in tha land, they can see things most can't. Let it show you the way, laddie."

With that, the old dwarf was gone. The twinkling moonlight swirled, carrying the ancient king to the afterlife. Gabriel watched as the sparkling bits of light, that was once the dwarf king, fade into the darkness, then he went inside his tent, feeling reassured that what they were doing was the right thing and they had a chance at succeeding. He prayed to the Gods to watch over his family and to keep his path lit with the wisdom to lead his people. Lastly, he thanked Fraener once more. He hoped to find his rest at the end of his journey.

24
Rauko' Sends A Message

Tired of the failures incurred by the demonic barkers created by Dori'naur, Rauko' and his hellhounds decided to go hunting. He used his skills to track the refugee army and found them camped outside of EL'Arsha.

"Look my loves, our prize awaits." He stroked the dirty mane of Shaaux. "Are you hungry my children?"

Rauko' stood, pulling his bow from his back and notched an arrow. As he pulled back on the string, the arrow ignited. With a swift release, the arrow flew through the air. Finding its mark in the center of a tent, the flames shoot skyward and the frightened refugees scattered about. "Feed my pets! We will find this old king and make him tell us where the vessel and Champion are hiding."

Varg and Shaaux ran rampant through the tents, stopping for an occasional snack. Rauko' walked slowly toward the people.

"Where is your so-called king? Your time has come, human ruler!" Rauko' bellowed.

Benzoete and Elos rushed to stop Gabriel, who was already

headed in the demon's direction. "You cannot defeat him my lord, he is a demon with great power," Benzoete pleaded.

Gabriel looked to his sword, then up to Benzoete. "Then give me great power, use whatever magic you have to infuse me. I have to face him or he will tear my people apart!"

Elos stared at the demon standing in the center of their camp. He shouted to Benzoete, "Use the Androdamos spell. He may have a chance."

"We have never used that spell on a human, we don't know if it will work properly!" replied Benzoete.

Gabriel pulled his sword from its scabbard. "With or without this spell, I'm going out there."

The old wizard nodded his head and looked toward Elos as they began the incantation. Gabriel felt a burning sensation flow through his veins. "What exactly are you doing to me?" he asked.

"The Androdamos is an ancient spell used on warriors to give them strength, agility, and increased haste. All of which you will need," replied Elos.

Gabriel shouted to the demon. "Rauko'! So, you come this far just to be sent back to Hell by a human?"

Rauko' laughed a loud demonic laugh. "Puny human, I am Rauko', the Hunter, I do not lose so easily."

"If it were easy, it wouldn't be worth it now, would it?" Gabriel saw the hellhounds flank their master now on each side of him. "Scared you cannot defeat me on your own, you need your mutts to help you?"

With a gesture of Rauko's hand, Varg and Shaaux backed down. Even if Gabriel defeated Rauko', he knew the hounds would still attack. He looked to Antoine and nodded in the direction of the hounds. Antoine, flanked now by Andrea, and Saduj, made their way closer to the evil hounds.

"Either way, these mutts have to be dealt with. When one of them falls, focus all effort on the hounds." Antoine told them.

"Have you prayed to the Gods mortal? I have met them, and they are not what you think they are. Pray for their protection, pray for victory, most of all, when you meet them tell them Rauko' sent you!" With that, the demon struck his blades together emitting sparks everywhere.

Gabriel pulled Fuascailte at the ready and whispered to it, "I may be seeing you again soon, Fraener."

King Gabriel gave a heroic battle shout and swung the blade, Rauko' meeting it with one of his own and with a swift kick, knocked Gabriel back. Rauko' advanced, spinning and leaping, coming down with great force on top of Gabriel.

"You disappoint me *King* Gabriel, you are not worthy of such title!" He lifted his right blade, about to strike, when Gabriel twisted and turned the attack on the demon.

"Never underestimate your enemy or you have lost already." Gabriel landed a flurry of jabs to Rauko's face, before leaping to his feet and hoisting his blade.

He landed a blow to the demon's body, opening up his armor.

"*Teray Rau Hauy!*" shouted the demon. A mortal has never left a mark on Rauko' before so he was furious now. With blades at either side, he ran straight for Gabriel. Dropping to the ground and sliding, sweeping at his feet. Being one step ahead of him, Gabriel jumped the blades and swung down with his own, catching the demon's hood and tearing it off. Rauko' stood and turned back toward Gabriel, revealing his skinless face and evil red eyes. "It ends now, human. I will let my hounds feast on all your people while your body is hoisted as my trophy!"

Rauko' lifted his arms, the winds swirling and the air thickened with dust and debris. Gabriel could hardly breathe or see. "Get the people away from here! Now!" Gabriel shouted to Benzoete.

He heard the stamping of the demon's feet coming toward him at a fast pace. Just as Rauko' was about on him, Gabriel felt the talisman heat up under his shirt. He pulled it into the open and saw that it was glowing. The power of the talisman silenced all the clutter clouding his vision and allowed him to see clearer than he ever had before. "I can see us fighting. I see us below on the ground, he's coming for me." Gabriel thought to himself.

It was as if the talisman showed him how and where to strike before it even happened. Almost as if it had slowed time itself, making it easy for Gabriel to see what he needed to do. As Rauko' came into range, Gabriel spun to the left thrusting his sword behind him. He felt the demon's blades brush by his face, barely missing their mark, but he could feel his own blade pierce the armor of Rauko's chest and enter the demon. Immediately, the winds died down where all could see. Rauko' stopped and looked down at the blade. Silence fell on the land.

"Go back to Hell," Gabriel told him, retracting his blade from the demon's chest and kicking him to his knees. "Tell your master, we will not roll over for him."

Antoine and the others rushed between the hounds and the two combatants. A loud howl erupted from Varg, piercing the air. Gabriel was in mid-swing, about to sever the smoldering skull from the demon's shoulders when Rauko' disappeared, vanishing along with Varg and Shaaux. An eerie laughter surrounded the remaining army.

"You bested me this time mortal, but you do not possess the full power to kill me. I now know you. I know who you are. We will take your world." Then Rauko's voice faded, and all returned to normal.

Gabriel fell to his knees, dropping his sword, and said a quick thank you to his new friend, Fraener.

Antoine rushed over. "My Lord, are you alright?" He motioned for Benzoete.

Benzoete and the others gathered around Gabriel who was holding his side, he replied, "Never better my friend, never better."

"I have never seen such bravery. You are truly worthy of the title king, and my brother by law." Antoine said. "What did the demon mean he now knew you?"

Before he could answer, he went limp with exhaustion. The men carried him to the main tent for Benzoete to examine his wounds.

Later that evening, when Gabriel awoke, he was sore but alive.

He and Antoine spoke with Elos about the talisman and its power.

"Truly amazing. Such power, given from beyond this life," said Elos, examining the talisman.

Antoine replied, "He couldn't have received it at a better time."

As the group went back to survey the damages, they made a grave discovery. Andrea came to the tent. "My Lord, Jackson, and Eduuine are dead, but not by the demon's hand. They were killed by a dagger to the back."

Jackson and Eduuine were two warriors of the King's Guard, the last two remaining. Gabriel summoned what strength he had, and burst from the tent. "So, we have a traitor in our ranks. Know this, when we find you out, it will not be pleasant!" he shouted.

Gabriel stormed back to the tent with Antoine close behind. "We have to find out who this traitor is. They are culling us out to get to you. There has to be a way to drive them out into the open," Antoine said.

Gabriel called for Benzoete. "I want you and Elos to devise a spell that may help us find the traitor. Use whatever means necessary. We sent a message back to The Remissum, we will fight and we will defeat them and we don't need someone on the inside giving aid to them."

Benzoete nodded, and asked. "What of Doochary? Do we still move as planned?"

Gabriel stood slowly and with a hardened look on his face. "Yes, we are going to end this. When Tradan and Zachery arrive. We will defeat them once and for all."

The battle between Gabriel and Rauko' the Hunter was the greatest victory the refugee army had yet. They had many more battles to come, but today, they won. The remaining members of the refugee army had renewed faith and hope in their king. Now, nothing would stand in their way. It has been a long journey and they have seen many friends and family die at the hands of the demons. When they finally reach the Tomb of the Elders, they will hopefully find new information on how to permanently defeat the Brethren and the master, Craotonus. They have come this far and only have four years left until Tradan reached his age of destiny so Gabriel is committed to keeping this world together until then.

25

Tradan Feels The Power

Tradan approached the age of fourteen and rapidly learned the ways of being a Champion of the Light.

"I know you have only been training for four years now, my prince, but you show exceptional progress," Benzoete told Tradan through the mirror.

Tradan puffed out his chest. "Why thank you, kind wizard! I look forward to tomorrow's lesson."

Even on a world without magic, he was bounds ahead of where he should be. Benzoete was highly impressed with the work he and Zachery have done to prepare for their battles with the demon brethren and Craotonus.

"Master Benzoete, I feel as though I am ready to join you and help save my people. Let me come home to join the fight side by side with my father," Tradan begged.

Benzoete peered from the other side of the mirror. "It is too early child. I know you have come a long way in your training, but we cannot disrupt the balance of power and risk everything we have accomplished. Continue your training, practice with Zachery for you two will be the turning tide to win this war."

With all the magic and training in magical practices, Natallia decided it would be best to move out of the town away from everyone, though they still kept in touch with Miss Lizzy and Cassy a lot, they had to for Zachery had fallen for Cassy.

"I want to tell her of my home, my family, my everything. I feel she would understand," Zachery stated.

Benzoete disagreed with telling her now, "Zachery, if she is truly your destined wife, I will allow everything revealed to her to before I summon you home. Let her decide her fate, If she feels the same I will try to get her here as well."

"I will do it your way Benzoete," he sighed. "I just hope she can handle the truth. I really hope she does."

With everything happening on my home world, would it be safe to even ask Cassy to come with me? I know it sounded selfish, and I know it would be putting her life in danger, but not having her with me would be worse than facing the demons. Cassy is intelligent and in another life, if she were born to my world, I could see her doing great things for the Light. Alas, she may be destined to do great things for this world and our paths would be separate.

***

Tradan and Zachery went to their favorite spot on their homestead; a place with many trees and rocks as well as a level, open spot secluded from outside view. Here, they could practice their training and not worry about prying eyes that is until they had to explain the weird lights people saw from all the way in town.

"Miss Lizzy, you know how young boys can be. Remember how Zachery was around that age. Billy was out there playing with fire and set ablaze some weeds that were soaked in some cleaning liquids I had in the house. Zachery helped him put it out, so all is well here." Natallia tried to sound convincing.

Miss Lizzy looked worried and kind of concerned. "Well, folks are starting to talk. They think you and your younguns are up to no good, moving out of town and all. Thinks yor hidin' something."

Natallia crossed her arms and shot Miss Lizzy a look. "Now you have known us for a long time, Miss Lizzy; you practically helped me raise both my children. Do you think we would be up to no good?"

The old woman smiled and gave a reassuring laugh, "No, no I don't. You folks helped me out a lot after you first got here. I kinda' miss havin' you around the saloon. You know Cassy misses having Zachery all to herself. I would have thought he would have popped tha question by now."

"Popped what question?" asked Natallia.

"You know, asked her to marry him. They both are sweet fer each other. I have an eye for these things, those two will end up together." Miss Lizzy just smiled and swatted her knee. "I just love seeing young people in love."

Natallia told me what Miss Lizzy said about Cassy's feelings for me. I will not lie, I felt like I was walking on air. It was clear to me now that she was the one for me and we would be together, on my world or hers. If she could not live out her days with me on Amundiss, after we defeat the demons, I will come back to finish my days with her on Earth. I just hope my parents will understand.

Benzoete spoke to them and tried to speed up Tradan's training to ready him for the fight lying ahead of them. "We have to be ready. We are almost to the Tomb of the Elders and when we have the information from inside, I just know the Dragon Rider and Champion of Light will have to be ready. The tomb holds the remains of my mother—she had a sword that was used in the first War of the Gods. I hope it rests with her."

"What kind of sword was it?" asked Tradan.

"The Bloodblade. Forged by the Gods themselves of their own body. My mother was extremely gifted in the art of war, she handled that sword with sheer perfection." Benzoete seemed to drift off into a memory.

"Benzoete! You still with us?" asked Zachery very loudly.

"Oh! Sorry, yes, yes, I am here. Tradan, you have to be able to harness the Light. It is your birthright, your number one weapon against the darkness. I know you are in this world without magic, but the Gods see you there, so channel them, talk to them, ask for their help. Once you give your all to them, you can be used as a weapon of good."

Zachery was as advanced in his training as he could be in this world and so he concentrated on helping Tradan find his inner power. "We will be headed into the Path of a Thousand Eyes, I do not know when we will be able to speak next. You know your training, you know your power, harness that and put forth all effort on controlling it. Zachery, before I leave, your parents want to speak to you." Benzoete stepped aside to let George and Elizabeth come forward.

It has been longer than Zachery wanted since last they spoke, he bounced on the balls of his feet, excited to hear from them. "Zachery, my beautiful boy. Well, I cannot call you a boy any more, you are a man. Your father and I are so very proud of you. We are happy with the man that you have grown into." Within seconds, tears cascaded down from Elizabeth's eyes.

George kissed her and placed an arm around her shoulders, "Well, Son, your mother said all I needed to say. I am terribly proud of you. Also, we hear there is a maiden in your life?"

Zachery blushed. "Yes, sir, her name is Cassy. She is the granddaughter of Miss Lizzy you heard us speak of."

"What are your thoughts on telling her about where you are from and your destiny as the Dragon Rider?" asked George, cautiously.

"Benzoete has asked me to wait to tell her before we are to return and leave the decision to her." Zachery mumbled as he lowered his head.

"You do not feel this way?" George asked.

"I am not sure what I feel. My heart wants to tell her now, have her talk to you two, but my head agrees with Benzoete. If I tell her now and she does not understand, it could compromise everything we have done here."

George smiled. "You have truly become a man, my son. Finish the young prince's training, come home and bring your girl with you. I trust she feels the same and all will work in your favor."

I hoped what my father told me was true. I felt that Cassy was my true destiny. I also felt my calling as the first Dragon Rider in over three thousand years. We will overcome this and we will have our life together, as long as she felt the same way.

The next day the training began as it always had before and yet today was different, Tradan seemed more confident, more intense more like a champion. "What will be the focus for today, my prince?" asked Zachery.

Tradan gave him a sly smile, "Sit back my friend, I have something to show you." Tradan then held out his hands and his body began to lift up from the ground. When he opened his eyes, they were bright white, shining forth from the sockets. "Now the fun part." As he hovered above the ground, he moved his arms as if he were wielding a lead baton. He motioned to the trees directly in front of the boys and immediately they were uprooted and shot through the air. The trees made a formation around them. He pointed to his left, the ground opening up and water sprang forth encircling the trees. With another gesture of his hands, the skies turned gray and lightning shot from the heavens. Tradan lowered himself back to the ground, the skies cleared and he walked over to me. "Well? How was that?"

"That was amazing!" Zachery exclaimed.

26

Enter The Path of a Thousand Eyes

As the refugee army approached Doochary, Antoine asked Gabriel about the guarding warrior. "My Lord, you fought valiantly against the demon, and it took a lot out of you. Let me face the warrior who stands guard at the path. You need to regain your strength and ready yourself for the Path."

Gabriel knew Antoine was right, though he did not like the idea of anyone else facing this ancient guardian, he also did not like his chances of defeating him himself. "Very well, Antoine, you have the task on your shoulders. Please, you must defeat this challenge not only for us, but I will not deliver the news of your demise to Natallia."

Benzoete and Elos come riding up closer beside them. "My Lord, we need to rest and find shelter before advancing on the Path." Gabriel agreed with the wizard. The group found their way to a local inn. After they are settled, Benzoete and Elos consulted the Book of the Ancients once more, trying to find clues to lead them to the path and how to defeat the ancient warrior that guarded it.

"According to this, the path's entrance is in a low area beyond the woodland troops, its cover hides them from the normal eye. The evening sun lights the way and reflects the shimmer of immortal armor." They look at each other with utter confusion.

Elos tried to decipher the clues. "Well, it seems that we will have to wait for evening for the setting sun to show the way."

"Yes, but to where? Doochary does not have troops from the woodlands or otherwise. One would think normal eye means human, so we should have the advantage of seeing the way. If we only knew which way to look," Benzoete said scratching his head.

Antoine and Andrea were busy making sure all the horses and gear were properly put away and taken care of. "You are a positively intriguing woman," he said to her.

"I have been called many things, but intriguing has never been one of them," Andrea laughed.

"You are undeniably beautiful. I find it hard to concentrate while you are around me." Antoine started to blush with his confession.

"Does that mean you are asking me to leave? As to not distract you, that is?" Andrea asked coyly.

"As the brother by law to the king himself and commander of the guard, I would have the authority to do so." He slyly cut his eyes to Andrea. "Unless you give me a good enough reason to stay."

She smiled a smile she had forgotten she had. It had been a long time that Andrea felt joy, let alone love. He leaned in and kissed her on the cheek, "Stay my lady, stay for me."

She returned the kiss and placed her hands on either side of his face. "It would be an honor to be by your side, in war and in life as long as you would have me."

Antoine had found love and peace for the first time since Natallia left. He now had another reason to fight the good fight and lead them to the Path of a Thousand Eyes.

The next morning as everyone gathered for a warm breakfast,

Benzoete and Elos looked frazzled from a long night of interpreting the clues in the Book of Ancients. "We think we know around where to look for the path. We were up almost the entire night, but we are close," Benzoete said as he patted down his matted white hair.

"It's over the west ridge through a line of trees. The doorway is made of stone, standing alone at the back side of a clover field," Saduj said while reaching for a warm bread roll. All the others just stopped what they were doing and stared at him, "What? I asked the people who live here. They said thousands of elves and men have approached looking for the treasures. The few to make it into the path were never seen again. Real reassuring, right?"

"He asked. . .the. . . people. We were up all night, and he asked. . .the. . .people." Elos had this strange look in his eyes.

"There, there, Elos. The lad did well. Thank you for the information, Saduj." Benzoete said.

Saduj winked. "Any time. If you need anything else, just ask."

Benzoete placed his hand on Elos's shoulder to calm him.

"When do we head out my Lord?" asked Antoine, who was now seated next to Andrea.

"Now this is a sight for my eyes to behold. Antoine is happy!" Gabriel laughed and gave George a playful punch in the shoulder.

"Looks like someone has found something they needed on this trip, right Antoine!" joked George.

Elizabeth came up behind George and Gabriel both and gave them a pinch to the ears, "Leave him alone. I think it is wonderful. Everyone needs someone to fight for."

Saduj nodded his head. "You have never spoke truer words ma'lady."

"Do you have a wife Saduj?" asked Elizabeth.

"No dear lady, I do not. My someone is my father. He was taken from me at a young age and I fight for him; looking to give his name peace. That is my someone." The table fell silent for a moment.

"We have 'til the sun begins to set. Get some rest and we will prepare to meet this Ancient Warrior," Gabriel said as he stood.

The people took the day to reflect on what they fought for. Some remembered family lost or taken. Some had the promise of a future of peace without the demons. Others, a commitment to honor, vows of protecting the lives of Amundiss. All had a reason.

As the sun began to descend, the group had made their way to the opening in the clover field. "According to the people here, when the setting sun's light hits the stone doorway, he appears. That is when you must make your challenge." Saduj told them.

They rode up to the doorway and wait. When the sun's rays connected with the top of the door it shimmered.

"It reflects the shimmer of immortal armor," Benzoete recited.

The ground shook, the stone doorway swayed back and forth and suddenly, it moved.

"Dear Gods, the doorway IS the warrior!" said George.

They watched as the massive slabs of stone transformed into the ancient warrior himself. Each trace of masonry was etched as if a master blacksmith had crafted the armor from heavenly materials.

Standing before the group, he introduced himself. "I am Stolos, the Watcher. Who will honor me in battle?"

Antoine stepped forward. "I am Antoine of Tralla. I come on behalf of my King Gabriel. We seek the Valley of Ice Shadows."

Stolos was ten feet taller than all of them. He leaned in toward Antoine, "Then why does this good king not fight for himself?"

Gabriel slowly dismounted his horse. "I will if that is what is needed, good watcher."

"No, I have this battle. My king is not whole, he battled the demon Rauko' just yesterday, it would not be a balanced and honorable fight." Antoine demanded as he stepped in front of Gabriel.

"Rauko'! No wonder you seek the tomb. My task is clear I cannot allow you to enter unless you defeat me. Know this, if I am the victor, your life will be forfeited." The giant told them as he pulled a giant war scythe from his back.

Antoine looked to Andrea. They exchanged only a look. With

eyes still locked on her, Antoine said, "I understand noble one. After I defeat you, my group will have access to the Path which leads to the Tomb of the Elders?"

Stolos nodded. "Then let it begin."

He stepped back, and as the sun was all but set, the night was upon them. Torches suddenly appeared, lighting the battlefield. Antoine knew he had to be the faster, more agile one on offense. His purpose was to keep the giant off balance. He knew if he took a direct hit from his scythe, his life would be over.

Stolos charged forward, swinging level with the ground in an attempt to catch Antoine in the legs to slow him down. Antoine leaped over the blade, jumped off the handle of the scythe, and landed a hit to the giant's head with his blades. Landing on his feet behind Stolos, Antoine rolled between his legs, anticipating him to turn, and sliced at the giant's ankles. It was enough to shake the noble watcher, loosening his grip on the scythe and dropping it to the ground. As the weapon fell, the handle caught Antoine in the back knocking the breath out of him. Stolos sensed his chance, swung a mighty fist and connected with Antoine's head full force sending him flying through the air and landing with a thud in the middle of the clover. Stolos gathered himself, picked up his blade, and slowly walked over to finish off his wounded combatant. The group of refugees all looked on in dismay.

Andrea screamed for Antoine, "You can't end it this way! You have to fight! Fight for Natallia! Fight for Tradan! Fight for me!"

The giant Stolos stood over Antoine and raised his blade readying for the final blow. Antoine lay motionless. As the blade came down, Antoine rolled to one side and the blade sunk into the ground. He grabbed the daggers from his boots, ran behind the watcher and buried a blade into the flesh of the giant's leg. One right after another, each a little higher than the last, he climbed to the head of the warrior. In a flurry, Antoine sliced at the neck, bringing the giant down to his knees. With a flip, Antoine kicked against the back of Stolos impaling the giant with the handle of his own scythe. Stolos roared in pain, pulling himself off the weapon.

As he turned to face Antoine, immortal blood spilled from his chest when a flash of light burst forth and the giant was gone. He reappeared whole again at his original location. "Well fought, good Antoine of Tralla. You have bested me and gained entrance to the Path of a Thousand eyes. Follow this path to the end. You will not know time and time will not know you. When you see the skies open up and hear the singing of the whistling thrush, look for the Tomb entrance at the base of the four falls. Go in honor." With that, Stolos morphed into the doorway again, this time with the entrance open.

Andrea rushed to check on Antoine, "How are you? Can you walk?"

Antoine fell to his knees, grabbed Andrea around the waist, and pulled her close to him. "Your voice is what I heard. Your voice is what kept me going. Your voice is why I am alive. I never want to be out of range of your voice, ever." He stood and kissed her, before looking at Gabriel. "I told you I could accomplish this, let us go claim our prize."

The group entered the doorway one by one. The war had been hard, but they were not prepared for what lay before them.

27
The Brethren Unleashed

Rauko' made his way into the war room of Castle Whitehold and staggered to a chair. Dori'naur stood, looking out the large window with his back to the door.

"You are pathetic. You let a mere human get the best of you. You bring shame to the master and yourself."

"All this time, and you didn't know, brother? This is no mere human," Rauko' told him as he tossed a bloody piece of cloth on the table. "Smell the blood for yourself."

Dori'naur took the cloth and rubbed the blood between his fingers. Bringing it to his face, he slammed his fist through the table. "How could we have been so stupid. We had the perfect advantage right in front of us and did not realize it!"

Rauko' smiled slyly. "Best part of it all, he does not even know who he is. He used none of his powers, only fought with brute force."

Dori'naur picked the bloody cloth back up and clenched it in his fist. "Do you realize the favor we would gain from the master if we presented him with this prize?! We must go together to capture the dear King Gabriel. Where were they headed?"

"I left them in EL'Arsha, just outside of Doochary. We can catch up to them quickly if we do not have your barkers lumbering behind," Rauko' retorted.

"Ready your hounds. We have a trip to make. Looks like we are going to see an old friend." Dori'naur said.

The demon brethren set out for Doochary, unbeknownst to them Antoine had defeated the guard, Stolos, and already entered the Path of a Thousand Eyes. The speed at which they could move was unreal. Through the demonic brother's determination to destroy Gabriel fueled them to no end. Once inside Doochary, Dori'naur found the wounded refugees who had stayed behind, because the feared they would not make it inside the path. As the demons questioned them, the refugees found the same fate as the poor people of Weelinn.

"What now, brother?" Rauko' asked as he tossed the body of the last refugee to his hounds. The sight of Shaaux and Varg fighting over the parts was insufferable.

"We go visit the watcher. Do you think he will remember us?" Dori'naur replied.

Rauko' let out a roar of laughter. "I should hope so. I still have his eyes!"

***

As the king's group entered the Path, Gabriel and the rest of the refugee army had no idea what dangers lay ahead of them, or the closing in demon brothers. Benzoete suggested that they stay close to the entrance until he bandaged up Antoine's wounds and applied the healing herbs, "You fought heroically. Your ancestors would be proud. Try not to open these wounds, we need you with us."

Gabriel placed a hand on Antoine's shoulder. "I am glad you're still with us, my friend. I could see the angelic fates smiling upon you. I knew you were to be victorious."

Andrea was at his side and cast an uneasy look in his direction. "Angelic fates? There's something you're not telling me."

Antoine shifted uncomfortably in his seat. "I will explain all to you once we are out of this place." He kissed her on the forehead and stroked her dark hair. "We don't know how far this will lead us, but we do know it is going to be dangerous."

Saduj walked up and asked, "Do you need any help carrying your things? I am glad to help."

Andrea turned to him and declining shook her head. "I have him, thank you. The wizards may need help with their things."

With a nod, Saduj walked ahead. "Something about him makes me uneasy. I would swear I know him from somewhere," Andrea grumbled.

"Saduj has been a great addition to the army, his arrows are what keep us alive against the barkers. Now, let us catch up to the others, I'm sure Benzoete has some advice on how this path works." Antoine wrapped his arm around her shoulders and they walked forward.

Andrea stopped abruptly and looked straight into Antoine's eyes. "You can't leave me, not now, not ever. You get discouraged in here, you look to me."

Antoine smiled. "Yes, ma'am. You have my word."

Benzoete gathered the men around him. "From what I can gather from the Book of the Ancients, this path is not to be taken lightly. I do not know how long it is, nor exactly what lies ahead. This is the only passage I found about the path:

"A thousand eyes have seen, a thousand eyes have closed. The path to what is sought is the path of what is not. Seek redemption through the Path of a Thousand Eyes. The Tomb of your Elders at the end doth lie."

Gabriel heard these words and thought of the old dwarf who he helped find redemption, and in a way his own.

"What does this mean? What will we have to do?" asked George, who sat nearby with Elizabeth and Launa.

Elos stepped forward, "We can only guess at the meaning. What we believe is the eyes that dwell in the path are from the past travelers that have attempted to pass through. If you falter, you will become the new inhabitant of the path."

"You still have not told us what it is we will be facing in here," Antoine spoke up.

"That, my dear Antoine, will be yourselves." The group gasped and mumbled to themselves at what Benzoete just revealed.

"How will we face our self? I do not understand," asked Gabriel.

"I have heard tales of the path all my life. The legends are that you will be confronted with your inner self, all your wrongdoings and your self-worth. If you cannot face your most evil side, you will be lost."

A worried look followed across the faces of the people. Most thought themselves to be good people, but even the most divine had a dark side. Who would be strong enough to confront themselves and survive a trial of the soul?

"Stay close to each other. Try to help your fellow companion. We will need it. Inside here, time is forgotten, don't let your soul become forgotten as well," said Gabriel.

As the refugees made their way to the Tombs, Dori'naur and Rauko' stood outside of the Path of a Thousand Eyes, and called for Stolos.

"Stolos! Awake! We have a need to speak to you!" Dori'naur bellowed in an ancient language.

The stones began to shake and rumble, the mighty watcher, Stolos, stood before them. "Why do you come to me? You are not permitted to pass."

Rauko' walked closer to the giant, "Tsk tsk tsk, now Stolos, is that any way to treat old friends?"

The watcher lifted his mighty scythe from his back. "YOU are no friends of mine! You are the reason for my torment! You are the ones who put me here!"

Dori'naur started to walk to the other side of the giant to surround him. "We are not the ones who sided with the Temptress now are we?"

"You are the ones who sent her to me. It is because of you that I failed Akadius and suffered the fate of his wrath. I have spent centuries hoping against hope that our paths would cross again. I knew that this day would come. I saw that the son of my master, Akadius, would come needing to enter. When they approached me on yesterday's eve, I knew you would follow."

Rauko' glared at the giant. "You faced the demigod yesterday? How did he fair?"

Stolos backed away a little. "No, no. I faced the Elysian, and he fared much better than you will on this day." With that, Stolos advanced forward, his war scythe connected with Varg's neck sending him flying with a yelp, landing with a bloody thud.

"You will suffer for that, gargantuan!" Rauko' released his blades and charged the giant.

Dori'naur summoned roots from the ground to entangle the giant's ankles. Shaaux leaped for his throat. As they all converged, Stolos swung his blade in a whirlwind motion, striking all of his foes, knocking them all backward.

Breaking the roots with ease, he leaped for Rauko'. "You are the reason! You took my eyes! Now I will take your miserable existence! I am not mortal and I easily can end you!"

With one hand, he pressed the handle of his scythe across the throat of the demon while pounding his other massive fist into the face of Rauko'. Shaaux leapt on his back and gnawed at his neck. Dori'naur gripped his axe, readying for the charge.

Stolos reached back. "These mangy mutts are getting on my nerves!" He grabbed the hellhound by the nap of the neck, placed the other hand under its throat and used her as a war club to bash at Rauko'. Just as Dori'naur moved in close, he thrust his battle-axe and connected with the giant's back. A massive roar erupted from the watcher as he reared up and swiped at the demon with the hound. "I believe this is yours, Dori'naur!" Stolos pulled the blade from his back and hurled it toward the demon.

Just before the axe impacted, Dori'naur held up his left arm and his oaken war shield appeared. The axe buried its blade into the shield, the force sent Dori'naur flying back. "Now, where were we?" He turned back to Rauko' who still lay motionless on the ground. "Oh, yes, sending you back to hell where you belong! I may have failed the Gods, but I am still celestial, I can destroy you!"

As he approached, and leaned down for the killing blow, Rauko' opened his hand to reveal the giant's eyes that he took from him centuries ago. It proved to be just enough of a distraction to allow Rauko' to thrust his blade into the chest of the giant. "You were always looking in the wrong places dear Stolos."

With a twist of the blade, Rauko' was on his feet. He pulled the blade free, unleashed his second blade on his left hand and slashed upward, leaving a gaping hole in the giant. As the watcher stumbled back to regain his footing, a blade pierced him from the back and out the front of his chest. Dori'naur used Stolos's own war scythe against him.

"We came for the demigod. As you know, we get we want," Dori'naur told him.

Rauko' stepped toward the impaled giant, now on his knees, and crossed his blades at his throat, "This is for my children, you are relieved of your position."

With that he took Stolos's head. A celestial taking the head of a celestial, everlasting death. The massive body fell to the side. Rauko' walked over to the lifeless head, removed the seeing stones and inserted the giant's eyes back into their sockets.

"Tell Akadius and the others when you *see* them, we are coming for them. The heavens will belong to Craotonus and the Brethren."

Dori'naur told Rauko', "We will have the demigod for Craotonus to sacrifice. We will have revenge for your pets."

Rauko' grabbed his brother around the face with one hand and pulled him close. "They were not my pets you imbecilic bastard! They were my children!"

The bodies of the hellhounds lay at the feet of their master. With his head bowed, he motioned with his hands and the demon dogs were delivered back to their home in hell. "Rest my children. When we have victory, I will come for you. You will be with me once more."

With that, they stepped through the entrance and began their search for Gabriel and the other refugees. How would the path affect something that was pure evil?

28

They Find the Miscreant

They had been walking for nearly a full day, or at least what seemed like a full day, with no dangers—none that they could see anyway. As they came upon a tree in the middle of the path, they noticed it had carvings on the trunk, "Turn your people back now King Gabriel and ye all shall live."

Gabriel glanced at Benzoete. "Who could have put this here? How could anyone know we were coming this way?"

Benzoete's eyes grew very large, "It is the path! The souls have been watching us. They can see inside us. We have to have wipe our hearts of doubt. Trust in your fellow man! If you give into the fear of the whispers, you will forever remain here! MOVE! We must hurry through this part!" The people picked up their pace and sprinted through the winding path.

They could hear things as the path grew darker. Shouts from the back. "No, I had nothing to do with it! It was a lie!" Eduuard, swung wildly around himself, trying to shoo the whispers from his head. "Stop it! You know nothing!" He stopped in his tracks, stood perfectly upright, head tilting to the left. "It was not me. . ." His eyes turned black as night, filled with the darkness from the path, then suddenly disappeared from the man's face. His body fell lifeless to the ground as if his soul was taken.

"RUN! Faster, empty your minds! Do not listen to the whispers!" Benzoete yelled as loud as he could.

The people heard the whispers louder now, "You will not survive. . ."

"You are not worthy of this. . ."

"You have come a long way to die. . ." The voices rang through their heads trying to get them to doubt.

As the group ran, Elizabeth stopped. "Why are we here George? Why must we put our children in danger?"

"No! Do not listen to the voices! Concentrate on me, please," George pleaded with her.

"We are fighting a battle we cannot win, George. I just want to stop. I feel so tired. Put Launa to bed for me, and call Zachery inside." Elizabeth stared off into the distance, the blackness slowly filling her eyes.

George placed his hands on her face to get her to look at him. "NO! NO! NO! Stay with me, please! I need you to stay with me! I can't make this journey without you."

Benzoete grabbed George by the shoulders. "It's too late; they have her. Do not give in, we need you."

George watched as his wife's body fall to the ground. He draped himself over her and wept. Their daughter, Launa, was frantic with fear.

"Mother, wake up! Why won't she wake up?" Launa shouted.

"George! Look into yourself! You have to stay for Launa! Stay for Zachery!" Benzoete pleaded.

George looked up at his daughter and immediately ran to her. He pulled her toward him and picked the young woman up in his arms, "I will not lose you, too." He ran passed Benzoete and headed for the front, passing all the others. Gabriel felt the pain of his dear friend. He had lost his love for only a moment, but he had to watch as Elizabeth was taken from him forever. Gabriel raced to catch up to George to be with his friend.

As the path narrowed, the voices began to calm.

"Are we almost out of this wicked place?" asked Antoine.

Benzoete looked around. "I do not know, we do not have much information on this place. Just stay alert." The wizard slowed to help the others. The people past the old wizard trying to stay on the path.

Saduj walked slowly passed mumbling something, "Spoiled brat. Not good enough. Took all from me!"

Benzoete asked the man, "Are you alright, sir?"

Saduj turned to face him, his eyes darkening. "You poor soul, you almost made it out." It appeared that Saduj was about to lose the battle with the path when they crossed the threshold. Benzoete called for Gabriel and Antoine to join him.

"What will we do for him? Is he gone from us?" asked Antoine.

Just as Gabriel came into view, Saduj lunged for him. "You spoiled brat! My father gave all we had for you! It wasn't good enough for the new boy king!"

Gabriel stopped in his tracks, startled, "Boy king? What is he talking about?"

Benzoete touched the man's forehead and said some soothing words in Elvish. "Now, Saduj, what is wrong?"

With his eyes darkening and beginning to fade, Saduj told them the truth. "My father was the greatest bladesmith in the southern realms and was commissioned to make the new boy king the best sword the realms had ever seen."

Gabriel turned his eyes to Benzoete. "I never received a sword from the southern realms."

Benzoete laid a hand on the knee of Saduj. "Go on, what happened next?"

A hard, cold look came across his face. "Jadory, our leader, had come back to my father with the sword. He said 'Stupid Markel! Your sword shames our realm! The king turned from it, said it was not worthy to be in his kitchen much less on the hip of a king!' My father could not handle the news, it drove him mad. We lost everything when Jadory took the sword and all the coin back for the disgrace. My father began to craft sword after sword, trying to make it perfect, until he took his own life."

Gabriel now had a scowl on his face. "I now know why I have never heard of this. Jadory James was one of the most dishonest leaders of the free realms. He was removed and stripped of all power and title. He had the bladesmith craft the sword with no intention to honor the payment."

Saduj rocked back and forth, laughing. "I found him, killed his men and I will kill him, too. I will avenge my father. I will kill the boy king. I will spit on his body as it lay at my feet!"

"Well, we found our traitor," Antoine said. "What do we do with him now?"

Gabriel stood and looked upon Saduj with pity. "We can do nothing worse than what the path has already done. He is trapped inside his own horror. Will this end his life?"

Benzoete nodded. "It will, but I do not know when. It seems that since he is not on the darkened path, the soul lingers. I do know it will be pure anguish inside his head until the path takes him."

"I will not have him suffer," responded Gabriel, pulling out his sword.

Antoine gripped the king's arm. "This man tried to kill you. He killed good men to try to get to you."

"I have seen enough suffering to last me for the rest of my days. Go ahead of us, take the arrows. I will not allow him to suffer." The men rose to their feet, gathered the arrows made from the blessed rock, and walked ahead. Gabriel was a just and kind king and although this man harbored ill will toward him, his fate was sealed so Gabriel chose to end his suffering. He carried out the sentence for treason and showed compassion at the same time. Gabriel lifted his blade. "I am sorry. Find peace." The blade sliced cleanly. The man's suffering ended. His lifeless body fell to one side, Gabriel watched his eyes disappear, forever to be a part of the path.

Gabriel joined the others and took quick inventory of all those that remained. In all, twenty people were lost. To George it was just one. His world had completely been changed and his heart was as heavy as his spirit.

"I am sorry for this, my friend. She will not die in vain. I promise you this." Gabriel told him.

"It does not matter now. Whether it is in vain or we prevail in all out glory. Either way, she is lost to me, lost to her children," George sobbed.

Gabriel weeped with him, "We must fight on. This is bigger than we are, we have to fight for the ones still living."

George embraced his friend and wiped his tears. "I will fight on. We will bring these demons to their knees and I will be the one to send them back to hell. They will know pain, they will know sorrow. This I promise."

Benzoete walked up and embraced his grandson, "I am proud of you. You are a true warrior. We will make it through this and we will see Elizabeth avenged. I have a little payback myself for my mother that has been brewing for three thousand years."

The group walked in silence for a long while when they saw a bright, sunlit, opening. "We have made it through the path, we have come to the Valley of Ice Shadows," Benzoete sighed with relief.

Antoine looked ahead, "A very warm place that's called the Valley of Ice Shadows."

Elos explained him. "That is just the entrance. We will have to prepare for the valley soon. We will need to take rest before facing the terrors of the Valley of Ice Shadows."

"Can it be any worse than that damned path?" Gabriel asked.

"I'm afraid to even speculate what we will face there. The Gods be with us," Benzoete responded.

29

Time of the Champion

Natallia and Zachery had been in Southland, Georgia for over sixteen years. Tradan had embraced his destiny of being the Champion of Light and had progressed in his training. It had been a long time since Natallia and Zachery had a chance to talk to anyone from their home. Last they had heard, the refugees were on a journey to the Valley of Ice Shadows to find the Tomb of the Elders in hopes of finding more information on the first War of the Gods and how the first Elders defeated the demons.

"I've been hearing people talk about these strange folks up in a place called Kittyhawk. These crazy folks think they can make a flying machine. Ain't that crazy talk?" Cassy asked Zachery as they lay on a blanket beside the river.

"Doesn't sound too crazy to me. What if we could fly? I mean they already have a new railroad that stretched from Atlanta to Florida and all the way through Alabama. Times are changing, Cassy, I hope you can accept change and things you don't understand." He really hoped she could accept it. Soon, he was going to tell her about his home and the perils they faced, his calling as the Dragon Rider, and Tradan being the Champion of Light. He believed the Gods made many worlds, not just Amundiss, and from each world there was a champion. Zachery found it hard to believe that the Gods would put life here with no magic and expect them to survive if the demons were to show up.

"Well, I'll believe a man can fly when I see them in the air. What has you so sure they can do it?" Zachery looked to the dagger in his boot and was just about to confess his secret when they heard a horse coming up fast.

"Zachery! I need you to come with me quickly!" It was Natallia, and she had been crying. "Cassy, I'm sorry, but I need you to go back home for a bit, please. I need to talk to Zachery alone." Cassy kissed Zachery on the cheek and made her way home. They jumped on their horses and raced back to the house.

"What is wrong, my lady? You are scaring me," Zachery asked.

"Go upstairs to my room. Benzoete has made contact. He is waiting to talk to you." She told him, trying to fight back her tears.

The mirror was covered with a sheet so when Zachery walked up to it, he removed the cover to see his father standing alone. "Father, I am so glad to see you! Tell me, how was the Path of a Thousand Eyes? Benzoete said it would be one of your hardest obstacles."

George lifted his head so Zachery could see his face and see that he had been crying. Eyes red with little bags surrounding the bottom. "Zachery, we made it through the path, most of us did."

"Most of you? Why are you weeping father? Where are Mother and Launa? Tell me they are alright." Zachery's heart began to race as concern rushed his entire body.

George remained silent. The burning in his eyes was too much to hold back as hot tears rolled down his dusty cheeks. He sniffed his nose.

"Tell me they are alright!" Zachery ordered with such a demanding tone, his father jumped and wept uncontrollably.

George wiped the never ending tears away from his eyes. "Your mother. . .I am so sorry, she could not fight the whispers. She was overcome by the fears of the path. I could not save her. Launa is safe, she is resting."

Zachery felt the rage building up inside him, but he knew he must control his emotions. He ran out of the room past Natallia. Once outside, he fell to his knees and screamed to the Heavens. His hands felt hot as he slammed them to the ground, sending a trail of fire to a nearby tree, setting it ablaze. Natallia wrapped her arms around him, sobbing, telling him everything would be made right. She had heard her parents ripped to shreds by the orcs, she knew what he felt.

"We will make it through this. We will go back home to our families and we will fight. Save your anger, save your hate, save your emotion for when you are faced with the demons that put them there," she told him.

Zachery heard her words, knowing that facing the demons was what he held onto. She was right, if not for the demons, he would not be in this strange world, his parents would not have been on this journey, and his mother would still be with him. "We have to get back. Tradan is advanced. I have to see these demons suffer for this." But Tradan was still two years away from full power, Benzoete would not risk bringing them back now, and deep down Zachery agreed.

They went back to the mirror, George told him they were getting ready for the Valley of Ice Shadows, "Remember, you and Prince Tradan hold the fate of not only Amundiss, but Earth as well. If we fail, nothing will stop them from coming there and devouring that planet as well. We will talk when we can, hopefully it will be after we have reached the tomb and we have answers. I love you, my son, I am so proud of you, your mother was proud of you. Always remember that." With that, the mirror faded back to normal.

Zachery fell to the floor, Natallia tried to help him, but he shrugged her off. "I just need to be alone, I am sorry." He ran from the house, jumped on his horse and rode to the river spot he and

Cassy called their own. Zachery sat there while memories flooded his mind. He had almost forgotten her smell of wild lilies; she always had lilies growing around the house. She said the smell of lilies in the summer was like coming home from a long journey. She would never smell them again. How could he go back there with the knowledge that she would not be there waiting for him?

That was the saddest day of my life. I knew that with me being here for eighteen long years this was a possibility, but I never let that enter my mind. She was my reason. She was why I needed to save my world. Now I needed a new reason.

At that moment, Cassy rode up to check on him. "Hey, you okay? Your mom said you were pretty upset, but wouldn't tell me why."

"She is not my mother," Zachery mumbled under his breath.

"What?" Cassy asked as she climbed down from her horse. "What can I do to help?"

Zachery looked up from his seat on the ground. "Hold me and tell me everything I have done was for good. Tell me there is a reason to go back and save them all. Just hold me and tell me what I need to do."

Cassy dropped to her knees and grabbed him, wrapping her arms around him, "I will hold you until my arms fall off if need be. Even if you're not making sense. You are my reason for everything, all you need to do is tell me how to help and I will do it."

At that moment, Zachery knew. He knew his reason. Cassy was his reason. His father and Launa were his reason, too. If they could not stop the demons on Amundiss, his whole family would die, then the demons would come here even stronger, and Cassy would die. He would not let that happen. She was his reason. She was his hope. She was his love. "I need you to listen to me and not say anything until I am finished. What I'm about to tell you is going to come as a shock and I need you to stay calm. Can you do that?" Cassy nodded her head, sat back, and waited for him to start.

Zachery stood up, paced around clenching his hands together a bit then turned to her and just said it. "I love you."

Cassy laughed. "That's what you had so much trouble saying, silly boy? I know you love me. I love you right back."

Zachery placed his hands on her shoulders and gazed into her eyes. "That is not all I need to tell you. . ." Zachery told the whole story. From the tree in his garden to his real mother dying recently in the Path of a Thousand Eyes. Cassy seemed to take the news well. The two stayed by the river just talking. Once Zachery started, it seemed like he would never stop. The sun had started to set so they decided to go back. "Thank you for letting me get that off my chest, I have wanted to tell you for so long. Remember, you cannot tell anyone." Cassy smiled and nodded her head. He kissed her like he had never before, as if they were truly connected now. This whole time was a half truth, a lie and now he was bearing his soul to her. He loved her and because she stayed, he knew she loved him.He traced the side of her face with his fingers, smiling. He kissed her once more and then smacked her horse and she was off. Zachery felt like a giant weight had been lifted off of him.

Telling Cassy my secrets that day helped me more than anything else could. She took it very well, I half expected her to run in the opposite direction screaming! She truly is my reason for everything, my soulmate.

Back at the house, Tradan was in the backyard practicing his training. "You okay?"

Zachery smiled. "Yes, my prince. How goes the training?"

Tradan cut his eyes to him and said, "Watch this, I haven't told Benzoete I can do this yet." He took his over shirt off and did a quick look around. "You ready?" Zachery watched intently. Tradan closed his eyes, drew his sword from the sheath on his side. Tilted his head to the heavens, then Zachery saw the most spectacular site he had ever seen. . .wings. Tradan had wings that protruded from his back.

"OH MY GODS! When did you discover this?" Zachery

shouted.

Tradan hovered above the ground, swaying from side to side. "It was a couple of nights ago in my room. When they popped out they nearly knocked all my stuff over. They don't seem to bother my undershirt, but they break through anything else I'm wearing. I think the tighter to my body, the better."

Zachery went over to inspect them and Tradan shifted them forward, sending a gust of air that took Zachery off his feet, and Tradan straight up into the air.

"Come back down here. We do not want anyone seeing a flying teenager above our house!"

When Tradan landed, Zachery could see they were not the usual set of wings. They were not feathers, but almost wraith-like and hard to see up close. He reached out to touch them. They were cold with an odd feel to them. The closer to Tradan's body, the stiffer they became.

"Benzoete has to know about this, this is amazing!" Zachery exclaimed.

Tradan lowered his head and the wings retracted, and the two ran back into the house.

30
Place of Reckoning

As the brethren entered the path, it was as if an alarm had sounded. The whispers were now deafening, and only at the beginning of the path, the voices saying "Sons of evil, beware. . . Brothers of pain shall know. . ." surrounded them like a swarm.

Dori'naur swatted the air around him. "Blast these voices, do they not know we have no soul?"

Rauko' laughed, then let out a roar, "We are fear! We cannot be swayed by confessions. We know what we have done, and we love it!"

The demons traveled farther as the voices of the lost souls continued to chime in and bend their ear with warnings. The brethren were determined to reach the refugees and the Tomb of the Elders, capture Gabriel, and destroy anything and everything they found inside from the first war.

After walking for what seemed an eternity, Rauko' asked, "Do you hear that?" He then paused for a brief moment. "There are no voices. We must be close."

They came upon the tree in the middle of the path, this time the carvings read, "Brethren, remember who you were."

The demons looked to each other. "Who we were? We have always been what we are and always will be." Rauko' chuckled while readying his blades, "And what we are is evil."

A flash of light blinded them, as their eyes focused they see a man who stood in front of the tree. "You were not always evil, Rauko'."

Dori'naur drew his axe, "Well look who it is brother, this has got to be our lucky day. Akadius himself." The demons stepped back to prepare for battle.

"I have not come to fight," the God stated calmly. "I have come to remind you of what you were."

Rauko' snarled. "If you did not come to fight, you should not have come at all." He rushed in swiping his blades. Suddenly he was frozen in his tracks, unable to move.

"You know you cannot defeat me alone. I created you and I can destroy you," Akadius retorted.

"No, the rules have changed, or have the millennia washed your memory away? We may not be able to kill you, but when we chose to side with Craotonus, making him our God, you lost power over us. We are our own entity now." Dori'naur glared with hatred.

"You were once my most trusted. When you left, you took half of the angels with you, damning them to a life of demons. Where are they now? Craotonus sacrificed them for his glory. Do not be fools and think he will not turn on you. Do you not remember the good that was inside you?" asked Akadius.

"Craotonus offered us more than you ever did or would. We were overlooked by you and the other miserable so-called Gods. forgotten about until you needed something. Here we are feared by the mortals. He gave us power and for that we will offer up your son for his own gain." With that, Dori'naur hurled his blade in Akadius's direction.

With a slight movement of his hand, the blade stopped. "That is true, I cannot destroy you, but without the power of Craotonus fueling you, you cannot touch a true God." Akadius summoned lighting all around them, striking one then the other in furious motion. The demons were sent flying backward, hitting the ground with a thud.

They got to their feet and slowly walked back to the God. "We will pass you. You cannot interfere for long in the matter of mortals, that is your rule, dear Akadius."

Then they rushed each side of him. Akadius raised his arms, palms facing each demon, and time slowed down. Akadius used the slowed time to clasp his hands into fists and bring forth a sword of pure lightning in each hand. The demons, in the slowed down time, made their way into his reach. He moved back and as the demons passed by, he struck them repeatedly leaving burning, gaping wounds in their bodies. Time resumed and they fell to the ground, twisting in pain.

"I hope this has bought them time," Akadius grimaced to himself.

"We will strip the skin from their bodies for this!" Dori'naur shouted painfully.

"I believe in them. They will defeat you. They will find the pieces we gave them and end this." A bright, golden light shone, as the God faded from sight and left the demons paralyzed for the moment.

***

Inside the warm, sun touched area of the path, the refugees saw the Valley of Ice Shadows. "I have never witnessed anything like this. The land goes from sunlight and warmth, to snow, ice, and frigid weather." Antoine complained as he looked out in front of them.

"Your elders really wanted this place to stay hidden for some reason," Gabriel remarked.

Elos nodded his head in agreement. "That is what we are hoping for. The tombs have been sealed for centuries, since the first war. The elders should have their weapons sealed with them."

The people started preparing for their last journey, they have come this far and nothing will stand in their way. Gabriel walked over to George who sat quietly with his daughter and knelt next to him. "I am sorry old friend. You and Elizabeth are family to me, always have been."

"I cannot go on without her, Gabriel. She was my rock, my reason. Who am I without her?" George said while shaking his head.

Gabriel took one arm and draped it across his friend's shoulders. With the other, he pointed at Launa. "Her reason. That's who will be. She will look to you now more than ever. You have to be strong for her. Launa was just a girl of eight when the demons had come; all she has known is life on the run, and who has been there to protect her? You have. Now, we are almost to the end of this journey and she will need you more."

George buried his face in his hands as he wept, "I miss her already, Gabriel, but you are right. I know what I must do. Thank you for showing me who I still am." The two stood and embraced.

"I am always here if needed, my friend. We are family," Gabriel said.

George then hugged Launa tightly, and both wept in each other's arms. He took her hands to console her.

Gabriel walked to where Antoine and Andrea were standing. "We ready to do this?"

Antoine smiled. "Of course, we are. When we do this, it means we are one step closer to getting Natallia, Tradan, and Zachery home and we end this."

The wizards moved to the front to address the group. "We know little about this Valley, only that it is not the cold you have to fear. Be on the alert and keep your eyes open for anything," Elos started.

"We will go at a steady pace. According to the Book of Ancients, the Valley is more dangerous than it is long," Benzoete finished.

Gabriel walked to the front of the group and stood on a rock so he could be seen by all. "I would like to express my deepest gratitude for the ones who have come this far. My condolences for those who have lost loved ones. We are looking at the last leg of a journey that started almost seventeen seasons ago, and we have seen many unusual places. I plan on finishing this quest to the tombs to retrieve whatever may be there. If any of you wish to stay here, if you wish to wait for those of us who enter the valley to return, I will not stop you. You have the choice to stay and I promise we will send for you when we have made it through the tombs. We are a small number now, and I feel honored to have fought beside each and every one of you. If you wish to stay, my thanks to you for your service, if you will go and battle the valley with me, stand and let us finish this."

One by one the entire group stood to support their king. They would follow him until the breath leaves their bodies. Gabriel felt his body fill with pride and was also humbled to be able to lead such an honorable group of followers. The king stepped down from the stone and began their walk toward the boundaries of sun and snow.

***

As the demons regained control of their bodies and resumed the path, they were filled with rage. They were humiliated by Akadius and they sought revenge. They were so blinded by their own bloodlust that they did not notice the path forked and they took the wrong direction. Rauko' had lost their trail. The demons were in the middle of a dark forest with no end in sight. Dori'naur growled out a roar of frustration, one so loud the refugees heard it at the boundaries.

"Antoine, what was that?" Andrea asked.

"Just the path letting out its frustrations for us making it out," Antoine said as he took her hand and started through the boundary line.

Dori'naur and Rauko' continued through the dark woods until

they come to an opening where they saw a dark figure wearing ragged robes. The brethren stopped and fell to their knees. "Master, you have returned," Rauko' said. "Have you fully regained your strength, Remissum?"

The figure raised his head, pulled back his hood. "We are nearly complete."

Craotonus opened his arms, allowing a dark black and purple mist to swirl around his feet. The dark master sneered and opened his robe to reveal where his body had been formed by the souls of the devoured mortals they had taken over the centuries. He closed the robe. "We need to prepare. I need to feed to regain full power. That is how we will defeat them."

Dori'naur bowed his head. "We need to return to the castle. We can gather the remaining mortal souls and make you whole."

"How do we get out of this wretched place?" asked Rauko'.

Craotonus grabbed each by the shoulder. "Leave that to me." Evil wings adorned by the skulls of the fallen appeared on his back and they took flight.

With Craotonus almost at full power, the refugees were going to need all the help they could get. With Tradan almost to fruition, they had a chance to end the war, and bring peace to all the worlds that were created by the Gods.

31
Truth

After Zachery told Cassy about where he and Natallia had come from; Natallia being a half human, half angel queen; Tradan, or as she knew him, Billy, being the Champion of Light; and of course, his heritage of being the Dragon Rider, he thought she took the news very well.

"Zachery is crazy!" Cassy exclaimed to Miss Lizzy.

"Now why would you say that? He has always seemed to be a pretty stable boy to me," chuckled Miss Lizzy.

Cassy sat down with her grandmother and told her all that Zachery had revealed to her. "There is no way someone could come up with that stuff and be in good mental health." Miss Lizzy just sat there with a calm, but rather confused look on her face. Cassy shook her head and said, "Crazy, just crazy I tell you."

Miss Lizzy laughed her big booming laugh, "Sounds as if he does have a big imagination. What do you plan to do?"

Cassy smiled her big bright smile. "He's just messing with me, I know it. Although, he did sound convincing, I'll give him that. I know Zachery, he's just a jokester." She kissed her grandmother, got up and headed up to her room, laughing. Miss Lizzy sat quietly at the table, pondering what she was just told.

The next morning Natallia had come to Miss Lizzy for advice. "I need your help, if you please."

Miss Lizzy was stocking liquor under the bar of her saloon. "I'll be happy to help anyway I can, my lady."

Hearing someone call her that made a flood of memories rush into her mind. Startling her, nearly making her forget why she was there. "Oh yes. As you know it is almost Billy's seventeenth birthday and I want to do something special, not only for him, but for Zachery, too. The little brother always gets the attention and Zachery has been a little down lately. I had him so young, I did not know really what I was doing especially when his father passed. He needs to know he is still important, even now as a man."

Miss Lizzy rose up from her bottles. "You are exactly right. We can have a big shin dig for both of 'em. I'm sure Cassy will want to help. You know, I believe those two are made for each other."

Natallia smiled. "Great! We will get together on the details later. Thank you again Miss Lizzy, you have been a godsend to us."

The old woman smiled and watched as she walked out of the saloon. A look of concern furrowed her brow, "Gods send, huh? I need to find Zachery," she mumbled under her breath.

Zachery still worked for Miss Lizzy at the saloon. She went to head him off before he got there. She had questions of her own. Miss Lizzy mounted up her horse, spry for an elderly woman and went to Natallia and Zachery's house.

When she arrived she found Tradan, or Billy to her, on the porch with a makeshift sword prancing around, "Well, hello, Miss Lizzy! My mom is not home right now."

Miss Lizzy got down from her horse and slowly walked up to the boy. "I know, child, I have come to talk to Zachery." She looked very hard at the boy trying to get a vibe from him.

"You okay, Miss Lizzy? You ain't looking right."

The old woman just nodded her head and said, "I'm fine. You

gettin' ready for your big day?"

Tradan smiled so big, all his teeth showed. "Yes, ma'am. Mother said she was planning something special, a surprise."

"Yes, I've heard some things, but you won't get anything from me! I know how to keep secrets! Now where is that brother of yours hiding?"

Tradan pointed out toward the barn. "He's out there. I. . .I should go get him for you. It's a long walk out there."

"No, that's okay. I'll walk out there."

She slowly walked down the steps, heading for the barn Tradan knew Zachery was out there practicing his magic and had to warn him before Miss Lizzy saw something they could not explain.

He ran into the house, pulling off his over shirt as he went, straight out the backdoor wings spreading out and flew straight up, out of sight and to the back of the barn.

"Quick! Miss Lizzy is about to open the door! Hide your magic!" Tradan warned.

Zachery pushed everything under some straw as Tradan flew back out just as the front door of the barn burst open. "Good to see you Miss Lizzy. Mom is not home right now."

She squinted her eyes and peered right at him. "So I hear. I needed to come see you though."

Zachery being quick on his feet asked, "Oh, I'm sorry, did I do something at the saloon? I will fix whatever I did when I come into work, don't you worry."

She paced around the barn, circling the young man. Now, she was almost face-to-face with him. She reached up and grabbed his face with her hand as if she was examining him. She lets out a gasp, and the color left her. "I. . .I did not think it possible."

Zachery was scared now. "What is wrong, Miss Lizzy? You're worrying me a bit." Her eyes grew wide open, and she bolted for the door. Zachery ran after her and saw how easily she got on her horse and rode back to town. Zachery ran to the house shouting for Tradan. "We have to find Natallia, we have to do it now!"

Tradan looked to him. "She didn't see you, did she?"

"No, I hid all my materials before she entered, but I think Cassy told her about us."

Tradan's mouth dropped open in shock, "You fool! Why would you do such a thing?"

Zachery threw an overshirt at the boy. "I'll explain later, let's go find your mother." The two shot out of the house and searched for the queen. Zachery thought of how Cassy could betray him and tell anyone his secret.

Zachery and Tradan went looking for Natallia. They finally found her at the local market buying supplies for the party. "What are you two up to? Zachery don't you work with Miss Lizzy today?"

Tradan took his mother's hand and started to lead her out of the store. "That's what we need to talk to you about. We may have a problem."

They jumped on their horses and raced home dodging the new horseless automobiles that some were using now. The strange carriages moved around without a horse causing the trio to wonder if that world really was without magic.

If Miss Lizzy was panicking about the truth of our home, we had a big problem. We could not allow anyone in Georgia to tamper with our progress. With a little over a year left before Tradan would reach his eighteenth year, we might have had to become nomads and stay on the run until Benzoete summoned us home. I needed the old wizard now more than ever.

32
Valley of Ice Shadows

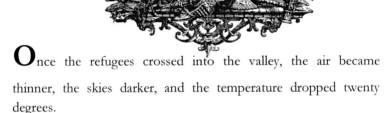

Once the refugees crossed into the valley, the air became thinner, the skies darker, and the temperature dropped twenty degrees.

Benzoete held a hand up, signaling for everyone to stop. "Do you hear that, Elos? The sound of cracking ice. It sounds as if it is right beneath us."

Elos tried to listen very carefully. "I hear nothing, Master Benzoete. Perhaps you are mistaken?"

Benzoete shook his head as if something were crawling on him. He dropped to his knees and started to brush the snow away from the ground. "Water! We are on frozen water and it is not holding us! Run! Get to the sides! Find solid ground and we will regroup!"

With Benzoete's warning, the group scattered, racing for solid ground. Antoine and Andrea quickly headed for the side with trees. As they approached a loud growling sound emitted from deep within.

"What was that?" Andrea asked. It was a sound that she had

never heard before.

Antoine was almost afraid to answer, "Dire wolves. We must be careful and remain calm. Sudden movements and they will pounce." Just as the words came from his mouth, they could see them, a pack of Dire wolves Antoine thought to be extinct. The lead wolf was a large, solid white male that had a chunk of its ear gone. "That is impossible," Antoine said. "They were killed in our village. My cloak is made of the white one's fur."

Andrea looked to Antoine. "They do not look dead to me. They not only seem to be alive, but also hungry and angry."

Antoine grabbed her hand and slowly walked backward, back toward the ice. "We have to put distance between us and them. We need to regroup with the others. I don't think we can kill them on our own."

As he turned to look for the others he noticed that the alpha had seen them. The white wolf caught their scent, angled his massive head to the skies, and let out a piercing howl.

"We have to move, NOW!" Antoine and Andrea ran back across the fragile ice to regroup with Gabriel and the others while the pack gained ground on them. "Guys, we have a problem!" Antoine shouted as he ran past George.

Benzoete turned toward the beasts, held out his hands to either side, and chanted a few elvish words. With a quick clap of his hands, the wolves were blown backward across the ice, hitting the ground. The force was too much for the ice and it started to break lose. Some of the pack fell into the water as the lead wolf and others started their chase over again running toward the refugees with the ice breaking behind them.

As the refugees found ground, the pack was on them. With some of the wolves swimming for their lives, the refugees weren't so outnumbered. Fangs glaring and claws swiping, the dire wolves attacked. George grabbed Launa and ran her to safety. Antoine and Andrea stood back to back with their blades acting as one.

Cold steel met the massive hide of the white dire wolf, slicing at the animal. With a swipe, the creature caught Antoine across the face and knocked him to the ground, dazing him. It sniffed the air, sensing the fur around the cloak Antoine wore as one of its own and flew into a frenzy. Andrea stepped in between the two at the same time the creature lunged. She pulled her blades in front of her as she bent backward so the wolf leapt over her to get to Antoine. With a thrust, the blades found their mark on the soft underbelly, opening a long cut, spilling blood all over her. A yelp is heard throughout the valley and the white wolf fell to the ground beside Antoine. When the others of the pack heard their leader fall, they retreated.

Andrea knelt next to the massive white animal, during its last moments. "None shall suffer. Die honorably." With that, she sliced across the throat, putting the great animal to rest. Andrea called to the others to see if they were all right, and to help her with Antoine.

Elos rushed toward them, "Here, try this." He said pulling a strange vial from his pouch.

Elos uncorked the vial and passed it under the nose of Antoine, with a jolt, Antoine leapt to his feet. "Where are they? What happened?" he asked in a panic.

"It is all right, they are gone," Benzoete reassured him.

Antoine lowered his fists and looked around. "Well you saved me again, dear lady."

Andrea tilted her head, "Again?"

Antoine being the dashing warrior he is, replied, "The first time was when you entered my life."

Gabriel laughed and slapped him on the shoulder, "We will have enough time for that later, we need to find this tomb."

As they come together, they heard George call from the distance. "Gabriel! I think you need to see this." They walked over to where George and Launa stood. "I think it's this way." George said as he pointed down a pathway between two solid walls of ice. At the end of the pathway a light could be seen. Sunlight.

"This place keeps getting stranger and stranger." Antoine grimaced, while rubbing his head. "We go from beautiful warm meadows to chilling ice and extinct wolves to sun again."

As he started to walk down the path, Benzoete stopped him. "Wait, Antoine, it cannot be this easy. We must be alert for anything. This pathway looks too inviting."

Gabriel agreed and drew his sword. "This valley has claimed countless lives, I can't believe the cold and wolves are the only thing here." The small remaining group followed their leader and readied their weapons. "Slowly, if we encounter anything, I pray to the Gods we are ready," Gabriel said a silent prayer to himself. "I pray to thee my Gods hear me now. We have come this close to finding your gifts, please do not forsake us now."

With that they started down the valley. With every step, they inched closer to the tombs. Benzoete's heart started pounding he was about to see the final resting place of his mother and the other two original elders of his people. As his mind wandered, he let his guard down for a moment and tripped over a stone.

Elos stopped to check on him. "Master, are you alright?"

"Yes, yes, I am fine. My mind got away from me for a bit," the old wizard replied.

When they reached the middle of the valley, the clouds vanished, revealing the sunlight. The warm beams shone down on them, casting their shadows on the walls of ice.

"I don't like this. Why did the sun come out all of a sudden?" Andrea questioned.

"Perhaps we are far enough through that we are safe now. Maybe?" George replied looking to Benzoete. The wizard furrowed his brow and shook his head. When they stopped, their shadows moved on their own.

"Look! My shadow has a mind of its own!" shouted Launa, pointing to the ice wall.

George turned in time to see her shadow step from the wall and come after her. He drew his blade and stepped between them. The shadows were coming to life and attacking them. It was almost as if the refugees were fighting themselves. The shadows moved like them and fought like them. Gabriel found himself fighting an exact copy of Antoine, only made of living ice. The battle suddenly favored the icey alley.

Gabriel could see his men being defeated and killed by ice copies of themselves. He gripped his mighty sword, Fuascailte, and let out a deafening battle cry as he thrust the blade through the ice warrior moving toward him. Once it entered the belly of his enemy, he turned and gave the blade a twist while lifting the blade, shattering the ice causing crystals to rain down. The mighty king ran to Antoine and Andrea. They were fighting a copy of Andrea and one of Gabriel when the king slid on his knees and swung. As the blade made contact, one by one it took the legs out from under the ice shadows. They fell to the ground, and gave Antoine and Andrea the opportunity to take their heads.

Gabriel was a killing machine. Lost in himself, all he knew was to protect his friends. George had destroyed the copies of himself and Launa, and now rushed to help the others. As he and Gabriel met in the middle, their blades were as kindred spirits. Benzoete and Elos had rooted the feet of some around them to the icy floor.

"Why does fire not affect them?" Elos asked.

"They are not made of normal ice. It is a magical element. We must slow them down," Benzoete retorted.

As George and Gabriel descended on them, the ice shadows fell to their flurry of blade strikes and melted back into the walls.

The two stopped and found themselves back to back. "Old friend I had no idea you could do that!" George said with a big smile.

"I heard a voice inside me, guiding me where to strike. I have never heard this voice before," said Gabriel.

"We will thank this voice later, my king," Benzoete said as he pointed toward another boundary line. They could see green grass and hear water flowing.

"The four falls?" asked George, "That is where we are to find the tomb?"

Gabriel took a glimpse at Benzoete. "You ready for this?"

Benzoete straightened his robes and ran his fingers through his stringy, white hair. "Yes, I am. I have wanted this for centuries. Let's go meet my mother, shall we?" The remaining few crossed over into the warm, sunny area and they saw lush green grass, tall trees, and a crystal clear river, full of life. "The Horizon River, what majestic beauty it holds. The waters of life flow from this place, no wonder they keep it locked away," Benzoete said in awe.

"Where do we go from here?" George asked.

"We follow the river to the Four Falls, the elders resting place will be there," Elos answered. "We have come to a sacred place, we do not know if we are entirely out of danger. Stay alert and be careful. If all goes to plan, Master Benzoete and George Morely will be the first to enter this place in over three thousand years. I have considered it an honor to have fought alongside each and every one of you."

Antoine stepped up next to him and placed an arm around Elos's shoulders. "Not bad for a bunch of humans, eh Elos?" They all laughed and started toward the falls.

33

Hell Comes To Whitehold

The fallen God, Craotonus, had returned. The demon brethren prepared to restore The Remissum to full power, even if it took every last mortal alive in Amundiss. Dori'naur and Rauko' knelt before Craotonus as he sat on the throne of Castle Whitehold.

"You will regain your place as ruler of the Heavens, my Lord. We will destroy the demigod king and his pathetic followers in your name," Dori'naur insisted while rising.

Rauko' followed suit, "Guide us, master. Your will shall be done."

Craotonus sat on a throne that was not his own, hood drawn over his face. "I need souls. Bring me the innocent. Bring me the untainted. They are the sustenance that powers me. Go my faithful, go and gather the souls for me. We will scar the heavens and let all know who we are."

With that, the demons left their master; one went east and one west, each with an army of barkers at their command. Each town they encountered, bloodshed and mayhem descended on the citizens like nightfall. With each kill, Craotonus grew stronger and stronger. When they found the priests that taught the people of the Light, they brought them to stand before The Remissum himself. The priests had a direct connection to the Light, and Craotonus wanted to savor every last drop of their mortality himself. The priests' blood was spilled across the floor as their lives were taken from them by the mindless barkers. Craotonus removed his tattered robes and kneeled, taking his hands and covering his body with their pure blood.

"Yes, I feel the tears of my siblings crying out for their beloved mortals. Feel my pain! Every one of you!" Craotonus shouted.

As the demons stormed through the towns, anyone who tried to stand up to them soon found their head torn from their body and placed on a spike as a trophy. Dori'naur and his group of barkers bombarded the town of Plomin.

Word had spread to the people of Plomin of the death and chaos and they agreed not to back down quietly. The city gates were blocked and sealed. Archers stood at the ready on the towers.

Dori'naur sneered as his evil army came to the gates. "As if these imbeciles stand a chance against me. Bring down the gates!" The order rang out to the barkers and they went into a frenzy. They rushed the gates using their bodies as battering rams. Just as they were to collide with the gates, they were swallowed by a gaping hole that was deep and filled with sharp stakes hidden in the front. The barkers found themselves impaled and trapped. This infuriated Dori'naur. "If you want something done right, do it YOURSELF!" His voice boomed and echoed throughout the city.

The people readied themselves for the second attack. Dori'naur knelt before the gates and touched the ground with the palm of his hand. Roots sprung up and wound toward the gates, entangling the bars and hinges. He quickly stood and with a swift flick of his wrist, the gates came tumbling down at his feet. With the gates breached, the remaining barker army rushed in, "Do watch your step, idiots." Since they watched the guard this time as they entered the walls, they missed the two massive blocks of rock that were mounted on the walls.

An officer of the city shouted, "Release the Shattering!" The giant slabs met each other, crushing with a shaking boom, the barkers between them.

With almost his entire army gone, the demon was infuriated. "I will crush you all beneath my heel! You will kneel before me and give your lives to your ruler, Craotonus, The Remissum!"

A voice rose up from the back of the main tower. "We serve King Gabriel, son of Owin, true ruler of these lands! You and your master will be delivered into Hell by his hands!" The magistrate stepped forward in full armor.

"You show bravery, my good man. You, I will kill quickly as to honor you." Dori'naur grabbed his mighty war axe from his back and instantly the kite shield formed on his arm.

The defenders of Plomin rushed in with weapons ready. The men fought valiantly, but one by one they fell to the demon. Bodies scattered all over the ground, blood flowed like water. Dori'naur walked toward the magistrate. "Kneel and I shall show mercy. I will swiftly take your head and deliver your soul to my master."

"You cannot deliver what you are unable to take. May the Light reign forever!" The noble magistrate proclaimed before thrusting his sword into his own heart, while looking deep into the burning eyes of the demon.

"NO, you fool!" Dori'naur shouted. "Bah! He will not miss one. Gather the women and children. We have a God to feed." As the barkers went to find the rest of the people, Dori'naur knelt beside the magistrate, "What a waste. You were a noble warrior, my master would have enjoyed your soul."

At that moment, one of the barkers scurried up to the demon. "Master, they are all gone. We can find no one."

Dori'naur sent the hobbled slave flying backward with a backhanded slap. "Find them, they cannot be far. We need them, we need them all! Craotonus needs the innocent!"

***

Rauko' was having problems of his own. The demon hunter took his army of mutated citizens into the city of Screel. This was a city filled with peace-loving people. Peace-loving yes, but when they had to defend their homes and their families, no one was as fierce and they were ready for this fight. They knew the odds of defeating the demon and his army were not in their favor, but they would never roll over and surrender. If Rauko' wanted them, he would have to fight for them.

As they approached the gates of Screel, a single, heavily armored knight stood just outside. "Lord Rauko' we were expecting you. We are the good people of Screel and we urge you to turn away and seek your mayhem elsewhere."

Rauko' laughed a very booming laugh. "You urge me to seek elsewhere? Now, why would I do that my good man?"

The stoic and stable knight replied. "You will seek elsewhere or prepare for doom."

As Rauko' looked on and listened to the knight, he shook his head, "Would someone bring me his head already?"

The barkers wildly charged the knight and yet he stood his ground. At the last moment before he was engulfed by the evil horde, he took a step back, drew his sword and kneeled. When the barkers got close they started to vanish.

Rauko' quickly lost his sneer and commanded the barkers to stop. "I can smell you now. Come out and face me. It has been what two, three thousand years since we last met?"

As the gates opened, the knight stepped back to take his place beside a beautiful woman with long black hair, standing in white robes. Her hands glowing with a yellowish haze, and her eyes fixed on the demon, she serenely said, "Rauko', turn your *things* around and leave this place. These are good people and I will not allow you to come in here to take their lives for your master."

The demon placed a finger at his lips like he was deep in thought, "Hmm my dear GailBen, why do you think we would turn around? I cannot be defeated by just a lowly wizard and her lackeys. You were a young elf when my master destroyed your elders. I see time has not made you smarter."

GailBen cracked an unnerving sneer, "Who said it was just me and some lackeys?" At that moment hundreds of warriors streamed from the buildings behind the two all armed and ready for battle. The most shocking member of the group was Sybillias, one of the remaining Gods. She stepped forward to stand beside GailBen, the High Elf.

"Sybillias! You cannot interfere with the mortals. That is Akadius's own rule. You dare defy him?" A furious Rauko' shouted.

The gentle God lifted her head, and removed her hood. "I am well aware of my place in the affairs of the mortals. I am also aware that I can bless those who pray to me and ask for guidance. I find these warriors worthy and just. They have my divine blessings." With that she looked to the heavens, stretched forth her arms and sent a bright light throughout the city. Sybillias looked to GailBen, "You are a worthy leader, dear friend. You have my grace. Show this hellion his way back to the ashes." Sybillias touched the hand of GailBen and the wizard's eyes begin to glow.

"Warriors! On my mark, escort these demons back to hell!"

Rauko' unleashed his blades, "Minions! Our master needs to feed. Let us fetch him a snack!" The demon charged straight for GailBen, while the remaining barkers rushed in to meet the holy warriors.

"Archers! Fire at will. Paladins! Attack! I am going to enjoy this."

The demon slashed downward with both blades. Swinging a blessed war hammer, GailBen blocked both blades to one side, sweeping the handle at Rauko' feet. As the demon jumped to avoid the strike, she spun and connected a blow straight to his chest with the head of the hammer, knocking Rauko' to the ground with a thud. GailBen raised the glowing battle hammer and she drove the weapon down; the demon rolling, barely missing being crushed.

The force of the mighty swing shook the ground, sending cracks running across the land. He delivered a quick blow to her back knocking the breath out of her. This gave the demon an opening to inflict a damaging blow of his own. As she was on the ground, Rauko' kicked her in the side, trying to slow her down. He raised his right blade and thrust down. Shifting to one side, the blade missed GailBen's face by inches, followed by the left blade, making the elf roll quickly side to side to avoid the demon blades. GailBen used her feet to grab at the knees of the demon buckling them and throwing him off-balance, giving her an opportunity to spring to her feet.

As Rauko' tried to rise, she slammed her hammer up against the side of his head putting him flat on his back once more.

She wiped the blood away from her mouth. "You have gotten slow Rauko', you're letting a woman get the best of you."

Rauko' moved slowly, but couldn't help laughing, "Dear woman, you forget who you are fighting." As he said this he clenched his fist and a barker ran into the back of the elf pushing her off-balance, forward toward Rauko'. He leapt to his feet, driving his blades into her chest. He leaned close to her ear and whispered, "I am not an honorable warrior, I do not fight by rules and I do not care for life!" He twisted the blades and GailBen shrieked out in pain. "My master will enjoy your soul. You will help him grow stronger. When you see Sybillias, tell her I am coming for her." Rauko' opened his arms, forcing the blades through either side of her body, tearing her to shreds.

The remaining Paladins fighting the minions had instructions that if GailBen fell in battle they must retreat and regroup. A horn sounded and the men ran out the gates. As they exited an archer sent a flaming arrow into a pile of boxes. An explosion rocked the countryside, sending barker body parts flying.

From out of the smoldering city walked Rauko'. "That is one less High Elf, we have to deal with." Clutching her battle hammer in his hand, "I believe this little trophy is mine." He returned to Castle Whitehold to ready more minions. He knew their time was running out. They had to get Craotonus to full power. This time, the heavens would fall and they would rule beside The Remissum for eternity.

MICHAEL LACKEY

34
Confession

Zachery and Tradan found Natallia and rushed to get back home.

She stopped them on the porch, "What is the emergency? What have you got yourself into Tradan?" laughed Natallia.

"We need to convince Benzoete to bring us home, Miss Lizzy has found out about us. I do not know how much she believed, but she definitely did believe part of it. She ran out faster than I have ever seen her move before." Zachery told her of their meeting in the barn and the look Miss Lizzy had in her eyes.

"Let's get inside before she decides to come back, maybe we can contact the others and see what's going on there."

As Natallia opened the door to the house and walked in they made a startling discovery, Tradan stopped in his tracks. "Um, guys. I think she already decided to come back." They look over toward the living room and there sat Miss Lizzy with a look on her face that they have never seen before, a look of bewilderment.

"Come in, I've been waiting for you."

The three entered the room a little uneasy. Here sat a person that they have seen every day for the past seventeen years and now she's been told that everything was a lie. "Now Miss Lizzy, whatever Zachery may have told Cassy, it was just a joke trying to make her laugh." Natallia looked to Zachery for help.

"Yes, I know she thinks of me as a jokester anyway. I tried to lighten the mood a little bit." Zachery raised his eyebrows and made a funny face. Miss Lizzy did not move, not even a smile.

Tradan stated, "I think I'm going to go up to my room. Looks like you need to talk about something."

"There is no need in that. I need you to stay." Miss Lizzy replied sternly. "Please sit, I need some answers."

The three sat around and stared at the old woman, not knowing what she knew or whom else she had told. They knew if she knew the truth and started telling people, one of two things would happen. Either they would think she was crazy, or they would turn on them and they would have to flee to another town and hide.

Why did I open my mouth to Cassy? Why did I let my emotions get the best of me? I had put us in danger and we were only months away from Tradan being eighteen. My love for Cassy clouded my judgment. I could not let that happen when we faced the demons. I must always have a clear mind.

"What kind of answers are you looking for? We will be glad to help with anything. As we told you, Zachery was kidding around like he always does," Natallia said.

"Tell me the story you told Cassy, tell me everything you know of this other world. Tell me what you know of Amundiss."

Zachery laughed. "It's a made-up place I told Cassy about. All in my head, I'm thinking of writing a book."

Suddenly, Miss Lizzy lunged forward and jabbed a dagger into the coffee table. "Lies! Tell me who you are!"

Zachery leapt to his feet. "Where did you get my dagger from?"

Miss Lizzy tilted her head. "Your dagger? I will ask one more time. Who are you?" Miss Lizzy now stood with her hands outstretched and glowing. "Tell me how you are here!"

Tradan sprung in front of his mother and pulled a blade from its sheath. "The question now is who are you? This is a world without magic, how are you capable of this?"

Miss Lizzy lowered her hands, "I am sorry. I do not want to alarm you. I just need answers, I have waited far too long for this to be a coincidence."

Natallia looked to the old woman very confused, "Coincidence? What are you talking about? You have heard of Amundiss before?"

Miss Lizzy sat back down and urged everyone else to join her. "I am going to tell you everything about me, everything. If what you say is not true, then I will seem just a crazy old woman. This will be my confession to you." The three sat back down, Tradan put away his sword, and they listened to what she had to say. "My name here in this place is Miss Lizzy, at home I went by another name; Aliz'Ra, the second seat of the elders of Eska'Taurn. My people were from the world you named, Amundiss. We were chosen by the gods to aid them in a battle against the fallen one, Craotonus."The look on the trio's faces was of utter shock. "I know this is a lot to take in. I assure you this is the truth."

Zachery stood, and walked to her, "You are Aliz'Ra? Benzoete's mother?"

Aliz'Ra's jaw dropped with so much shock. "My son lives? You know of him?"

Natallia smiled. "Know him? He is the reason we are here. He sent us here for our protection. My name really is Natallia, I am married to Gabriel, King of Whitehold, seat of Amundiss. This is Tradan, as you know, he is my son. Zachery is not my son, but the son of George and Elizabeth Morely. I believe he has something he can tell you that will really shock you."

As she looked to Zachery, he reached for the dagger still stuck in the table. "This dagger was given to me by my father. He told me it was the only thing he had that belonged to his mother."

Aliz'Ra looked confused. "I don't understand. This dagger was forged by my husband's father's hand guided by the Gods. He was the first chosen by the Gods to lead our people. How do you have it?"

Zachery smiled. "My grandmother passed it down to my father. He never knew his mother, he was told she died shortly after he was born. My grandmother's name is Valindra, she is the daughter of the High Elf wizard, Benzoete. That would make you my great-grandmother." Zachery bowed to her.

Aliz'Ra's eyes started to fill with tears. She cupped her hands around Zachery's face. "All this time. I had my own flesh and blood here with me, but you're human?"

"Half human. That's why my father never knew of his mother or his bloodline," Zachery replied.

"This doesn't tell us how you are here. Benzoete said you were killed in the Great War," Natallia said.

"Ah, he never saw what happened. He was terribly young when the war began. We were fighting the minions of Craotonus when we saw the evil one himself. I was given the Bloodblade and wanted to end the war then and there. I sent Benzoete and the others to retreat and I went after the fallen god. We fought for several moments, when he realized I had bested him, the coward tried to flee from me.

"He opened a portal and as he entered I followed before it closed. We ended up here, fighting still, I knew I wounded him, I should have killed him and sent him back to Hell, but we were wrong. The Bloodblade was not strong enough to kill him. I buried the blade deep where his black heart was and had him laugh at me. He destroyed my amulet, which gave me most of my power, so I was stranded here with no way to communicate or go back home."

Tradan sat quietly by when he spoke up, "What is this Bloodblade you speak of? And also does Cassy know this?" Zachery's love for Cassy made him blurt out the question, but what if they were to be relatives?

"Cassy does not know, she thought you were insane when you told her your story. Also, she is not my blood granddaughter. Her parents were close friends of mine and when they died in a fire, I took her in as my own family. I moved around a lot as to not draw suspicion." Zachery let out a sigh of relief. "The Bloodblade is a sword crafted by the Gods themselves from their own blood. They thought it would be enough to kill Craotonus but he was more powerful than even they knew. He had bonded with the shadows of Hell, they gave him strength beyond measure. I failed my people. I thought because of my mistake the people of Amundiss had all perished."

Natallia sat down beside her, wrapped her arms around her and said, "No. It was your act of bravery that saved everyone that day. You sent the demon back to Hell for long enough that we could have Tradan, the Champion of Light, and Zachery, the Dragon Rider. Benzoete told stories of you, he kept your memory alive and all of Amundiss has rejoiced your name."

Aliz'Ra smiled and looked to Zachery. "Is it true? You are of the blood of the Dragon?"

Zachery tugged at his shirt and said, "Yes ma'am. According to Benzoete, the bloodline skipped to me and I have the power to call forth the dragons once more. He sent us here to harness our power so we could defeat the demons once and for all, and now with you by our side, I know we will not fail."

Aliz'Ra felt a swell of pride, "I have watched the Champion of Light grow before my eyes and did not know it. That means my dear Natallia, you are a Vessel of Light, a direct descendant of the angels. It is an honor." Natallia smiled and just nodded her head.

It was a shock when I found out my grandmother was an elf and still alive, but now here I was sitting and talking to my great-grandmother who everyone thought was dead. Her magic was still a part of her so that would explain why we were able to learn our magic so easily. I couldn't wait for my father and the others to reach the tomb of the elders, they were in for a shock when they entered and found only two elders buried there.

"Do you speak much with my son and the others? If he sent the Champion of Light and the Dragon Rider here for protection that means one thing. Craotonus is back. I need to tell him I have the

Bloodblade," Aliz'Ra said.

"We have not been able to talk to them for any length of time for a few months now. They briefly told us of my mother's passing right before they entered the Valley of Ice Shadows. They are going to the Tombs of the Elders to retrieve any information that could help them."

Aliz'Ra looked puzzled, "Tomb of the Elders? My dear comrades, I am sorry, I failed you," she said in a low prayer.

Tradan puffed out his chest. "I feel strong enough now to go and face the demons. I know with Zachery and now you, together we are enough to defeat them."

Aliz'Ra said, "You can't underestimate their power. I did and it nearly cost me my life and one of the most powerful weapons the Gods have ever given us. I will help you with your training, both of you. I need to speak to Benzoete as soon as you can reach him. I will go get Cassy and we will stay here with you."

"Yes, Cassy. How will she handle this?' asked Zachery.

"She is a strong girl and I'm sure she will be all right." Aliz'Ra gave him a wink.

Aliz'Ra left them and went to find Cassy and gather some of her belongings that she thought she would never need again.

One of the most powerful beings from Amundiss still lived. Zachery and Tradan had a full-time teacher now and Craotonus had a battle coming his way

35

Tomb Of the Elders

As the refugees back on Amundiss followed the flowing waters of life, they came to an area with four majestic waterfalls, all flowing into the mouth of the Waters of Life. According to the Book of the Ancients, that is where they would find the Tomb of the Elders.

"This is the place though I do not see any place for the tombs," Gabriel said while looking around.

"We have to be careful. This place is beautiful and holy, but it is also deadly. We have to find the entrance without disturbing the surroundings," Benzoete said as everyone spread out, in search for clues.

Antoine and Andrea started toward a large group of trees hoping to find something useful. "Hey, Antoine look at this," she said as she bent down and reached for a shiny, metal object.

"Don't touch it!" Antoine shouted, but it is too late. As Andrea picked the object up a rumbling was felt under their feet. A crack opened up in the ground and they saw four large creatures ascend from the depths. "Ice golems!" shouted Antoine. The others rushed to them as the elemental beings stared them down, silently watching them.

"Maybe they are not malicious," Gabriel whispered. Just then all four raised their arms. Streaming from the sky came thousands of razor-sharp ice shards.

"Hurry! Come to us!" shouted Elos.

As the group hovered around the wizards, Benzoete and Elos raised their hands to the heavens and summoned fire above them. As the shards came close, they harmlessly melted. The ice golems lowered their arms and in unison, held out their right arms and formed massive ice sabers. The four charged the group as one.

"Scatter and keep moving! Do not let them strike you!" George shouted as he grabbed Launa by the arm and led her away from the group.

Everyone headed in different directions, confusing the giant creatures. Andrea stopped and pulled one of the blessed arrows from her quiver. "Let's see if you like steel," he said as she let the arrow fly. She found her mark in the upper thigh of one of the golems. As it hit, all four stop. "I only hit one, why did they all stop?" she asked Antoine.

That sparked an idea in the warrior. "They are connected. I bet if we stop one, we stop them all." He told Andrea to focus all her attention on the one closest to them. "Gabriel! Follow my lead!" he shouted.

As the two met, they started slashing at the legs. With a mighty swing, Gabriel sliced clean through the massive leg and cut it off. As the ice giant fell, so did the other three. With them down and immobilized, Elos and Benzoete closed in and rained fire on them. The fire weakened the mighty ice golems, and the group moved in to deliver the final blows. George plunged his blade into the neck of the one closest and watched it return to water and flow to the river, each one followed.

"All things are in the circle of life's waters," Benzoete said.

As they gathered themselves, George walked over to the waters.

He leaned over and peered in, "Elos, Benzoete, come look at this." George pointed to a golden, glowing symbol at the bottom of the river.

"By the gods, George! You found it!" Benzoete said while patting him on the back.

The symbol he saw was a fully bloomed tree with a golden serpent wrapped around the trunk. On the serpent's back are the words, '*Quis te est.*'

"What does this mean?" George asked Benzoete.

Elos walked up beside them. "It is asking who you are"

Benzoete looked deep into George's eyes. "You have to believe in yourself and me. I fear that the door will not open unless we fully believe."

George walked closer to Benzoete. "I have seen many, many marvels. Things I would not have believed before I met you. I know you are my mother's father. I know my place and my heritage. I also know that I have to accept this in order to save my family."

Benzoete smiled. "Then let us go meet my mother and the original elders of our people."

They grasped each other's hand and walked slowly toward the water's edge. Just as they are about to step in, the water began to bubble. The symbol under its surface glowed even brighter now. As they stepped down, the water parted and their feet settled on dry land. With every step they took the waters moved farther back.

When they reached the spot where the symbol rested, Benzoete looked to George. "Are you ready?"

George turned and saw Launa standing on the shore, "Let us end this."

With that, they both laid a hand on the tree symbol and the ground shook. Walls shot up from the ground holding back the waters, the serpent seemed to magically move and slither away from the trunk as a doorway appeared.

"We did it. We found and opened the Tomb of the Elders. This is a historic day!" Benzoete laughed and motioned for the remaining group to follow them down. Benzoete told them, "We will enter first. When we call for you, slowly enter."

As Benzoete and George entered the Tombs, a musky smell hits them. "Wow, you can tell this place has been sealed for three centuries." George waved his hand in front of his nose.

Benzoete snapped his fingers and a row of torches lit up the room. He called back to the others. As everyone entered they saw a table in the center of the room. Around the walls were several paintings dictating the great battle between Craotonus and the Heavens.

Gabriel walked to the table. "Benzoete, is it possible this day was foretold to the elders before they were laid to rest?"

Benzoete rubbed his scraggly beard. "It is possible, why do you ask?"

Gabriel pointed to the chairs sitting around the table. "There are twelve chairs around the table, and eleven of us made it here."

The old wizard looked really puzzled now. "All things are possible, my king. Why the extra seat is the question?"

At that moment, a rumble came from the back of the room. They saw a wall slowly descend to the floor. Three coffins stood along the wall. Above each was the name of the one enclosed inside. First read Malotorin, the brave. Second read Aliz'Ra, the relentless. Over the last read Chrin'lolas, the eternal.

Benzoete started to tremble, "No, this cannot be!" The sarcophagus with his mother's name stood open and empty. "They didn't bury her here? Why would they not lay her to rest with the other two elders?"

Then they heard a voice. "Because, like myself, she did not perish in the great war."

Everyone was startled and drew weapons. From the shadows behind the sarcophagus stepped a terribly fragile, extremely old and worn elven man. Benzoete rushed to him, "Chrin'lolas! You live? How?"

The old elf made his way to the table and took a seat. "The Gods chose to let me rest and wait for you to find this place. I was awakened when you entered the valley. I have much to tell you and to prepare you for the Demon Lord."

Elos stood by trembling. "It is a glorious honor just to be in your presence, dear Elder."

Chrin'lolas smiled and gave a nod of his head. "My time is short. I was to die in the battle, but the Gods let me live for this reason. Once I fulfill my destiny, I will take my place beside my fallen comrade."

Benzoete asked the elder, "You said my mother did not die that day. If she did not, does she still live then?"

Chrin'lolas replied, "Yes, but I am not sure where or how. I only know that when we were chosen as first seats of the Elders, our essence was fused together. I can sense their life force. Alas, dear Malotorin's is extinguished, but I feel Aliz'Ra still."

Gabriel whispered to Antoine, "We need to try and contact Natallia and Zachery, let them know we made it in and tell them the news of Aliz'Ra. If we can find her that would swing more momentum in our direction."

Antoine nodded. Benzoete, Elos, and George sat with Chrin'lolas while the others set up a makeshift camp inside the tombs. Andrea studied the paintings when she saw Aliz'Ra wielding a strange-looking sword. "If I may ask, what is that blade she has in her hand?"

Benzoete looked up. "Oh, I can answer that, she had the Bloodblade. It was a sword made from the blood of the Gods. We thought it would be enough to kill Craotonus, sadly it was not."

"That is why it is important to find her. If she still has the Bloodblade we need to equip it with this," Chrin'lolas said as he opened a box mounted in the wall next to his sarcophagus. "This is a gem given to me by the Gods. It is named, Heaven's Tear. When the Gods saw how evil Craotonus had become, they wept. As their tears flowed to the floor, they formed this gem. It has the power of pure Light, love, and compassion. If we combine it with the Bloodblade, it will make it powerful enough to destroy the immortal demon forever, ridding him from the shadows."

Antoine came over to them. "We have everything set up. You can try to contact Natallia now."

Benzoete walked to the area with his candles and mirror; with a snap of his fingers the candles light. He took a small green amulet out from under his robes, closed his eyes, and concentrated. The mirror started to ripple like water. Antoine, Gabriel, and George watched anxiously, they desperately wanted to see their family.

Suddenly the mirror ran red like blood and a face appeared. Instead of their family members, Craotonus appeared. "Ah, my dear Benzoete how long has it been? I just want to thank you for showing me where you hid the Champion. I will show my gratitude with the gift of your loved one's heads delivered to you by my minions."

With an evil laugh, the mirror faded back and Benzoete was knocked backward off his feet. "We have to get them back here now! They are not prepared for this on Earth!" shouted Gabriel.

Elos helped Benzoete to his feet. The wizard brushed himself off. "Chrin'lolas, can we hide the Champion of Light for a few months or more until his eighteenth season day?"

Antoine clenched his fists, "We have no other choice! You heard the demon as well as we did. They have to be brought back."

Chrin'lolas paced back and forth, rubbing his long beard. "There is one way we may be able to bring them here and to keep the child safe."

Andrea was now with Antoine, sliding her hand into his. "Well, it is more than we have with them alone in this other world. Whatever needs to be done, we will do it. We have beaten the odds on every challenge we have faced."

George spoke up, "What about Earth? If we bring them back here the demons will tear that world apart looking for them. All those innocent lives, gone."

Benzoete looked as if he would be sick. "We need for them to know we are bringing them here. Not hiding them, but protecting them."

Chrin'lolas nodded in approval. Gabriel shook his head, "You are talking about suicide. It would be a full war with all his minions and a fallen God. We are not ready for that."

"They are not ready either. If Craotonus were at full strength, he would have already come for us. We have to act fast and get them here," Benzoete said.

George asked, "I don't know much about the prophecies or lore of the elven people, but could Prince Tradan be strong enough before his eighteenth season day? Could he have trained and have learned all he can? Or must we wait for that day?"

"It has been centuries since the last Champion of Light. Even before master Chrin'lolas. We do not have all the information either, just what the Gods revealed to us through the Book of the Ancients." replied Elos.

Chrin'lolas turned to Benzoete, "You have the Book of Ancients with you? That could be the key to all our questions!"

Benzoete opened his satchel and handed the book to Chrin'lolas. The old elder walked over to the table and quickly opened it up, flipping to the back.

"I do not understand, the pages are blank. What is it you are looking for?" asked Gabriel.

Chrin'lolas closed his eyes and smiled, "You shall see my new friend. You shall see." As the elder passed his hands over the pages, words began to form:

"The Champion shall pass from one world to the next. His power has been proven. He is the chosen one. Call him, and the Rider to face the task. Take the castle, take your world for it is written. With my son at their side, the warriors shall not fail."

Seeing this written before their eyes brought a hush over everyone. Then Elos broke the silence, "Who is the writer and who is this son they speak of?"

Chrin'lolas closed the book, "My good people, that was Akadius, lord of the Gods and Heavens, and you have been in the presence of his son this entire time." He shifted his eyes to Gabriel.

Antoine's eyes widened. "You are the son of a God? Did you

know?"

Gabriel, who was seated now, replied, "I did not know. My father was Owin, King of Whitehold, and husband to Jacquelin. This is a mistake."

Chrin'lolas shook his head, quite calm. "There is no mistake, my king. It was written by the God himself. This sheds a much needed light to this dark situation. You are the Champion's father correct?" Gabriel nodded his head, finding words were too hard to come by right now. "Then we have an unstoppable force. The son of Akadius fighting alongside his son, the Champion of Light as well as with the first Dragon Rider in centuries. Bring them home Benzoete. Bring them home and put an end to this."

Antoine jumped to his feet, a giant smile on his face. "Let us bring our family home!"

36
Coming Together

After finding the Tomb of Elders, the refugees felt that they were finally on the right track to defeating the evil Craotonus and his brethren of demons. The original elder, Chrin'lolas, who was still very much alive, set them on course to bring Zachery, Natallia, and Tradan home. Given a second chance at life, Chrin'lolas could not leave the tomb. He had fulfilled his debt to the Gods and his time was over.

Meanwhile, Aliz'Ra was with Zachery and Tradan helping with their training when she felt a jolt run through her that sent her to her knees.

"Aliz'Ra! What is it?" asked Tradan.

"This cannot be." And with that, she wept.

Zachery tried to comfort her. "Let us help you, tell us what had happened."

She slowly stood up. "When the Gods chose us to be the first elders of our people, we were given great power and our essence was fused together. I just felt the life force of Chrin'lolas fade. He died in the original war."

"Or so you thought. Everyone thought you were dead to, remember," Tradan told her.

"We need to try and contact my son and the others. I feel they have news we need to know."

***

On Amundiss, Chrin'lolas used his last power to send the brave refugees back to Doochary. The noble elder had earned his rest and he knew that the Champion of Light would soon take his place and eradicate the dark demons. As they exit the entrance to the Path of a Thousand Eyes, they saw the body of Stolos motionless on the ground.

Antoine walked over and bowed his head. "Rest now, noble one. You have earned your place in the Heavens."

They had to find a place to set up camp in Doochery and contact Zachery on Earth. Chrin'lolas, before passing, had given Benzoete the knowledge of how to bring all of them back to Amundiss.

"We cannot stay here long. The demons know we were inside the path, we need to be far away from here," said Elos.

"I agree though we also need to find a way for Craotonus to figure out that we are bringing Tradan and Zachery here without it looking like we meant for them to do so. We cannot have the demons going to Earth, they would devastate that world," Benzoete said.

Gabriel had an idea. "Craotonus knew you were contacting them through the mirror, so this time do not try to hide it. We will contact the others, tell them they are coming home and Craotonus could hear the news."

Benzoete silently nodded his head, tapping his fingers together in front of his mouth. The old wizard had a plan of his own brewing in his ancient mind.

***

On Earth, Alis'Ra needed to find a way to tell Cassy the truth. She took Zachery's news pretty well mostly because she did not believe him. Aliz'Ra went to find Cassy. She was at the saloon talking to some of the patrons.

"Here she is now. I told Mr. and Mrs. Mitchell you should be here any time now" stated Cassy.

"I am sorry, Maybelle. You and Eugene have anything you want on the house, me and Cassy have to get going."

Cassy looked confused. "Going where? Don't ya want to hear their big news?"

Maybelle spoke up. "We are having a baby, Miss Lizzy! We came to tell everyone good-bye. We will be leaving to go to Atlanta tomorrow."

"Yes, Maybelle and I want to raise our child there to give her a better opportunity," said Eugene.

"Her?" asked Miss Lizzy.

"Well, we're not certain, of course, but we would like a little girl named Margaret. It sounds good, doesn't it?" replied Maybelle.

Aliz'Ra, or Miss Lizzy to them, composed herself and gave them her biggest smile. "I hope ya'll the best, and that your little girl has everything the wind would blow her way. Now, me and Cassy have to go." She grabbed Cassy by the arm and they headed out.

Once outside, Cassy stopped. "Why do we have to go so fast and where are we going?"

Aliz'Ra took a deep breath. "I will explain everything once we get back to Natallia."

Cassy was not one to talk back to her grandmother, but she needed answers. "No, ma'am. I need to know what's going on."

Aliz'Ra stood straight, brushed herself off, looked Cassy dead in the eyes. "My name is Aliz'Ra, second seat of the elders of my people, not Lizzy. My home is a planet called, Amundiss, and everything Zachery told you is the truth. They need our help and we must give it to them."

Cassy stood there with her mouth wide open, gave her a nod of the head. "Well, let's go then."

Once Aliz'Ra and Cassy returned to Zachery and the others, Cassy had to get all the answers. "Okay, please tell me this is some kind of joke. You're all in on it, right? Zachery, what's going on?"

Zachery motioned for her to sit down. "As I told you before, we come from a place called, Amundiss. It is a place filled with magic that would awe you. Aliz'Ra is my great-grandmother and is also an elf."

Cassy looked to Aliz'Ra who nodded her head in agreement, showing Cassy that what Zachery just told her was the actual truth. "So, does that mean I am an elf, too? I thought they were just in stories."

"No, my darling, it does not. I love you as if you were my own blood, but I took you in after your parents lost their lives in a house fire when you were just a baby. You are a true Earthling," says Aliz'Ra.

"Why are you all here? What is going on with your home?" asked Cassy.

Natallia spoke up, "Demons. Our home is in danger from demons. They are led by a fallen God by the name of Craotonus who wants to destroy the remaining Gods and take control of the heavens."

"I fought Craotonus in the first War of the Gods over three thousand years ago. I followed him here and thought I had bested him. His power is stronger than we realized. He destroyed my amulet of power that would enable me to return home. So, I have been moving from place to place trying to stay out of the way," Aliz'Ra told her.

They all sat around the table and told Cassy every detail, introducing themselves to her truthfully now. Zachery sat there with one burning question for Cassy, "After hearing all this, I have something to ask you. Are your feelings for me still what they were, and are you willing to go back with me? I cannot go back without you."

Cassy blushed. She was madly in love with Zachery and although the news seemed to be too much, she was glad to know he was not crazy. There was a huge risk if she chose to go with him, but she knew she did not want to be without him either. "Yes, of course, I will go back with you. You have become the most important part of my life, I will follow you anywhere you want to go."

Now that everything was out in the open, secrets revealed to the most important people here, we all felt complete. Cassy and I could actually have a life back on Amundiss. It was always in the back of my mind that we were too different, that we were meant to live our lives apart. But that gave me hope. That was another reason we had to destroy Craotonus and his minions and I couldn't wait to introduce her to my father, I know mother would have loved her as much as I do.

37

Orc Rising

At Castle Whitehold, the demons discussed what needed to be done to ensure Craotonus's full recovery, as well as how they intend to handle the demigod son of Akadius.

"My bargain with the Shadow Lords are still strong. I feel their presence inside me, stirring, wanting to choke the life from our enemies," said Craotonus as he peered out the window.

"My lord, what do the Shadow Lords need from us? We will do everything in our power to further the cause." Rauko' said as he kneeled before The Remissum.

Dori'naur sat at the table, running his finger along the wooden top, slivers of wood cut from underneath his fingernail fell to the floor, "Something troubles you Dori'naur?" asked Craotonus.

"These Shadow Lords are willing to help us destroy the Gods and watch the heavens crumble. At what cost to us? What do we sacrifice for their involvement?" asked Dori'naur.

Craotonus looked at him. "Not what we sacrifice, it is what we gain! We gain power, we gain respect, we gain. . ."

Dori'naur leapt to his feet, eyes glowing red. "We already have these things, thanks to you. You are a God, and we are your loyal subjects. What do they offer that we do not already have?"

Craotonus slowly walked to the table, leaned over, and braced his hands on top. "The way."

Rauko' and Dori'naur looked toward each other rather confused. "The way to what, master?" Rauko' asked eagerly.

"The way to destroy the Heavens and get my revenge on the ones who shunned and mocked me. The way to have Akadius groveling at my feet, begging me to spare his pathetic existence."

"Are we and our minions not enough?" Dori'naur asked. "You are a God. . ."

At that moment, smoke filled the room, swirling about them. As the black and purple smoke dissipated, a hooded figure stepped forward.

He could have passed for a cleric if not for the sense of death that spilled out from him. "The offer we gave your master was simple. Be our pawn, our vessel of darkness, and see the Gods at his feet," the Shadow Lord said.

"And in return?" Dori'naur questioned,

The Shadow Lord turned to look at Craotonus, "In return, eternal servitude."

Rauko' slammed his fist down on the table. "I will not become a slave to you! I serve my master by choice."

Suddenly, the Shadow Lord reached towards Rauko'. Shadowy tendrils wrapped around the demon's throat, moving up to his nose and mouth. "But you do have a choice, dear Rauko'. What was it you told the good people here Dori'naur? Serve me or suffer." The tendrils started to tighten, cutting the life force from the demon. Rauko' tapped on the table in submission, nodding his head in agreement.

"Enough, Malonox! We understand," exclaimed Craotonus.

"Good. Glad you chose to see it my way!" the Shadow Lord said with an evil laugh. Malonox released his grip on the demon and Rauko' fell to the floor gasping. Malonox then turned to face Craotonus, "As long as we understand each other, all will be well. I will have the head of Akadius for my trophy or yours will be on my dinner plate." Instantly, he was gone.

Craotonus lowered his head and said in a low mumble, "What have I got us into? Have I gone too far?"

"What now?" Dori'naur asked. "If you cannot break your bond with the Shadow Lord, we have to succeed. Why did you not tell us of your deal with them?"

Craotonus paced back and forth shaking his head. "I was a fool. My hatred for Akadius and the other Gods drive me mad. They thought they were better than me because the mortals loved them more than me. They looked at me with pity; but I am Craotonus! I need no one's pity. Malonox came to me, told me he could give me great power, enough power to defeat my siblings and take the heavens for my own. When I agreed to join him, his essence infused with my own, filling me with shadows. There was no turning back."

Rauko' was back on his feet now, rubbing his throat. "So were we just pawns in your game?"

"No, you were my most trusted friends here. I did not know, or I would not have asked you to join me."

Dori'naur walked to Craotonus. "We will follow you to the end. You will lead us to victory once you have regained full strength. What is our next move?"

Craotonus replied, "I am close to whole. We also know where the Champion of Light is. His power is not established yet. I will send you two there to Earth to take care of him. First, we will need an army, an army great enough to destroy all in their path."

"Where do we find this army?" asked Rauko'.

Craotonus smiled an evil smile, exposing his jagged teeth, "It's time to summon the orcs."

Dori'naur looked to Craotonus, "Will they follow us? Can we trust them?"

With a nod of his head, Craotonus said, "Yes, they are creatures of the shadows. They have been the ones that have sought out the Vessels of Light over all these centuries. They will follow us and help us destroy the Light. One more thing, Rauko', you do not seem whole. I have a gift for you, from the Shadow Lords." Craotonus raised his hands and said some words in a language the brothers did not understand. Suddenly, in a puff of smoke, there stood Varg and Shaaux.

"My children!" shouted Rauko'. The hellhounds leaped on their master. "Thank you, my Lord! How did you bring them to me?" asked Rako'.

"I have new power over the shadows, and the place where the most shadows abound is in the depths of Hell. I released their bonds and brought them here," said Craotonus.

Dori'naur replied, "Now, where do we find these orcs, and where do we kill the Champion?"

***

Outside of Doochary, the refugees had set up camp so Benzoete could contact the others on Earth. "This time, do not block your message. We need Craotonus to hear," said Gabriel.

Benzoete agreed. "Once this message goes out, they will know where we are. When I finish, we must be ready to move."

Antoine came to them and said, "We are ready. Are we sure this will work?"

Benzoete shrugged his shoulders. "I certainly hope so. It may be our only chance. Everything has to go as planned; do exactly as I say." They gathered in front of the mirror. Benzoete pulled his amulet from his robes and waved his hand in front of the mirror.

On Earth, Natallia felt a slight buzzing and realized it was her amulet. "They are alive! They are trying to contact us. Quickly, we must get to the mirror." As the group ran inside, Natallia told Aliz'Ra and Cassy to stay to the side out of sight, "We want this to be a surprise. I will motion for you to come forward. I can't wait to see Benzoete's face when we tell him." As they settled in front of the mirror, they see it start to ripple.

As always there was Benzoete looking back at them, this time his face was not all smiles. "Benzoete, what is wrong? You look distraught. Is everyone alright?" Zachery leaned in, "My father and sister, how do they fare?"

Benzoete held up his hand. "Everyone here is well, for now. We need to bring you back home to Amundiss, Craotonus has discovered where you are and we fear he will destroy that world looking for you. We know that Tradan is still months away from fruition and full power, but we hope that we can stay hidden in Doochary long enough to wait them out."

As Benzoete finished stating his plans, Zachery noticed George behind the old wizard holding a piece of paper with something written on it. Zachery realized it was a message written in the language that he and his sister had made up as children while playing. He read:

Dubo nubot subay ubanythubing. Thube dubemubon ubis lubistubenubing. Rubeubady ubevuberyubonube tubo cubomube hubomube tubomuborrubow ubevubenubing. Prubepubarube thubem, fubor wube wubill bube ubon thube mubovube. Wube lubovube yuboubu my subon.

After Zachery read that the demon was listening, he leaned into Natallia and whispered in her ear, stood up and walked over to Aliz'Ra and Cassy to let them know. "Now is not the time, my lady. Follow me and I will explain," Zachery whispered.

They walked out of the room as not to be seen in the mirror. Once in the other room, Aliz'Ra wondered what was going on.

"Craotonus is listening. He knows where we are. We will be leaving for Amundiss tomorrow. I saw my father holding a sign up behind Benzoete that said 'Do not say anything. Ready everyone there, we will be bringing you home tomorrow evening. Prepare everyone, we will be on the move. We love you, my son.' With the mention of we, at least that tells me my sister Launa is alive as well."

Just then Natallia walked in, "What is going on? I know what

Benzoete told me is not correct."

Zachery told her and Tradan what the sign said and they would need to be ready.

"Sounds like it's time to face my old foe once more," Aliz'Ra said. "We have to gather weapons and be ready for anything."

We were going home. Would I even know my home after all these years? I was just a boy when we left, and now I stood a trained man, a Dragon Rider. I knew it would be bittersweet seeing my family again since I could not tell my mother good-bye. I was taking this fight to the demons that forced us into this in her name. I wanted revenge for her life.

Craotonus sat in front of a huge mirror when Rauko' stepped in. "It appears we do not need to go to Earth after all, not yet. They are bringing the Champion here to us. It might be a trick. If they do not bring him, we will open an all out war on the people of Earth until we find him. There is one thing that concerns me now knowing they were on that wasteful planet."

"What could possibly concern you on a planet without magic?" Rauko' asked,

Craotonus stood to face him. "That is where I left Aliz'Ra to die. She had the Bloodblade with her. If by chance she still lives and has made contact with him, she will be coming as well. It cannot be a coincidence they were sent to that backward planet."

"We will be ready, my Lord," Rauko' assured. Our army is more than we could imagine."

Craotonus walked out to a large balcony overlooking the enormous courtyard. Standing in formation were hundreds of mighty orcs who were war hardened and battle forged by the shadows. Standing before him was a mass of killing machines. "Good, Malonox would be pleased. We will ride for Doochary at first light. Ready the minions." With that Rauko' and Craotonus gathered the barkers and the horde of orcs. War was coming.

By this time, the refugee army was reduced to only eleven people. They were not much of an army any longer. Now, they had to be smarter than the demons, outthink their enemy and be one step ahead of them at all times. They packed up their camp as soon as the conversation with Natallia was over. Moving as fast as they could, they found themselves ahead of the coming demons. They set up Benzoete's conversation chamber once more and prepared for him to call for the others.

"Are we far enough away to call them?" asked Antoine.

"We are for the moment. Once I summon them here, we will have to make our way to the mountains of Casterton. We will need to enter my secret library and make plans to recruit as many people as we can. We will need to have an army, for I am certain the demons will. I will start the process as soon as we get the signal from Andrea and the others that all is clear."

The group sat quietly for what seemed to be an eternity. Each one silent as they thought of the lives they have seen lost. What once stood an army of followers, now was barely enough for a family reunion. Antoine thought about what it would be like to have his sister and new nephew back, and to introduce them to Andrea. Gabriel sat alone thinking about Tradan and Natallia, finally getting to embrace his son and kiss his wife. George sat with Launa as they tried to find peace in knowing Zachery would soon be with them once more, though still feeling as if a piece was missing with Elizabeth gone.

Liam was just a simple tradesman, living not far from where they were at that very moment. He sat staring out toward his former homestead where the barkers took his family from him. Benzoete and Elos sat quietly in a meditation state, pondering life's balance and how to restore it. Last was Nola'sha, a young elven woman who had been with the group since Weelinn. She served in the tower of Benzoete and has been loyal to the end. Nola'sha knew harmony from her childhood days right after the first war. She longed for those days again, wanting to raise a family in peace.

They sat there gathering their thoughts when a call rang out it was Andrea and the other two riders. "We rode out for at least twenty lengths, and no sign of anyone following us," Andrea said.

Benzoete rose to his feet. "Now, it begins! Ready yourselves."

The old wizard and his apprentice linked hands around a cauldron. Liam brought over the mirror and laid it on its back in front of them. Benzoete and Elos both with their free hands took hold of their amulets and chanted an ancient elven spell. Natallia and the others were waiting in the room with their mirror.

Suddenly Zachery noticed it glowing. "Look! It is time!" he shouted.

They all stood up and made their way to the mirror. They heard the voice of Benzoete, "The time is now, step forward through the glass. Do not stop or wander. We can only hold this portal for a short time."

Natallia was first to step through, followed by Tradan. As the next figure stepped through the room turned silent. Aliz'Ra and Cassy came into sight, followed closely by Zachery. It was a good thing Zachery was quick because the sight of Aliz'Ra shook Benzoete and he almost closed the portal. As the reunited mother and son shared hugs and kisses, Benzoete broke down and wept at the sight of his mother.

Aliz'Ra wrapped her arms around her son, wiped his eyes and said, "It is a sight to behold. My son, a man! I have longed to see you with my eyes every day for I have seen you with my heart every second. You were never far from me, even though you were worlds away."

Zachery grabbed both his father and sister at the same time, and tears flowed between them. A family mourning the loss of a mother, though delayed, is a powerful and sad reunion. As they cried for the passing of one, they embraced and welcomed another. Cassy smiled and came closer. Zachery introduced her to his family as his saving grace while on Earth.

Gabriel and Antoine ran to where Natallia and Tradan were. Gabriel, the strong king, the ruler of Whitehold trembled at the sight of his wife and son.

"Well, are you going to kiss me or not?" asked Natallia.

Before she could even finish her words, Gabriel had pulled her close to him, kissing her as if it was their wedding day all over again.

"My heart cannot take you leaving me again, my Lady. I will never let you go," said the king.

Antoine stood close with Andrea by his side. "Lord Tradan, it is an honor to finally meet you. I am Antoine, your Uncle." Tradan smiled and wrapped his arms around the big burly man. Natallia came over and joined in. "I am so glad to have you back sister. I have someone I want you to meet. This is Andrea Aravena, her love has saved me more than once on this trip."

Natallia smiled at Andrea, "It is a pleasure to meet the woman who melted the ice away from my brother's heart. I look forward to hearing stories of your adventures."

Even though the air was filled with joy and love, Benzoete spoke up, "I am sorry to cut the reunions short, but we must be moving. We have to be long gone before the demons come."

The group packed the remaining items and rode as fast as they could for Casterton.

A new era had dawned on Amundiss. I saw King Gabriel rejuvenated with the return of Natallia and Tradan. The Champion of Light was here and the good people of Whitehold would have their king soon. I could only imagine what stood in store for us. May the Gods be with us.

38

Training Ends

The refugees made it to the foothills of Casterton Mountain safe and sound. Again Benzoete headed to the door and opened the passage. Everyone filed into the musky old library and found their way to the tables for rest.

"We will rest a moment then we will need to map out our next move," announced Benzoete.

This gave Zachery time to talk to his father and sister more as well as let them talk to Cassy for the first time. "Did she suffer?" asked Zachery. "Was she in pain, when it happened?"

George felt hot tears forming in his eyes once more, but he pushed them away for Zachery. "No, she was not in any pain. It was almost like sleep fell upon her. I had her in my arms and could feel her life essence leave her body. If not for Gabriel showing me I still had a reason to push on, I too would have ended there in the path with her." With those words, he pulled Launa closer to him. "You helped me focus on life. The more I focused on you, I thought of Zachery. I knew I had two of the most important reasons in all the worlds to carry on."

Cassy leaned forward and laid her hand on Launa's. "If you need to talk woman to woman, I'm here. I lost both my parents when I was little. I'm willing to talk if you want to."

Launa smiled and the two stood up and walked over to a corner to sit on the floor, out of the way.

"She has a good heart, son. She seems special," George said.

"She is the one for me. We come from two different places, but it already feels as though our hearts are one." Zachery replied.

George patted his son on the shoulder. "Have you told her that?"

Zachery lowered his head, "Not in all those words."

"Then, do it. Do not waste any time. Love is precious, let nothing stand in the way," George retorted with a hearty grin.

I had missed these talks with my father so much. Just hearing his voice was good, but to have his comforting presence with me was truly a blessing. I wished my mother could have met Cassy for I know she would have loved her as much as I did.

"Gabriel, you and young Tradan come here please," murmured Aliz'Ra, who was seated with Benzoete and Elos at the end of the table.

"We were discussing how advanced the young prince was in his training. My mother explained he is almost ready for battle. Also, that you have a special trait not known to past Champions. What, may I ask, is that?" Benzoete questioned.

"I really don't know much about the past Champions, just what I have learned from you and Miss Lizzy, I mean Aliz'Ra. I can show you the part I like best," Tradan said with a smile.

Zachery overheard the conversation and told his father he needed to watch. The group gathered around as Tradan removed his overshirt. "Ready? Stand back now." Tradan closed his eyes and concentrated. When his eyes opened, they had turned a bright white. He opened his arms and his magical wings appeared from his back and he started to hover. "I don't understand why they don't rip through my undershirt, but they tear anything else I wear."

Benzoete was shocked and Aliz'Ra looked up at her son. "Any idea why his power is as evolved as it is?" Benzoete nodded his head as he watched Tradan shimmer and glow, lightning arcing from his fingertips. Aliz'Ra laughed her hearty laugh and said, "All right, Tradan, enough for now. You can show them the good stuff tomorrow. Now, what do we not know?"

Benzoete told her they recently found out that Gabriel was the demigod son of Akadius. The enhanced power of a demigod mixed with the fact his mother was a direct descendant of angels made for an interesting Champion of Light.

"He could be ready. With the advanced genes and the fact his grandfather is Lord of the Gods! He may be ready," Elos said with such excitement in his voice.

"How will I know if I'm ready?" Zachery asked. "I have done marvelous things and achieved powerful magic, but without dragons, my training is incomplete."

Benzoete patted him on the shoulder. "You are home now, Zachery. Fill your thoughts of Amundiss. Let the magic of our home fill your senses. When you feel it, you will be ready. Now, we need to rest. No one knows what lies ahead for us tomorrow."

When I feel it, I will know. Benzoete's advice has helped me before. I never doubted myself on Earth, but now I'm home and that means it is close. The demons will be coming, and I had to be ready.

As the new day began to break over the mountaintops, each person inside the secret library stirred. The look on Gabriel, Antoine, and George's faces was clear. They were elated to have their family home.

"Mother, I have a question to you." Benzoete walked up to Aliz'Ra. "You had the Bloodblade when you followed Craotonus into the portal. Any chance you kept up with it all these years?"

Aliz'Ra replied, "I don't know what happened. I drove the blade into his chest all the way to the hilt. It hurt him, I could tell that, but he just laughed and pulled it free. He had somehow became more powerful. It was not enough then, though I still have it." With still very quick reflexes, Aliz'Ra shifted backward and pulled the blade from beneath her clothing. "At least it will help with the minions," she said.

Benzoete held out his hand. "May I please?" She handed him the Bloodblade and watched as he reached into his side satchel. The old wizard pulled a shiny gem from his bag after placing the sword down on the table. He placed the gem in the center of the hilt and it began to glow. Everyone watched as the gem seemed to sink into the hilt of the sword, binding its power with the blade.

Covering it with both hands, he recited the words taught to him by Chrin'lolas. When he removed his hands, the gem was now enclosed inside the Bloodblade. "Now one last thing. I do apologize mother, but this is no longer your blade." Benzoete tossed the newly gemmed Bloodblade to Tradan. When the boy's hand closed on the handle, the blade erupted in flames.

"Our champion is well equipped now," Antoine said in amazement.

"I believe it is time to see what these good lads can do." Benzoete smiled, waved his hand and the door opened wide. The group exited the library into an open area to the south.

Gabriel walked over to Benzoete. "Do you really believe them to be ready? We have waited all these years, surely we can wait a few more months."

Benzoete flashed his wild smile. "My king, Tradan is the offspring of an angel and the son of Akadius, with his advanced bloodline, I believe he was ready months ago. As for Zachery, he has one last task I need for him to do." Benzoete motioned for his mother to join him. They walked over to where Zachery stood. "Zachery, do you remember many years ago when we first met? We were in my library in Weelinn and I asked you to hand me your dagger. You were so surprised at the fact I even knew you had it. I placed it into the skull of the dragon and asked you to concentrate on what made you happy. You had your magic then and you trusted in my words and believed in yourself. Now ask for help from the Gods, and follow them."

I trusted Benzoete from the moment I met him and I trust him now even though I've always doubted myself. I do not want to disappoint all these people.

Aliz'Ra could tell Zachery needed a little push of encouragement. "My boy, I have known you for over half of your life. Even though I did not know you were the Dragon Rider, I always knew you were amazing. I am honored to be your great-grandmother, but mostly I am honored to be your friend. Let go and trust yourself. I do." She punched him on the arm, gave him a wink and walked back to Benzoete and Cassy.

As Zachery stood there in the open area, he asked the Gods for guidance. Suddenly, a tree sprang up from the ground. A tree full of life and on its trunk the words: *Quis Te Est.* "What does this mean? I don't understand."

George smiled. "I do. We saw it on the tree at the tomb. It is asking who you are, Son! Tell it. Shout it. Believe it!"

Zachery closed his eyes and clenched his fists. Fire began to form around his closed hands and he opened his eyes to reveal a fiery soul. With a loud voice that seemed like it was not his own, he shouted, *"Eccoita Angulòcè!"*

Aliz'Ra gasped and started to cry. "He called them, they will hear his voice."

The mountains started to rumble and quake. A loud shriek was heard from what seemed to be realms away. Zachery turned his head skyward, reached for the heavens, and a pillar of fire shot into the clouds. "Hear my voice, heed my call. Awake and come to me!" Zachery shouted. The shriek was heard again, only this time it was deafening. A large shadow flew over them. Zachery lowered his hands to the ground, a circle of pure fire formed around him.

The people watching backed away as a majestic creature descended. Before them now sat a creature everyone believed to be extinct. Large, gleaming black scales covered his enormous body like armor on the most fearsome knight. His wings were large enough to darken the sun. Long, sharp claws dug into the ground. The creature was enormous. It reared its head, spewing dragon fire into the skies. As Zachery walked toward the beast, it bowed before him as a show of respect for the Rider. "Good to see you," Zachery said as he rubbed the scaled skin on its head. "His name is Barrok, the Black."

Cassy stepped forward. "How do you know that?" she asked.

"He told me. We are as one now. We can communicate through thoughts." Zachery climbed up on the dragon's back, up close to his neck. "All right, Barrok. Let's fly." With one powerful push of his wings, they were airborne, soaring through the skies with ease. Zachery found two trees standing away from everything else. As quickly as he thought it, Barrok knew. They started to dive down, toward the trees. At the last second, they pulled up, but not before Barrok lit the trees on fire with his fiery breath.

The refugees cheered wildly. Finally, there was a Dragon Rider soaring through the skies over Amundiss once more.

Tradan laughed and said, "A real dragon! I knew we would see many marvelous things, but this is the best!" The young Champion ran toward Zachery, dropping his overshirt to the ground once more. He leaped into the air and his magical wings sprung forth and carried him up into the air. "My turn Zachery! Try this."

Still holding the Bloodblade, Tradan soared down to the ground in a spiral. He hit the ground with a thud, landing on one knee and planted the blade into the soil. Where the blade was buried into the ground, a ring of fire emitted outward from the Champion charring the ground and engulfing the surrounding trees. The blast was so intense the shockwave knocked Elos off his feet. "Oh, sorry Elos. I didn't mean to do that." Tradan chortled with a sly grin. Antoine tried to contain his laughter as he helped Elos to his feet.

Benzoete clapped his hands wildly, "Well done, well done indeed! Your training has advanced more than I could ever have hoped for. Just remember, a real battle is not just burning trees and shrubs, you must have the conviction to defeat your enemy. They will try to end your lives so you must not falter from your knowledge of the Light. You cannot hesitate to take theirs given the opportunity."

Just as Benzoete had finished his words of encouragement, Barrok reared his head up and sniffed the air. Zachery shouted, "He smells orcs closing in! They have found us!" The orcs were close. Craotonus had sent them to find the refugees, and test their new champion.

"Pawns! This group of orcs are just pawns. He's testing us." Gabriel informed them.

Antoine grabbed an extremely large axe, "Well let's see how we do with this test, shall we?" He extended his hand to Andrea who gave him a sly wink. "I never liked tests. I may have to peek at your paper."

The two laughed and started out to the left, Benzoete spoke to Tradan and Zachery, "Tradan, follow your father and do not take on more than you can handle, not this early. Zachery, I need you and Barrok to fly ahead of us and lay down cover fire. Elos and I will take George and the others to the high ground to the right. May the Gods shine on us."

Barrok opened his mighty wings and took to the sky again. "We need to lay a line of fire between the orcs and the others, give them time to get into position." Barrok snorted and shook his head. "What do you mean you need a snack?" Just then, Barrok dove toward the oncoming army. The orcs saw the massive beast and froze in their tracks.

It had been centuries since anyone had seen a live dragon. With a swoop, Barrok grabbed two of them in his mouth and quickly disposed of them. "Feel better now? Can we lay the cover fire now?" Zachery laughed and patted the dragon. On their second pass, Barrok and Zachery both set a long path on fire, blocking the orc troops from the refugees. The orcs stopped and tried to figure out a way to get to the refugees when a shout was heard from the left.

Antoine, with his war axe held high, came leaping through the flames catching them by surprise. His blade landed the through the skull of an unexpected orc taking half of his head off. "Hello boys, I have someone you need to meet!" he chuckled as he knelt low beside the body of the slain orc. A volley of arrows came through the flames and smoke like rain. Andrea slung arrow after arrow, each one finding its mark in the chest of the unsuspecting orc warriors. Antoine gave the signal to Gabriel and he jumped to his feet.

A large, brownish-green orc named Xago walked toward him. "I smell the angelic blood in your veins. You're one of the light bearers we searched for. You smell like your father, he fought well trying to protect you. He died honorably by my blade. So, shall you this day!" Xago was a seasoned war hardened warrior. He stared at Antoine, waiting for him to move when an arrow flew past, headed straight for Xago's heart. Without even a flinch, the orc snatched the arrow from the air and broke it like a twig.

Antoine charged. Every move he could think of, the massive orc had a counter. Swing after swing, neither combatant gained ground. On the other side of the fields, Gabriel and Tradan charged in. The two fought as if they were the same person. Tradan connected the Bloodblade with the neck of an orc and returned him to dust. Gabriel blocked a sword swipe and his boot landed on the orc's chest sending the creature to the ground.

In one motion, the mighty blade Fuascailte was planted in the fallen orc, while Gabriel swept the feet of another to the ground. He pulled his blade from the dead orc and slashed the other. Tradan's eyes began to glow bright, his wings were at full width, and he flew from orc to orc, taking their heads in a bright blur.

Elos and Benzoete looked down from the higher ground and started to chant elvish words. Crows flew in from every direction attacking the orcs and serving as distractions.

Liam and George stood at the ready to defend the women if needed. By this time, Antoine and Xago had moved from the others and still fought furiously. Xago thrust his mighty sword barely missing Antoine, causing the orc to go off-balance and leave his back exposed. Antoine pulled a small dagger from his boot and jabbed it in the shoulder blade of the orc. Xago let out a bloodcurdling howl. He spun with his free hand and his massive fist hit Antoine in the head, knocking him backward. Andrea rushed to where Antoine fell.

Pulling the blade from his shoulder he said, "Foolish girl, you cannot stop me. I will have his head."

Andrea pulled an arrow from her quiver and notched it. "Then come get it."

Xago charged toward her and leapt into the air. Just as she was about to let the arrow fly, a very large claw grabbed the orc and flew off. She watched Zachery and Barrok carry Xago away and toss him to the ground. She let out a sigh of relief and turned back to check on the motionless Antoine.

Tradan was surrounded by orcs when he heard his father shout, "Tradan! Circle of fire again, son!" With a grin, Tradan shot straight up into the sky. Now, the Bloodblade burned with a bright white fire. Holding the blade above his head and pointing his left fist toward the ground, he dove straight down and smashed the ground. This time it was not ordinary fire that encircled him, but a shockwave of pure light. The circle of light spread out from the Champion engulfing every orc around him in holy fire. Gabriel could not stop himself from feeling a swell of pride.

Aliz'Ra stood with her son and Elos, and helped them enhance their powers when she was suddenly she's overwhelmed by a presence. "Oh, no, it cannot be."

Benzoete turned to her. "What is it, Mother? What do you feel?"

Aliz'Ra began to tremble and whispered, "Malonox."

As she muttered his name, a dark figure appeared behind Natallia, grabbing her around the waist.

"Foolish demons had one task: kill the vessel. Sometimes you have to do things yourself."

Liam and George rushed to help her, when Malonox raised his hand and sent them flying backward.

"This battle is not over. I will have the Gods at my feet. They will feel my wrath." With that the Shadow Lord plunged a dark blade through her back until it pierced through her chest. She cried out in pain. "We will meet again Champion," stated Malonox as he disappeared into the shadows. The remaining orcs fled and Gabriel and Tradan rushed to Natallia's side.

"Help her! Don't just stand there, do something! You must do something!" Tradan shouted with tears slipping down his cheeks.

Gabriel held her in his arms and stroked her hair, she tried to speak he just placed a finger on her lips, "No my love. Words are not needed. I loved you from the moment I saw you and I know you loved me." He could see the shadows overtaking her. "You completed my life. Go to your rest and know I will see you again." He kissed her lips and wept uncontrollably.

Tradan was on his knees at her head and she reached for his hand. He held her hand like he did when he was little and could not sleep; it had helped him know she was there, so now it was his turn to let her know he was there for her. As the life faded from her, a light appeared. Angels had come to take her home. She had been the first female angelic to live past maturity in centuries; now was her time to rest.

The others made it to where yet another tragedy had struck. As George and Liam were hurled backward off the hilltop, Liam fell on a broken tree and was impaled. They found his body hanging lifelessly. The refugees suffered major blows that day. Now, they knew how Craotonus had become so powerful. They also knew that they had to seek out any remaining citizens of Amundiss willing to fight for their lives alongside the Champion. The demons had an army thirsty for blood, and the refugees needed the same. They were not given much time to grieve, but their loved ones will be missed. Queen Natallia, with her true beauty and grace; Liam

Traxton, who lost his family and wanted to serve his king. May the Gods be with them.

We lost a great leader that day, and I lost a friend. May she find my mother in the afterlife and she will find a friend.

39

The Refugees Fight Back

As the group mourned their queen and loyal friend, the burial fires could be seen for miles.

"They will pay for this, Gabriel. I promise you this," Antoine vowed with tears streaming down his face.

Gabriel embraced and held him tight. "We have to win this war for her. We cannot let her and all the others die in vain." The stoic king pushed back and looked him dead in the eyes, "We must rally an army and hit the demons where they stand. We need to take back what is ours; our land, our homes, Castle Whitehold. We hit them when they least expect it."

George stood nearby. "Where will we find such an army? The demons have ravaged this land, those that are left are scared and hiding."

Aliz'Ra stood facing the fires as tears filled her eyes for her friend. "We open the doors of Eska'Taurn. Allow the elven people to fight for their world like the days of old. Most are skilled fighters and will be ready to fight."

Benzoete and Elos stood in shock. Turning to his mother, he asked, "Can we do this? The elven people have not been a part of Amundiss for centuries. Only a few have chosen to venture out."

Elos then spoke up. "Also, Madam Aliz'Ra, the bond holding the doors is secured by elder magic. Can we override that?"

Aliz'Ra looked to them. "Do you forget who the elders were that put that foolish spell in place? I am the last remaining original elder of Eska'Taurn. With my son's help, I will right the wrong I put in place all those years ago. We, the elven people, need to be a part of this world. We need to fight once more."

"How long will this require? We will try to find as many here to help," questioned Gabriel.

"Not long, we will gather the necessary items and begin. We will need to have our minds in perfect unison. Once we unlock the spell, our people will ride to our aid," answered Aliz'Ra.

Antoine, whose face was still streaked with tears, assured her, "When they get here, we will be ready."

***

The next morning, Gabriel was still standing by his wife's ashes. George headed to his longtime friend. "Gabriel, you need to eat," he advised. "You will need your strength."

The king looked to his friend. "How did you do it? How did you find the strength to go on from the Path after it took Elizabeth? I have visions of revenge for her and at the same time I want to lie beside her and join her. I do not know how I can focus now on our task."

George placed an arm around the shoulder of Gabriel and walked him over to the side of one of the tents. "You have to do the same thing that you told me. You have to find your reason." As George repeated this, he pointed down to the edge of the meadow where Tradan knelt in the sunlight. "All he has ever known was his mother. He needs his father now. He may be the Champion of Light, but he is also a young man who just lost his mother. Go to him. Go to him and find your reason to go on."

Gabriel embraced George and thanked him for being such a good friend for so long. He walked to the meadow and took a seat next to his son. "We will see her again you know. When our time comes, we will gather with the other followers of the Light that has passed on to the afterlife. That is the eternal plan by the Gods."

"I spent the first half of my life in a world thinking the worst thing to fear was a harsh winter," Tradan began. "The one thing that was constant in my life was my mother. I will be with her again. We will end this and have revenge on the demons that did this."

At that moment, Gabriel gazed into his son's eyes and saw a man looking back at him where a boy once was. "You are my reason now. George told me that when Elizabeth died, he had to find a reason to continue. His reason was Zachery and Launa. I still desire peace for our world, but you are my priority now. I was so focused on having my world back, I forgot that that included a son." Gabriel stood and extended his hand to help Tradan up. "We need to eat and check in on the others; we have a long journey ahead of us." As Tradan pulled himself up, Gabriel pulled him close and wrapped his arms around him, "I truly love you, my son. We have lost a lot in the years you were on Earth, but understand this, I stand with you, for you, and together Amundiss will flourish again."

***

At Castle Whitehold, Craotonus was in council with the demon brethren. A cloud of smoke filled the room and Malonox fell to the floor. "Lord Malonox! Are you alright?" asked Rauko' as he tried to help him from the floor.

Dori'naur pulled a chair over and helped him to sit. "You killed a mortal, did you forget the pact?" inquired Craotonus.

"I remember that idiotic pact you cretin. I did what had to be done, the fool that was guarding her, unfortunately, found himself on a spike as well. I did not plan on that."

Dori'naur and Rauko' were confused now. "What is wrong with him?" asked Dori'naur.

Craotonus walked to a chair and motioned for them to sit. "Malonox is one of the Prime, a group of six eternal celestial beings. They had no beginnings or end. They were the ones who created the Gods to oversee the worlds as needed."

Rauko' made him come to a halt. "There are more of him out there? They are the ones who created Akadius and the others?"

Craotonus nodded his head. "Myself included. Malonox was sent here and he is the one that created us. We are his children."

"What happened then?" Dori'naur questioned. "Why are those fools the ones still in the heavens and not Malonox?"

The Shadow Lord was starting to regain some of his strength and replied, "Because when you let your children become more powerful than you, and let them have free reign, they will turn on you."

Craotonus told them. "The mortals became afraid of the shadows, shunned away from Malonox and sent their prayers to us. The more they prayed, the more Akadius convinced us that Malonox had gone mad and needed to be banished, that we needed to be in power. We confronted him and used our joined powers to overthrow him. We were convinced he was wrong and could not be trusted. Akadius made a magical pact that kept Malonox from the heavens and barred him from killing the mortals. In that pact, it also stopped the Gods from stepping into mortal affairs.

"If Malonox kills a mortal directly, it takes his power, if he kills more, it could remove his entire existence. Akadius was made Lord of the Heavens when Malonox fell. His word was and is law."

Dori'naur asked. "So, what will happen if the Gods meddle with mortal affairs?"

Craotonus lowered his hood, revealing his disfigured face. "We become banished from the Heavens and live our days as a demon. It could lead to our demise."

"So, this is why we have the army," Rauko' declared. "We

invoke our will to the orcs so Malonox will not be directly involved."

Malonox slowly stood now. "Exactly right. We need more of the very essence that feeds dear Craotonus and myself to follow our cause. If the Heavens are to fall, we will need to start with the son of Akadius and this Champion of Light." The Shadow Lord looked to his followers. "We will have this world as our own, and every other world we choose."

***

Benzoete, Elos, and Aliz'Ra were busy going over the plans to unlock Eska'Taurn. "Can we really do this?" asked Benzoete.

Aliz'Ra nodded and replied, "Any door that is locked, can be unlocked. We will need to use the power of the Book of the Ancients has, along with our own to do this. Elos, I need you to watch over us as we channel the spell; we cannot be interrupted."

Elos bowed before her. "Anything you ask, madam elder, it shall be done."

The three walked toward Gabriel, ready to instruct him it was time. "My King, we will be taking our leave now. We have most of the necessary items, the rest will be acquired along the way," said Benzoete.

"May the Gods be with you every step. We will make our way to the outskirts of Weelinn. When you have unlocked Eska'Taurn, you and your people shall meet us there. I hope along the way we can find more willing to fight for the Light." Gabriel bowed before Aliz'Ra and bid them farewell.

"You are a noble king. You and all of these people with you are the reason Eska'Taurn will be opened once more.

We will fight our enemy and crush them beneath our boots, once and for all." Aliz'Ra told him.

Benzoete turned to George, "With the doors of our homeland opened, you will meet your mother. No illusions this time. I know she will be ready, but will you?"

George smiled. "I have seen many marvelous things on this journey. I've discovered who I really am. This will be a final piece to my life, I am ready."

The two embraced, then Benzoete turned to leave. As he reached his horse, Benzoete called out, "Zachery, take care of your sister." The old wizard smiled and gave the two a sly wink.

Antoine shouted, as the elves mounted their horses and started on their way, "Godspeed friends, we will be waiting for you. As for the rest of us, we need to head out. We have a long journey to Weelinn."

Weelinn, the city where everything started to take place for me. They had told us the demons raided the city and killed a lot of people while searching for us. How many of its citizens were still there? We didn't know, but we prayed there were some.

Antoine, George, and Gabriel rode side by side as they made their way to the city. "Look at us. We have been friends our whole life. You are the grandson of a great elven wizard, and me the son of Akadius himself. Then, I marry the love of my life and she turned out to be direct decedent of the angels," laughed Gabriel.

Antoine asked, "How is it that you are a demigod and do not know of it? Well, I do understand the not knowing part, really, but how did this happen?"

Gabriel just shook his head and said, "I don't have an answer for that, my friend. I have always been Gabriel, son of King Owin and Queen Jacquelin of Whitehold. Even Benzoete and all his knowledge did not have an answer for me."

"Well, I, for one, am glad to have such an honorable friend," said George. Gabriel placed a hand on his shoulder and smiled.

Meanwhile the elven trio made their trek to Eska'Taurn. After leaving Mordit City, formally known as the elven city of Terra'Fayoak the elves made their home in the north. This is the place where the original elders sealed the doors to the outside world.

They believed that the outside world of Amundiss had become corrupt after Craotonus and the brethren started the first War of the Gods. The elves only allowed access to the outside world to a chosen few. The new elders chose to keep the seal intact for the safety of their people, but now see they need to help the humans fight for Amundiss. If the outside world fell to the demons, they would soon have the power to break down the barriers of Eska'Taurn. They just hoped that the elves of Eska'Taurn felt the same way.

"Will the elves fight alongside the humans?" asked Benzoete.

Aliz'Ra replied, "We will show them that the humans have changed. They are worthy now, not just a narrow-minded young race. They will overlook the past and see the need to work toward a future."

Elos, who rode in silence, spoke up and asked, "Were the humans as bad as the stories? I have spent the last eighteen years fighting alongside them and now consider them brothers. My opinion was based off of our people's dislike for them."

"As I said, they came a long way since the first humans were here. I will tell you this. I have watched the humans of Earth for the past three thousand years. I have seen them at their very worst and yet they always seemed to care. Always appeared to find a way to rectify what their past leaders have besmirched. I believe the human race has evolved past their ancestor's transgressions. They are a good and just race, and I will fight to help protect them and our world." Aliz'Ra avowed with confidence.

Benzoete let out a little chuckle. "Now do not get me started on dwarves!" The three shared a laugh and continued on their way.

***

Weelinn was just three days of a ride and along the way, the refugees managed to find close to fifty new recruits wanting to fight for their homes and families.

"I hope we can find more inside Weelinn," remarked Antoine.

"If anyone is left alive. The demons tore that place apart," added George.

"Have faith my friends," Gabriel reminded them. "The Light will show others to our task, and when it does, we will be ready."

Zachery and Tradan scouted ahead from the air. The new recruits buzzed about seeing a real dragon, and a flying man! Everyone in Amundiss had heard stories of the Dragon Riders, but most felt they would never see another in their lifetime. Zachery and Barrok landed in front of the group. "There is a rider coming. Barrok sensed no evil. Tradan is going to escort him in."

Gabriel, Antoine, and George rode ahead to meet him to put some distance between the group in case it was a trap

As the men waited for the rider, Antoine confessed, "It has been a pleasure and honor to fight alongside you. You are two of the noblest men I have met."

George squinted his eyes. "I am just a simple farmer, trying to save the world." He stated this with a stoic look on his face, the other two turned to look at him. He then followed with laughter. "I didn't think I could say that with a straight face."

Gabriel slapped him on the back with a hearty laugh. "Now there's the George I know! Now we are ready for some fun!" Antoine shared in the laugh, as they observed a lone rider in the distant view.

The man and his horse rode up to the trio, and Tradan landed beside him. "Gentlemen I give you, Kegan Kadrisson, King of the Iron Army."

Kegan was King of the dwarven army. The dwarves were an anchorite society. They chose to dwell in the mountains of the north in search of treasures. They differed from their distant cousins that lived in the south. The Iron Army were highly skilled warriors.

Gabriel dismounted and walked closer to the dwarven king. "It is an honor to meet you King Kegan. I am Gabriel, King of Whi. . ."

"I know who you be. That's why I been looking fer ya. I am not here on some social visit, lad. I be here to offer ya the honor to fight alongside the finest warriors this land has seen, the Iron Army."

Antoine tensed up. "This is the King of Whitehold you are talking to. The honor would be yours to have him."

Gabriel waved his hand to Antoine motioning him to stand down. "Forgive us, good Kegan. I would be terribly grateful to have you and the Iron Army join us."

George was not accustomed to royal affairs and asked, "Why would you come this far alone? How will your army join us in time?"

Kegan let out a booming laugh, "Aye, my friend, I not be alone. I only showed you what I wanted ya to see." With that the noble king pulled a horn from his side and blew three loud charges. In an instant, the ground started to shake and Barrok with Zachery took to the skies to get a better view.

"By the Gods!" Zachery yelled down to his father. "There are thousands of them! Coming from every direction!"

Soon standing before them was a magnificent army, armorclad and awaiting orders. Gabriel dismounted his horse and knelt before the dwarf king, "Oh, great Kegan Kadrisson of the Iron Army, we are your humble comrades. Join us, and help us crush this threat that is upon us."

"Like I told ya, that's why we be here laddie!" Kegan chuckled at Gabriel.

That night in camp, Gabriel lay awake in his tent and prayed a prayer of thanks to the Gods for leading this great army their way. "I offer my thanks to you, leaders of the Light. Help us defeat these demons and restore this world to the glory that you intended it to have." He thought about all he had been told. He was the son of Akadius, leader of the Gods of Light, and yet felt odd to be praying to him now. "Why did they hide this from me? How did this happen?" he pondered as he drifted off to sleep.

As he slept, Akadius greeted him in his dreams. "Dear Gabriel, I am here to answer your questions and give you comfort in the decision of your parents," said Akadius.

"My parents asked for this?" asked Gabriel.

"Your father was one of the most honorable and noble men ever to grace this world. He found favor with the Gods as he led his people with kindness and yet was firm when needed. Alas, he needed an heir and could not father a child of his own."

"My father was sterile?" asked Gabriel.

Akadius stretched forth his hand. "Walk with me." Gabriel took his hand. When they started to walk, Gabriel found himself at Castle Whitehold. He saw his father, Owin and his mother Jacquelin alone in their chambers.

"I have been told by the doctors I cannot give you a child. My family line ends with me," Owin confessed as he covered his face in shame.

"Do not despair, my love. We will find a way," Jacquelin told her husband wrapping her arms around him.

Gabriel found King Owin alone on the balcony, kneeling before the Heavens. "I come to you in a time of need. I offer myself to you as a servant of the Light. My lineage ends with me unless you can intervene and help. Please, I beg of you, do not let my bloodline end."

As Owin prayed, the Gods listened. They knew he was a just man, perhaps the closest to the Gods any mortal had ever been, and they wanted to help him. A light appeared before him, and the voice of Akadius was heard. "Owin of Whitehold, you honor us with your loyalty. You stand as an example of what the Light should be. Go to your wife, tell her I will give you a son, if she is willing. Your son will stand as the symbol of this world. People will look to him as a great leader. He shall be known as Gabriel, meaning strength of the Gods."

Owin wept, overcome with joy that his prayers were being answered. "Go, speak to your wife. In three days, I will come to her as a white owl. If she would have me, we will give you a son."

As the two traveled, Gabriel saw his mother and father discussing the offer of Akadius. They clasped hands and leaned into one another, shedding tears of joy. On the third night, Jacquelin wore an exquisite gown of white. As promised, a white owl landed on their balcony.

"My answer is yes, Lord Akadius. I do this for my husband, and all of Amundiss. No one is more deserving a son than Owin." She walked to the bed and took her place.

The owl took flight and morphed into a man. That night, Owin and Jacquelin received their gift.

Akadius looked towards Gabriel. "You see, you were destined for greatness. Your legacy will outshine all others."

"I do not want to outshine anyone, I just want peace and prosperity for the people of Amundiss."

Akadius smiled. "And that is why you are the greatest king to grace this world. You are here for a purpose. Protect your people. Let the Light inside you shine for all. Craotonus will not be easily defeated, but you hold the power to defeat the shadows."

Gabriel woke to a feeling of calmness. He knew what his parents had gone through, and he understood. He readied himself and went to find the others. They had the world to save, and he knew they would succeed.

40
New Weelinn

Weelinn, once a powerful city full of life and vitality, and it now was just a shadow of what it once was. King Gabriel and his army rode in hoping to find any signs of life, but what they found was truly devastating.

"This place smells of death, laddie, don't be gettin' yor hopes up," Kegan grimaced.

"I failed this city once; I will make sure its demise was not in vain." The destruction was almost unbearable for Gabriel.

"You do know it was not your fault. We did what we had to do," stated Antoine.

Gabriel replied, "Yes, I realize hard decisions had to be made. For that, we will need to bring this city and all cities touched by evil, redemption."

As they dismounted, Kegan told the Iron Army to spread out and look for anyone left.

"We need to get to Benzoete's tower. When they unlock Eska'Taurn, they will head there to meet us." Antoine explained to the others.

They walked the streets and observed a small child running toward a doorway.

"She was not old enough to have been here when the demon destroyed the city. There are families here!" Gabriel started for the doorway.

"How can people be living here? This place is a heap of rubble."

"They found some way to survive, and we need to find them," Gabriel told Antoine.

When they reached the doorway, Gabriel told Kegan and George to stay outside, and to keep their eyes open for anything. He motioned for Tradan and Zachery to circle above and warn them of any oncoming attacks. "When we enter, do not do anything that might frighten these people. The Gods only know what hell they have seen over these years." Antoine nodded his head in agreement. The two walked inside to find just an empty room, no people, animals, or furniture of any kind.

"This was the right door, wasn't it?" asked Antoine.

"I am certain of it. There must be a hidden passage. You go left and be careful." Gabriel and Antoine didn't know what they were looking for, but they knew what they saw.

"Gabriel! Here, I may have something."

The king rushed to where Antoine was kneeling, "Where? All I see is a pile of sticks and stone."

Antoine pointed to a small beam of sunlight streaming in from the cracks in the roof. "Notice the smoke coming from somewhere behind the pile. Can't you smell it?"

As Gabriel leaned in to get a better look or rather better smell, a smile crossed his face, "Is that eggs I smell?"

Antoine grinned. "Let's see who's home." They searched around the pile and found a handle—the door was hidden very well. Gabriel reached out slowly and pulled up. When the door opened they saw a tunnel. Suddenly, an arrow flew between their heads, barely missing them. The men fell backward and retreated from of the line of fire; Gabriel quickly slammed the door shut. It burst open again and a massive elf warrior barreled out, holding a rather huge sword and came to stand over them.

"Who are you and what business do you have in Weelinn?" the elf asked.

Gabriel, held his hands in front of him showing they meant no harm while slowly standing "My name is Gabriel, King of Whitehold, this is Antoine. We mean you no harm. We search for survivors and anyone willing to help us fight the demons. How many of you remain?"

The elven warrior stood his ground, "What proof do you have to your claim? The brethren have many bounty hunters looking to claim new souls to feed to their master."

Gabriel opened his arms, "All I have to offer is myself: I am whom I say. We have an army waiting on the outskirts. If you and your people want help, we will do anything we can while we wait for Benzoete to return."

The warrior lowered his weapon, "Master Benzoete lives? We lost contact with him after he left the city."

Antoine smirked, telling the elf, "You are in for one hell of a surprise then."

Gabriel said to him, "We can help you. In return, you can help us. We need to reach Benzoete's tower."

The elven warrior sheathed his sword and held out his hand, "My name is Hatholon. I was captain of the defense for master Benzoete. I, and what remained of my comrades, helped lead as many as we could to safety when the demon arrived."

Antoine shook his hand. "You and your men are very brave. How many people do you have with you?"

Hatholon replied, "I would have you see for yourself. You are the first outsiders to set foot in our camp."

Gabriel called for Kegan and George. The two introduced themselves and the group entered through the hidden door. They followed a tunnel lined with torches and markings they did not understand.

"What do these markings on the wall say?" asked George.

"It is what we are calling this place. Welcome to New Weelinn." The group made it to the end of the tunnel, which opened up to a massive underground city that was truly amazing. "It has been eighteen years since the destruction of Weelinn. We managed to save one hundred people that day, a fraction of how many once lived here. Over the years, we have flourished in hiding. We have families here. People living in harmony. I would not see them destroyed by Craotonus."

Kegan was in shock. "How could ya survive down here laddie? Away from tha surface for so long."

Hatholon told them. "We did what we had to do, we adapted. We have groups that patrol the surface and gather needed supplies. There are some who were born here that have never seen the surface."

Gabriel clenched his fist in anger. "I vow to you we will restore Weelinn. We are planning our assault on the demons now. Once Benzoete has returned we will be ready. Do you have any able to join us?"

Hatholon pointed to a small building to their left, "That is our barracks. We are few, but those of us that are battle ready are fierce. Most are from the original defense unit and we are thirsty for revenge." They walked to a nearby building where the passing people stared at them. It had been many years since they have seen outsiders. "This is our town hall, you will meet with Gannon. He is our elected leader."

Upon entering, the group was introduced to Gannon, who was a tall, lanky man with long blond hair. Surprisingly, he was human.

They walked over to him. "My name is King Gabriel of Whitehold. We mean no harm to you or your people. We seek volunteers to fight alongside us in defeating the demons. I see you have an army of your own."

Gannon rose from his seat. "I remember you from the first time you came here, all those years ago. You came to see master Benzoete, you were in hiding, but I knew you. I was just a common houseboy then, and yet you spoke to me like I was a royal visiting your home. You and your people showed us respect and in return, it shall be shown to you. Anything you need that we can provide will be given. Know, though, that the people here have the power of free will, they will choose to fight with you or not."

Kegan saluted the man, bowing with his arm crisscrossing his chest, "You are a wise and thoughtful leader laddie. I 'ave not met many humans like you. It be my honor to stand with ya." Gannon nodded at the dwarf king.

"I would like to address your people then, with your permission, to ask for volunteers," said Gabriel.

"Hatholon will sound the horn letting the people know there is a town meeting. Thirty minutes after the sounding of the horn, they will be gathered in the square. You can make your proposal then." They heard the sound of the horn ring out.

George asked Gannon, "You're sure that can't be heard from the surface? It was pretty loud."

Gannon turned to him, "We have taken every precaution. This city chamber is lined with sound dampening materials. We've made plans for our survival, I assure you."

The people made their way to the town square. It was an astonishing sight to see so many that had survived. Gabriel stood on a balcony overlooking the forming crowd. A clamor rose from the people about the new outsiders, but Hatholon raised his arms and the crowd went silent.

"My name is King Gabriel of Whitehold. We came asking for volunteers. Join us in the fight for freedom. We are readying to face the demons and will reclaim our lands. I understand why you would want to choose not to fight, we have all lost people we love, and that is just one of my reasons to see these demons be returned to hell."

A voice from the crowd yelled out, "How can we destroy these creatures?"

Another spoke up. "You have already lost your castle, we are unseen here, why should we risk our lives?"

Gabriel was about to answer when George stepped forward.

"My name is George Morely and like most of you here I am just a simple farmer. My whole life was my family and my farm. But then the demons took my farm and my wife. Who here has lost someone to these monsters? For that reason alone we must fight. If we do not succeed, others will fall."

Gabriel embraced George then turned back to the crowd, "The choice is up to you. We will not force you to go. We will be at the Town Hall waiting for those who will fight to join us there."

The group walked back into the Town Hall. Gabriel thanked Gannon for his time and hospitality.

Hatholon stepped forward. "I would like to join you. I lost good people in the attacks on Weelinn. I want to see them vindicated."

Gabriel extended his hand. "It will be an honor to have you."

Antoine heard a commotion outside and peered through a window. "Gabriel, you should see this."

The king walked to the door. "Bless the Heavens." There, outside the Town Hall, stood fifty or more men. "You honor us with your presence! We will face the demons and their horde headlong. You men, along with the Iron Army and the Elven Army of Eska'Taurn fighting side by side with the Champion of Light, we shall be victorious!"

A cheer rose up from the crowd, fists pumping in the air. They prepared to follow the group to the surface.

As they walked, Hatholon asked Gabriel, "You mentioned an army from Eska'Taurn. How is that possible? Those of us that left when the new elders were named are all that is left. Eska'Taurn is locked and can only be opened by the elders."

Antoine laughed. "That is the surprise I was telling you about. Seems that Benzoete's mother is still alive and we found her."

Hatholon stopped in his tracks. "Aliz'Ra lives? I have heard so many stories of her! I was but a young elf when the battle waged between the heavens and Craotonus. How did she. . . Where was she. . . What is. . ." He just kept mumbling to himself all the way to the hidden door.

Once they all were back to the surface, a large shadow appeared overhead. The new recruits braced for what they were sure was the demon army.

All of a sudden, Barrok and Zachery landed in front of them. "There you are. We were getting worried." At the sight of the creature and its rider, everything went silent. Some of the younger men had never been to the surface and definitely none had seen a real dragon before. "Didn't I mention we had a dragon?" laughed Gabriel. "We must go to Benzoete's tower. We will wait for the others there. Kegan, you and Hatholon take the men to the ridge with your army, see if we have enough armor and weapons for everyone." The dwarf king nodded his head and led them away. Zachery circled above them searching for signs of Benzoete or the others.

"I hope they are alright. We should be have heard from them by now." Zachery told Barrok.

I had seen Benzoete and Aliz'Ra do many things, but opening the doors to Eska'Taurn and convincing the elves to take up arms may have been a task too great. The end was near I could feel it in my soul. We were going to rid this world of the demons, I knew we were.

41
Nightfall Begins

Craotonus grew stronger every day. With the guidance of Malonox, he had become even more powerful than the refugees could imagine.

"The mortals are mounting an attack. They have grown in number and will pose a problem," Malonox muttered.

"Dori'naur and Rauko' are preparing the orcs and *new* soldiers of seed, barkers I think they call them. I am almost complete. Let them come!" Craotonus howled as he pounded his fist on the table.

In the courtyard, Dori'naur had a group of barkers returning from the outskirts. They were returning from collecting enough souls to complete Craotonus and make him whole. It was getting harder and harder to find anyone left to sacrifice without venturing out for long distances. The people of Whitehold and all surrounding cities were either hiding or dead. The demons spread over the land like a plague, killing all that stood in their way, delivering the souls to their master.

"Today is a glorious day! You, my good people, are the newest additions to Lord Craotonus's army. You will serve him with your life and your death!" Dori'naur spread out his arms, and roots entangled the feet of all the people. They struggled to break free while the demon laughed at their struggle. He slowly walked through the crowd, "Do not fret. I assure you it is painless." He thrust his hands downward and the roots pierced the skin of the people. Screams of pain echoed throughout the courtyard. "Well, I have been known to be wrong!" The skin ripped from their flesh was replaced with bark-like armor. Their souls are torn from their bodies and delivered to Craotonus. Their free will was taken away and they were turned to mindless, bloodthirsty monsters.

Craotonus stood in the center of a large, round room as he soaked in the last of the souls. He fell to the floor, writhing in pain and pleasure. Pure darkness swirled around the room, pouring into his evil body. Tearing at his flesh, shedding his outer rags, he stood before Malonox completely exposed. "I am yours to command. I am whole and complete, use me."

Malonox walked to the fallen God, placed his hands on his head. "*Malonorey terio rigorer. Falkea no reato.* Blood of my blood, flesh of my flesh."

The corrupt lord handed him a robe of pure shadow. Donning the robe, dark smoldering embers formed in his burning eye sockets. The robe locked itself around him, shrouding him in evil.

"We will take back what is ours. Akadius will feel my hands around his throat, squeezing the light from him. My master, you will be at your rightful place and all shall kneel to your might," Craotonus told him.

The two walked out to the courtyard to meet Dori'naur and Rauko'. Once there, Craotonus motioned for the brethren to join him; they fell to either side of him.

"Today, we stand united. Today, we are shrouded in shadow and it shall deliver us to victory. The humans think they can overcome us, and dissipate the shadows. They do not know what they face." Craotonus lowered his head and opened his new midnight black wings.

"You shall be witness to the rebirth of this world and when we are finished, the other worlds will have no choice but to kneel before us!" He swung his mighty wings forward, spreading a dark shadow over the warriors like a blanket, filling their very souls with evil.

Rauko' and his reborn hellhounds were working with the orcs. After Craotonus gave his address to the Dark Army, they knew they had to be ready for war.

"You have some of the finest looking warriors I have seen in centuries. They are equal to the blessed humans of the first war. I look forward to seeing them face the dwarves and their Iron Army. They will be ready, won't they?" Rauko' asked a figure standing on the edge of the courtyard.

From the shadows, a large brownish-green orc stepped into the light. He carried a large scar across his chest and one down his face. "They will chew up this so-called Iron Army and crush them like children," Xago said. "My people are what wars are fought for. They are always ready."

Rauko' shot a hideous smile. "Good. I look forward to seeing them rip the son of Akadius into pieces."

"The demigod is mine," Craotonus said as he approached them.

"When do we strike, my master?" Rauko' asked.

"We wait. They will come to us. Have the orcs lay in wait, come in from behind them and crush them."

The demons were ready for war. They longed for it. Everything they had worked for, the centuries preparing, all came to this.

The refugees, on the other hand, had a new sense of confidence. They had outlasted the demon forces for eighteen years now. Tradan matured in power and wisdom. Zachery Morely went from a wide-eyed farm boy to the first Dragon Rider to emerge in centuries. The mighty and noble King Gabriel found out he was the son of Akadius with an unknown power. Aliz'Ra, one of the first Elders of Eska'Taurn, still lived. They were joined by some of the mightiest warriors to walk Amundiss. The sting of loved ones lost could still be felt throughout the people. Mothers, fathers, daughters, sons, wives, and husbands, all lost to the evil holed up in Castle Whitehold. They were ready, finally ready.

***

Aliz'Ra, Benzoete, and Elos made the long trek to the boundaries of Eska'Taurn, a long forgotten land of the elves, hidden from the eyes of others. Eska'Taurn was sealed to protect the elven people from the outside world; only a few chose to branch out into the world were used as contacts.

"It has been a very long time since I have laid eyes on my home. Will they allow us in?" asked Elos.

Aliz"Ra's eyes filled with tears. "While I was on Earth, I looked to the heavens and thought of this place. When we moved from Terra'Fayoak to Eska'Taurn, we had everything we needed. Then the demons came. I helped make the decision to seal this place in hopes of saving our people, and now I am asking them to help save all of us."

Benzoete stared at the entrance. "I saw all this coming. That is why I set them in motion. We have to save Amundiss. If we fail, I fear others will fall as well. Our people are a race of good, they serve the Light, they will not fail us." He affirmed with a look of determination in his eyes.

Aliz'Ra stepped forward, "*Mendowa tero yesatay.*" She pulled a dagger from her robes and gently opened the flesh of her hand. "Bound by my blood no more. I release the bond." She placed her hand on a nearby tall tree. Elos took a small wand and dipped the tip into a vial of magical herbs they had gathered on their way there. He handed the wand to Benzoete. The old wizard drew symbols around the tree and they began to glow brightly. With the last symbol in place, Aliz'Ra recited, "*Dentrey maleno* tero yesatay. " The air seemed to shimmer and ripple around them. As the doors opened, the illusion faded. A glorious city lay before them.

"Home," sighed Benzoete.

The trio entered the city walls, leaving all that saw them gasping and whispering.

"We are here to speak to Lanlose. He is still leader of the people, is he not?" Aliz'Ra said loudly. "Where may we find him?"

"You may look in the city graves, my lady. He has passed to the afterlife, where we thought you three had gone," a voice from an alleyway replied.

"Who do we have the pleasure of speaking to?" asked Benzoete.

"Not very sure if it is a pleasure, but you are speaking with me." The man stepped out into the open.

"Kallen? Is it really you?" asked Elos.

Kallen was a close friend of Elos and had been a student under Benzoete before the entrance was sealed. He had chosen to stay in Eska'Taurn, blaming the humans for the War of the Heavens. "Hello, Elos, Master Benzoete, it pleases me to see you among the living. Lady Aliz'Ra, there are no words for having you here. Welcome back to your home."

Aliz'Ra nodded. "Kallen, we need to speak to whoever took master Lanlose's place. Eska'Taurn, and all of Amundiss are in jeopardy."

Kallen pointed to a majestic tower in the center of the city. "You will find Meno' there, he was chosen to lead us. He will not be easily swayed to help the humans."

"How do you know that is why we are here?" asked Elos.

"Master Meno' hears the wind as it blows from city to city. We know Craotonus has returned, we also know of Valindra's grandson and his gift. Do you actually believe he can be a stable Dragon Rider with human blood coursing through his body?"

Benzoete stepped closer to Kallen. "I have seen this *human* show more honor and bravery as a boy than most of the civilized elves living here. Now as an adult, he is the Dragon Rider, and he will aid this world in defeating the demons. Did the winds tell you that?"

Aliz'Ra tugged on Benzoete's sleeve, "Dear Kallen, take us to Meno'. I need to speak with him."

Kallen led the group to the Pellucid Towers, a tall structure made entirely of mirrored glass. Meno' was at the top floor of the tower. Aliz'Ra had her work cut out for her in convincing him to help humans; she hoped she could make him realize that fighting was not just for the humans, but also for all the people left on Amundiss and other worlds to come.

Coming the top floor, they entered a grand hallway leading into a room filled with a large table and chairs. Standing behind the head chair was a tall, slender elf with long white hair, and a deep scar across his eyes.

"Welcome home, I have been expecting you," Meno' said in a low whispered voice.

"We wish to address the elven people, with your permission, of course. The demon Craotonus has returned and is at full power now. We need to band together with King Gabriel to defeat these creatures." said Aliz'Ra.

Meno' stepped from behind his chair and walked to where they were standing. "You do not know me, do you, dear Aliz'Ra?"

She searched her memories, but could not recall him.

"Of course, you do not. Why would you recall a frail old man that the council disregarded and thought of as dead for over two thousand years? Now you want me to allow my people to aid the ones who imprisoned me?" Meno' laughed and his eyes cut to Benzoete. "Your mother was a proud warrior of the elven people. *Was.* Now she's a puppet of the humans."

Benzoete stepped forward, only to have Aliz'Ra stop him. "I know you now. We did not disregard you, we banished you! You call yourself Meno' to these unsuspecting people; but I know you as Relinquo, the one that turned his back on our people for the sake of self-promotion!"

Elos gasped and took a step back. "I have heard stories of you in my training. Relinquo was to deliver the humans to the place the elders were stationed. He wanted them dead in order to put himself in power. When they arrived, the Elders left and the humans took him instead."

"They kept me locked in that cell for centuries! As one imbecilic king died off, another took his place. Each one with new ideas on how to study me and receive immortality. As the War of the Heavens began, I took my chance to escape. I had barely made it into Eska'Taurn when it was sealed. Now, I am at my rightful place." Meno's voice reeked with anger.

"And did you come into this position the same way you tried the first time?" asked Benzoete.

The guards around the room stirred. "I am Aliz'Ra, chosen first Elder by the God's hands. Your position is relieved," she said with fire in her eyes. "The people of Eska'Taurn have the right to choose their destiny, not to have it chosen for them by a deceitful, self-propelled leader. The banishment is still in effect, please escort Relinquo away from this place."

Eska'Taurn had been led by corruption and deceit for all those years. Aliz'Ra had many repairs to make with very little time. The elven people would get a choice: either to keep the disguised Relinquo, or to choose a new leader. With or without the elven army, Benzoete knew they had to meet Gabriel and the others in Weelinn soon, though he had someone he needed to find before the vote took place. Valindra was there in Eska'Taurn, and he knew she would want to go and meet George. Leaving the tower, Benzoete walked to a large building on the south side of the main city. It was a school for gifted children. He knew that Valindra made the choice to be without her son, and the man she loved, so she had surrounded herself with children every day.

Nervously, Benzoete walked in and watched the lovely woman at the desk as she prepared a lesson. "Hello, my beautiful one."

She looked up from her work and tears instantly flowed from her eyes. She leapt from her chair and ran to him. "How are you here? Is George all right?"

Benzoete kissed her on her forehead chuckling, "I love you, too. I am just fine."

She turned red and squeezed him even harder.

"Yes, George is fine. Also, he and the others are waiting for us in Weelinn. We came here to ask the elven army to aid in the battle against Craotonus." he said.

"We? Did Elos return with you?" she asked.

"Yes, and another. One thought to be lost to us." Valindra looked confused. "When we opened the portal to bring Queen Natalia, the woman who carried the new Champion of Light and the others back to Amundiss, we discovered my mother, Aliz'Ra, was alive and living on Earth. She is here with us." Valindra could not find words, she stood there stunned. Benzoete laughed, "Come on, we need to go find her and Elos and prepare to meet up with George." He took her by the hand and walked her out of the school. "The entrance is open, you can come and go as you please," he told her.

"It has been too long for to simply come and go. We must coexist with the humans and other races. We have been separated far too long." she said with a smile.

Aliz'Ra was ready to address the elven nation, stepping out on the balcony of the reagents building. You could hear several people whispering about the great elder coming back from the dead. "Good people of Eska'Taurn, you have been led in deceit. The man you knew and trusted as Meno' is in fact named Relinquo, a known traitor," anger stirred in the group, "I was stranded on another world, much like our own, since the last War of the Heavens. I am back now and here to ask you. . . to ask you to join me in battle to save our world once more. The humans and dwarves are not as you once knew them. They are honorable, trustworthy and are sacrificing themselves for the good of our world. I ask you today, rise up and fight. RISE UP AND FIGHT!"

Cheers from the crowd shook the very foundation of the city.

"We must go now. Gabriel and the others will be waiting for us in Weelinn. The time is now, our time to take back Amundiss." Benzoete told Elos and Valindra.

42

The Light's Crusades

On the balcony at Benzoete's tower in Weelinn stood Gabriel, Kegan, George, and Antoine. They spoke of strategies and prepared for war. They knew this would be no ordinary war; more lives would be lost and bloodshed would be everywhere. This world had not seen a full-scale War of the Gods in centuries.

"How long do we wait for Benzoete and Aliz'Ra?" asked Antoine.

"I have faith they will convince the elves to aid us, but we cannot wait for too long. I feel Craotonus is aware of our presence and the longer we wait, the better prepared they will be," said Gabriel.

Kegan pounded his mighty war blade into the floor, "We go bustin' through tha front gates, with or without em. If your wizard is as good as ya think, they will na' be far behin'."

Tradan walked up to the group. "I know I am new to battle and war strategy, but I think we should do as Kegan says."

Gabriel turned his head. "Were you listening in on us?"

Tradan lowered his head. "I am an important part of this, and I just wanted to know what we were doing."

Gabriel smiled. "You are absolutely correct, my son. We should have included you and Zachery. Do you know where he is at?"

A burst of air blew from the nostrils of Barrok who was perched on the roof above the balcony. "My apologies, but we are closer than you think," voiced Zachery.

"Well since we all are here, why not gather the men and get ready to end this," Antoine stated with a stern look upon his face.

As the group was leaving, Antoine stopped Gabriel. "I have a request of you, Gabriel."

"We have a request," said Andrea as she walked toward them.

Antoine took her hand in his, "We wish to be married. We don't want to face this battle as two separate people. We have given our hearts to each other, and now we want to be a union in the sight of the Gods."

Gabriel beamed with delight. "Wonderful! We will gather the people and have a grand ceremony!"

"No, Gabriel. We wish to keep this simple. We were also hoping you could do it now," Andrea said with a nervous laugh.

Gabriel nodded. "I understand. We need a witness and rings first."

Suddenly, Justin walked in. "That's why I am here, my Lord." He held a small, wooden box Justin had become like a brother to Antoine. Once a squire to the King's Guard, now witness to a blessed union. Besides Gabriel, Antoine could not ask for anyone more.

Antoine took the box from him and opened it. "I had the blacksmith craft two rings from the blessed rock of Terra'Fayoak. I felt that I am blessed to have such a woman by my side, it was only fitting."

Gabriel held his hand to accept the rings. "Let us begin then, shall we?"

They walked out on the balcony, Antoine and Andrea stood side by side in front of Gabriel, with Justin to the side.

"The Gods never intended for their people to walk alone in this life. They want us to take up a partner.; a partner who we can share all things with. You, Antoine, and you, Andrea, come before the Gods as two, but shall leave as one." Gabriel handed the rings to each of them. "Live life in the Light. Love each other truly and with passion. You are warriors in every sense, now be warriors for each other."

Antoine slid a ring on her finger. "Wear this as a symbol of my love and devotion to you. You have saved my life more times than I can remember. Save it once more by accepting me as your husband."

Andrea took the other ring and placed it on his finger. "I joined this war hoping to help spread peace to all the people of this world. I didn't realize I would find my peace and happiness amidst all the chaos. Forever, you will be in my heart."

A tear slowly rolled down Gabriel's cheek. "As your king and ruler of these realms, I pronounce you to be husband and wife."

Antoine took his battle-hardened hands and gently pushed back Andrea's coarse curly hair. He placed a hand on each side of her face, cupping it, and gazed deeply into her warm, chestnut eyes. She smiled and they leaned toward each other for their first kiss as man and wife.

"Natallia would be so proud," Gabriel said.

Justin let out a chuckle. "Don't enjoy the marriage chambers too much. We still have a war to win tomorrow."

The group shared a laugh and went to finish the day.

The Refugee army combined with the Iron Army stood at three thousand strong warriors. They hailed from every corner of Amundiss, but had one common goal: send Craotonus and his minions back to Hell for good.

Zachery and Cassy patrolled the skies the next morning. Cassy loved being with Zachery and Barrok flying. "I will never get used to this," she said.

"Once we end this war, we will fly everywhere, I have so much to show you. Amundiss is a beautiful world, much like Earth, just with magic." Barrok snorted, "Oh yes, and dragons!" said Zachery as he patted the great beast.

"Do you really think we can defeat the demons?" asked Cassy.

"We must have full faith in King Gabriel and the Light. If we do not, we have already lost." Zachery said with a smile.

Cassy wrapped her arms tighter around him, "We just started our life together and hopefully working toward forever."

Meanwhile, Gabriel stood with King Kegan who was dressed in his finest armor, ready for battle. They faced the armies who were awaiting orders. "Today we change history. Our world will be ours again, and the demons will be returned to Hell where they belong. It has been eighteen long years that we have been under the heel of Craotonus and his minions. Today, that ends! Today, we join forces and fight!"A loud cheer erupted from the crowd Kegan stretched out his hand and settled them down. "We dwarves have been outsiders long enough. King Gabriel and the others 'ave showed us there be humans worth fighting for. It is our time to crack some heads and show 'em why the Iron Army be one of the mightiest on Amundiss!" The mass of people cheered once more.

George and Antoine poured over a map of the castle, marking every possible place where they could enter and catch them off guard.

"I did not live at Castle Whitehold for very long, but I made it my duty to know every nook and pebble of that place. We can enter at the eastern side, flanking Gabriel and leaving the others to divide their forces." Antoine said.

"Good. We will need every advantage we can get. Does Andrea know what she is to do?" asked George.

Antoine nodded. "She has her group headed for the south embankment, they are ready. They will be waiting for your signal." Antoine placed his hand on George's shoulder. "How are you holding up?"

George tried to seem strong, but he just sat down, placing his face in his hands. "I am scared to death. Not for myself, but Launa. She has already lost her mother, what if I fall, or worse, what if I cannot protect her?"

Antoine said, "I cannot make promises that I do not know if I can keep, but I will vow this to you, I will try with all my might to protect her. Have faith in the Light and the Gods, today, we will have our vengeance against the monsters who tore our families apart."

George stood and wiped his eyes. "My entire life, I have had one true friend in Gabriel. Now, I am honored to call you a friend and family. Let's finish this." He took up a sword and placed his helmet on his head.

Antoine smiled. "The honor is mine, elf farmer." They shared a laugh and walked out to meet with their soldiers.

Launa came running up to her father. "Let me come with you father, please. If today is our last day, I want to spend it with you and Zachery, not hiding in a hole somewhere."

George looked to Antoine, who simply shrugged his shoulders. "I need you to be safe."

"Where else would I be safer than with you and Antoine?" she questioned.

Antoine told George, "If she will stay to the side, but still in our sight, we could watch out for her." George gave Antoine a stern look. "Come on, George. She is an adult now."

George felt his heart sink. "All right, but you stay clear of any trouble. If you see us fall, promise me you will run, run as fast as you can and hide. I need you to live. Promise me that." Launa hugged her father and promised. "Now can we get started? I hear we have some demons to kill." George retorted.

***

At Castle Whitehold, preparations were also being made. Craotonus was at full power and filled with shadows. Malonox could not engage in the battle himself, but his will and thoughts would be carried out by The Remissum.

"Give me the power, I pray thee, dark master. Show me the way to defeat the Light to bring you back to your rightful place as ruler of Amundiss." Craotonus knelt in his chambers.

From the shadows stepped the Dark Lord, Malonox himself. "Rise, my dark Champion. Today, you will serve as my right hand. You will usher darkness into this world forever!"

He laid a hand on the head of Craotonus, causing shadows to engulf him, weaving in and out of his skin, forming a living armor, surrounding him. Craotonus stood, holding out his hands as if receiving something. Malonox closed his eyes and started to whisper a demonic chant. As the words spilled from his lips, he pierced his own body with his hands, removing a bone from his chest. The bone was black, gnarled, and looked to be rotting.

"The Shadow Bone will protect you against our enemies. It is the only defense against the Bloodblade, use it wisely."

As Malonox handed the bone to Craotonus, it shifted from a rotting bone to a bone handled blade. The blade looked like it was made of pure shadow, evil resonated from the weapon. "I shall lay the heads of our enemies at your feet. Our path is clear, our mind is as one. We will be victorious."

Malonox nodded his head in approval. "Gather the minions, the time has come. The mortals are stirring. Strike them hard, do not give them any openings to defeat you."

Craotonus bowed his head. "Your will, my Lord, we will not disappoint."

***

The time had come. The armies were ready and willing to follow King Gabriel and the Champion of Light into battle for the sake of Amundiss. Everything hung in the balance of this battle. The people of Amundiss had been slaves to the evil Craotonus and his minions for too long. If Tradan could not defeat the fallen God, all would be lost. Not just for Amundiss, but every world would be in danger.

Akadius and the other Gods surely would not just sit by and let the innocent people fall to darkness. They had a vow to not interfere, but this was different, was it not?

The balance of good and evil, Light and Dark, could not be weighed by mortals against Gods, Akadius would be there. The people prayed to the Gods for encouragement, they prayed for vision, but most of all they prayed for their king. King Gabriel of Whitehold had led them with courage and wisdom. Today, he would not fall; today, he would lead them to victory in the name of the Light.

I had seen many things from the time the Demons entered my life. I had new friends, met new family, and met the love of my life from another world. If we failed to end this, we failed everyone. My newfound power of being a Dragon Rider was in no comparison to the burning need to protect Cassy and my family. Barrok and I acted as one, our souls are forever linked and we, along side Tradan and the others, would try to rid our world of the demons and bring Light to the people. This I swore upon my life. This war ends here. This is our finale. The shattering of Amundiss and its' people will come to an end.

MICHAEL LACKEY

43

The Shattering

The time had come. Kegan ordered the sounding of the war horn. A low, loud tone flooded the land. A second horn was heard, and then a third signifying they were in place and ready.

Gabriel looked to his son. "Are you ready for what lies ahead? Are we ready to put an end to the pain and suffering of our world?"

Tradan pulled the Bloodblade from its sheath, holding it high above his head as the blade ignited in flames. "I am ready, Father. We must end this once and for all!" With a shout, his wings arched downward and he took to the skies. A rumble of cheers came from the armies as they moved forward. George, Zachery, and Cassy were with a company of the dwarves on the eastern side, with Antoine and Launa behind them.

"That is our cue! In the name of our king, we take back what is ours! Ready yourselves!" Zachery called out. The mighty dwarves stood stoic and awaited their orders, watching Antoine step forward.

"We wait for the signal to charge forward. We know that they await us and have a company of orcs defending the castle." As Antoine said this, one of the dwarves cursed orcs and spat to the ground.

"We will show them the way back to Hell!"

Another low tone rang out over the hills. "Iron Army! Move forward and await my command!"

The mighty dwarves started to march forward to the highest point above Castle Whitehold.

Zachery and Cassy climbed onto Barrok and took to the skies. "We are ready, Cassy. I feel it. We will see victory this day."

Gabriel and Kegan mounted their horses and led the bulk of the refugees toward the front of the castle. Gabriel told Tradan to fly back and meet up with Andrea and her unit of soldiers since they were the surprise group. The Champion nodded to his father and soared through the skies. The sound of the men and horses was like thunder. What a glorious sight it was to watch the army set out for Whitehold.

As they marched the long, dry road a loud, strange noise came from the trees. Gabriel held his right arm up signaling for the men to stop.

"Did you hear that?" asked Gabriel.

Kegan looked around. "Aye, but I don' know what it was."

Suddenly the trees shook and a roar was heard as the sea of green poured out of the forest.

"Orcs! Take up yer blades!" shouted Kegan.

It was an ambush. The demons wanted to end this early. The warriors clashed in a flurry of steel and blood. Gabriel leaped from his horse, kicking an orc to the ground. With one swipe of his sword, the orc's head departed from his body. Kegan ran toward a group of the green skins that had two of his men surrounded. In a flurry of controlled madness, the good king opened the stomach of the first orc, turned and found his dagger planted in the throat of a second. In a split second, the blade was retracted and thrown, finding its mark between the eyes of a third. The two dwarves stood in shock, watching their older king completely dismantle the orcs with little effort. The fourth orc turned and ran.

"I don't think so, ya green bastard!" Kegan shouted. He launched his short sword through the air, striking the fleeing orc in the neck, slicing clean through with enough force behind it that it landed in the chest of another unsuspecting orc, dropping him to his knees. "Well, don' just stand there laddies! Get ta killing!" Kegan barked at the two astonished dwarves he saved. He looked down and observed a massive war hammer left behind by one of the departed orcs, "This will do nicely!" He picked the hammer up, it was a one-handed weapon for an average orc, but for Kegan, it made a deadly two-handed hammer of death.

Gabriel found himself in awe watching the old dwarf king in action; he felt a deep connection to Kegan. They both wanted what was best for their people, no matter the cost. Gabriel made his way through the orcs, each one that encountered his blade intensified the hatred in his soul. He repeated the scene over and over in his head of when Malonox took Natallia from him, which allowed Gabriel to lose himself in the battle and unleash a power even he did not know he had.

His eyes glowed a bright white, his senses heightened, allowing him to think two, maybe three steps ahead.

"Come to me Malonox! Meet your end!" he shouted as a group of orcs rushed him at the same time.

The green skins closed in, but Gabriel steadied his sword beside him and his eyes got brighter as if they would burn out of his head.

Just as the orcs were about to reach him, Gabriel shouted, "NATALLIA!"

He gripped his sword and plunged it into the ground sending out a shockwave, completely disorienting all the orcs. He pulled the blade from the ground, and in one circular motion, he beheaded all that stood around him. As the bodies hit the ground, he was already focused on his next target.

Kegan laughed. "I never knew you humans were so much fun laddie!" He crushed the chest of an oncoming orc.

One by one, the orcs fell. All but one and Gabriel grabbed him by the throat and lifted him high in the air, "Run, tell your master we are coming! Tell your green-skinned kinsmen they will also fall this day. The Light will outshine any and all that oppose it." He slammed the orc to the ground with a thud.

As he stood up, Kegan gave him a swift kick to the backside, "Run laddie! An' hope we don' catch up to ya!"

Gabriel looked around to assess the damage to their men.

Kegan came over to him. "I didn' know you had that kinda power lad. It was truly amazin'!"

Gabriel looked at his hands holding the Fuascailte blade. "Neither did I, Kegan. I do not how I did it."

Kegan slapped him on the back. "Eh! Doesn't matter, just keep doin' it!"

The small battle was not an attempt to stop them, it was merely to slow them down. Gabriel worried that the other groups would be hit hard also.

Gabriel called for two of his men. "Samuel, I need you and Justin to find the fastest horses we have and warn the others of possible ambush. Explain all plans stay the same, just be on alert for orcs. God's speed men." The men mounted their steeds and raced off for the others. "As for us, we march for Castle Whitehold. I have a demon I need to see."

To the East, George and Antoine rode side by side now. No words were spoken as the two stayed focused on the day. Zachery and Barrok landed right in front of them.

"My Gods, Son, you have to give us warning before you do that!" George exclaimed.

"I am sorry father, but a rider is headed our way fast. He is one of ours."

As Antoine rode toward the rider, he could hear Samuel call to him, "King Gabriel sent me My Lord, orcs staged an ambush!" As he said the last word, an arrow found its mark in the man's chest, then another. Before the poor soul fell from his horse, five arrows were lodged through him and orcs poured from over the hills.

"For the master! Leave no one alive!" The orc's battle cry was heard.

Antoine pulled his sword and shouted to Zachery, "Give us some cover! I want to smell burning orc flesh!"

Zachery and Barrok pushed to the skies and straight for the oncoming horde. Arrows bounced off of the scales of the mighty dragon. "They tickle? Really? I love you even more Barrok." Zachery pointed to the front line and instantly an inferno of dragon fire engulfed the orcs in their tracks.

Shrieks and cries rang out as the green-skinned assassins fell into ash, which bought the two men enough time to ready themselves. Antoine took Launa to the side and told her to stay out of sight. She knelt behind a large tree and watched as Antoine quickly sliced and diced an on coming orc. The orc fell to his death right in front of her.

Launa saw the orc wielding two finely crafted swords. "I can't rely on father and Antoine to come to my rescue every time. I am not some helpless little girl," she mumbled to herself. Launa crawled on her hands and knees to avoid being seen. Carefully, she went to pick up one of the swords, when the shiny gem in the handle of the other one caught her eye. She picked up the blade and returned to her tree. Once there, a strange feeling overcame her, visions of wars she had not been a part of poured into her mind. She held the blade to her chest and waited as the visions began to fade.

Out on the battlefield, George, who started out as a farmer, had learned to be one of the best fighters in the realm, with Gabriel and Antoine's help. He twirled his two-handed broadsword like it was made of straw.

Two orcs confronted him. "That's a nice blade for such a pitiful little human."

George smiled, "I'm glad you like it, you are about to see it up close." George dodged, moving toward the orc on the right, but slicing at the unsuspecting one on the left. As his blade narrowly missed the orc's face, he kicked the mouthy orc in the stomach. He bent over as the breath rushed out of him. George connected the hilt to the back of the orc's massive skull sending him to the ground. "Did you get a good enough look? No? Do not worry, you will get another chance."

He delivered a swift kick to the orc's side as the second lunged for him. George turned and blocked the strike with his blade. The orc's delivered a flurry of attacks as both were now on their feet. Sparks flew as the blades clashed together. Another kick to the stomach by George sent one stumbling backward and to the ground providing an opening.

George swung his sword upward and connected with the exposed midsection of the standing orc, opening up a gash that resulted in his seeing his own insides flow out. George thrust the end of the blade up and under his chin. As the blade entered through, he sneered, "Take a long look. Feel free to admire the craftsmanship." George dug the sword in all the way to the hilt and looked the orc directly in the eyes, "I told you that you would get a closer look." He retracted the blade and spun to block an oncoming strike.

George pressed forward, driving the orc back. Swing after swing, George countered every strike. Finally, he found an opening. As the orc swung high, George went low and through the massive legs of the orc, springing up behind him. With a quick thrust, the blade found its mark between his shoulders. The orc howled in pain and leaped forward. As he turned to face George, he found the blade pressed into his chest. A quick twist of the blade sent the orc to the dark afterlife.

Zachery and Barrok took a swipe through the middle of the group. "I never knew father could do those things! But he and Antoine can't handle them all, let's show them what we can do." Barrok rolled right, unleashing a horrific roar. Some of the orcs froze in their tracks, terrified of the mighty dragon.

Zachery concentrated on a single orc in the center of a group. He raised his hand and summoned a pillar of flame to fall on the poor bastard, filling him with a holy fire. The flames consumed him, making him a living bomb. As the flames burned out of his body, the fire spread from orc to orc dropping each to ash. "Head toward Antoine, he may need our help," Zachery said.

Antoine was not lacking in skill. "Flank them from all sides! Contain them to one spot and leave none alive!" he called to the dwarves.

A massive orc stood at the edge of the chaos, just staring at Antoine. "Angelic one! Come to Kodar, I will send you to your afterlife to meet your Gods."

Kodar the Clanslayer was one of the generals in the orc clan named Firefist. Kodar walked methodically toward Antoine, smashing everything in his path, even his own men.

"Kodar! You want me, you got me!" Antoine rushed through the field straight for the orc.

When they met, Kodar raised his war mace above his head and sent it flying down. Antoine slid with his shield held up. The mace connected with the shield, sending sparks flying everywhere. Antoine made it to Kodar's feet with the shield still up. Another massive strike was on its way when Antoine pulled his dagger and planted it through one of the orc's feet. Kodar shrieked and Antoine discarded his damaged shield, pulling two short swords from their sheaths. As Kodar bent to release the dagger, Antoine met him with a dual swipe gashing across his face, two deep lines.

"I thought you were better than this, great Clanslayer! I have heard stories of your power and might, all I see is a weak child." Antoine mocked him.

"It is now my time, little human!" Kodar pulled the dagger from his foot and sent it hurling through a dwarf standing to the side.

He picked up the mace and charged. The swing went low and Antoine jumped, avoiding the spiked head of the weapon. As he was airborne, Kodar connected with a fist to the chest, sending Antoine flying back knocking orcs and dwarves to the ground.

"One hit and you break? Now who is the child?" Kodar bellows.

Slowly, Antoine stood to his feet. "I am just getting started, you will leave this life today."

He picked up a broadsword dropped by a fallen orc and headed back to the fight. As they met again, Antoine blocked the mace with the sword and spun away from the force of the blow. He leaped again, this time landing a kick Kodar's head. The kick sent the orc's helmet flying off his head exposing a gnarled, knotted head lined with Clan Firefist tribal tattoos.

Kodar turned his eyes to Antoine. "A valiant death awaits one of us this day. It will be my honor to kill you, you are a worthy human."

Antoine lowered his sword in front of him and placed his arm across his chest in a salute, "You are truly the Clanslayer and a worthy adversary. May our Gods welcome us home."

A quick bow of their heads and the battle waged again. Blow after blow each warrior seemingly knew what move the other would make before they moved. Antoine rolled left picking up a small dwarf shield. When he leapt to his feet, he sent the shield flying. Kodar swatted it away, leaving himself exposed to the dagger flying behind it. The dagger found its mark in the center of Kodar's massive chest. He let out a deep growl as he grasped the dagger's handle.

"It will take more than that tiny blade, angelic one!"

Antoine used that as a distraction and made his way behind Kodar.

He thrust the point of his sword into the leg of the orc. "That's why I kept this one."

Kodar dropped to one knee, Antoine delivered a strong kick to Kodar's back forcing him to the ground. Another kick to the side and Kodar found himself struggling for breath. Antoine leaped on Kodar's back as if he were a horse, reaching toward his own sides and pulled out two more daggers. Reminiscent of his battle with Stolos, he plunged the blades into the neck of Kodar, over and over, blood filling the orc's mouth. The orc stood and threw Antoine over his shoulder hard to the ground.

Kodar spat out a mouth full of blood. "You make me taste my

own blood? Not many have done that."

Antoine looked up in amazement, what did he have to do to defeat the creature? He stood and gripped the hilt of the broadsword so hard his hands ached. Back and forth they fought, each one trying to find an opening. As the battle waged between these two epic warriors, Antoine grasped at any advantage. The wounds around his neck still poured blood and the blood loss was starting to take its toll on the orc. His swings slowed, and Antoine felt fatigued but still took his chance. As Kodar swung his mace, Antoine stepped back and the mace missed completely, knocking Kodar off-balance. Antoine stepped forward and swung upward catching him directly under the chin opening up a gash in the orc's throat. Kodar dropped his weapon and fell to his knees holding his wound.

Antoine readied his blade. "You are truly a master warrior, and the best I have faced. May you find rest." With a slice of his blade, he took the head of Kodar and fell to his knees exhausted.

Zachery saw Antoine fall and told Barrok to get close enough to grab him. Just as they made it to the fallen warrior, a group of orcs tried to claim a prize that was not theirs. In one swoop, Barrok glided in, picked Antoine up gently in his massive talons, and a nice snack of orcs crunched in his mouth. "That is just disgusting Barrok, you do not know where they have been," Zachery chuckled. The remaining orcs turned and retreated toward the castle.

, "Don't allow them to escape!" George shouted to Zachery. "Take them down!"

Zachery motioned for Barrok to head them off. In a blast, the mighty beast ignited a line of fire, stopping the gross creatures in their tracks. The dwarves came in behind them and ended the skirmish quickly.

George found Launa still behind the tree grasping her sword. "We need to go, sweetheart, follow me." George looked at the blade in her hands, "Are you alright? Are you harmed?"

Launa looked to her father, "No sir, I feel great." She showed him the sword and he placed his arm around her and agreed to let her keep the blade as they rejoined the group.

As they walked from the tree line, he saw several dead orcs, "I'm glad to see you were protected in my absence."

On the other side of the castle, Justin rode to find Tradan, Andrea, and the others.

As his horse galloped into their sight, Tradan flew to meet him. "Sir Justin, you bring news?"

"Orcs laid an ambush for the King's company, we survived with minor loss. His Majesty sent word that all was to plan, just stay alert and safe."

Andrea had made her way out to them and heard the news. "What of Antoine and George's group? How do they fare?"

Justin answered, "I do not know, my lady. King Gabriel sent Samuel to warn them and myself in your direction. I am to stay with you and aid you in any way needed."

Andrea had a look of concern come across her face, worried that Antoine and his men were also ambushed and could not overcome them.

She looked to Tradan. "How fast can those wings take you? I need to know Antoine's fate."

The Champion knew she would be filled with concern and her mind would not be as sharp. "Get the men into position, and wait for the signal. I will return in time to meet you as you head to the walls."

Andrea thanked him and took Justin to fall in with the others. Tradan hoped to find all was well. The demons must be worried, that is why they sent the ambush. Andrea led the group to a well-hidden area just outside the southern wall. Antoine had told them of an area that was the weakest in the castle. He told them how an army that came through the wall would be noticed, but a small group of warriors could be unseen, especially when the attention was drawn to the two armies to the front and east.

44
Redemption
Comes

The past eighteen years had brought heartache and pain. War had plagued Amundiss and threatened all of its citizens. Now, the time had come for the people to reclaim their world, or all would be lost to Craotonus and the demon brethren. Aliz'Ra and Benzoete still had not returned, and the time had come to storm Castle Whitehold. Fueled by their survival of the two earlier attacks with the orc armies, the refugee's focus burned even hotter than before. They knew they had Malonox worried, they had more than a chance in defeating the evil.

When the king's company of soldiers marched to the top of the hill overlooking Castle Whitehold, a bright light flashed before them. When their eyes cleared, Akadius stood before them, the Lord of the Heavens. The God of Light blessed each and everyone and vowed to be with them through the end. Akadius could not take up arms against the mortal orcs fighting for Malonox, but he could bestow upon these good people his guidance.

"I know it has seemed that the Light has deserted you. The

world has grown into a dark and evil place, overrun with weeds of darkness. Thank you, good people, for your continued faithfulness, you will be rewarded."

Gabriel dismounted, walked toward him, and fell to his knees, "My father I beg you, protect my people. They fight in your name and the Light, do not let the ones who have passed to the afterlife go in vain."

Akadius motioned him to rise. "This is why you are the leader you have become. Let the Light guide you all, trust your instincts for I will be with you." He unsheathed his sword, pointed toward the crowd of soldiers, and a warm glowing light washed over them. Akadius nodded at Gabriel and vanished in bright flash.

Zachery and the second group had made their way to the eastern side of the castle. Antoine came around after his hard fought battle with Kodar.

"Careful, Antoine, you don't want to roll off a dragon while in flight," Cassy told Antoine.

He shook his head and looked around, "Feels like a mountain fell on me. Is everyone alright?"

Zachery turned around, "We had a few casualties, but once they saw Kodar fall, the orcs turned and ran. You were an inspiration, even to the Iron Army! Plans are still the same, we wait for Gabriel's signal."

Antoine glanced down at the castle below. "Are the men in position? If so, let's land and get to work."

Barrok circled high above, swooping down and landing light as a feather behind a line of trees where the men waited to storm the walls. The Iron Army dwarves were ready to bring the wrath of a thousand years of exile. They were a legion of warriors very few had walked away from.

"Thank the Gods you are alright. When we got the news of the ambush we were worried," said Tradan as he landed beside them.

Zachery pointed to Antoine. "We are all right, a few lost, but you should have seen Antoine and my father! I did not know the ancient ones had it in them!"

The two laughed as Antoine made a face at him. Tradan told Antoine of Andrea's concern, "Take care of her please, and tell her I will see her soon."

Tradan smiled and took to the skies to join Andrea and the small group. He flew high above the clouds avoiding detection from the orcs patrolling the walls of the castle. Quietly, he landed and made his way to Andrea's position. He told her Antoine is safe and he sent his love.

Andrea smiled. "Let's make this fast. I need to kiss that man." Tradan shook his head, smiling.

Gabriel and Kegan rode their horses to the main gate of Castle Whitehold and called out for the demons to show themselves. A loud boom filled the air and black and purple smoke formed in front of them.

As it disappeared, Malonox appeared before them. "Son of Akadius, and the noble King of the Iron Army dwarves. You can't possibly be foolish enough to believe you can defeat me. Darkness is eternal. The shadows will prevail when nothing else can. I will have your heads this day, and my dark kingdom will be whole."

Kegan laughed. "I was hopin' you would say dat! The Iron Army does not know defeat!" The dwarf made a slight motion with his left hand and an archer from the middle sent an arrow soaring right for Malonox's head.

In a calm and effortless motion, the demon caught the arrow inches from his face, and broke it in half. "You will see glorious death this day. Tell your Gods the darkness is coming, and no one can stop us." In a cloud of smoke, he was gone.

Atop the towers, flags arose. Blood red with a black tree in the center. A horn sounded from inside the castle and the gates dropped. A thousand orcs stood at the ready with blades flashing in the light.

"Fall to position! Wait for them to advance!" Gabriel shouted the order.

Kegan turned to the other side, "Battle formation! Short wall!" As he bellowed the orders, all the Iron Army dwarves formed a barrier around them with their shields.

Human archers set up position behind the warriors in rows of two. First row with arrows notched in position, second row knelt, waiting their time. The orcs flooded out of the gates and headed for the refugees.

"Wait for them! Wait for my command!" Gabriel shouted. As the orcs reached halfway across the entrance road, Gabriel ordered, "Fire at will! Make your marks!"

Arrows flew, each one felling an orc. First row knelt as the second stood and let loose their arrows. Just as the first, the row of orcs fell. This continued until the mass of bloodthirsty orcs reached the Iron Army wall.

"Dwarves! It's bone crackin' time!"

Just before the green skins reached the wall, the dwarves pushed their blades forward. As the first wave collided, they found themselves on the wrong end of the dwarf steel. They retracted their swords and clashed with the horde of orcs. Humans and dwarves banding together, fighting for the Light.

Gabriel stormed through the oncoming orcs, slashing his way to the gates. He reached the back of the mob and found a group of barkers waiting inside the courtyard.

In the center of the mindless killers stood Dori'naur. "Welcome home, former king. Do you like what we have done to our castle?"

Gabriel gritted his teeth and snarled, "This is my home. I will take it back. Your head will adorn my mantle."

"I had hoped that was your answer." Dori'naur motioned his hand and the barkers made their way toward Gabriel.

He took a step back, thinking of a way out when he heard a voice behind him.

"We are with you, lead us."

Hatholon stood with a large group of the dwarves and humans.

Gabriel smiled. "Strike hard, strike fast, they are slower than most."

The group charged forward as the barkers leapt for them. The battle-hardened dwarves started to slice through the barkers.

Hatholon and Gabriel stood shoulder to shoulder as the minions encircled them and Dori'naur slowly stalked toward them.

"Your time has come to meet your father face-to-face. You will fall to the master."

"I have met my father and I have his blessing. You are about to meet your end." Gabriel swung low, sweeping at the feet of the barkers nearest him, and they leapt straight up to avoid the strike. Hatholon swung high and separated their heads from their bodies.

They turned their attention to the demon Dori'naur and slowly walked his way.

"You will pay for the lives you have sacrificed," Gabriel said.

"It is a price I gladly pay," Dori'naur said, turning away and disappeared in a cloud of smoke, his laughter ringing throughout the courtyard.

"We need to give the signal to Antoine and George. Once they have started their attack, we will signal Tradan and Andrea." Hatholon nodded and pulled a horn from his satchel. A low, loud tone echoed through the air.

"Do we press forward and search out the demon, my lord?" Hatholon asked.

Gabriel paused to think, "Not just yet. We need to keep the focus on us and Antoine's company for now." They ran back toward the battle to give the others time.

At the Eastern wall, the signal horn was heard. "That is our signal. Company to position!" Antoine shouted.

"Group B, on my mark!" George ordered.

"Group A! Ladder men and blades! GO! GO!" Antoine followed behind a group of men carrying large ladders and watched as they leaned them against the walls.

Several orcs seen atop the walls were alerted to their presence.

"Group B, archers! Clear those walls!" George shouted.

As the orcs prepared to push the ladders, a stream of arrows pelted the top of the castle wall, instantly dropping several defenders and pushing back some of the others. Volley after volley, the arrows flew. The ladder men knew when to advance and when to hold back. Under the cover of fire from Group B, the blades on the ladders made it to the top and over. As each one made their way over, the last of the group gave the signal wave to Group B to join them.

"Group B! Time to climb!" George shouted the order and the warriors advanced to the wall.

Once over the wall, they spread out through the hallways and corridors taking down any orc or barker that stood against them. George was the last atop the wall, but before joining his men, he blew his signal horn alerting Andrea and Tradan to move their group forward on their mission. George felt a rush of emotions and memories as he stepped inside the castle. It was the first time he had been inside since the demons held him and Elizabeth eighteen years ago. Much had happened in those years, much had been lost.

George took a deep breath. "This is why we are here, for all the people we lost, for you Elizabeth. I am glad Launa is safe outside." With that he drew his sword and ran in to join his men.

As George blew his signal horn, Tradan and Andrea readied the few warriors to advance on the Southern wall.

"Antoine said there was a spot where the trees hung close to the walls and offer easy access to the top. We can quietly enter from behind and find Malonox and cut the head from the serpent," said Andrea.

The group ran from the tree blind and rounded the corner of the walls.

"This is not good," Justin replied as the group came to a quick stop.

The trees burned to blackened stumps, leaving nothing behind.

"Change of plan. It will take a bit longer, but just as effective." Tradan grabbed Andrea by the arms and flew to the top of the wall.

They made a quick sweep to check for lookouts. One by one Tradan flew the group to the top.

"All right, we know what we have to do. Be quick and be safe."

Andrea reiterated the plan to the group as they separate and search the castle. The refugees and the Iron Army were slowly working their way into the castle courtyard, drawing the attention to them and killing as many of the orcs as they could. This gave the smaller groups cover to search for the demons.

Tradan turned a corner and caught sight of Dori'naur as he stood with a group of his new and improved barkers. "Welcome young Prince, or should I call you Champion? Your training is not enough for what you will face today. Are you prepared to die so young?"

Tradan gripped the Bloodblade. "My training will be enough to end your life."

Dori'naur cut him off. "My life may come to an end by your hand or someone else's today, alas you are not enough!"

With that, he sent the barkers after them. Tradan set his mind while Justin and the others engaged with the minions. The young Champion opened his eyes and he lunged forward without hesitation, thrusting his blade to the right, catching a barker in the back of his head. With a flick of his wrist, he separated the barker's head from his body, dropping it in a heap of ash. In a fluid motion, the blade swung left, connecting with a minion slicing completely through them. Calmly and methodically, he walked through the fighting group, dropping barker after barker until it was just Dori'naur.

"No one interfere, he is mine."

The demon let out a wicked laugh. "Stupid boy, did you really think it would end here? Our time will come, patience is a virtue." As before, in a puff of smoke, he was gone.

"We will find them, my Lord," Justin repeated.

Tradan nodded his head. "I know we will. I also know we will end their reign of horror."

Meanwhile, Andrea and her group entered a corridor, but Rauko' stood at the end, with his demon dogs. "Ah, what do we have here, a welcoming group? Well then let me introduce you to two very important parts of my family. Shaaux and Varg, make them feel at home."

The hellhounds bared their teeth and charged the refugees. Shaaux leapt for Andrea, knocking her to the floor. Varg circled the group, snarling at his prey. Justin reached for a torch that was still lit from the night before. He waved the torch back and forth in front of the demon dog, not to intimidate him, but hoping to prove a distraction. As Varg focused on him, the pause allowed the others to spread out and form a plan. Andrea had her hands full with Shaaux, hacking and slashing at the beast.

A loud howl of pain echoed through the halls, as the human Sherman slipped in unnoticed, buried his blade into the hindquarters of the hellhound. Shaaux turned her attention away from Andrea, unleashing a blood curdling bark, causing Sherman to freeze in his tracks long enough for her to pounce. Shaaux sank her teeth deep into him, the sound of his bones being snapped was soon drowned out by his screams of pain. A quick twist of her head and poor Sherman was no more, torn to shreds by her razor-sharp teeth, and scattered them across the floor in pieces. Varg, saw the human scraps fly and turned his attention to the floor for a quick snack.

Andrea regained her senses and sent a dagger flying toward the beast. It found its mark, cutting a rope that secured a large candle fixture from the ceiling. Both hounds were too busy chewing their snack to realize it before it came crashing down on top of them.

"Now! While they are dazed, go for their throats!" Andrea shouted.

The group rushed in, blades slashing. The hellhounds howled in pain, their master could not bear their cries.

"I will not lose you again!" Rauko' shouted as he unsheathed his blades. The demon rushed to his pets' aid, spearing one of the refugees in the back, lifting him high above his head, and then slammed his body to the floor.

"Take care of those mutts, I'll take the demon," Andrea bellowed.

She swiped hard at the demon, but his left blade blocked the strike and he slashed high with his right. Andrea barely ducked out of the way. He kicked her to the ground, crouching above her.

Rauko' laughed, pulling back his hood and asked, "Stupid girl, did you really think you could defeat me? The dark God of the wild? DID YOU?"

She looked deep into his burning eyes, "No, I just wanted to keep you busy for him."

A loud yelp was heard. Rauko' turned to see Tradan standing with the head of Varg in his hand and the Bloodblade through the neck of Shaaux. He hurled the beast's head at Rauko', as it landed it returned to ash.

The demon lept to his feet and straight for Tradan. As Rauko' slashed at Tradan, his blade still ablaze, he blocked the demon's moves.

"Get them out of here, stay to the plan find the others."

Andrea led the group out searching for Malonox and Craotonus.

"You should have kept them here Champion. You will need them to carry your lifeless body to your father."

Tradan gripped the blade, spinning to his left catching the demon's chin with the hilt. Rauko' staggered back, Tradan spread his wings, "I will see my father when I deliver your head to him."

He thrust his majestic wings forward, sending a burst of wind in the demon's direction. Flying behind the gust, he landed a punch to Rauko's face, but it barely stunned him.

"I hope you have something better than that. I want to enjoy killing you for what you did to my children." Rauko' grabbed him by his special made chest plate, "You want to fly? Feel free." In a flash, Rauko' had Tradan pushed through an open window. Shadows emitted from the demon's armor, swirling around Tradan, trapping his wings close to his body. "I will see you at the bottom champion. Do not die until I get to you." He pushed Tradan from the window, and disappeared in a ploom of smoke.

As Tradan fell from the tower, he stilled his breath and said a few enchanted words. His body slowed in the air until he came to a complete stop, hovering just above the ground. His eyes glowed bright and the shadows started to fade.

Rauko' appeared just as the shadows broke and Tradan stepped to the ground. "Well, I may have underestimated you. No longer." Rauko' unleashed his blades and swiped for Tradan.

The Champion was unphased. He brought the Bloodblade up, stopping the strike short. The blade ignited, and Tradan's eyes grew brighter as he smiled. "Your days will come to an end. You will pay for your sins against this world and every single life you have taken." He pushed the demon back, delivering a flurry of strikes, each one countered by Rauko'. Sparks flew from the cold steel as they struck at each other.

Rauko' removed his hood revealing his horrid bone face. "My master will reign once more over this world and the heavens. You will fall, dear Champion, just as all the others before you."

Tradan heard these words and wondered how many have tried and failed? Why did Benzoete not tell them of the others? A sharp pain filled Tradan's arm, Rauko' had opened his flesh during his distraction. The pain snapped him back to the task at hand. The demon swung wildly, slashing at him. The pain grew in Tradan's arm, but he matched every swing, every slash, and every thrust. The battle took them into the midst of the courtyard where the armies were still battling for control. The site of the Champion of Light brawling with a disciple of darkness attracted most of the attention from the armies.

"Rauko' the Hunter! You will pay for the suffering you caused the city of Weelinn!"

The voice was Hatholon, who now stood with Tradan.

Rauko' delivered a kick with so much force it sent Tradan flying backward.

"I can still smell the death of your people on my blades. They were worthless."

Hatholon stepped forward, slashing the head from an oncoming orc. "My people were living in peace until you nearly wiped them from existence. They gave you what you wanted. . .

what you asked for and you still slaughtered them, my sister gave you the answer you asked and she was fed to your beasts!" Hatholon now stood face-to-face with Rauko'. Tradan fought his way back to them. "If I fall here, avenge the people of New Weelinn." Hatholon told Tradan. He then pushed his blade toward the demon's head. The edge of the steel slid just under Rauko's' chin.

Rauko' sensed an easy kill, he advanced swinging in a diagonal arc, "My turn." Hatholon staggered back.

Hatholon gathered his balance under him and slashed low, catching Rauko' right above the knee. It slowed the demon, startling him for a moment. Hatholon stepped into his battle stance and took advantage of the surprise. Slash and hack, strike after strike, Hatholon was filled with eighteen years of hatred. He could hear his sister's voice playing over and over when she was at the mercy of Rauko's beasts while he was hidden away. He vowed that day to kill Rauko' and today he was determined to fulfill that vow. A strong swing of his broadsword severed Rauko's' left hand and retractable blade off when he tried blocked the strike. The demon howled in pain. An orc came at Hatholon to protect his master, the elven warrior hurled his sword finding its mark in his chest. He grabbed his bow from off his back, and fired a stream of arrows at Rauko'.

One by one the demon cut them from the air with his fist blade of his right hand, some of the arrows slipped through and found their mark. Rauko' looked down at several arrows lodged in his chest as a burning sensation coursed through his body.

"What is this magic? This is no mortal weapon." He pulled the arrows from his body and watched his blood drip from the tips.

"You will suffer! These are weapons of the Gods blessed by Akadius himself." Hatholon yanked a sword from a dead orc and ran toward Rauko'. Again, he attacked with a vengeance.

Weakened by the blessed arrows, Rauko' fought on the defensive for survival. "Minions! Come aid your master!" The surrounding orcs rushed to help Rauko'.

Tradan had stayed out of the battle between Hatholon and Rauko', but the orcs were tipping the balance. He stormed forward to cut them off. Gabriel saw Tradan and ran to help him.

"Kegan, push inside. We will find you."

Kegan shouted to the Iron Army as he pulled his war hammer from the face of an orc beneath him. "It's time boys! Show 'em why we don' back down!" The Iron Army all grunted in unison, pushing toward the main entrance of the castle.

Tradan and Gabriel held the orcs off as Hatholon and Rauko' battled behind them. "If you need us, we are here."

"This is my fight. Live or die, I do on my own," he said and Gabriel gave him a nod.

Hatholon grabbed a blade. "One of us, demon, will leave this world now."

The elf had tears streaming down his face. His mind flooded with the memory of his sister and the people of Weelinn as they were destroyed by this demon and his minions. The warriors faced off for the last time, Hatholon swung the blade catching Rauko' in the abdomen. Rauko' grabbed the blade of the sword with his one hand and punched him in the face with the remaining stump on his left arm. Hatholon stumbled back and Rauko' pulled the sword from his stomach and plunged it into the chest of Hatholon.

"When you see your sister, tell her Rauko' sent you to her."

With a smile, Hatholon looked deep into his face. "We can tell her together."

He had grabbed a short sword from where he fell, as Rauko' looked down, he felt a sharp pain. Hatholon had the sword pushed to the hilt through his chest. Hatholon spat blood into the demon's face, "Now, the people of Weelinn can rest in peace."

Rauko' leapt to his feet, grasping the sword. Could a mere elf defeat the mighty hunter? He pulled the blade and watched his life flow from the wound. Rauko' fell to his knees, "Master, forgive me. . ."

Gabriel rushed to Hatholon as Tradan landed behind Rauko' and used the Bloodblade to sever his head. The power instilled inside the Bloodblade meant the end of Rauko' the Hunter, never to return.

"This was my destiny, my fate," Hatholon coughed. "I can go to my sister, with my head held high."

Gabriel smiled at the brave warrior. "You earned your rest, go to your family."

As the last breath left Hatholon's body, Dori'naur appeared from the Shadows of the main doorway. "NO! It does not end this way, human!" A sea of barkers flooded past Dori'naur and into the battlefield. "Destroy everything that moves!"

MICHAEL LACKEY

45
New Day For Tomorrow

Infuriated by the loss of his brother, Dori'naur sent all the barkers on a rampage.

"Bring me the head of the Champion, destroy everything else."

As the sea of barkers came lumbering out for the king and his son, a single arrow flew over the wall, striking the lead minion between the eyes. As the first one dropped to ash the sky turned dark. Gabriel looked up and grabbed Tradan and pulling him back just in time to see thousands of arrows rain down on the barkers. Gabriel turned to Kegan to see if this was his plan, when Zachery and Barrok came soaring over the wall and sat down between them and Dori'naur with a roar.

"Better late than never my king, I am sorry for the delay," Benzoete said as he dismounted Barrok.

"By the Gods you made it!" Gabriel exclaimed.

"My mother and the others are taking care of the remaining orcs outside. Elos is with Antoine," Benzoete said.

Gabriel shot a smile to Tradan thinking perhaps the balance had just been tipped in their favor.

Dori'naur pulled his war scythe from its sheath, "I will deliver your heads personally and we will kill your people slowly."

Tradan stood with his father and Benzoete. "You will try."

Dori'naur thrust his hands toward the ground, causing roots to cover the ground. Tradan stepped forward, wings fanned out, shimmering brightly in the sun's light. With the Bloodblade in his hand, he bent to one knee and pierced the ground. A white light emitted from the blade and engulfed the evil roots, choking them out. "We have tricks of our own," said Tradan.

The demon gripped the scythe tightly and charged for Gabriel. Sparks flew as the two blades connected. Dori'naur would not be defeated easily. Gabriel stepped back, avoiding Dori'naur's strike, then spun forward with a hearty swing of his own. Dori'naur had a plan for everything. He pointed his left hand in the direction of Tradan. A long chain of bones shot out around the Champion, pulling him in front of the strike. Gabriel had to use all his strength to divert the swing away from his son. Dori'naur used that to his advantage to connect with Gabriel's face. Tradan sent an elbow to the demon's chin knocking him backward.

Benzoete was busy trying to clear the way for Elos and the others when he heard whispers in his mind.

"My time has come, wizard."

Benzoete tried to shake it off.

"Your mother could not defeat us. She is stronger than you."

Again, he shook off the whispers. "You will not best my mind!"

Craotonus tried to conquer the wizard's main weapon: his mind. Benzoete waved his hand sending a group of orcs flying against a wall.

A loud roar was heard as Barrok soared once more into the courtyard. Zachery pointed down to a group orcs circling around the wizard, and quickly Barrok snatched them up in his massive talons. "Find Craotonus! We have to stop him!" Zachery and Barrok slammed the minions to the ground outside the castle where some of the Iron Army made mincemeat of them.

The scene outside the castle gates was pure chaos. The refugee army and elven army were dealing with the orcs and barkers. What a sight it was to have Aliz'Ra standing on top of a ridge commanding an army of elves against a horde of demons. It was a flashback to three thousand years ago. "I will not let you slip from my grasp again." she whispered under her breath as she sent a fireball into a group of orcs. "Using my magic again feels good!" She made her way from the ridge to the castle to find Malonox.

Antoine and George had their group over the eastern wall and were pouring into the waiting group of orcs.

"I never knew there was this many orcs in existence! Where did they all come from?" asked Antoine.

George explained to him they were summoned by the darkness. "Malonox is their master and they heed his call. Cut the head off the serpent and it dies."

George turned to see an orc archer aiming for Antoine. He grabbed a spear from one of the wall racks and hurled it through the air. The spear caught him in the chest, pushing him back.

The orc let the arrow loose, striking one of his own comrades in the back of the head. Antoine slid down a ladder with a sword in each hand. On the ground, he slid between two orcs on his knees, slicing their legs. As they fell, he buried the blades deep in their backs. George followed Antoine into battle, swinging his broadsword. Left to right, slice and dice, orcs fell to their death.

Suddenly, a booming voice called out. "Angelic one! We have unfinished business. One of us dies today!" Xago stood alone just inside the archway. Antoine looked on in disbelief. "Did you think me dead? I am a God amongst the filth, you cannot defeat me." He stepped into the light, his body scarred from the talons of Barrok.

"I will send you to your Gods, Xago!" Antoine shouted.

Xago laughed. "And I will let you see your father again!"

Antoine asked George to find Andrea and then ran straight for Xago, swords at the ready. He lept over a dwarf and stretched out both arms. Each blade struck the necks of the orcs, flanking him as he planted his boots at Xago's chest sending him to the ground. With amazingly quick reflexes for a warrior his size, Antoine was already positioned at Xago's head before he could get to his feet. He thrust his blades down piercing Xago's shoulders to the ground. Xago let out a monstrous howl of pain.

Antoine leaned down, face-to-face. "I am in no mood for you today, orc." He was close enough for Xago to land a massive headbutt, sending Antoine sprawling.

With a low growl, Xago stood, breaking the blades off at the ground. "I told you little human, I am a GOD!" He pulled the hilts of the swords from his body and tossed them to the ground.

Antoine stood, shaking his head, "As your master will soon find out, even Gods can die. You will just find out first."

The orc pulled a broadsword from his back sheath. Antoine, now without his swords, pulled two daggers from his boots.

Xago gave a great big booming laugh. "Little human with little knives."

Antoine slowly walked toward him, twirling the blades in his hands. Coming forward, the two met. Xago swung downward while Antoine crossed his daggers and blocked the strike above his head.

Before the orc could recoil his sword, Antoine delivered a quick kick to his midsection, followed by a swipe with the left dagger, which caught Xago's chest-plate strap and dropped one side loose. "What happened Xago? Did you drop something?"

The orc grew furious, slamming the armor to the ground.

The battle was spread out all over the grounds. Tradan and Gabriel were busy with Dori'naur while the others dealt with the minions and searched for Craotonus. Tradan hovered above the ground and grasped the Bloodblade as it ignited. As the two exchanged blows, the sound of the Bloodblade striking the blade of Dori'naur's scythe was like thunder. Gabriel worked his way behind Dori'naur and swung for his head. Dori'naur lifted the handle of the scythe and blocked the king's strike behind his head while landing a kick to the Champion.

Tradan took flight and landed beside his father. "We have to strike together, he's stronger now."

Gabriel lifted his head to the heavens and asked his father in a silent prayer for help.

The demon laughed at his challengers, "We will rule this day!" He saw signs of readiness for their next strike. Dori'naur held out his left arm to form a massive oaken shield upon it.

Barrok and Zachery came flying back over the walls and engulfed the demon in dragon fire. Through the smoke and flame, they saw him walking out. "I have walked through the fires of Hell, given my life to the burn of darkness, do you think dragon fire would stop me?"

What stood before them was not the Dori'naur they had known. He no longer controlled the mutated body of the noble Sir Rodderick. The dragon fire was not enough to stop him, but it did burn away his outer shell, leaving his true form. What they saw now was a grotesque, vile creature with roots surrounding his body acting as living armor.

Andrea and her group came running outside now. "My Lord, no sign of Craotonus or Malonox." she shouted as she and her men joined the attack on the minions.

"This will not end until we destroy Craotonus," Gabriel told Tradan. "To do that, we must kill Dori'naur."

Walking slowly toward them, the demon boasted, "We are eternal, we are as one now. His strength powers me."

With that said, they knew why Malonox was not found, he was within Dori'naur. That is where his added power came from. They knew if they killed Dori'naur, Craotonus would have to show himself. The father and son duo charged forward, eager to end it. Dori'naur raised his shield and held his battle scythe at the ready. Tradan waved his hand and sent a wave of holy fire at the demon, he blocked it with his shield. After the blast, Gabriel followed in with Fuascailte gleaming in the sun's light. His blade found its mark and opened a gash in Dori'naur's side. Wincing from the pain, he lowered his shield and knocked Gabriel to the ground. He raised the scythe's blade to deliver a blow to the downed king.

"Aye, you be an ugly bastard ain't ya!" Kegan exclaimed suddenly, catching the demon in the back with his war mace, drawing his attention and anger.

"Enough from you, little man!" Dori'naur spun, catching Kegan full force with his shield.

The blow sent the dwarf flying into the air where Dori'naur speared him with his spinning blade, driving him to the ground. Kegan's life rapidly faded and his skin turned black from the scythe's darkness of death.

Dori'naur leaned in. "My master thanks you for the donation."

He retracted the blade in the nick of time, blocking a strike from Gabriel who was back on his feet. Upon seeing the lifeless body of the King of the Iron Army, Tradan and Gabriel got their second wind. Gabriel was overcome with emotion at seeing his friends and allies fall to their death.

Gabriel heard the voice of his father Akadius in his mind. "Trust in your power. Trust in the Champion."

He knew what had to be done. They would not win a brute force battle against Dori'naur and Craotonus. Gabriel decided a prayer to the heavens might just be the unexpected turning point in the battle they needed. He lowered his sword and knelt on one knee. Letting Dori'naur see his opening.

He closed in on the defenseless king, left his shield at his side to get an unencumbered swing. The instant before the blade claimed its prize and in a blazing bright blur, Tradan flew between them. He grabbed his father's sword with his left hand in anticipation of the demon's blade and blocked the dark scythe out of the way. His right hand held the Bloodblade piercing Dori'naur's black heart as he thrust deep. Gabriel opened his eyes, plunging his hands to the ground and sending a shockwave throughout the courtyard, knocking all the minions off-balance.

Dori'naur looked down at the blade in his chest, locking eyes with Tradan. "I am eternal. I have the master's power...his will."

Tradan twisted the blade, and the demon screamed in pain.

"Your master will soon follow you." He retracted the blade and placed it against his throat.

Dori'naur dropped the weapon to the ground, "Master, do not forsake me!"

Malonox appeared behind the demon, grasping the scythe from the ground, "You are not worthy of mercy." The fallen God used the forsaken blade to remove Dori'naur's head. "I hold out hope your master will prove better." A blinding light emitted from his stretched out hands. As the group regained their sight, they found Dori'naur's headless body and no sign of Malonox.

Back inside, Antoine and Xago had beaten each other senseless.

Xago could not believe he hadn't killed Antoine yet. "You are truly a warrior angelic one, but you shall not last much longer."

"That is the same thing Kodar thought as well, just before I killed him." George had found Andrea and the two rushed for Antoine. "This is between us, no one is to interfere."

Andrea called to him, "Please, we can help you! We are in this together."

George pulled her back, "He has to do this on his own, and we have to let him. We need to help Aliz'Ra and the others." George tossed Antoine his sword and nodded. They rushed out, leaving the two warriors to finish their personal battle.

"Now, we finish this," Antoine smirked as he twirled the blade at his side.

Xago slowly walked back and forth, switching his sword from hand to hand. Antoine ran for the orc, sword held high. Xago stood his ground, waiting for the right moment. Just as Antoine slashed forward, Xago stepped forward and caught Antoine flush with his boot, sending him flat on his back. The orc descended upon Antoine, pushing his blade down upon him. He desperately held the massive arms of the orc up, trying to free himself. The blade inched down at him, but Antoine delivered kick after kick to Xago's back, the final one landing on the back of his head. With the orc dazed, Antoine twisted and knocked him off. He rapidly crawled away, making his way back to his feet. Antoine pulled another dagger from his belt and hurled it at Xago. The dagger found its mark deep in the orc's stomach. He pulled the dagger out and threw it back at Antoine, who barely moved out of the way.

"What do I have to do?" Antoine muttered to himself.

"Do not worry little human, I will kill you quickly if you wish." Xago started for him again, but this time Antoine knew he could not stand against him with brute strength.

Xago brought his sword down as Antoine rolled forward digging the dagger into the orc's massive thighs. Xago was bleeding badly now with another open wound. The blood loss made him see double and Antoine took advantage of his disability. Xago swung wildly trying to connect. Each missed swing drained him; Antoine just had to make sure he was one step ahead. Xago missed and Antoine was behind him, plunging the dagger repeatedly into the orc's side, then lept out of the way of his swinging elbow.

"Do you see your end Xago? Today belongs to the Light."

Xago unleashed a furious roar, turning and jabbing one right after the other, but Antoine blocked each one. He dropped and swept the orc's legs out from under him. He fell with a thud and Antoine climbed on top of him, driving the dagger into his chest over and over. Antoine slowly rolled off his motionless body, trying to catch his breath.

Andrea had been watching from a distance, she ran to see if he was all right. "Antoine! Can you move? Speak to me!" Tears flowed staining her ebony cheeks.

Antoine let out a low grunt. "I'm fine. We need to help Gab. . ."

As he said this, Xago planted a blade into his shoulder, barely missing Antoine's head. Andrea screamed, jumped to her feet and beheaded the orc. Even in death it took all Andrea had to pry his hand from the hilt. Once she pulled the blade from Antoine's body she helped him up.

George had sprinted outside to help Aliz'Ra with the minions. He found more than he expected. "Aliz'Ra where do you need me?" George asked and saw a beautiful elven woman look his way.

"George? By the Gods, it is you." He did not recognize this

woman.

"Do I know you? Have we met before, my lady?" George asked. His mind flooded with an illusion he saw in Casterton. Could this really be his mother, not some vision of her?

"Yes, I am your mother and I have waited a long time to talk to you again."

George lowered his sword and lost where he was for a moment as he walked toward her. He smiled and held his hand out to her. She gave him a reassuring glance and reached for him. Just as they are about to embrace George's eyes widen and he looked down. An orc had speared the unsuspecting warrior and the tip was through his chest.

"No!" Valindra shouted.

Aliz'Ra pointed at the orc and burned him to ashes. George dropped to his knees as Valindra held him.

"Please, hold them back for a moment," she asked Aliz'Ra with tears filling her eyes.

Elos had said that in the bloodlines of the elves everyone had a gift. Valindra's gift was that of a healer. She pulled the spear from George's back and his blood started to spill everywhere.

"I never knew you, but I've always loved you." Valindra touched his lips to his forehead and told him to not talk and lay still. She placed her hands over the wound and started to chant a series of magical words. The elven healer began to glow warmly.

"Valindra, are you sure?" Aliz'Ra asked.

"He is my son, I would gladly give everything in me for him." She closed her eyes. As the tears ran down her cheeks and fell from her face they took flight around them like fireflies at night. "*Nala shon, ella teka. Nala min, teh ife.*" Valindra spoke these words and George inhaled the magic flying around them.

His wounds started to close and the bleeding stopped. George opened his eyes and saw Valindra holding him, "What happened? Are you alright my lady?"

She smiled and said, "I am now, my precious boy." Those words echoed throughout his memories, he remembered hearing that as a baby. George smiled at her and was out again from the pain.

"Get him to safety until he can regain all his strength," Aliz'Ra ordered.

Valindra helped him to his feet and led him to a tree line out of sight. As the battle waged on, Aliz'Ra's focus shifted to a stranger fighting against the orcs. He left none standing as he walked toward them. She recognized the blade he was using, it was an ancient guardian blade, used by elven warriors who were blessed with extraordinary powers. The blades harnessed the power to unleash the warrior's inner juggernaut. When they held the guardian blade they were unstoppable warriors, but they were long killed by Craotonus in the first War of the Gods. Who was this stranger?

Elos saw Andrea helping Antoine from the battlefield as well as fight off other minions. He rushed over and put Antoine's other arm around his shoulders and helped to move him.

"He is bleeding pretty bad, we have to stop it," Andrea exclaimed.

Elos took his sword and held the blade in his bare hands, the steel turning red hot. "Hold him steady, this is going to hurt." Elos pressed the blade against Antoine's skin fusing the wound closed. "Here, make him take these herbs, they will help him regain his strength faster." Elos gave Andrea a pouch and a flask of water, "I must see to the others." He ran back to the battlefield helping whoever he could.

Barrok and Zachery landed in front of the castle gates, readying a barrier the minions could not pass. "We need to make sure all these guys are dealt with." Zachery told Barrok, who unleashed a bloodcurdling roar and a swipe of his tail sending a group of minions crashing into a wall. Zachery asked Cassy to hold tight, he patted Barrok and said, "Let them have it!" Barrok sent a pillar of dragon fire into the mote, setting the water to boil.

Every minion that tried to cross the fire was instantly killed. A loud, resonating sound filled the air and black and purple smoke swirled above the castle courtyard.

Craotonus stood in the center. "I have had enough fun this day. The time has come to end this!" He held the Shadow Bone blade pointed toward Barrok. A bolt of pure shadow hit the beast, knocking it away from the gates, sending Zachery and Cassy flying from his back. "Honor your master! Kill them all, feed me their souls." Craotonus spread his wings and held the Shadow Bone high in the air. All of the minion's eyes began to smolder, as if they were on fire. Every one of them left the fight and ran for the courtyard, surrounding their master. "Son of Akadius, when I feed on your soul, I shall become invincible!"

Gabriel stepped forward. "Sorry to disappoint you, but my soul is staying with me today." He looked to his friends and allies who now stood with him. "We came this far, will you follow me to the end?"

A thundering cheer erupted from the people.

"My king, we are here to bring the Light back," Benzoete told him.

Gabriel turned to his right. "Are you ready, my son?"

Tradan glared straight at the fallen God, "I most certainly am father."

Craotonus motioned his hands forward sending the minions into a frenzy. Gabriel shouted orders to focus all on the minions because Craotonus could not kill on his own. He could not kill, but he could mettle. Winds, lightning, smoke, and debris crashed against the warriors. The skirmish between the minions and refugees waged all around. Gabriel saw this as an opportunity to catch Craotonus off guard.

Zachery rushed to try and get Cassy to a safe place as he and Barrok shook off the effects of the shadow bolt from Craotonus. "Stay here out of sight. Launa should be just over that rise, go to her and stay there. If we do not come for you run, run anywhere far from here."

Cassy pulled him in close and kissed him, looking deep into his eyes. "We will see each again soon. I believe in you and the others." She kissed him again and turned to find Launa.

Barrok exhaled, blowing Zachery's hair. "Oh hush, she loves me. I owe her my life." They took to the air and headed back to the castle.

The herbs Elos had given Antoine had him back on his feet even though he was not fully himself, but half of Antoine was still better than most warriors in the land. He and Andrea stood by Tradan, fighting off the orcs and barkers best they could. Aliz'Ra made her way toward Craotonus, vowing to right her wrongs of the past.

She did not have the Bloodblade this time, but she would make her presence known. "Craotonus! Face your doom!" she shouted at him.

"Foolish, Aliz'Ra, have you not learned? You cannot best me, not three thousand years ago, not now, not ever," he replied.

"I have learned from my mistakes, and I had a long time to ponder on them. I thought I could defeat you on my own back then, now I know we have the power." When she finished her sentence, a bolt of light hit Craotonus, knocking him backwards.

Tradan was close enough to connect with holy fire, burning the God where he stood. Craotonus now knew Aliz'Ra was just a distraction she had no intentions of engaging against him. He turned and fired off several bursts of shadow bolts, each one finding its mark, each one wrapped around the refugees, asphyxiating the life from them. Each death weakened the fallen God, but each soul fed his power.

"No!" Gabriel screamed. "You shall not have my people!" He leapt with his blade held high.

Craotonus used the Shadow Bone to block the strike. "I need your soul, son of Akadius. You will make me invincible."

Gabriel twisted his blade and took a step back. Left then right he swung, slash after slash they met head on. With every slice, Craotonus grew more confident. He lunged forward, thrusting the Shadow Bone at Gabriel's midsection. The king, using the hilt of his blade as leverage, twisted the Shadow Bone free from his hands, dropping it to the ground. Craotonus looked at him in shock, then waved his hand sending shadows to grip Gabriel's throat. The king dropped his blade and started to rip at the shadows gathering his breath.

Craotonus leaped behind him, grabbing around his body. "You are mine now, son of Akadius. I can smell your soul!" He buried his claw-like fingers into the stomach of the king, trying to rip the very soul from him.

Tradan saw his father in danger and instantly fanned out his wings to fly toward him when he felt a sharp pain in his back. An orc had severed one of his wings, grounding him. Gabriel screamed out in agony now. Tradan pulled his injured wing in close to him and quickly opened the orc's stomach, spilling out its contents in front of him.

He locked eyes with his father, "Father! Take the sword! You have the blood of the Gods inside you!" Tradan gripped the hilt and the Bloodblade ignited. One last effort, the Champion hurled the blade for Gabriel to catch it. The noble king stretched out his arm and snatched the blade from the air. "Strike him down! You have the power to destroy him!"

Gabriel hoisted the sword above his head, the flames of the blade changing to a bright white aura. Craotonus sensed the new power of the Bloodblade and cowardly crouched behind Gabriel. One last act of honor. One last selfless deed for his people. Gabriel looked to his son, who had dealt with the orc and was coming toward them, he smiled and plunged the blade through his own body, pushing out through his back piercing the black heart of Craotonus.

"Father, no!" Tradan screamed.

A thunderous howl erupted from Craotonus, the blade burned his cursed heart. Gabriel fell to his knees, still clutching the blade inside him. Desperation started to flood the mind of the fallen God, he had to have Gabriel's soul to buy him time to get away and find Malonox. He found the Shadow Bone and raised the blade ready to strike when he was whisked away. Craotonus found himself in the clutches of Barrok.

The dark life force was rapidly escaping him. "Release me, beast!"

Zachery looked down at him. "I am afraid we cannot."

Craotonus swung his blade. "Release me or I will strike you down!"

Barrok turned to give Zachery a sly smile, "You heard him Barrok, release him." The dragon clenched his mighty talons, crushing Craotonus's wings, then opened them and dropped him.

The dark one had to use the last of his power to try to sustain his life. Barrok had flown up higher and higher so Craotonus dropped through the air and landed with a thud in the middle of the castle courtyard.

Tradan stood over him with tears streaming down his face, "I've lost my mother because of you, I've lost my father because of you, I will not lose my world to you. Not today, not ever."

The sky darkened, smoke-filled the courtyard, Malonox appeared before them. "Young Champion, do you realize the shadows are strongest when the Light is brightest?"

Tradan held the Bloodblade to Craotonus's throat and replied, "Yes, but what happens when you remove the obstacles?" He removed the head of Craotonus. "You have only the Light again."

The Shadow Lord walked around the courtyard. Darkness trailing behind every step. "Your destiny was written eons ago. Like your father, your time ends here today."

Aliz'Ra stepped in front of Tradan. "I have been alive for eons and have seen the pages of time rewritten."

Malonox laughed, "Ah, yes, the last elder of the great elven people. We created your kind first, alas, you became so obsessed with your magic that we were just an afterthought. We decided to create the stone image dwarf, again you turned from us and focused on steel and treasure."

Antoine shouted, "We do not need a history lesson."

Malonox pointed to Antoine, "And we come to the humans,

last of the free will. Your kind has become so self involved that even most of the other races shunned you."

Tradan asked, "So this is a genocide for you to start over?"

Malonox clasped his hands together in front of him, "Start over? No, dear boy. We have the orcs that have proven to be far superior. We have been working on a new race, a more work focused race. We just need to eradicate you and your kind." Malonox opened his arms, sending shadow tendrils across the courtyard snaring all that stood there to the ground. Benzoete used his magic to burn the shadows from his body, but to no avail. "Now, seeing as I cannot end your life myself, I will leave that to the new leaders of Amundiss."

The orcs charged in to claim their prize and put an end to this battle when a bright light flashed across the sky, thunder rang out, and the ground quaked.

Standing before Malonox was Akadius, Lord of the Heavens. "Enough of this Malonox, this ends now."

The Shadow Lord looked down to him. "You are correct, soon so shall you and your siblings end. You placed me in that hole, but left me the sight to see everyone that loved you still. I will regain my throne."

Akadius looked across the courtyard. He saw the fallen body of Gabriel, he knew the sacrifice he had paid for his people; and he saw the Iron Army, holding their weapons at the ready. Even faced with certain demise, they would fall fighting. Akadius waved his hand and sent light streaming across the courtyard trapping each and every orc and barker that remained in a cocoon of light. "You are the creator of the creators. I am so sorry for your fall into the darkness." He closed his hands and the cocoons shrivel up with the minions still in them.

"You fool! You know if you interfere and take mortal lives it will be your demise. Do not take the joy from me of taking your life!" Malonox bellowed.

Akadius charged fast as lightning toward the Shadow Lord. With one hand, he grabbed the arm holding the Shadow Bone, holding it steady. "I know the price I have to pay, it does not compare to the price we have already paid for allowing you to exist, thus giving you this chance to wreak chaos. I am ready to pay the price, are you?" Akadius clenched his hand into a fist, gripping tighter and tighter until it began to glow.

Zachery felt his dagger vibrate. He pulled it from his boot to see that it was glowing. "Forgive me, father." The dagger flew from Zachery's hand to Akadius.

Akadius then plunged his fist into the chest of Malonox and summoned his power of pure Light while inside the dark one. He took Malonox's hand that held the Shadow Bone and thrust the dark blade deep into his own chest. The shadows fell from the refugees as they looked on in disbelief. The Light purged the very skin from Malonox's body. Shadow and death spread across Akadius.

Tradan sprinted to Akadius's side, "My Lord, what do I do?"

The fading God looked to the young Champion, "Lead the people as your father would."

With that both the Lord of the Heavens and Malonox, the Eternal Prime, was gone. The life force had escaped them both.

The dagger passed down from Aliz'Ra's father was the first gift of the Gods ever bestowed to mortals. It was created by, and given with pure love, by Malonox. That was the key to mortality's salvation: love.

46

The Champion's Reign

After all had settled and the shock of what had happened wore off, Tradan rushed to his father's side.

Benzoete and Antoine try to comfort him. "He was the bravest man I have ever known," Benzoete said.

Antoine placed a hand on his shoulder, "He did what had to be done, and he did not hesitate. How many of us could have done that?"

Tradan tried to be brave, "What do we do now? How can we move forward without him?"

Now with everyone gathered around their fallen hero, they mourned the loss of a true leader. Aliz'Ra and Valindra were still with George.

"He is coming around now," Valindra said.

Aliz'Ra leaned in, "George? George, can you hear me?"

George rolled over and held his chest, "What happened? I saw the spear go through me."

"You can thank Valindra for that?" George looked up at his mother for the first time that he could remember.

"You saved me? How?" he asked.

Aliz'Ra answered, "She used her gift, all of her gift." She then stood up. "I will let you two talk, I need to go find that stranger with the Guardian sword."

As Aliz'Ra walked away, George sat up, "What gift was she speaking of?"

Valindra sat down beside him, "Our bloodline is one of the oldest of all elven kind. Each one of us have a gift. My father, like his mother, is a powerful wizard. My gift was of healing."

George stopped her, "You said was."

Valindra held her head high. "I used my gift of heritage to heal the infected or wounded. I could not bring anyone back once they crossed over to the afterlife, but I could stop one person from tasting death if I truly needed to." She told him.

George rubbed the place on his chest where he saw the spearhead pierce his body. "I was going to die and you used your gift to save me. What will happen now to your gift?"

Valindra smiled and held his hand. "You do not need to worry yourself with that. We should go find the others." She helped him to his feet and he pulled her in close and hugged her tight.

"I am proud to finally be able to embrace my mother." They shared a smile and walked toward the castle.

When they stepped into the courtyard they saw everyone standing around a man's body.

"That's Gabriel's armor!" George shouted as he tried to run through the crowd. He fell to his knees and clutched his friend close to him. Tears streamed down his face, "It was not supposed to end this way. We have endured too much to fall now!" Antoine consoled him and told the others to take the king inside and prepare him for his rest.

Zachery pulled his father off to the side. "We have experienced loss beyond measure, but Amundiss is free! That is what King Gabriel wanted, that is what mother wanted. We must honor them by living the life they gave their lives to protect."

"I'm the father, I was supposed to give you the advice and help."

Zachery smiled. "You have, my entire life. Now, it is my turn to help you. Let's go find Cassy and Launa, we have much to do now."

Aliz"Ra had found the mysterious warrior that had the Guardian blade standing off to himself still clutching the hilt. She wondered who this brave man was and more important, where he got the sword. "Hello there, brave warrior! Have we met?" she asked. Receiving no response, she walked closer, being as careful as she could to not startle him. "Young man, may I inquire whereabout you came across that sword?"

Aliz'Ra touched the man on the shoulder and then had to duck several wild swings. She waved her hands and sent the warrior flying backward. As he hit the ground, the sword was knocked from his hand and his helmet flew off his head. "By the Gods! You're not a man at all!" The young woman turned to face Aliz'Ra, "Launa! How did you. . ."

Launa stared at Aliz'Ra, "When I held that sword I was not myself. I did not know I could move the way I did, do the things I did. I. . . killed."

Aliz'Ra held her tight and tried to calm her down. "You did what you had to do, deary. They would have killed you if given the chance." She leaned over and picked up the sword, "Now tell me, where did you get this?"

Launa explained finding it on a dead orc.

"This is a blessed Guardian sword. They were given to the Guardians of Terra'Fayoak. The Guardians were a special breed of elf with very powerful abilities brought to life by the blade itself." Aliz'Ra looked hard at Launa, "This means the elven bloodline did not skip you. You are a Guardian!" She took Launa by the hand. "We will tell the others when the time is right. We have other things to do right now." The two walked back to find George and the others.

***

The next day, word had already spread to all that remained in Amundiss of the bravery of King Gabriel and the refugee army. The fight was over. Everyone could begin rebuilding their lives. The courtyard of Castle Whitehold had been cleared and made ready to lay the mightiest that have fallen to rest. An altar was made for King Kegan of the Iron Army, who led his men with honor, with no fear. One was made symbolizing everyone that lost their lives in the fight for freedom. An empty one was made, honoring Lord Akadius, who stepped in and broke the rules of the Heavens to stop Malonox.

The last altar held the body of King Gabriel, the noblest and most compassionate king in history. As night began to fall, torches lined the courtyard, circling around the altars. People made their way toward the altars to thank all that sacrificed everything to free their home from evil. The Iron Army stood stoically by their king in respect, saluting their leader and friend. George and Antoine were with Tradan inside the castle throne room.

"He was to take this throne and lead us to a brighter future. I came into life as a normal kid thinking my father had died. You would think I would be used to it."

George sighed. "This journey has twisted everything we all knew into a new way of life."

"Do not forget, we are here for you. You will lead in your father's footsteps." Antoine added.

"You and Zachery are my most trusted friends and family, but I still wish Father were here." They turned to prepare for the funerals.

As night fell, there was a mixture of joy and sorrow. Tears flowed from every eye in attendance. Barrok sat in the back with Cassy. Zachery didn't want him to scare the people.

Tradan and Antoine stood before the people. "We are here because of sacrifices, not only by these honorable people behind us, but of the thousands of souls taken before their time. We were fortunate to have them in our lives, and I for one feel lucky to have called them friends," Antoine began. "Behind us rests more than one king. King Kegan Kadrisson of the Iron Army led his brave men against the demon's army when we needed them the most." Antoine turned and saluted the dwarves. "I thank you for your service and know your king was proud to be an Iron Army Dwarf!"

A loud battle cry of "*ANG THRONG!*" rang out from the mighty dwarves. Tradan stepped forward, "King Gabriel of Whitehold. I knew him for a very little time, but I know he stood as a fixture in this kingdom. He was not only the noblest king this land had seen, but he was also my father. His presence will be missed."

Just as Tradan was about to continue the eulogy, the sky was filled with small, fluttering lights. Four pillars of light formed in front of the altars. There stood the remaining Gods themselves, Sybillias, Hagorith, Artoga, and Hypotios. They were dressed in all white with purple and silver trimmed attire.

Sybillias stepped forward as the people bowed before her, "Arise good people. We came here today to honor our fallen brother, alongside you. As he made his choice to break the laws of the heavens, he came to us. He wished to fill his place among us. Someone to take his seat and help us govern the worlds before us."

The people below murmured to themselves. "We are here to announce a new God will join us, if he so chooses. A man known for his goodwill and justice." Sybillias opened her arms and a shimmering form of a man stood before her. It was Gabriel! "King Gabriel of Whitehold, you are offered the position of immortal God of the Heavens.

"You are of the bloodline of Akadius and have shown your honor and compassion." Sybillias, the God of the North, produced Akadius' crown in her hands. "Do you accept our offer to take your rightful seat amongst us?"

Gabriel turned to Tradan and asked, "How will this affect him? How much a part of his life can I be?"

Hypotios answered, "He will take his place as king and ruler of these lands, and will most definitely need advising." She gave a wink to the young king.

Gabriel smiled, "Then I accept your most gracious offer."

Immediately Gabriel's mortal body vanished from the altar. He appeared next to the other Gods dressed accordingly.

Sybillias turned to the people. "All hail Gabriel, Lord of the Heavens!"

The crowd cheered Gabriel's name and the celestial beings were gone.

Zachery walked over to Tradan, "This is fabulous news! Gabriel as the Lord of the Heavens, he can visit you when you need him most!"

Tradan took a deep breath and felt a new sense of relief come over him. He smiled. "He can also talk to me, he is with my mother watching over us."

Zachery looked to the Heavens. "This is a new start for Amundiss. A new era of Light and peace."

The people cheered for their new king and the thought of a new beginning. They set the altars ablaze, wishing the good King Kegan a peaceful journey through the afterlife. A new chapter unfolded for Whitehold, all knew of the ones that gave their lives, and a monument was to be erected in their honor as a tribute and reminder. A reminder to always be mindful of the shadows.

The eighteen years Amundiss was held captive by the demons almost broke the people's spirit. In the end, Light will always prevail against darkness. We have a long road of recovery and rebuilding ahead of us, but I know it will be a joyous adventure. Cassy and I are to be married and we will have our farm outside of Whitehold, with a place big enough for Barrok of course.

My father, at the encouragement of Antoine, will take his place on the King's Council. Speaking of Antoine, Andrea came to him later on and told him they were expecting a baby. She also reminded him that twins were highly possible in her family. Benzoete, Aliz'Ra, and Elos decided to return to Eska'Taurn and lead the elven people in the new era. We discovered Launa had the gift of Guardianship, which was awakened by the power in the sword when she grasped the hilt. She will learn more in Eska'Taurn with their heritage scholars. She promised father she would visit Whitehold every chance she could. My grandmother Valindra chose to stay at Whitehold with my father, though her time was to be short. When she used her gift of healing to stop death from taking father, it took her immortality and she will taste death as a mortal. Our time is precious—spend it with the ones you love.

Battle for the Heavens

47
Shadows

As the good people of Amundiss mourned their losses and
celebrated their new beginning, a dark figure was seen walking to
where Malonox had been buried. The man plunged his hand into
the ground and pulled the evil skull from the grave. As he held it
close to his face, the outer skin and darkness fell from the bone
leaving a bright white skull.

"Poor Malonox. You should have known not to battle the Light
alone, brother. We will avenge you." He placed the skull inside his
dark robes and sank back into the shadows.

The Prime's death was felt within his brethren. The burial site
of Malonox would forever be a barren and sad place. This marked
the beginning and end of a maker. Could he truly be gone?

Once the maker's were bathed in the Light. Now darkness
shadows their souls. Evil can never be truly defeated, but trust in
the Light to show you the way.

ACKNOWLEDGEMENTS

As a writer, words are supposed to come easy, but finding the words to express the gratitude I have for these people is near impossible. When you decide to take the journey of writing, you better have a great team to guide you:

Annette Terrell is the gifted photographer responsible for my cover photo. Never stop chasing the dream.

Along with Kristyn McQuiggan who is the talented designer who took the photo and made book cover magic. Find her at drop.dead.design.com

Josh Rhoades is the first person to hear of Amundiss and the heroes that live there.

The main support for a writer is having someone believe in you. From day one, my family never doubted me, even when I doubted myself.

April, my gorgeous wife. I love you and thank you for standing by me.

Christian, my beautiful daughter. Thank you for pushing me to be the best I can be.

Marshall and Frances, my parents. Through your example, taught me about the Light. Because of you, I can see the way.

Lastly, two of the best friends I have never met. Your constant support, kind words and willingness to help means alot to me. @TimWilliamsArt and @microstakeshero Keep Twitter going guys!

Thank You.

ABOUT THE AUTHOR
MICHAEL LACKEY

Michael Lackey (1973-) was born and raised in the heart of Dixie, Alabama. Always a dreamer and believer in things that most found silly, Michael loved to pretend as a child. He imagined himself in a land of monsters, where he was the only one who could save the world from utter destruction. He mapped out stunt courses for Hollywood. Raised his sword high and proclaimed himself the champion and slayer of the mystical beasts that plagued his land.

Like most over imaginative children, life set in for Michael. Work. Adulthood. Family. He never really grew out of his imagination. Now in his forties, his stories and love for fantasy spring forth onto pages.

CPSIA information can be obtained
at www.ICGtesting.com
Printed in the USA
FFOW04n1520130518
46538567-48513FF

9 781640 841